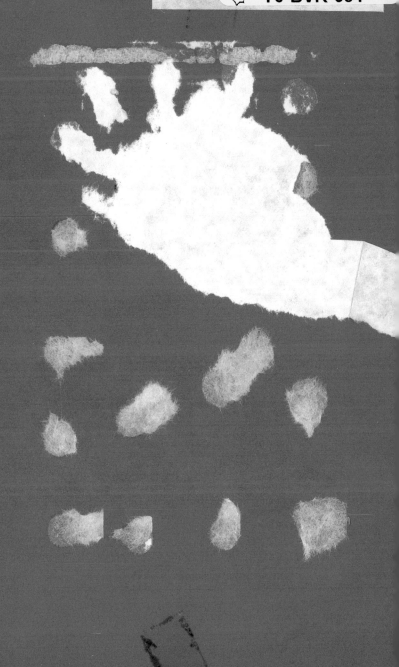

THE
CRYSTAL MAN

THE
CRYSTAL MAN

LANDMARK SCIENCE FICTION

by *Edward Page Mitchell*

Collected and with a biographical perspective by
SAM MOSKOWITZ

Doubleday & Company, Inc., Garden City, New York
1973

ISBN: 0-385-03139-4
Library of Congress Catalog Card Number 73–79697
Copyright © 1973 by Sam Moskowitz
All Rights Reserved
Printed in the United States of America
First Edition

ACKNOWLEDGMENTS

There are still exciting discoveries to be made in the thrilling historical panorama of science fiction and the rediscovery and publication of such a pivotal master of the art as Edward Page Mitchell ranks high among them. The clues that led to this event and the painstaking search that rescued an important literary figure from anonymity would read like an adventure of Sherlock Holmes to science fiction scholars, but would probably have less than that effect on even the enthusiast. Suffice it to say that three years have gone into it, accompanied by considerable secrecy, but enrolled in the search were bibliophiles Lester Mayer and Joseph Wrzos, both of whom have little appetite remaining for further perusal of the worn microfilm files of research libraries. An integral part of the reconstruction of the material was Rhea Finkelstein's typescripts, copied from the less-than-ideal surfaces of giant photoprints in turn made from microfilm negatives.

The discovery of these stories, all that are known to have been published by the author, necessitated a reevaluation of the outline of American science fiction, which has been accomplished in the biographical perspective, radically changing the picture of the major influences in American science fiction and presenting an altered view of Jules Verne's position. It also introduces the thought that American science fiction may have anticipated and even influenced H. G. Wells.

Sam Moskowitz

CONTENTS

Lost Giant of American Science Fiction—
A Biographical Perspective
by Sam Moskowitz

Science Fiction

Unknown-Fantasy

Supernatural

Neo-John Collier

Future War Farce

LOST GIANT OF AMERICAN SCIENCE FICTION—
A Biographical Perspective

By Sam Moskowitz

The "Missing Link" in the history of American science fiction, the most thematically important author in the genre between Edward Everett Hale's landmark story of a manned artificial satellite, *The Brick Moon*, in 1869–70 and Edward Bellamy's *Looking Backward* in 1888, has been discovered. He was Edward Page Mitchell, for over fifty years an editor on Charles A. Dana and Frank A. Munsey's New York City daily THE SUN, and quite possibly a major influence on H. G. Wells, whom he anticipated.

Why is he important?

He wrote the earliest known story utilizing a theory suitable for faster-than-light travel, and in 1874.

He wrote a time *machine* story in 1881, seven years before H. G. Wells presented his earliest version of the theme in THE SCIENCE SCHOOLS JOURNAL in 1888.

The first fictional concept of a neo-electronic *thinking* computer functioning in the head of a human was his in 1879.

Even earlier he had published the premier science fiction in which matter is broken down into energy, transmitted over a distance, and coalesced into matter again.

There is no previous story on record of the creation of an invisible *man* through scientific means than his in 1881, and the scientific explanation and at least one of the incidents are very close to that of H. G. Wells's, which it preceded by sixteen years.

The first use of freezing by a mechanical process so that a person can be revived at a later date was his in 1879.

In 1885 he was probably the initial author to employ the story idea of a child born a mental mutant, capable of instinctively inventing new devices to order.

His 1883 literary masterpiece of a highly evolved tree-sized floating plant has to be the closest thing to the initial story of a friendly alien yet found.

An 1880 effort of changing a man's personality and viewpoint through a surgical operation on the brain was not likely to have had antecedents.

What is more, the man was a stylist and had a delightful sense of humor.

How could so important a figure in the history of science fiction remain so little known?

He wrote and had published initially all but one of his stories anonymously, and those in a newspaper.

If those were the circumstances, how could his works conceivably have had any influence on anyone?

The newspaper they were published in had the largest circulation in the world and it had also formed the world's first fiction syndicate which permitted reprinting by members.

There was no international copyright law at that time, so foreign publications were able to reprint without compunction.

Since the stories were anonymous, pick up without credit was common by newspapers and publications in other parts of the United States, and a change in title was an effective disguise.

Why would a newspaper provide a haven for such advanced scientific ideas, in an age when the average reader had relatively little education?

Only one newspaper in the United States was likely to and that paper was THE SUN. The reason it was receptive was that it owed its eminence and profitability to a science fiction short story, and therefore was inclined to extend good will toward scientific tales of imagination.

The first issue of THE SUN appeared September 3, 1833 (misdated September 3, 1832), founded by Benjamin H. Day, a twenty-three-year-old printer who had been employed by THE JOURNAL OF COMMERCE. Assisting him was George W. Wisner, an unemployed printer who tried his hand as a reporter and writer.

Most papers in New York of that day sold for six cents and had a very limited circulation, usually among the business and professional class. Day took a crack at issuing a one-cent paper aimed at the workingman. The early editions were only four letter-size pages in their entirety, but were popular because Day concentrated on printing news of murders, court trials, and executions, as well as five-week-old European war and political intelligence.

His paper's first illustration was a line cut in the September 14, 1833 edition. Two columns wide, it showed the forty-foot telescope with the 48-inch reflector of the late Sir William Herschel, who became one of the greatest astronomers of all time, primarily as a result of he and his sister Caroline Lucretia grinding the lenses for the finest telescope then produced. The forty-foot telescope was underwritten by a grant from George III.

Herschel was the discoverer of Uranus, of several of its moons, of over eight hundred double stars, sun spots, the lunar mountains, and such a vast addition of knowledge to the science of astronomy that linking his name with an astronomical discovery went a long way toward general acceptance with both the scientific world and the general public.

The illustrious name of Herschel gained further honors in the history of astronomy through the work of his son John, the father having died in 1822.

A second story which was of importance in conditioning readers' minds to the amazing hoax THE SUN was soon to spring on them was found in the October 16, 1833, issue. That story gave substantial space to the flying experiments of the Frenchman, a

Dr. Durant, and, discussing his balloons, the paper commented: "May we not therefore look to the time in perspective when our atmosphere will be traversed with as much facility as our waters?"

The publisher of THE SUN, while attending the sensational trial of Matthias the Prophet, who was accused of killing Elijah Pierson through the use of poison, was greatly impressed by the reportorial work of Richard Adams Locke of New York's COURIER AND ENQUIRER. He engaged him on a free-lance basis to prepare a series of feature articles on the life of Matthias. These were first run in THE SUN and then reprinted and sold as pamphlets. When Locke's paper learned he had been "moonlighting," they fired him.

Fortuitously, George W. Wisner was then leaving THE SUN because of reasons of health, and Day hired Locke to take his place, paying him a salary of twelve dollars a week.

Locke was a descendant of the great British philosopher John Locke. It was not commonly known that he had been born in East Brent, Somersetshire, England, in 1800. He studied at Cambridge, entering there in 1819. Lack of knowledge about his ancestry (deliberately suppressed to save him from anti-British feeling) has prevented proper determination of where he obtained the basic concepts for his soon-to-be-perpetrated "Moon Hoax."

While at Cambridge he was a contributor to THE BEE, a Liverpool semi-monthly subtitled *Fire-side Companion, & Evening Tales*, which was launched in 1820. This lively anti-American, anti-Semitic review contained a potpourri of stories, articles, essays, reviews, and news items both original and reprinted from the press of the world. As was the custom, most of its material was published anonymously. A short satire on the United States titled *America in the Year 2318—A Quiz*, appearing in Volume I Number 4 in 1820, mentioned an automaton physician, a robot "filled with a quantity of highly rarefied air brought from the moon." The story, written in the form of a diary, following the city-line of Baltimore, December 1, 2318 read:

As many of our readers in distant parts of the country have doubted whether the voyage to the moon ever did take place, we do again assure them, upon our veracity, that the information was literally correct. This aerial journey must indeed appear to many who hear of it a most extraordinary undertaking; particularly when it is recollected that in the dark ages of English credulity, it was imagined that tubes two hundred and forty thousand miles in length, besides being exposed to many other insuperable objections, would break with their own weight. Yet such were the tubes used by our adventurers, and such were absolutely necessary to supply them with air from the dense atmosphere of *our* earth. At the period to which we allude, when every science was fettered with adamantine chains of system, it was also thought impossible for goose-quill, or any other wings, to be of service where the air was so rare as to offer no resistance. This idea the undertaking now under consideration has fully disproved . . . Before we take leave of this interesting subject, we must correct an error that crept into our paper of this day month. It was on the *first*, and not on the fourth, of April that Messrs. Sharpe and Airbuilder departed on their journey.

There is no proof that Locke was the author of this particular work in THE BEE, but the reference to both a moon journey and to winged flight in a magazine that we know he contributed to, plus the fact that it was an April Fool's *joke*, must be considered.

It was in 1816 that Thomas and Joseph Allman, London, had issued a new two-volume illustrated edition of *The Life and Adventures of Peter Wilkins, A Cornish Man*, by R.S. (since attributed to Robert Paltock) and originally published in 1751 by J. Robinson & R. Dodsley. For writing skill, story, and imagination, this was probably the finest science fiction novel up to the date of its publication, and for narrative value could be read for entertainment today. These outstanding attributes were effusively acknowledged in a sixty-three-page critique in the Volume 7, No. 1 (1882) edition of THE RETROSPECTIVE REVIEW, a publication which Richard Adams Locke would have had access to while at Cambridge. This unique publication, edited by Henry Southern, who founded it in 1820, was dedicated to printing lengthy reviews of "curious, valuable and scarce old books."

The importance of *Peter Wilkins* to Richard Adams Locke, as Edgar Allan Poe was later to observe in an essay on *The Moon Hoax*, was considerable. In *Peter Wilkins*, the hero, shipwrecked on an island leading to an underground world, discovers a race of flying humans, with the wings of batlike membranes extending from their legs all the way to their heads. Locke's Lunarians in *The Moon Hoax* would have almost identical wings, and the illustrations of the two stories bear considerable similarity.

THE RETROSPECTIVE REVIEW also published, in Volume 8, Part 2 in 1823, a review of Bishop John Wilkins' *Voyage to the Moon* (the new title of *A Discourse Concerning a New World*), in which the author was taken to task for the poor science of the story. It is believed that the lead character in *Peter Wilkins* was deliberately named after John Wilkins, because of the renown of the moon story which, while originally published in 1638, enjoyed a new British edition in 1802.

Another source for Locke's idea was surmised to have been an article by Dr. Thomas Dick in an issue of NEW PHILOSOPHICAL JOURNAL, an Edinburgh publication, in the year 1826. The article contained a facetious piece about communicating with the moon through special arrangement of stone symbols, and Locke is said to have owned the issue with the article while in the United States.

The idea for *The Moon Hoax* was proposed by Locke himself to the publisher, Day. His motive was to earn more money. A teaser announcement in the August 21, 1835, issue read: "CELESTIAL DISCOVERIES—The Edinburgh *Courant* says— 'We have just learnt from an eminent publisher in this city that Sir John Herschel, at the Cape of Good Hope, has made some astronomical discoveries of the most wonderful description, by means of an immense telescope of an entirely new principle.'"

On August 25, 1835, the feature front-page story of THE SUN read: "Great Astronomical Discoveries. Lately made by Sir John

Herschel, LL.D., F.R.S., & c. At the Cape of Good Hope." The source of the story was given as "From Supplement to the Edinburgh Journal of Science."

The first chapter told of discoveries to be revealed of life on the moon, planets around distant stars, "and has solved or corrected nearly every leading problem of mathematical astronomy." A fascinating part of the build-up was establishing that in order to get his remarkable close-ups of the moon, Sir John Herschel had perfected a method of employing artificial light (lasers). Details of the casting of the lens of the telescope were told.

As the days progressed, the public got descriptions of moon vegetation, lunar lakes and inland seas, animal life, volcanoes, and many other details of the satellite's landscape. By the third day, August 28, 1835, interest had grown so immense that the circulation of THE SUN at 105,000 was claimed to be the largest of any newspaper in the world!

The circulation continued to climb as the winged human-like creatures were revealed and the state of their civilization described. The most amazing part of the hoax was that virtually no one seriously doubted it. At the worst, competing newspapers failed to mention the story, but many of them not only mentioned it but copied it and praised the revelations. When the series ended with the edition of August 31, 1835, a pamphlet was readied for the presses to sell for twelve cents, and a set of lithographs showing scenes at the moon was made available at twenty-five cents.

When the newspapers arrived in France, there were three separate reprintings of the entire story in pamphlet form. In Great Britain, it was reprinted by firms in London, Edinburgh, and Glasgow.

THE JOURNAL OF COMMERCE decided to rerun the entire story for its readers. When Locke heard about it, he told a reporter from the JOURNAL OF COMMERCE not to be too hasty, since he had written the story himself. THE JOURNAL then exposed the hoax, but THE SUN played coy for two weeks before letting the other shoe drop.

No one seemed very angry. A diorama (a painted moving transparent backdrop for a lecture which gives spectacular illusion of color and movement) was put on in the City Saloon called *The Lunar Discoveries; a Brilliant Illustration of the Scientific Observation of the Surface of the Moon, to Which will be added the Reported Lunar Observations of Sir John Herschel.* A tongue-in-cheek play, *Moonshine, or Lunar Discoveries,* was presented by Thomas Hamblin at the Bowery Theatre and was favorably reviewed. The paintings for the diorama and the playbill for the theater performance would make fascinating collector's items if still in existence.

The one man who wasn't pleased was Edgar Allan Poe.

Writing to John P. Kennedy of Baltimore (the benefactor whom he had originally told of his own moon story) on September 11, 1835, he said: "Have you seen the 'Discoveries in the Moon?' Do you not think it altogether suggested by *Hans Phaal?* It is very singular,—but when I first proposed writing a Tale concerning the Moon, the idea of *Telescopic* discoveries suggested itself to me—but I afterwards abandoned it. I had however spoken of it freely, & from many little incidents & apparently trivial remarks in these *Discoveries* I am convinced that the idea was stolen from myself."

Hans Phaal—A Tale had appeared in THE SOUTHERN LITERARY MESSENGER (of which Poe was editor) in June 1835, only two months prior to the publication of *The Moon Hoax.* Poe claimed that he had intended to write a sequel, but that Locke's work anticipated him.

Fuel to his belief was the action of the New York TRANSCRIPT in publishing Poe and Locke's stories side by side, after the hoax had been revealed, as evidence that Poe might have written the story. So much did this matter prey on Poe's mind that when *Hans Phaal—A Tale* was collected in *Tales of the Grotesque* in 1840, Poe attached an essay titled *Note on "Hans Phaal,"* in which he painstakingly listed the many scientific errors in Locke's story that should have revealed it as a hoax to the informed reader. Later, he did an article titled "Richard Adams Locke" for the June 8, 1844, COLUMBIA SPY, in which he stated that he believed Locke when that reporter said he had not read Poe's story before writing the *Hoax*, and spoke highly of Locke, but in so overdone a manner as to smack of derision. He also recounted the scientific errors in *The Moon Hoax* that he had published in his earlier note.

Poe's annoyance was not so much in the possibility that Locke may have used an idea similar to his, but sheer envy at his success. After all, Poe had used it first and nothing spectacular had come of it.

Poe's reactions were a bit of sour grapes, but from Europe there came another reaction to *The Moon Hoax*. The story wasn't written by Locke at all, asserted Augustus De Morgan, a mathematics professor at University College, London, and father of the novelist William De Morgan. He did not believe that Locke possessed sufficient scientific knowledge to make such a story convincing and asserted that the job had actually been done by Jean Nicholas Nicollet, a French astronomer who had come to the United States and been employed to explore the tributaries of the Mississippi. This suggestion sounded great to the French, so they echoed the claim.

Edward Page Mitchell was to put the question to the first publisher of THE SUN, Benjamin H. Day, during an 1883 visit. There was no question at all in Day's mind that the sole author of *The Moon Hoax* was Richard Adams Locke both in conception and execution. Only the fact that Nicollet spoke English and that it was within the realm of possibility that Locke could have met him gave the story any substance. There was no evidence ever produced that the two men had ever met or communicated.

Richard Adams Locke now felt he had the formula for starting a successful newspaper. In partnership with Jared D. Bell and Joseph Price, he launched on October 6, 1836, a competing penny newspaper titled THE NEW ERA. For it he wrote another hoax, *The Lost Manuscript of Mungo Park*, which purported to tell the unrecorded adventures of a then-famous Scottish explorer. Either the lie wasn't big enough or people weren't going to be taken in twice. THE NEW ERA failed within thirty days. Locke then took a position as editor of THE BROOKLYN EAGLE and would eventually leave journalism altogether for a position in a customs house. Though he lived until 1871, he failed to again appear in the limelight.

Unlike Locke, Edgar Allan Poe was not to disappear from the public eye. Moving back to New York with a sick wife and his mother-in-law on April 6, 1844, he arrived with less than five dollars in his pocket. Utterly desperate, he went down to see Moses Y. Beach, the new owner of THE SUN, and broached to him the idea of another hoax. The time was right, it was almost nine years since the last one, and the readers would not be expecting it.

"We stop the press at a late hour to announce that by a private express from Charleston, South Carolina, we are just in possession of full details of the most extraordinary adventure ever accomplished by man," the April 13, 1844, issue of THE SUN stated. "The Atlantic Ocean has actually been traversed in a balloon, and in the incredibly brief period of three days." The same day, at 10:00 A.M., an extra appeared with the elaborate headline: "Astounding News by Express, *via* Norfolk! The Altantic Crossed in Three Days! Signal Triumph of Mr. Monck Mason's Flying-Machine!!! —Arrival at Sullivan's Island, Near Charleston, of Mr. Mason, Mr. Robert Holland, Mr. Hensen, Mr. Harrison Ainsworth, and Four Others in the Steering Balloon Victoria, After a Passage of Seventy-Five Hours from Land to Land—Full Particulars of the Voyage!!!"

To be ever after known as *The Balloon Hoax*, the short story told of the construction of a spring-powered dirigible, with a rudder, which started from Penstruthal, North Wales, England to cross the British Channel, when the propelling device broke.

A wind carried it swiftly across the Atlantic to Charleston, South Carolina. The early part of the story is taken up with detailed descriptions of the scientific aspects of the balloon. The latter part is in the form of a diary, relating the balloonists' experiences during the trip.

Poe stationed himself outside THE SUN building and reported what he saw in the May 25, 1844, issue of the COLUMBIA SPY:

> On the morning (Saturday) of its announcement, the whole square surrounding the "Sun" building was literally besieged, blocked up—ingress and egress being alike impossible, from a period soon after sunrise until about two o'clock P.M. . . . I never witnessed more intense excitement to get possession of a newspaper. As soon as the first few copies made their way into the streets, they were bought up, at almost any price, from the news-boys, who made a profitable speculation beyond doubt. I saw a half-dollar given, in one instance, for a single paper, and a shilling was a frequent price. I tried, in vain, during the whole day, to get possession of a copy. It was excessively amusing, however, to hear the comments of those who had read the "extra."

Poe hoped that "The Balloon Hoax" would endure and bring him notoriety comparable to that of Locke's, which he might translate into cash. Those hopes were dashed when the story proved a twenty-four-hour sensation, and within forty-eight hours THE SUN implied that the story might not be valid, and within a week admitted the hoax.

But Poe's *Balloon Hoax* had an effect destined to alter profoundly the course of science fiction. On February 8, 1860, Jules Verne came home to a surprise birthday party at which was present Félix Nadar, the first man in history ever to take an aerial photograph. Since the photograph had been taken from a balloon, the talk turned to the future of air travel, and it was Félix Nadar who suggested that someday Poe's *Balloon Hoax* would be accomplished in fact. Verne then sat down to do some calculations on what hourly speed a balloon would have to make to

reach the United States in three days, and the possibilities en-
thralled the two men until late in the evening.

Verne had been intrigued by Poe for many years and his career as a playwright had been going poorly. A series of his plays
had been produced, but none of them was lasting many performances. A chance second meeting with Nadar on the streets of
Paris resulted in a conversation in which the photographer told
him of plans to build a balloon which would have a kitchen, sleeping bunks, a dining room, and, because of his interest in photography, a darkroom. He would call the vessel *The Giant*, and,
through exhibiting her, raise enough money to experiment with
a heavier-than-air machine, possibly utilizing the helicopter
principle.

Filled with the idea, Verne sat down and began to write a history of ballooning, which he finished in 1862. When he took it to
Pierre Jules Hetzel, French publisher, he was told to rewrite it as
fiction. The result was *Five Weeks in a Balloon*, which upon its
publication in 1863 would establish Verne's reputation. As his
novels appeared in book form and were translated, Verne was
to make science fiction a popular form of entertainment in most
of the Western nations of the world. *Five Weeks in a Balloon*
was followed by *Voyage to the Center of the Earth* in 1864, *From
the Earth to the Moon* in 1865, *The Adventures of Captain Hat-
teras* in 1866, and *The Children of Captain Grant* in 1868, but
none were published in the United States! When Jules Verne
visited America in 1867 as a passenger on *The Great Eastern*,
the giant side-wheel steam-powered passenger boat, he was literally unknown. He traveled in the United States, greatly impressed
by the sights and the people he saw, but outside of an occasional
copy of one of his books in French or copies of translations from
England, his popularity and influence were minuscule.

The first book of his to be translated and published in America
was *Five Weeks in a Balloon*, published by Appleton, New York,
in 1869. It is commonly believed that the American dime novel
was imitative of Verne, predominantly because in later years the

leading author of such works, Luis P. Senarens, was called the "American Jules Verne." Nothing could be further from the truth. The American dime novel was a native creation, *and it in- fluenced Jules Verne,* just as Edgar Allan Poe, and through Poe, Richard Adams Locke, had channeled Verne's thinking.

The first science fiction dime novel, *The Steam Man of the Prairies,* was written by Edward S. Ellis and appeared in August 1868 as Number 45 of *American Novels* published by Irwin, Bea- dle. The invention of a steam engine, shaped like a mechanical man, to pull a steel wagon in which adventures in the great West would be experienced, was the seminal stream of the American dime novel. Edward S. Ellis was one of the most noted of dime novel writers and would become a leading historian as well as superintendent of schools in Trenton, New Jersey. His story ap- peared a year before any of Verne's works were published in the United States.

Harry Cohen, writing under the pen name of Harry Enton, took his cue from a successful reprinting of Ellis' novel in 1876 and produced *Frank Reade and his Steam Man of the Plains* for Frank Tousey's BOYS OF NEW YORK, February 28 to April 24, 1876. It was a copy of Ellis, featuring a man-like steam robot pulling a metal wagon invented by a teen-age genius who would take his ma- chine and companions out West to follow the trail of adventure. Harry Enton would end up a medical doctor.

With his second Frank Reade story, Harry Enton graduated to steam horses. He quit writing them after the third, and the series was continued by the fourteen-year-old Luis P. Senarens in 1879 (who would eventually gain a law degree, but never prac- tice). Senarens had received through his publisher a letter from Jules Verne complimenting him on his steam men and steam horse stories. Almost immediately afterward, Verne published *The Demon of Cawnpore, a story about a steam elephant!*

In France, Verne's novels were first serialized by HETZEL LE MAGAZIN D'EDUCATION ET DU RÉCRÉATION. In England, they were

frequently serialized in various boys' magazines before hard-
cover publication. Their popularity influenced other boys' magazines to cultivate authors who could write effective imitations,
and therefore created a school of writing of the Jules Verne
variety. In fact, *The Scapegrace at Sea: Or, The Adventures of
Dick Lightheart on the Sea, Underneath the Sea, on the Earth,
and in the Centre of the Earth*, which ran in YOUNG MEN OF GREAT
BRITAIN beginning with Number 260, 1873, introduces Captain
Nemo from *Twenty Thousand Leagues Beneath the Sea*, and his
famous submarine, *The Nautilus*, in a long, extremely well-done
sequence.

In the United States, a successful "invention story" formula
for the boys' weeklies had been created by Edward S. Ellis, Harry
Enton, and Luis P. Senarens *before* the translations of Jules
Verne. They did not need Jules Verne. Furthermore, the boys'
weeklies tended to run primarily original stories written to order
during the seventies and eighties.

The landmark post-Civil War story in science fiction was not
influenced by Jules Verne but by Richard Adams Locke. The
story was *The Brick Moon* by Edward Everett Hale, the longest
portion of which was serialized in three installments in THE
ATLANTIC MONTHLY October, November, and December 1869, and
a short sequel, *Life on the Brick Moon*, in THE ATLANTIC MONTHLY
for February 1870. This was the first work of fiction ever to deal
with an artificial earth satellite, and the first work of fiction or
non-fiction to discuss more than a theory which would make
orbiting an earth satellite possible. In the introduction to *The
Brick Moon* in Volume 4 of his collected works published by
Little, Brown, and Company in 1899, Hale stated that "The account of the first plan of the moon is a sketch, as accurate as was
needed, of the old chat and dreams, plans and jokes, of our
college days before he [his brother, Nathan] left Cambridge in
1838." In the collected works, he put in a footnote attributing the
questions to his brother Nathan, which did not appear in earlier

printings, and the pre-1868 vintage of the story and its origin at Cambridge is mentioned in the text.

Writing to his son Charles on August 8, 1869, Hale reveals he has finished the story prior to that date, as he chattily informs: "I am now sitting while I preside over the manufacture of a kite by Arthur. I do not think you took much to kite building. I was rather famous for it, the scientific, sedentary, and solitary character of the amusement comporting with my taste . . . Parallel with this taste you will say is my story of the Brick Moon of which the first part will be in the Atlantic for October. It is the success and failure of our great enterprise of sending up from township No. 9 a Brick Moon to assist in fixing the longitude. The story has spun out into three numbers and will need another for its completion."

The imaginative achievement of publishing a story about an earth satellite in 1869 made a great impression on Hale's contemporaries. Sixteen years later, William Sloane Kennedy, writing in THE CENTURY for January 1885, bowing to Hale's great originality, said:

> His stories of imagination or extravagance are full of the most delightful escapades and *tours de force*. Give him the least bit of *pou stó*, and, by sheer force of genius and fancy, he will project you into the air a full-blown romance, which shall keep touch with the base earth of reality by said pivotal *pou stó*, and nothing else. How he revels in the wild play of his fancy in these tales! He reminds you of Jules Verne rather than of Poe, and does not merely climb, but soars away into the ether; he constructs a Brick Moon, and by the aid of vast water-power machinery projects it into space with its inhabitants as easily as a prestidigitator tosses a ball into the air; and when he has got it revolving there in the meridian of Greenwich, as a celestial beacon for all lost mariners, what does he do but set his brick moon inhabitants to leaping two hundred feet or so into the air, in long and short jumps, by way of a Morse system of telegraphic signals to their friends on the earth!

Poe journeys off leisurely to the moon in a balloon, but Hale

makes his own moon, and gets astride of that for a ride; the mountain in this case comes to Mahomet. There is more deceptive
verisimilitude in the adventures of Hans Pfaal, but that of "Colonel
Ingham" is more thrilling.

Sloane further makes a point of a little-realized fact when he
continues: "I have said that Hale reminds you of Jules Verne; but
it is to be noted that when the American began to write in this
vein the Frenchman had produced only one or two books, which
were untranslated outside of France."

It now becomes obvious that the tremendous importance of
Richard Adams Locke's *The Moon Hoax* on the development of
science fiction has up to now been missed. It has been treated as
a sport, a freak happening of interest primarily because it fooled
so many people for so long a time with so big a lie. The truth is
that *The Moon Hoax* directly aroused Poe to write *The Balloon
Hoax* and through Poe influenced Jules Verne to begin writing
science fiction. In the United States, it was the direct cause of
Hale's writing of *The Brick Moon*, itself a landmark and contemporary influence in science fiction. Peripheral influence of its
translations into French and its reprintings in England have yet
to be adequately appraised.

Jules Verne did not become popular in the United States until
1873, when *Around the World in Eighty Days* was serialized
early that year in the French daily newspaper LE TEMPS. The idea
of a race against time to circle the globe by conventional methods
of transportation in eighty days acted upon the imagination of the
world like a sporting event. Each daily installment of the novel
in LE TEMPS, or a review of it, was telegraphed by foreign cor-
respondents to their newspapers. All over America, newspapers
ran a daily account of the progress of Verne's English hero,
Phileas Fogg, as he strove to complete his journey in time to win
his audacious wager. As he reached the final part of his trip by
fictionally crossing the United States, the fires of public enthusiasm flared. Boston publisher James S. Osgood, striking while the

public fancy was at its height, published a pirated edition in 1873. He was followed by another Boston firm, G. M. Smith, which, in 1873, printed the first American edition of *Twenty Thousand Leagues Beneath the Sea*. This was Verne's masterpiece, a work of such imaginative plotting and superb characterization as to rank among the world's permanent adventure classics.

In Philadelphia, J. B. Lippincott rushed into print *In Search of the Castaways,* three connected novels in one volume, related to *Around the World in Eighty Days* by theme, since the plot involves the children and friends of the lost Captain Grant circling the globe by ship in search of him.

Yet it was SCRIBNER'S MONTHLY, under its original publisher and later continuation under the name of THE CENTURY, that played a major role in popularizing Verne's fiction in America. Any publisher could pirate Verne who wished to, but Scribner's became the printer of the authorized editions in the United States. For a few years, almost as important as Scribner's in American reprintings of Verne was Henry L. Shephard & Co. of Boston. Both of these firms were the first to put Jules Verne between the covers of popular magazines in America.

Scribner, Armstrong and Company had moved swiftly into the publishing of Jules Verne, arranging for authorized editions with Messrs. J. Hetzel & Co. of Paris and with Sampson Low, Marston & Co. of England, the latter owning English translations. Their first title was *From the Earth to the Moon Direct in Ninety-seven Hours, Twenty Minutes; and a Journey Around It,* which they published in 1874. To promote it, they ran an adaptation by Frank R. Stockton, then a member of the staff of SCRIBNER'S MONTHLY, in that publication for January 1874, under the title of *The Great Air Line to the Moon,* with six illustrations from the book. This is the first *magazine* publication of Jules Verne in America yet established.

SCRIBNER'S MONTHLY was founded in November 1870 as the result of a merger of PUTNAM'S MAGAZINE and HOURS AT HOME. Dr. J. C. Holland, a Scribner's (book company) author, and Roswell

Smith, a Western attorney of considerable means, had a sixty per cent interest in the magazine, and Charles Scribner a forty per cent interest. By 1874, it was already one of America's leading publications, and by the end of the decade would be the leading American publication.

With the great public enthusiasm for the works of Jules Verne, the magazine was receptive to such material from outsiders, all the more so since its associate editor, Frank R. Stockton, later to evolve into one of America's leading science fiction writers, was understandably partial to such material.

At Bath, Maine, a young man of twenty, named Edward Page Mitchell, was just learning that while he had permanently lost the sight of one eye, he would retain vision in the other, and occupied the time on his hands by writing a five-thousand-word short story which he titled *The Tachypomp*. His visual problem had occurred through a strange accident. While returning home from Bowdoin College on a train, a hot cinder had swept in through the window and landed in one eye. For weeks they tried to save the sight in the damaged eye, and then, through a sympathetic reaction, the uninjured eye lost its sight. The burned eye gradually recovered, but the other had to be removed and was replaced by a glass eye.

The story he had written was a highly advanced one for the time. A wealthy young student seeks the hand of his mathematics professor's daughter in marriage, but is so inept at figures that he fears he will be turned down on that account. In applying to the professor for her hand, he is told that consent will be given only if he either squares a circle, invents a perpetual motion machine, or comes up with a formula for infinite speed. He seeks out a private tutor, Jean Marie Rivarol, who is a mathematical genius. Rivarol feels that squaring the circle is too easy, does not want to give away the secret of perpetual motion, but will come up with a device for infinite speed. To indicate his qualifications, Rivarol has a partially successful android in the closet that can do simple mathematics and compose verse, and has keyed his staircase so that at various pressures meters in his room record the weight, height, and complexion of an arriving visitor coming up the staircase. An accidental discovery, resulting from a cave-in of the cellar while burying a dead cat, reveals a shaft going right through the earth.

The idea Rivarol has for our hero is based on the familiar debate of whether a man walking up the aisle in a moving train is traveling faster than the speed of the train. He envisages building a series of trains, the bottom one of which will be two miles long, with tracks laid on its top, a second one-and-three-quarters miles long with tracks on top, for a height of eight, sixteen, or thirty-two trains. Each train will be slightly shorter than the one below it, and since all would be powered by alternating current electrical engines for instant acceleration, they would all move at the same speed. Therefore, each train would arrive at the destination simultaneously, but each layer of trains adding its speed to those upon which it was riding. Theoretically, infinite speed could be attained by this device.

The two set out to find a place west of the Mississippi where they can erect a prototype, but our hero accidentally steps into the hole through the earth and is saved only by awakening in the parlor of the mathematics professor, who, having checked his character, gives his blessings for the marriage of the daughter.

The main weakness of the story was the effort of a young Mitchell to write at the top of his form and therefore rendering a story much too archly constructed, though with a redeeming leavening of humor.

Mailing *The Tachypomp* with "fear and trembling" to SCRIBNER'S MONTHLY, Page "was transported to the twenty-seventh heaven when there came back from New York a prompt acceptance and a pleasant note from Richard Watson Gilder, followed by a check then beyond the dreams of literary avarice." The story was published anonymously in the March 1874 issue of SCRIBNER'S MONTHLY, only sixty days after that magazine had run its first Jules Verne piece, and so was launched the strange literary career of Edward Page Mitchell, who would become the most original, one of the most important, most widely copied, and most skillful producers of science fiction in America, and yet literally remain virtually unknown.

Edward Page Mitchell was born March 24, 1852, son of Edward H. Mitchell and Frances A. Page, in the small city of Bath, Maine. He wrote *The Tachypomp* (which translates as "quickly to send") in a Windsor chair brought from Leyden to Plymouth, Massachusetts, by ancestor Experience Mitchell on the *Anne*, the third ship of settlers to that famous colony. Believing the chair brought good luck, he kept it, and it still remains in the family to this day.

Page was born and lived the first eight years of his life in the home of his maternal grandfather. It was a home religiously puritanical, yet filled with a great quantity of fascinating books and long runs of popular magazines. He was not permitted to read anything secular on Sundays, but the other six days of the week there was a richness of information and imagination that he would treasure and remember with affection to the end of his life.

At the age of eight, his family moved to New York City and occupied a house between Forty-first and Forty-second streets on Fifth Avenue, directly across from the present-day site of the main New York Library. At that time Croton Reservoir occupied the location. He attended Grammar School 35 in New York City and George W. Clarke's Mount Washington Collegiate Institute. His idol during New York days was P. T. Barnum, whose life he had previously read. One of the most vivid memories of his life was the draft riots of New York in 1863, when an estimated two thousand people died. He was an eyewitness to many of the sickening aspects of the event, and was later to describe them in his memoirs.

The following year his father moved the family to the Bryan Grimes Plantation in Tar River, North Carolina, where he unsuccessfully tried to grow cotton in 1866 and 1867. A series of letters the young Mitchell wrote to THE BATH TIMES in Maine at the age of fourteen were his first published efforts. Returning to Bath, he was entered at Bowdoin College in Brunswick, Maine, in 1871, with the intention of becoming a doctor. He changed his mind, and his greatest distinction was writing the school song, *Phi Chi*, graduating in 1874.

To help finance his college work he taught elementary school during Christmas vacation. A letter from General Joshua L. Chamberlain of Maine, the officer who accepted Lee's surrender at the close of the Civil War, got Mitchell a summer job on the Boston DAILY ADVERTISER. Most fascinating part of the job for Mitchell was the presence of Edward Everett Hale, who had been former editor-in-chief of the paper, and who was in and out of the office on a regular basis. Mitchell was invited to the home of Hale, and writing of that occasion, he commented: "The creator of the brick moon and of Philip Nolan came in." The note reveals that Mitchell had read *The Brick Moon* and his placing of it first in listing, before *The Man Without a Country* (which featured Philip Nolan), speaks for itself.

THE DAILY ADVERTISER gave Mitchell a wide range of experience in journalism, which was supplemented by writing for the BOSTON COURIER, a Sunday paper with a distinguished list of contributors.

Mitchell so loved newspaper work that all desire for the discipline of medical school evaporated, and he was satisfied to major in the humanities.

THE LEWISTON JOURNAL (in Maine), which had enjoyed a long and distinguished history under the editorship of Nelson and Frank Dingley, found itself in urgent need of a newspaperman when Nelson was elected governor. With editors not being in excess supply in that small community, they recalled that a young fellow named Edward Page Mitchell had previously applied to them for a position. Frank Dingley wrote him on November 11, 1873, offering him a trial if he showed "immediately." The job proved a happy one for Mitchell, who in addition to the routine, was permitted to do an assortment of human interest features, including sleeping in a haunted house.

In those early days and for several decades afterward, Mitchell had a strong interest in the occult and was attracted by anything suggesting strange phenomenon. While still working on the Boston paper, he had enjoyed his first encounter with the supernatural in a schoolhouse in nearby Newburyport. A respected schoolteacher and a room of sixty students reported seeing the ghost of a young boy, who proved intangible to the grasp, repeatedly enter the classroom. He would enter even when the doors were locked. Additionally, there were invisible locking and unlocking of doors, loud noises in the space above the ceiling of the schoolroom, fluttering window shades, and a wide variety of other inexplicable manifestations. Mitchell, with a party of newspapermen, stayed the night at the schoolhouse, shortly before George Washington's birthday. The only sound in the schoolroom was the large, ticking clock.

After hours of boredom, about twelve midnight, one of the newspapermen addressed the otherworldly spirits, and challenged them to give some sign if they were present. Instantly the clock stopped ticking! Examination of the clock indicated that it had wound down.

While working on the Lewiston paper, Mitchell agreed to spend a night in a haunted house in Springvale, where an itinerant pedlar was believed to have been murdered by three residents whose ghosts had been purported to have been seen by later occupants of the house. Additionally, there was the usual collection of slamming doors, rattling shutters, sounds of a scuffle with no one present, and similar reports. Accompanied by his cousin Albert G. Page, and with courage fortified by a revolver, the two slept the night in the house with nothing more ominous than the branches of trees scratching on the roof serving to frighten them.

Starting in Boston and continuing in Lewiston, Mitchell attended every type of séance or supernatural concord that he learned of, in an effort to find a single circumstance that could not be explained. He exposed a number of hoaxers and, after twenty-five years of research, including investigations in New York and Philadelphia, asserted never to have found a shred of evidence of the existence of either the spiritual world or the supernatural. This intellectual disenchantment with mysticism reached the point that when he died he was not a member of any church nor did he make any religious profession.

This penchant for the supernatural was to be the making of Edward Page Mitchell's career. For as one of the editors on the Lewiston paper, he used to receive on an exchange basis the nationally famous THE SUN from New York City, now edited by Charles A. Dana. The lively journalistic style was the wonder of the newspaper world. It was the claim of the paper that all the news worthy of print could be gotten on four pages (they kept increasing the physical dimensions of the pages to maintain their claim). They featured both stripped, condensed news writing, which would be applauded today, and they also *fictionized* the news, *literally* wrote it like fiction with characters, dialogue, plot, and sometimes in the first person.

Dana's purpose was to *entertain* first, and inform secondly. His paper was the cheap entertainment of the masses in a day when there was no radio, television, or moving pictures, and when the price of a quality magazine was twenty-five cents in the age of the twelve-hour workday and laborers' salaries sometimes six or seven dollars a week.

This paper utterly fascinated Mitchell, and he submitted short, snide, and satirical pieces to it, which were accepted and paid for. At that time he had felt his fifteen dollars per week was pretty good, but he found himself getting more money than that for a relatively short contribution to THE SUN.

Since the primary purpose of THE SUN was to entertain, it had, as a matter of policy, run fiction as an occasional part of its content.

It was in THE SUN that Horatio Alger, Jr., in 1859, found publisher Moses Beach receptive to a series of anonymously published short stories with titles such as *The Discarded Son, The Secret Drawer, The Gipsy Nurse,* and *Madeline the Temptress.* It was the same publisher of THE SUN who introduced Horatio Alger to Street & Smith and helped him thereby establish a new market for his novels.

If any paper was partial to fiction it was THE SUN, and if any paper had no built-in prejudice against *fantastic* fiction, it was THE SUN. Sensing this, Mitchell, after selling a few short essays and editorials, submitted the humorous spiritualistic story *Back From That Bourne,* claiming to be a letter from the island of Pocock, off the coast of Maine. Using the background of a séance aboard a yacht, a shiftless, no-good character known to the islanders as Johnny Newbegin, recently dead, is materialized. When the séance is over he refuses to return to the spirit world and takes up where he left off in his past life, except that he has undergone a complete turnabout in character and is now a solid citizen. Conditions in the spirit world are so bad that not only does he refuse to speak about them, but he has no intention of going back. The world is now faced with the problem of what to do if any quantity of the dead decide to return.

Charles A. Dana loved the story, printed it on page one of the December 19, 1874, issue of THE SUN, and decided he would some day offer Mitchell a job on the strength of it. Many of the other papers did not take the story as fiction, and ran their own versions of it. Fifty years later, Dorothy Scarborough, Ph.D., author of one of the best books on weird fiction, *The Supernatural in Modern English Fiction* (Putnam, 1917), selected it for inclusion in her anthology *Humorous Ghost Stories* (Putnam, 1921), picking it up from the original source with no apparent knowledge of who the author was, since she also ran it anonymously.

Dana's delight with Mitchell's contributions meant more sales, one of them fiction. The piece titled *The Story of the Deluge* ran in THE SUN on Thursday, April 29, 1875. It purported to be an account of newly discovered records from Noah's Ark, and with considerable humor, sheds revelatory light on the Bible. One entry is loaded with significance. It states: "Water falling rapidly. Ate our last pterodactyl yester . . . Bitter ale and mastodons all gone." Also amusing is the "new-found" record of a second successful ark. Dana thought the piece "first rate," but asked for more satiric emphasis so that no one would think it was an anti-religious attack.

Steadily employed, with a writing future ahead of him, Mitchell married Annie Sewall Welch on October 29, 1874, and received an increase to twenty dollars a week from the Lewiston paper. When a later request for twenty-five dollars a week was refused, Mitchell began correspondence with Dana on the possibility of work in New York, and on May 14, 1875, received a letter stating: "I have no doubt we shall be able to give you as much work as you want, and of whatever kind." By the time negotiations were concluded, it was agreed that he was to start work October 1, 1875, and that the salary would be an incredible fifty dollars a week. It is hard to interpret just how much money that was in terms of yesterday's buying power, but it had to translate in value to something like twenty-five thousand dollars a year in today's terms.

Mitchell rented a flat on Madison Avenue, New York City, and moved in with his wife. He would never leave THE SUN and his complete life and dedication would be that paper. As the years progressed, he would be handed more and more responsibility, and eventually become the virtually unknown pivot of the paper, but for the next ten years there would still be time to turn out a few stories which now must be recognized as milestones in the history of science fiction. To judge them adequately, it is important to understand what was happening in science fiction in America when his stories began appearing anonymously in one of the world's most widely circulated and copied newspapers.

When Mitchell began his writing, the Jules Verne boom had made the French author a household name across the United States in only a few years' time. Vying with Scribner's for leadership in the publication of Jules Verne, Shephard, in 1874, was the first American company to issue *A Journey to the Center of the Earth,* one of the best and most imaginative of Verne's early novels. The sales of Verne's and other successful titles made them feel that they should have a magazine for promotion and prestige purposes as did Scribner's, their major competitor. A likely-looking Boston magazine that could be had reasonably, because of a series of disastrous fires, was AMERICAN HOMES. The publication had been launched with the November 1871 issue by two Massachusetts men, Colonel Charles H. Taylor of Somerville, and A. M. Lunt of East Cambridge, and the firm was known as Chas. H. Taylor & Co. The magazine sold for fifteen cents in contrast to the twenty-five-cent price of most of the leaders such as HARPER'S, ATLANTIC, and SCRIBNER'S, and the annual subscription rate was one dollar and twenty-five cents. It was an immensely readable magazine, both in fiction and non-fiction, and it was a family publication and not a decorating or woman's magazine as the title might have indicated. Its standards were not as intellectual as many of its competitors, but it was far less stodgy.

After a shaky start, it hit upon the idea of giving a color print, suitable for framing, of a cat and a dog called "The Two Pets" as a premium to subscribers. Such prints were called chromos, because they were printed laboriously with the manufacture of eighteen to twenty stones, each stone to impress a different color or shade. This was the most impressive type of color print that existed. Paintings were expensive, and if a family wanted a nice color picture for the wall, this was one of the few inexpensive ways to get one. The same aesthetic need was to account for the immense success of Currier & Ives in the sale of its lithograph color prints, and even to this day, famous subjects in full color in a newspaper centerfold will often be later found pinned up like a painting on hundreds of readers' walls.

On November 9, 1872, the Great Boston Fire wiped out the offices of the magazine, its press rooms, its chromos, much of its mailing list, and even the establishments of its suppliers. Just about when they had new quarters and presses, they were hit by a second fire. Unable to rally again, the company was sold to Shephard & Gill, with Charles H. Taylor remaining as editor. The first issue under the new arrangement was November 1873, at which time the indicia carried the legend "Published by American Homes Publishing Company." The entire facilities burned out again in February 1874, and readers were sent a notice giving them the new catch-up publication dates.

The magazine had run only a few works of fantasy and science fiction up until that time. The earliest was *An Oxy-Hydrogen Courtship* by Edwin Ballard in the December 1871 issue, where a marvelous device for making photographs seem to appear on the surface of a mirror is built by using "an oxy-hydrogen lantern and such a complication of lenses and mirrors, concave, plane and convex, that I fear I could not describe them if I should try.

"The figures I had seen were thrown upon a thin muslin screen between the frame and the mirror and were but the images of photographs."

The device is used to project a young man's proposal of marriage in writing to a girl in the audience whom he loves, and she accepts.

A well-illustrated story published anonymously, *A Young Crusoe,* appeared in the January 1872 issue, and involved Charles Crusoe, fourteen, living in Bombay, who is shipwrecked with his father and servant Sambo while on a return trip to England, and relates how they make out on a desert island.

By far the most oustanding early story was *A Chesapeake Wonder Tale* by George Alfred Townsend in the February 1872 issue. A gravestone in Newark, Delaware, gives off a ticking sound when one's ear is held to it. The story behind the ticking is that the British government in 1714 had offered twenty thousand Pounds to the man who could come up with an accurate portable timepiece which would help determine latitudes while at sea. John Harrison got the award for the chronometer, but Charles Mason, a master of timepieces and a scientific man, had begun work on the project in 1764. He had built a tiny, compact ticking masterpiece, but a two-year-old boy, William Minvit, the son of a Finnish-Dutch fisherwoman swallowed it, and Mason the rest of his life deplored that "a child had eaten up 20,000 Pounds belonging to him at a single mouthful."

The heat of the baby's body keeps the device ticking, and when the boy grows up he becomes a master watch repairman. His bride is frightened by the sound of the ticking on their marriage night, but eventually reconciles herself to it. Now, long years after his death, the marvelous timepiece keeps ticking away underground, apparently the temperature still such as to require no compensating balance. Townsend was a fine stylist, and this warm and moving story was later collected in his *Tales of the Chesapeake* published in 1880.

The first mention of Verne in AMERICAN HOMES came in the same February 1874 issue in which they ran a favorable, though somewhat flip review of *A Trip to the Moon in Ninety-seven Hours,* their distortion of Scribner's title.

"If the object of the author was to impart scientific knowledge in a highly popular form," Taylor wrote, "it must be conceded that he has amply gained his end." However, in a comment made almost a hundred years ago, the fallacy of which is revealed by the fact that it is still being made today after we have already achieved moon flight, he also states: ". . . We may well question whether it will not be most seriously considered by many of our enthusiastic minds . . . While there are still so many problems to be solved in our own terrestrial globe, it is as well, perhaps, not to encourage more curious enthusiasts."

The lead story in the June 1874 number was *A Floating City*, a condensation and adaptation of Jules Verne's book concerning his trip on the cable-laying *Great Eastern*, the huge ocean-straddling paddle-wheeler. The same issue contained an advertisement for Jules Verne's *Adventures in the Land of the Behemoth* with twenty illustrations for $1.50. The August number promoted Verne's *Meridiana*, illustrated and printed on tinted paper for only 25¢. It also announced that *Journey to the Center of the Earth* was available. This last was characterized as "a work of thrilling interest. It contains much popular scientific interest. It is externally very beautifully embellished."

A full-page advertisement in November 1874 hailed Jules Verne's "Masterpiece! The rival of *Robinson Crusoe*," the first part of *Shipwrecked in the Air,* with forty-one illustrations for $1.50.

In that issue, with much fanfare, it was announced that the well-known editor, writer, and newspaperman, George Cary Eggleston, would become the new editor of AMERICAN HOMES and Charles H. Taylor would take a position with the BOSTON GLOBE. George Cary Eggleston was the talented brother of Edward Eggleston, who authored *The Hoosier Schoolmaster* in 1871. In fact, that book was based on the early experiences of George Cary. Edward Eggleston and George Cary Eggleston had taken over the editorship of HEARTH AND HOME, a failing farm weekly, with the issue of August 19, 1870. It was in this magazine that *The Hoosier Schoolmaster* was first serialized. Frank R. Stockton was hired as an associate editor at the end of December 1870, and the magazine's contributors included Edward Everett Hale, Rebecca Harding Davis, Sarah Orne Jewett, Harriet Prescott Spofford, Mary Mapes Dodge, and Harriet Beecher Stowe.

When the publication was sold in 1873, George Cary Eggleston went back to free-lance writing. Based on his experiences as a soldier in the Civil War for the South, his *A Rebel's Recollections,* a superbly written piece on the war as it looked to the Confederate soldier, was well received in 1874. Henry L. Shephard talked him into lending his name and talents as editor of AMERICAN HOMES. Apparently, Shephard also talked him into advancing a substantial sum of money to the magazine.

When he came to the publication, it had already begun serialization with pictures of *The Mysterious Island* by Jules Verne in its September 1874 issue. The version run was abridged and

adapted by Hawley Lee. In reviewing the hard-cover edition of
the first volume of *The Mysterious Island*, subtitled *Shipwreck
in the Air*, Eggleston wrote for the December 1874 AMERICAN
HOMES one of the most historically important and revealing statements in print on the precise comprehension and understanding
of the special qualities of that fiction which today we call science
fiction:

> The appetite for the marvellous is a universal one, and from the
> earliest dawn of literature until now there have always been wonder
> stories eagerly read of all men. Ours is a scientific age, however, an
> age of easy unbelief, a questioning, doubting, faithless age, and we
> do not readily accept, even in the half-hearted, constructive way in
> which fiction must be believed to be enjoyed, any thing not borne
> out by hard-visaged fact. We use gas and kerosene, and do not be-
> lieve any longer in wonderful lamps, the scouring of which brings
> faithful genii to our presence as promptly as the tapping of a bell
> calls (or ought to call) Bridget or John Thomas from the kitchen.
> We cannot find Lilliput or Brobdingnag on the map, and so we turn
> all these things over to the children nowadays. We want wonder
> stories quite as our forefathers did, but we cannot get up the
> pseudo-belief in them which is absolutely necessary to their enjoy-
> ment. Science has destroyed the work of the classic wonder-
> mongers, not by proving the stories impossible, for that we knew
> already, but by creating in us mental habits fatal to their enjoy-
> ment.
>
> No sooner was this evident than the world began to ask of science
> herself something in place of that which she had taken away, and
> Bulwer, with his remarkable faculty of discovering and adapting
> himself to new conditions, made more than one effort to create a
> new order of wonder stories suited to modern habits of thought. In
> "A Strange Story" and "Zanoni" he wove Rosicrucian dreams of
> science into a web of modern romance, and, failing in this, he con-
> jured up the terrible "Vril-ya," by supplementing the development
> theory with imagination. Even in this, however, he was only partly
> successful, and the modern wonder story—a wonder story which we
> practical, hard-headed, inquiring, fact-full people of today could in

some sort believe—was not born until M. Jules Verne made a congenial marriage between science and fancy. By dint of using actual scientific facts and processes where they are at all practicable, and keeping his imagination in lines exactly parallel with those of science, when science itself will not do, he has succeeded in creating stories more marvellous than any of Scherherazade's, but which nobody can help believing as he reads them. He uses actual, well-known things so constantly that his inventions never seem to be other than the most familiar facts of every-day life . . . He never ignores a difficulty likely to present itself to the mind of the reader, but calls attention to it instead, and provides against it in one way or another. Thus, in his account of the "Journey to the Moon," he explains that the concussion produced by the sudden launching of the shell from the immense cannon would mash its occupants to a jelly in overcoming their inertia of rest, and provides an elaborate water cushion arrangement to break the force of the blow . . . The most utterly preposterous things are told with an attention to detail which makes plain, everyday fact of them.

George Cary Eggleston would try his hand at several short science fiction works while editing AMERICAN HOMES. *Who is Russell?* in the March 1875 issue was a strange story of a man named William Russell, a soldier in the Confederate Army, who simply appears one morning at roll call, modest and unassuming until one day when the men are doing gymnastics he takes the stage and gives an extraordinary exhibition of professional strength and skill. When a man has an arm blown off by an explosion, he borrows a surgeon's kit, amputates the man's arm with expertise, and gives precise instructions for the man's care. He seems to know nothing about the sea, but one day asks to be permitted to take an examination for admission to the navy as a lieutenant. He passes, is put in command of a boat, and wins honors in battle. After the war he shows up in New York as a partner in an outstanding law firm, and asks his war buddy to call on him. When his friend arrives at the designated address, he finds there another man with the precise background Russell had claimed for himself but the man has no knowledge of Russell. The mystery remains unsolved as the skillfully written story ends.

Another of Eggleston's fantastic tales was *The True Story of Bernard Poland's Prophecy* in June 1875. "What we call past is not past,—and what we call future is not future. All things that have been, or shall be *are*," asserts Bernard Poland to his southern friend. "Memory and prevision are only different ways of knowing *a fact which now is*," he stresses shortly before he turns pale as he faces a knoll. In answer to the worried inquiries of his friend, he says that he saw himself running ahead of a group of soldiers being fired on with canister shot, only to be hit himself and fall before reaching his objective. He knows he will die there, but not when. Years later, a letter is brought to his southern friend by a comrade of Bernard Poland's. The circumstances and the place turn out to be identical with his prevision.

Eggleston attracted to AMERICAN HOMES former contributors to HEARTH AND HOME who sometimes wrote works that could be termed science fiction. John Esten Cooke, considered second in his time after James Fenimore Cooper as a writer of historical novels, and the man who is held responsible for "poetic idealization of the ante-bellum South," contributed *A Magnetizer* in the December 1874 issue, concerning the ability to perform painless major surgery on a hypnotized subject and the powers of clairvoyance that might accompany hypnotism. Rebecca Harding Davis, an early realist who exposed slum conditions of her times and was the mother of the famous journalist Richard Harding Davis, contributed *The True Story of Wolfenden,* a story of a strange vendetta, curse, and disappearance into the polar wastes of an enigmatic and pathetic man in the May 1875 number. Edward Eggleston himself contributed to the magazine, but his only known work of science fiction would appear years later in the December 31, 1887, issue of HARPER'S WEEKLY, titled *A Prospective Retrospective.* It purported to be an article written in the year 1987, which derided the fashions of 1887 and showed a United States turned into a social appendage of Great Britain due to inadequate copyright legislation which made it more profitable for publishers to run British than American authors.

Though Eggleston definitely displayed a predilection to admit fantastic fiction to the pages of AMERICAN HOMES, it was his publishing firm's commitment to Jules Verne that would supply some of the most historic sidelights.

The first furious exchange had been reported before Eggleston's coming in the "Publishers' Department" of the July 1874 issue. It had been the practice among the better publishers that when one announced a book not covered by American copyright, the others would hold off with the same title for a respectable period of time. Shephard had issued *Adventures in the Land of the Behemoth* by Jules Verne for $1.50, and almost instantly Scribner, Armstrong & Co. announced a cheaper edition under the title of *The Adventures of Three Russians and Three Englishmen.* When contacted by Shephard for an explanation as to this breach of publishing ethics, Scribner's replied they had announced the book seventeen months earlier through proper channels under the title of *Meridiana.* The pros and cons of announcing a misleading title had raged in letters to THE NEW YORK TRIBUNE and later in Boston's SATURDAY EVENING GAZETTE.

Now followed an even more bizarre aspect of competitive publishing. SCRIBNER'S MONTHLY had begun an illustrated serialization of *The Mysterious Island* in its April 1874 number. Vindictively, Henry L. Shephard began serialization of his own adaptation and condensation of the same work in the September 1874 issue of AMERICAN HOMES. The novel came in three sections, and SCRIBNER'S MONTHLY would run it continuously—skipping only their May 1875 number—through October 1875. A different translation and adaptation of the same novel with the same illustrations *was running simultaneously* in AMERICAN HOMES. This extraordinary competitive situation obtained until George Cary Eggleston cut the novel off without a word in the middle of the story in the issue of February 1875, after six installments had been run.

The reason for the abrupt termination was found in a brief filler in the back of the April 1875 issue, headed simply *The Mysterious Island*. It was announced that a synopsis of the remainder of the story would appear in a later issue and that "For the gratuitous flings at the Southern people which are found in this French author's story, however, we are in no way responsible. We began translating and printing this story as soon as its publication was begun in France, with no thought that a foreigner writing a romance could by any possibility make it politically offensive to any part of the American people."

The May 1875 issue offered a two-page article titled *Jules Verne and His Work* with a sketch of Verne and a facsimile of his handwriting. Eggleston was now critical of Verne, whom he termed "a dabbler in science, who, finding its wonders vastly entertaining, doesn't care to go deeper for the sake of greater accuracy or thoroughness . . . but he has made himself very interesting, and every one of his realistic wonder stories is well worth reading, when one has an idle hour for that purpose. He hit upon a totally new device in the outset, and has used it masterfully, so that with a trifle more of patience and care he might have made for himself a permanent reputation in his peculiar vein . . . Unluckily he has sacrificed a good deal to haste, and it would now seem that he is about to sacrifice still more to greed."

What Eggleston was referring to was the fact that Verne had divided *The Mysterious Island* into three short novels, and it bid to run forever. He felt this was a deliberate ploy and that he would present the remainder of the story in synopsis form for those who were interested in its outcome, but he didn't think it fair to have numerous new readers starting a story with no beginning and seemingly no end. The attack on Verne was undoubtedly a sop to Southern readers as had been the discontinuation of the serial.

With the September 1875 issue, AMERICAN HOMES abruptly ceased publication. Eggleston gave his explanation many years

later in *Recollections of a Varied Life,* published by Henry Holt
& Co. in 1910, when he wrote: "a peculiarly plausible and
smooth-tongued publisher, a gifted liar, and about the most companionable man I ever knew, had swindled me out of every dollar I had in the world and made me responsible for a part at least
of his debts to others. Another 'secret' partner, honest, sent to jail
and the man began a religious magazine."

SCRIBNER'S MONTHLY ran the first two volumes of *The Mysterious Island* in eighteen installments, concluding in October 1875.
The third part of the novel was run in condensed form in
the March and April 1876 issues.

SCRIBNER'S MONTHLY would not become the Mecca of
nineteenth-century science fiction, but in 1874 and 1875, in addition to the novels of Jules Verne, they had run Edward Page
Mitchell's first science fiction; Edward Bellamy had started his
series of short stories that would lead up to *Looking Backward;*
Frank R. Stockton was editing and writing for them; George Cary
Eggleston had been and would become again a contributor, and
some of the stories of Henry James were of the supernatural.

There were other threads woven into the fabric of science fiction of the time.

A considerable furor had been raised in northern California as
the result of an exclusive story published May 13, 1871, in the
SACRAMENTO UNION, a morning paper and for decades the leading paper in the state. The story, submitted by a San Francisco
correspondent with the initials "W.H.R." purported to be a post-
humous manuscript of one Leonidas Parker, who tells of meeting
with Gregory Summerfield, a seventy-year-old scientist who then
demonstrates to a group of the most distinguished men of San
Francisco a formula he has invented, which would make the
oceans inflammable and thereby destroy the world. He demands
one million dollars in tribute to restrain himself from doing so.
Half the money is raised in San Francisco, but on a pretext that
the other half will have to be raised in New York City, Summerfield is induced to take a train east with Parker. When the train

makes a brief stop part way up a mountain, Parker pushes Summerfield over the edge of a cliff in front of witnesses. When taken to trial, Parker is exonerated. The story, published as *The Case of Summerfield*, though fictionized in the manner of THE SUN, was so convincing, particularly in its simulated legal briefs, that thousands of Californians were convinced it was true and, far from being relieved at being saved from a horrible fate, were quite frightened.

The SACRAMENTO REPORTER, a competing evening paper, reprinted the entire story verbatim, crediting it to the SACRAMENTO UNION, that very same afternoon, which was a Saturday. However, the following Tuesday May 16, 1871, the SACRAMENTO REPORTER exposed the story as a hoax under the heading of "A Caxtonian Triumph." "Caxton" was the pen name of the San Francisco lawyer William Henry Rhodes (though the relationship between the headline and the identity of the writer was not further spelled out in the exposé). "The UNION of Saturday contained a story which attracted considerable attention and enabled the proprietors of that sheet to sell very readily all the extra copies they had struck off," the REPORTER bitterly complained. "It is a thrilling narrative," they continued, "and probably we ought not to object to the pains taken by the writer to make the public accept as true that which is pure fiction; but we do object to the attempt to hoodwink the people, made by the UNION in its preface to the POETIC romance, which reads thus: 'We are indebted to a correspondent at San Francisco for the particulars of the most interesting case that has ever come within our observation as public journalists.' If the UNION was itself deceived, or if it believes still that 'The Case of Summerfield' is not unadulterated romance, let it say so. It is certain that the UNION's correspondent deceived it, or the UNION attempted deliberately to believe it was the UNION that was deceived, as the semiunconscious state in which its recent great reverse has thrown it rendered it easy to impose upon it.

"If the UNION's contributor could achieve a few such triumphs over the press generally, he would no doubt be tempted to exclaim, as did the creature of his brain, when he produced the villainous compound which was to destroy the earth: 'I feel like a God! and I recognize my fellow men but as pigmies that I spurn beneath my feet.'"

Far from being crushed, the SACRAMENTO UNION responded with a rebuttal from "W.H.R.," who, after calling the editors of the REPORTER to task for lack of imagination, stated: "But if the veracity of that report be questioned by any honest inquirer after truth, and he will pay me a visit at my office in this city, at No. 21 Wright Street, adjoining the City Hall, I will engage to exhibit to him the positive proofs of the chief facts stated therein. I have the original draft of poor Parker's confession in my possession, with the names of the committee in full, and also a list of the subscribers to the 'Summerfield fund.'"

This kept the populace frightened and paved the way for a follow-up story titled *The Summerfield Case Again,* in the Saturday, June 10, 1871, edition of the SACRAMENTO UNION. It was enough to make fright turn to panic, presenting meticulously phrased letters and documents to the effect that a notorious criminal known as Black Bart had found the body of Summerfield where it had fallen and removed from it a vial of the substance which could make water inflammable. It stated that a ten-thousand-dollar reward was being offered for Black Bart by the governor of the state of California. A highwayman was eventually captured named Black Bart, but he claimed he had decided to use the name as a result of reading *The Summerfield Case Again!*

The story eventually was verified, that the author of the dual hoax was actually William Henry Rhodes, a San Francisco attorney with a literary flair. He had for many years written poems, essays, features and sketches for San Francisco and Sacramento newspapers and had been a contributor to the California magazines GOLDEN ERA and THE HESPERIAN, among others. He frequently used the pen name "Caxton," which accounted for the manner in which the SACRAMENTO REPORTER had headlined its column referring to his story.

Even more important, we can now trace the newspaper hoax as a definite branch of American science fiction, exerting tremendous influence and attaining widespread readership. Many of the stories of the nineteenth century which seem self-centered on the wonderful idea to the exclusion of characterization or plot were deliberate attempts to gain verisimilitude through giving the impression of factual reporting and do not represent any deficiency in the ability of their authors. We must also realize that we have only heard of the *very famous,* and successful hoaxes; there undoubtedly were others.

Rhodes was born July 16, 1822, in Windsor, Bertie County, North Carolina, the son of Colonel Elisha A. Rhodes and Maria Ann Jacocks. He was educated at Princeton University, Harvard University, and Harvard Law School, obtaining his LLB in 1846, the same year his first book, a volume of poetry titled *The Indian Gallows and Other Poems,* was published in an illustrated edition by Edward Walker, New York. Most of the poems were about Texas and they were a tribute to the Red Men, who "are rapidly passing away, and soon they will live only upon the pages of the Historian and the Poet."

He returned to Bertie County to practice law, but finding it unrewarding, left for Galveston, Texas in 1846 (where his father had been appointed United States Counsel), to serve as a probate judge there for one term. With the Gold Rush booming San Francisco, he moved to the vicinity of that city in 1850 and in the years that followed resided in Oroville, Red Bluff, San Francisco, and Sacramento.

Through all the changes he continued to practice law, but halfheartedly, not too adequately supporting his wife Susan Harrison, whom he married in Oroville on December 29, 1859.

The only thing he liked as well as writing was talking and he gained a reputation as a brilliant orator who could be counted upon to compose appropriate verse for any group he was called upon to address. As a founder of the Bohemian Club, a Mason, an Odd Fellow and a member of the American Party, among others, he was called upon frequently. His greatest bar to literary success was said to have occurred when Bret Harte, who had been a fellow contributor to the GOLDEN ERA, became the editor of the OVERLAND MONTHLY in July 1868. The OVERLAND MONTHLY was a literary magazine composed entirely of original contributions. It paid for everything it published, a rarity among California magazines, but Bret Harte decided that Rhodes did not fit the policy. He had done the same to the poet Edward Rowland Sill, on the basis that the man did not write on western topics.

Rhodes had to seek out various newspapers for his efforts, but despite this gained an extraordinary local reputation, his short story *The Summerfield Case* being cited in chemistry classes "as utilizing for dramatic purposes the curious fact that by the use of potassium, water may be set on fire." The main legal thrust of the story, is a man justified to murder for the sake of saving the world from disaster, was discussed by thousands in the years that followed.

If there was any question that Rhodes had gotten his idea for *The Summerfield Case* from Richard Adams Locke's *The Moon Hoax*, it was dispelled when he wrote *The Telescopic Eye* for the SAN FRANCISCO EVENING POST in 1876. Written in the style of a new story, it concerned the investigation of a San Francisco boy thought to be blind because he could see nothing close at hand, but who was actually born with optics capable of defining clearly objects to the utmost detail on the moon's surface. He describes the human life and geography of the moon in considerable detail. The account ends with his great joy at finally focusing his orbs on a Martian city! This had been preceded in a newspaper by *Phases in the Life of John Pollexfen*, which also implied that it was a true story of a San Francisco photographer who made a fortune by extracting an eye from a young man to use as the lens of a camera which would be the first in history to take color exposures!

These stories were given the stamp of truth and authenticity by the incorporation of official-reading legal documents, very precise dates, familiar streets in San Francisco, and other fastidious accouterments of newspaper hoaxes, though after the first few most accepted them for what they were, a documentary style of science fiction. A similar method was employed in the story *The Earth's Hot Center*, which was presented as a series of official reports from John Flannagan, the United States Counsel at Bruges, Belgium, to Hamilton Fish, the Secretary of State of the United States, telling of an experiment in determining the composition of the earth's depths in which a shaft, over a period of twenty-five years, is sunk seven miles deep. The story ends with the matter-of-fact report of the creation of a new volcano that threatens to inundate the European lowlands with lava and fill in the English Channel.

When Rhodes died, on April 14, 1876, his friends rallied to leave a literary monument to his career which would also bring a few extra dollars into the hands of his widow. It took the form of a memorial volume published in 1876 by the outstanding San Francisco house A. L. Bancroft under the title of *Caxton's Book*. The collection was edited by the West Coast poet and writer Daniel O'Connell, but a very important introduction was written for it by his legal colleague W. H. L. Barnes, renowned for his exposure of the inhuman conditions accorded seamen on sailing ships in the famous "Sunrise Case."

Referring to Rhodes writings while still at Harvard, Mr. Barnes stated: "His fondness for weaving the problems of science with fiction, which became afterwards so marked a characteristic of his literary efforts, attracted the especial attention of his professors; and had Mr. Rhodes devoted himself to this then novel department of letters, he would have become, no doubt, greatly distinguished as a writer; and the great master of scientific fiction, Jules Verne, would have found the field of his efforts already sown and reaped by the young Southern student."

The book contained all the science fiction previously discussed

and in addition *The Aztec Princess,* in which a time warp is
utilized to take the protagonist back to the reign of the ancient
Aztecs. The story is especially fascinating for its claim that the
Aztecs were once part of European and African civilization
separated when the land split and the continental drift created
the New World! *Legends of Lake Bigler,* in the same volume,
could also be considered science fiction, telling of an aquatic race
of humans and ends with the apparent discovery and killing of a
mermaid in "modern" times.

A big land such as America, with relatively poor transportation
and communications systems after the Civil War, with thousands
of newspapers and magazines published regionally because national distribution was difficult, developed not regional literature
but literature in regions. Otherwise talented and influential voices
spoke their piece unheard by most of the country and disappeared from the scene. The need of a widow and the popularity
of Verne had prompted friends of Rhodes to assemble a collection of his tales, essays, poems, and sketches with the emphasis
on science fiction. They knew what science fiction was as precisely as we do today. They came close to calling it that when
they termed his work a combination of "science and fiction" and
specifically called them works of "scientific fiction."

Rhodes wrote before and contemporaneously with Verne, yet
his themes were not mere adventure stories; he had begun to introduce moral and philosophical concepts to accompany his more
speculative ideas. His friend Barnes had urged him to drop law
and devote himself full time to writing, "But he dreaded the venture; and like a swift-footed blooded horse, fit to run a course for
a man's life, continued on his way, harnessed to a plow, and
broke his heart in the harness!" There is strong intimation in that
passage that his death may in some way be attributed to
despondency.

What prompted Rhodes to write science fiction? There was
only Edgar Allan Poe and Nathaniel Hawthorne in that tradition
in this country when he began. The fact that his biggest successes

were deliberate science fictional hoaxes, and the fact that the long-visioned boy in *The Telescopic Eye* goes into considerable detail on the human civilization and geography of the moon, requires no elaboration. When he left eastern schools and eastern legal practices for the West, he was already profoundly influenced by Richard Adam Locke's *The Moon Hoax*.

The inchoate state that American publishing was in during this period made it quite possible that a major thematic figure in the history of science fiction could arise, publish prominently, be copied directly, exert influence through forgotten printings, and still end up with his brilliance completely eclipsed. Edward Page Mitchell, just moving into his writing stride when *Caxton's Book* appeared, was unquestionably such a man.

THE SUN was the ideal medium for a man with a storytelling gift and a leaning toward humor. THE SUN wrote its longer news stories in *fiction* form. Many of the stories that appeared in that paper—even front page stories—were *literally* fiction. There were clues for the observant, but the naïve were presented with headlines, decks, and city datelines in the traditional newspaper format. That was the presentation given to Edward Page Mitchell's imaginative interview *The Soul Spectroscope*, which appeared in the December 19, 1875, issue, concerning a certain Professor Dummkopf, "a German gentleman of education and ingenuity," datelined "Boston, December 13." When interviewed, Professor Dummkopf was engaged in experiments on photographing odors. He also expounded on his theories for bottling sound, so that great operas and speeches could be preserved for the future. The project he was most excited about was the perfection of a "soul spectroscope," a machine that would fundamentally act as a lie detector, analyzing the emanations and radiations from the body and determining the character of the individual.

The Inside of the Earth in the February 27, 1876, edition of THE SUN was the same type of tongue-in-cheek farce, this time an exposition on Symmes' theory through the guise of an imaginary interview with an old man designated as Claltus. "A Big Hole

Through the Planet from Pole to Pole" was the deck of the story. The man interviewed has a model of the hollowed earth, showing the location of the lands inside. He believes there may be men living there, projects the type of life they may lead, and sums up the many experiences of sailors that seem to confirm the truth of his hypotheses.

Both of these were slight pieces of nonsense, fillers written by a clever man with great intellectual scientific curiosity and an even greater sense of humor. The humor was also present in his next story, *The Man Without a Body*, in the March 25, 1877, number of THE SUN, ladled on so heavily that it diminished the work, but nothing could diminish the idea. This story is a sequel to *The Soul Spectroscope*. While broadly farcical, it is a true short story, with a beginning, a middle, and an end, not a pretended interview. The reporter, while browsing through the old Arsenal Museum in Central Park, is startled to see the apparently decapitated head of Professor Dummkopf sitting on a display shelf. When he looks carefully at it, the head winks at him. The head had been presented to the museum as that of a notorious French murderer, but it seems that the bizarre situation of the professor is due to his invention of the Telepomp. This machine is capable of breaking matter down into atoms, conveying them as energy through a wire, and re-forming them at the other end. The machine works to perfection. When a cat is transmitted and re-formed alive and well, the professor decides to transmit himself.

The experiment initially proceeds well, the head and neck of the professor materialize at the other end, but then the process stops. He had not put enough sulphuric acid in the battery, so it ran out of juice to complete the transition. Medical students find the head and give it to the museum, but when the story ends the reporter is sneaking it out to a questionable freedom.

This story is a landmark. It is the first fictional exposition yet discovered of breaking matter down into energy scientifically and transmitting it to a receiver where it may be re-formed.

Mitchell's first son, Ned, had been born the year before, which may account for his interest in the miracle of birth. In *The Case of the Dow Twins*, in the April 8, 1877, edition of THE SUN, two boys are born joined by a piece of tissue. Though cut apart following delivery, they both seem to know what the other is doing. Jehiel is the good, obedient boy and Jake a no-good hell-raiser. When Jake is cutting up somewhere, Jehiel is frequently awakened from a sound sleep and forced to repress a desire to act in the same way.

When Jake is killed, Jehiel is suddenly transformed into a hellion, leaving his intended and ending up in jail. Apparently the two personalities now reside in the one body, with Jake the ascendant. This story is a slickly written, well-handled addition to the considerable literature of dual personality.

Exchanging Their Souls in the April 27, 1877, edition of THE SUN was a very effective variation on the theme. Again, the presentation was made with newspaper headlines but the storytelling format was this time very strong. A Russian prince suddenly begins behaving like a Georgian wheelwright and a Georgian wheelwright begins behaving like a Russian prince (even speaking in four languages). It appears to be an exchange of personalities, but a mesmerist reverses the situation, restoring both to normality. The mesmerist alleges there actually was a case of temporary insanity and that he has only duped the prince into behaving normally, but the evidence strongly supports something far more unusual.

A few months later, *The Cave of the Splurgles* in the July 29, 1877, issue of THE SUN revealed a Mitchell who had evolved into one of the cleverest and most original short story writers of his decade. In 1939, a magazine would appear under the title of UNKNOWN, printing off-beat fairy tales for adults so delightful that its file of thirty-nine issues is treasured and the term "UNKNOWN-type" has become almost solidified as a generic classification for fiction. *The Cave of the Splurgles* seemed to have anticipated that style of fiction. Perhaps something of Lewis Carroll's lead in *Alice in Wonderland*, another fairy tale for adults, which had first appeared in 1865, and its sequel, *Through the Looking Glass*, in 1872, may have influenced Mitchell. The uncharacteristic moralistic finale of the tale added a touch of Nathaniel Hawthorne or Edward Everett Hale, but with those possible acknowledgments the theme of a man being pulled into a hole and finding himself in an underground world where the Devil and all his demons have *retired* was original with Mitchell. Regional dialects were a trade-mark of a Mitchell story, as was the silkiness of his transitions in dialogue. He presents the famed devils, friends, and demons Ahriman, Beelzebub, Moloch, Pretas, Typhon, Baal, Belial, Asmodeus, Leviathan, Nergal, Belphegor, Rimnon, Dagon, Kohai, Behemoth, and Antichrist. He even introduces Lilith.

The sundry devils and demons try to make a pretense of fierceness and evil, but they have become too civilized and humane to hope to compete with the monumental wickedness of humans; that is why they do not permit anyone who falls into their world to return and destroy their reputation.

In this story, and in others like it to follow, we see the influence of Mitchell on Brander Matthews, a contemporary of almost the same age whom he knew well. His *A Primer of Imaginary Geography*, with its marvelous retinue of legendary and literary characters—which first appeared in SCRIBNER'S MAGAZINE December 1894, and then led off his famous collection *Tales of Fantasy and Fact* (Harper & Brothers, 1896)—is an imaginative extension of the type of things attempted in *The Cave of the Splurgles*. John Kendrick Bangs' best sellers *A Houseboat on the Styx* (1895) and *Pursuit of the Houseboat* (1897) also employ the device of humanizing famous legendary figures and mixing with them departed great men of history and notable characters from the literary works of other authors in light fantasy. Bangs, additionally, wrote a number of outstanding ghost stories, but his familiarity with Mitchell stemmed from the fact that he did a regular column for the EVENING SUN in 1888 and 1889 titled "Spotlets." Further, his major vice was collecting stories of the strange and supernatural, which made up a large part of his

library. There is virtually no chance that he did not own copies
of Mitchell's stories from THE SUN.

Mitchell's short tale, *An Extraordinary Wedding*, in the January 6, 1878, issue of THE SUN, impressed another author renowned
for her strange philosophy, Madame Helena Petrovna Blavatsky,
whose cultist "bible" of the Theosophical Society, *Isis Revealed*,
had appeared in a handsome two-volume edition from J. W.
Bouton the previous year. Madame Blavatsky had collected to
her bosom all the "secrets" of the ancient religions, sects, and philosophers, not excluding Atlantis, astrology, reincarnation, the
Kabbala, and virtually every other popular unexplained miracu-
lous event. She presumed to give them a reasonable interpretation, at the same time attempting to find a common denominator
for the bizarre potpourri of religion, science, legend, occult, and
humbuggery. Madame Blavatsky read the adroitly done tale of
spiritualism, *An Extraordinary Wedding*, dealing with a Scottish
girl possessing bonafide occult powers, who in the presence of a
distinguished group of people, including the local minister,
causes the shapes of a man and a woman to manifest themselves
in the shadowy substance issuing from her breast. The man asks
that the clergyman present marry him to the woman. When this
is done, the two of them slowly dissolve into nothingness. The
man, it is discovered, was a suicide who had fallen in love with
the image of Cleopatra as rendered in a portrait by Hans Makart,
and shot himself to death in the east corridor of the Imperial
Gallery of Vienna where the painting hung. The woman was unquestionably Cleopatra herself, who was united in marriage with
the spirit of a man who lived long after she died.

Colonel Henry Steele Olcott, one of Madame Blavatsky's
closest friends in the United States, at her request tracked the
anonymous story to Mitchell. He was issued an invitation for a
visit. Mitchell did go up to see Madame Blavatsky, who was then
residing "above a saloon at the southeast corner of Eighth Avenue and Forty-seventh Street." Madame Blavatsky attempted to
ascertain from Mitchell whether his employer Dana was influ-

enced by high-placed Roman Catholic friends and what his views might generally be on religion and mysticism.

During the course of the conversation, the fat, homely, sloppily dressed woman snatched at the air over her head with her hand, opened it to display a tiny piece of paper, read it, and claimed it was a message from a Gobi oasis. Madame Blavatsky on later occasions corresponded with Mitchell in a more conventional manner, seeking to enlist THE SUN in her cause. While Mitchell admired her as a truly outstanding woman of ability, he made it unequivocally clear that he regarded her as a fraud.

It has often been said that weaknesses are the other side of strengths, and Mitchell's humor, which sometimes transformed individual stories into delights of sophistication, frequently damaged otherwise powerfully developed themes. The sardonic humor in *The Devilish Rat,* published in THE SUN January 27, 1878, has the opposite effect, resulting in one of the grimmer supernatural stories by an American author, anticipating the method of John Collier in its handling. An American visiting the Rhine stays at an old castle where he involves himself with the theory of the transmigration of souls. The rats there are so numerous that he sleeps in a wire cage. Each night there is among them a gigantic specimen, the size of a small terrier, incredibly ancient and gray, who comes to glare at him. Frustrated at any progress in his experiments, he lunges out of his cage one night and grabs the very old rat from behind, killing it with his bare hands. He then falls asleep and wakes feeling invigorated. When his mentor, Professor Calcarius from Bonn visits him, he overpowers him, binds him with wire, and leaves him behind so he will be eaten by the rats. The girl who has been bringing him his food, learning that he is leaving, asks him, on his way through Cologne, to visit her betrothed, whom she has sent money to further his career. She wants him told that his uncle has died leaving him an inheritance enabling them to get married. He visits the soldier, telling him instead that he is now the girl's lover, and provokes such anguish that the boy throws the money at him and breaks into tears.

It is now evident to the protagonist that he has a new soul which was transferred to him from the great gray rat he killed. At first he was hopeful it might be that of Socrates or some other learned man, but as he realizes that is not the case he displays undeniable satisfaction as he states, "I believe it to be the soul that once animated Judas Iscariot, that prince of men of action."

The Pain Epicures, which appeared in THE SUN for August 25, 1878, is a tale which John Collier would have been proud to have written. A young man suffering from neuralgia is envied by a friend who has helped organize an association which trains people to cultivate a taste for and enjoy the delights of pain. The rationale of the members is that since life is full of physical pain, let us learn to like it. In his tour through the club, a wide variety of self-torture is exhibited. Each member tries to outdo the others. He is appalled by a prestigious wealthy member who has imported a rack from Spain and employed a Negro to stretch him on it. The limit is reached when the observer discovers the aunt of his girl friend with her bare foot in a basket of hornets, which she has covered to prevent them from escaping.

The last piece of fiction by Mitchell to appear during 1878 in THE SUN was *The Terrible Voyage of the Toad,* a humorous story of a group of men who set out to visit the Paris Exposition in a worn old sloop they call *The Toad,* and the various "supernatural" manifestations which prevent the successful completion of the voyage, with major emphasis upon Beelzebub, a sea monster with seven heads and ten horns (named in *Revelations*), who proves too formidable for them to defeat after their rum gives out. This was printed in the October 20, 1878 issue.

The parallels with today's writers, modern philosophy, and current themes are particularly fascinating in examining the writings of Edgar Page Mitchell, none more so than *The Devil's Funeral,* a short philosophical fantasy which appeared in THE SUN for March 15, 1879. It is only a few years past the time that the "God is Dead" movement was at its peak in the United States, and there have even been several pseudo-scientific works of fiction derived from the concept. *The Devil's Funeral* was based on the implications of the death of the Devil. It is a philosophical fantasy in which the narrator finds himself borne down the ages "at the end of Time, under a blood-red sky more awful than the deepest black." At this moment the bier of the Devil is surrounded by his worshipers, many men of great repute. They bring their gold to be consumed in a magic fire at his funeral pyre and his last will and testament is read, in which hell is closed and the remaining torments are divided among his worshipers. This is one of the most serious of Mitchell's works and though the writing is superb, the potentialities were not adequately exploited in the brief compass of the tale.

Many of the preceding tales were frankly supernatural or fantasy, but *The Facts in the Ratcliff Case* in THE SUN for March 7, 1879, was quite deliberately framed against the background of a medical school and strong speculation of a hereditary mutant with unusual mental powers is offered where a supernatural explanation would have been easier. The focus of the story is a woman whose eyes and presence seem literally to have the effects of a drug on those upon whom she focuses her attention. Her father walks around in a perpetual daze and the young doctor who meets her and whom she attempts to persuade to permit her to attend a surgical session with the students is similarly affected. Years later she is on trial for killing her husband with drugs. She is saved by the doctor she had met previously, when he offers the testimony that there is no trace of drugs in the dead man's system. In appreciation, she offers her late husband's fortune and herself to the doctor, but he will have no part of either. "What was the mystery of the noxious influence which this woman exerted through her eyes?" he asks. "What was the record of her ancestry, the secret of the predisposition in her case? By what occult process of evolution did her glance derive the toxical effect of the *papaver somniferum?* How did she come to be a Woman-Poppy?"

It is a frustrating process trying to trace the possible influence of a man who writes anonymously for a daily paper, who may be reprinted anywhere in the world, even under a change in title, with no record that it has occurred. Let it be said that A. Conan Doyle's superb short story, *John Barrington Cowles,* collected in *The Captain of the Polestar and Other Tales* in 1894, and published in magazine form earlier, has a striking similarity to *The Facts in the Ratcliff Case,* concerning as it does a woman with a strange power in her eyes and some secret of will-possession that drives at least three men to their respective deaths.

A story that Mitchell originally titled "Twenty Flasks' Baby," but which was published as *An Uncommon Sort of Spectre* in THE SUN for March 30, 1879, certainly lives up to its title. A ghost from the *future* comes back to the past to visit his father in the fourteenth-century Rhineland. The only other important literary ghost from the future before this time appeared in Charles Dickens' *A Christmas Carol* (1843) and there is considerable question as to the legitimacy of that ghost since he appears in a *dream* and not while Old Scrooge is awake. In speaking to his father (known as "Twenty Flasks" for his ability to consume that amount of alcoholic beverages nightly), the ghost from the future points out that since no one ever heard of an apparition from anywhere but the past, it must be his sire who is actually the ghost! The tale is cleverly constructed and delightfully handled.

The sparks of originality that Mitchell was now striking were to flame into brilliance in the course of the next few years. *The Ablest Man in the World* certainly deserves to be so categorized, for in that story, published in THE SUN for May 4, 1879, a watchmaker improves on the primitive arithmetical calculators of the period to the point where he develops a machine that can be fed information as well as numbers, and that can reason. He transplants this thinking machine into the head of an idiot and that individual becomes one of the world's outstanding men. The story is well presented and thought out, the only omission being mention of the power that operates the brain, though this would require little more than the actual electrical energy of the body. This story was one of two by Mitchell selected by the editors of a ten-volume set of *Stories by American Authors* published by Charles Scribner's Sons in 1884, to demonstrate the finest works of contemporary American authors. It was included in Volume 10 and "The Tachypomp" in Volume 5. Among contemporaries to be so honored were Edward Bellamy, Henry James, Frank R. Stockton, Brander Matthews, Thomas Nelson Page, Rebecca Harding Davis, George Parsons Lathrop, and Lucretia P. Hale. The story deserved the distinction, for no earlier *scientifically explained* thinking calculator has yet been uncovered in science fiction.

A few months later, in THE SUN for July 27, 1879, Mitchell scored with another extraordinary forecast in *The Senator's Daughter*, where he utilized mechanical low-temperature freezing units to preserve humans who would be revived at some future date. That story takes place in the year 1937 in a United States that travels by pneumatic tube, heats by thermo-electrodes, has newspapers printed in the home on continuous strips like ticker-tape, eats food pellet concentrates, boasts great lighted fountains and international broadcasts. Things have changed sociologically, the yellow race has won by battle the right to vote and to participate in the government. They also are the proponents of Vegetarianism. The white race has established into law that no Caucasian female under thirty may marry a Mongolian without written consent of her parents or guardian. The penalty is suspended animation in a freezing chamber until she is thirty years of age.

When a white girl under the age of thirty is refused permission by her father, who is a member of the Senate, to marry a Chinese boy, she voluntarily submits to freezing for ten years. She has seen insurance company projections that show her father will be dead in that time and unable to combat the marriage.

The concern over the Chinese who were flooding into the western states following the Civil War has today all but been forgotten, but Mitchell was not alone in expressing this fear in a work of science fiction. P. W. Dooner's novel *Last Days of the Republic,* published by Alta California Publishing House, San Francisco, in 1880, tells of the conquest of the United States by China, and provides adequate testimony to the attitudes which some Americans of that period held toward the yellow population.

Mitchell's next story, in the February 22, 1880, edition of THE SUN, found him still on his scientific bent. *The Professor's Experiment* offers surgery on the brain as a method of altering a person's viewpoint. When a young man finds that his philosophical opinions stand in the way of marriage to the girl he loves, he agrees to submit to a brain operation to change his outlook to one that conforms to hers. The girl and her previously obdurate father learn of it, burst into the operating room while he is under anesthesia, and demand that their minds be operated on to conform to his. He comes to while they are arguing and explains with delight that he has explored the precepts of Brahma under anesthesia and has come around to their point of view (a sort of dig at Madame Blavatsky); therefore the operation will not be necessary after all.

Our War With Monaco, published in THE SUN for March 7, 1880, was little more than a light farce involving the introduction of poker in the gambling rooms of the principality of Monaco by an American, which causes such strained relations that a virtual state of war comes into being. The situation is resolved when the American, in a sight-seeing balloon, threatens to drop cans of dynamite on the city, causing the prince to "forget" his grievance.

Of far greater significance was the appearance of *The Crystal Man* in the January 30, 1881, number. This is the earliest story so far located of a *human being* rendered invisible by scientific means. *What Was It?* by Fitz-James O'Brien, published in 1859, involved an apelike creature whose natural state was invisibility. Guy de Maupassant's *The Horla,* which also concerned a creature who happened to be invisible, would not appear until 1886. H. G. Wells's *The Invisible Man,* the most famous story on the subject, was not due until 1897, yet in its rationale and one of the sequences it has strong similarity to *The Crystal Man.* Both stories go into extensive scientific explanation on the necessity for bleaching the pigments of the body, including the pigments of the retina of the eye and the red corpuscles themselves in order to achieve complete transparency. The only other major invisible man story that employs the same method of invisibility is *The Murderer Invisible* by Philip Wylie, published in 1931, in which the author acknowledges his debt to *The Invisible Man,* and which was eventually combined with Wells's novel for the shooting script of the motion picture.

Mitchell's hero succeeds in making cloth invisible in his early experiments, as does Wells in similar experiments of his character. Mitchell specifically suggests the humor of a seemingly unoccupied suit of clothes prancing about, and Wells actually utilizes such a situation for comic relief in one chapter of *The Invisible Man.* Mitchell's lead character finds himself in a situation where he must remain invisible the rest of his life. "My life is living death; my existence oblivion," he states. "No friend can look me in the face. Were I to clasp to my breast the woman I love, it would only be to inspire terror inexpressible." Seeming irreversibility of invisibility and the aloneness of an invisible man is a potent part of Wells's novel. The ending of both stories is tragedy and death. Mitchell's character commits suicide and Wells's is killed. It is the previously mentioned bleaching method of invisibility, however, which is so extraordinarily similar that it raises the question if by some means Wells might have had the opportunity to have read *The Crystal Man.* Circumstantial evidence will be presented that makes the possibility worth researching still further.

While it is known that Wells was not the first to write of time travel, it is generally believed that he was the first to use a *machine* for that purpose. It is the *machine* that marks the great advance in Wells's concept over that of other authors, because it permits him unlimited flexibility of action within a frame of logic that can sustain "willing suspension of disbelief." It now appears that Wells was not the first author to utilize a time machine, that a prototype of his device appears in *The Clock That Went Backward*, published anonymously by Edward Page Mitchell in the September 18, 1881, issue of THE SUN. An eight-foot-high clock, an heirloom from sixteenth-century Holland, apparently not functional, has been left to Harry, a cousin of the narrator of our story, by their great aunt Gertrude of Maine. The narrator gets the rest of her estate. The clock has only been seen to run in any fashion just once. Late one night, the two boys had observed their aunt quietly leave her bedroom and proceed to wind the weights. The hands of the giant clock began to move—backward. She hugged and caressed the timepiece with a great display of affection. Suddenly it stopped. With a final gesture, she had pulled the hands back to their original positions and then stiffened in death!

Their aunt's will has provided for their education in Holland and they take the clock with them. One of their professors bears an astonishing facial resemblance to Aunt Gertrude. Visiting with them one evening, while a storm is in progress, he proceeds to wind the clock. As it moves backward, there is a tremendous burst of electricity and the two boys find themselves in sixteenth-century Leyden, under siege by the Spaniards.

There, Harry, through his acute observation, draws attention to a breach in the wall which results in saving the city from the attackers and changing the entire course of history, including that of the United States. Wounded during the battle, the narrator loses consciousness to find himself back in nineteenth-century Holland, arm bandaged and with the clock. Harry has stayed behind and will become one of the ancestors of their aunt. The professor is back lecturing in class: "Does the law of heredity, unlike all other laws of this universe of mind and matter, operate in one direction only?" he asks the students. "Does the

descendant owe everything to the ancestor, and the ancestor
nothing to the descendant?"

What the narrator cannot thrust from his mind is the scene of a
man dumping molten lead on the invaders above the breach in
the wall, who is identified by the townspeople as Jan Lipperdam,
the man who built the strange clock which can carry a man
backward and forward in time. When for a brief moment
Lipperdam turned his face toward the boy, it was that of the
professor who had wound the clock that carried the two of them
back into the past!

The Crystal Man and *The Clock That Went Backward* are
remarkable anticipations in the manner of H. G. Wells, who
would not write his earliest, juvenile version of *The Time
Machine* until the serialization of *The Chronic Argonauts* in
THE SCIENCE SCHOOL JOURNAL in the issues of April, May, and
June 1888. Remarkable, but by what stretch of the imagination
might a linkage be shown between them and H. G. Wells?

The clue is to be found in the publication history of *The
Balloon Tree* by Edward Page Mitchell, in many ways his finest
literary effort, published in THE SUN for February 25, 1883.
Scientific researchers on an unnamed island (though its description more approximates Australia than any other locale) are
searching for evidence of reports of a migratory plant which has
the capability of inflating itself with hydrogen and floating from
place to place in search of water, normally difficult to find in its
parched and desert surroundings. Such a plant, it is reasoned,
must have an advanced nervous system and intelligence.

One of the searchers is separated from the group and lost.
Exhausted, his water gone, he collapses and waits for death.
Then, something "Majestic if not beautiful, humane if not human,
gracious if not a woman," picks him up. He sees a massive trunk,
flexible branches, "a wreath of strange foliage and in the midst
of it a dazzling sphere of scarlet." He has the impression of being
conveyed through the air for a long distance, and when full
awareness returns, he is on the seashore with his friends about

him, "and there to the south was a bright red spot on the horizon, hardly larger than the morning star—the Balloon Tree returning to the wilderness." He had been conveyed one hundred miles to safety by this strange, intelligent, feminine plant.

Mitchell's ability to create the proper mood, his admirable restraint in narration, creates here a literary classic in the canon of science fiction. Possibly the earliest story of a truly alien, friendly intelligence that is not a sheer fantasy or fairy tale.

The Balloon Tree was reprinted in the British fiction weekly, SHORT STORIES for December 14, 1895, under the house name of Richard Sibert. The establishment of this reprinting is of major importance. First, it proves that Mitchell's stories were "copied" not only in the United States but in England. Since the publication in SHORT STORIES was twelve years after its initial appearance in THE SUN, it raises the question as to where it had been found by the editors of SHORT STORIES, and whether other of Mitchell's stories were not reprinted in England during the same period. Secondly, a link to Wells derives from the fact that SHORT STORIES was published by C. Arthur Pearson as a companion to PEARSON'S WEEKLY. *The Invisible Man* would appear in PEARSON'S WEEKLY roughly eighteen months later, starting in the issue of June 12, 1897. Beyond that, Wells was writing to order for Pearson for the monthly PEARSON'S MAGAZINE, his first story, *In The Abyss*, having appeared in the July 1896 issue and serialization of *The War of the Worlds* begun with April 1897. To connect Wells with SHORT STORIES further, in his book *The War in the Air*, he credits as a major inspiration George Griffith's future war novel *The Outlaws of the Air*, which was serialized in SHORT STORIES beginning with the issue of September 4, 1894.

The only recent uncovering of the actual titles of Mitchell's stories, the possibility that they may have appeared under other titles and by-lines (SHORT STORIES reprinted Fitz-James O'Brien's famous classic *The Diamond Lens* as *The Eye of the Morning* by "J. O'B" in its November 2, 1895, number), the rarity of copies of SHORT STORIES, the possibility that Mitchell's stories might also have appeared in some other publication, make understandably difficult the job of pinpointing the appearance of a tale as similar to Wells's *The Invisible Man* as *The Crystal Man* in England of almost eighty years past. The discovery of *The Balloon Tree* in SHORT STORIES creates the distinct likelihood that *The Crystal Man* may also have appeared there or elsewhere and may have been read by Wells.

Some of Mitchell's stories blossomed from newspaper experiences. Such a tale was *The Wonderful Corot*, which appeared in the December 4, 1881, issue of THE SUN. The year of the publication of the story, Mitchell had visited a Philadelphia banker who spent ten to twelve thousand dollars a year in researching the occult. In the process, he housed at one time or another scores of spiritualists, mediums, magicians, and other practitioners of strange and mysterious arts. On his visit, Mitchell was shown a painting which was said to be the work of the renowned deceased French landscape artist Jean Baptiste Camille Corot (Mitchell was to become one of the nation's leading devotees of art) and told it was painted with the assistance of spirit influence. In the story, Mitchell gives a superb description of the unusual people who are guests in the home of the Philadelphia banker, and the romantic landscape is confirmed to be unmistakably the work of that master, Corot. As a guest in the house overnight, he is awakened by a sound, to discover some of the spiritualists in the act of theft. To cover themselves, they move to strike him down. Suddenly the voice of a girl, whose fraudulent spiritualistic performance of the night before he kindly had overlooked, shouts to him to save himself by leaping into the landscape of the Corot. He does and emerges in the location in France where the painting was made.

Though again one might feel Mitchell was imbued with the spirit of Lewis Carroll's *Through the Looking Glass*, the story is a splendidly told fantasy whose unusual twist could not have been anticipated by the reader. It is difficult to fault on originality.

The responsibilities given Mitchell by the paper continued to increase and the frequency of his stories was curtailed. His sole appearance in 1882 was in the April 16 edition of THE SUN with *The Last Cruise of the Judas Iscariot*, a story of a bad-luck ship whose owners take her out to sea, loaded with stones, in an attempt to sink her in deep water. A storm comes up and the ill-fated ship tacks back sixty miles against the wind to beach herself with the jib boom driving itself through her captain's window!

In addition to widened responsibilities on THE SUN there were also more responsibilities for Mitchell at home. A second son, Dana, was born December 17, 1881, his wife traveling to Bath, Maine, to give birth. Dana would later become an architectural draftsman.

With their Madison Avenue apartment now overcrowded, Mitchell began a search for larger quarters and finally settled on Bloomfield, New Jersey, a suburb of Newark. He rented a home on Clark Street, and there, on September 29, 1883, a third son, Frank, was born. On September 14, 1885, a fourth son, Robert, was born to the Mitchells.

This, combined with increased commuting time, helps to explain why in 1884 the only story he contributed was *The Flying Weathercock*, a supernatural tale in the April 13 issue. In that story a weathercock atop a church, stimulated by the Devil, flies the structure from the top of a hill down into a marsh.

Charles Scribner, the publisher of the ten-volume set *Stories by American Authors*, which had proven a phenomenal sales success, arranged for a dinner of those writers who had been represented in it, at the Union League Club on March 21, 1885. Mitchell was invited since he had two stories in the set. He was at the time possibly the youngest of the group, but far from unknown. Frank R. Stockton asked if he had come to the affair on a tachypomp. Stockton would register a stunning success on turning from writing fairy tales to science fiction with *A Tale of Negative Gravity*, which would be published in the November 1885 issue of THE CENTURY, America's leading magazine. This proved a delightful story of a man who invents several anti-gravity devices and for fear of having the harmony of his marriage destroyed by the business problems of marketing them, utilizes the devices for his personal pleasure until his strange physical feats get people to doubt his rationality. He then floats the devices off into the blue.

It can be said that Frank R. Stockton and Edward Page Mitchell formed a common school of science fiction writing. Both had a superb command of the English language, were consummate stylists, original and imaginative in their concepts, and leavened their efforts with a light touch of humor. Mitchell's fiction-writing career was drawing to a close, but in the next fifteen years Stockton would become one of America's leading science fiction writers.

Birds of a feather flock together, and at the gathering Mitchell was particularly fascinated by Edward Bellamy, whose *Dr. Heidenhoff's Process* (1880), in which a method is found for blotting out cancerous memories that destroy people's lives, and *Miss Ludington's Sister* (1884), where the theory is projected that the body is inhabited by a variety of souls at different periods in its life and that a medium may restore the spirit of youth, had already appeared. The next year Bellamy would write *The Blindman's World,* a utopia of the Martians who cannot remember the past but can the future. Bellamy's repeated theme was that our accumulated memories are the chains that bind us and ultimately blight our lives, and to rid ourselves of them would be true liberation. Two years later, in 1888, his *Looking Backward* would appear, swinging the entire direction of American science fiction briefly towards the utopian and even winning the unreserved endorsement of Madame Blavatsky as the ultimate design of her Theosophy.

At the meeting, too, was Brander Matthews, who much admired Mitchell, and George Parsons Lathrop, who had married one of Nathaniel Hawthorne's daughters and would later write science fiction under the influence of Bellamy.

Not at the meeting, because his fiction writing days were still in the future, was a man who had been working as night editor on THE SUN ever since Mitchell had come there and would remain a friend the remainder of his life. That man was Garrett P. Serviss, the popular science writer, who would emerge as one of the leading American science fiction writers of the turn of the century. Serviss much admired Mitchell's fiction and his career was to take a similar direction, since his first major work of fiction, *Edison's Conquest of Mars*, a sequel to H. G. Wells's *The War of the Worlds*, was serialized in *newspapers*. The novel appeared in early 1898 and is known to have been carried in THE NEW YORK JOURNAL and THE BOSTON GLOBE at the very minimum, and probably in others. His second novel, *The Moon Metal*, was also first syndicated in newspapers in the Midwest in 1900, the year of its appearance in hard covers.

The implications of newspapers being an important vehicle for the publication of important new science fiction during the nineteenth century is a chillingly nightmarish thought for any serious researcher into the history of the genre.

There was a pickup in Mitchell's fiction production in 1885, but it was to be almost the last flurry before other duties made it impossible for Mitchell to continue to produce the imaginative and delightful tales which he was to refer to with great love and fondness to the very end of his life. *The Legendary Ship*, in the May 17, 1885, issue, tells of a vessel that sets out from old New Haven to establish trade with England and never returns. The townspeople pray for some sign of what may have happened to her. One day the ship is seen swiftly moving into the harbor, sailing *against the wind*. As the ship nears the shore, suddenly the sails and masts are torn aside, the ship dives into the water, and a smoky cloud hovers over the place where she disappears. As the mist clears, there is not the slightest ripple on the surface. The people realize they have witnessed a replica of the disaster that overtook the vessel and that God has answered their prayers.

Though sticky sentimentality was the order of the day, Mitchell's stories were usually free from it due to his somewhat cynical sense of humor and his reporter's objectivity. An exception was *Old Squids and Little Speller* in the July 19, 1885, issue of THE SUN, which is so well handled it almost makes a case for sentimentality and is in many respects a distinctly superior work. The story takes place in the early part of the nineteenth century when toll roads were common. A young tollkeeper, who has acquired the nickname of Old Squids, runs one of the collection sites. The driving ambition of his life is to be able to paint a new sign listing the correct tolls for various wagons and animals. Despite extraordinary application, the feat proves beyond his ability. One night a woman with a child seeks lodging. When morning comes the woman is gone, leaving the baby behind. Old Squids adopts the tot, who soon develops to be of a brilliant and unusual intelligence. In modern science fiction the child would be called a mutant. In a touching sequence, the tiny youngster with limited help from Old Squids, masters spelling and arithmetic easily and paints the sign that Old Squids has worked on in vain for many years. The boy then invents an automatic tollgate far in advance of anything previously seen. When a milling factory opens up near by, he fashions out of pieces of wood a machine design embodying an entirely new concept for the weaving of cloth. It revolutionizes the industry.

While working on a more efficient method of transmitting power to the mill than the water wheel, the boy accidentally falls into the gears of one of the machines and is fatally injured. The mill workers carry him back to Old Squids to whom the boy lisps, "Thid, I shall never work it out." The light that had glowed so brightly in the life of Old Squids goes out and the model of the boy's milling machine provides the last tangible reminder of the wonderful child he had so pridefully loved.

John Collier's method is again forecast in *A Day Among the Liars*, in the August 23, 1885, issue of THE SUN, wherein a man pays a visit to a sanitarium set up by a rich man to cure liars. The trip through the foundation carries with it a rich and exotic harvest of tall stories and a disquieting taste of the less-than-desirable qualities of complete candor of those who have been cured.

The last verified story by Edward Page Mitchell known to have appeared was *The Shadow on the Fancher Twins* in THE SUN for January 17, 1886. In this story, Mitchell returned to a theme that had absorbed him through a large part of his writing career, the interchangeability of personalities. He had previously dealt with it in *The Case of the Dow Twins, Exchanging Their Souls, The Devilish Rat, The Clock That Went Backward,* and now in *The Shadow on the Fancher Twins.* The Fancher twins are brothers vastly different in personality but seemingly one spirit in two bodies. Whatever one does, the other feels and senses. When one falls in love, both do. They realize this is an impossible situation and enlist in the Army to evade their fate. One is court-martialed on the charge of desertion. Actually he has been visiting the girl he loves. Facing the firing squad, he implores his brother, who has been selected for it, to fire first and penetrate his heart. His brother does so and after the shot goes over to the lifeless form and falls across him dead.

The almost biblical beauty of the style brings home the realization that when Mitchell turned from occasional preoccupations with fiction forever, America may have lost a potential master of the short story.

Professionally, Edward Page Mitchell was to grow in stature as a newspaperman until he would be recognized as one of the nation's greatest editors. He was the right arm of Charles Dana until that famed man's death. On July 20, 1903, Mitchell was made the full editor of what was probably the leading newspaper in America. In December 1909 he took over complete administrative control of THE SUN, relinquishing it in December 1911 when William C. Reick gained majority interest in the paper and became president. Mitchell continued as editor, but it seemed inevitable his career would end when Frank A. Munsey bought THE SUN on June 30, 1916, for he rarely left staffs as he found them. Several things happened to alter the inevitable. First, Munsey remembered that Mitchell's telegrams were among those he had transmitted while working on his first job in a telegraph office in Lewiston, Maine! Munsey then proceeded to buy out some shares of the stock Mitchell had in THE SUN at a generous price. Then, with uncommon good taste and delicacy, Munsey asked Mitchell to stay on. At the same time an offer was conveyed to Mitchell from Adolph S. Ochs to come over to THE NEW YORK TIMES. With so many years already invested in THE SUN, it was easier for Mitchell to stay. Yet, unless we are to consider Mitchell a complete hypocrite, his feeling for Munsey must have been reciprocal, for his published statements of praise and affection for that controversial publisher are the most fulsome yet uncovered.

Perhaps his feelings were influenced by a generous pension and the ego-inflating remarks made by Frank A. Munsey at Mitchell's retirement dinner held at the Waldorf-Astoria on January 7, 1922. In attendance were 650 guests, literally every major newspaper editor of importance from Maine to Washington, D.C. Eulogies were delivered not only by Frank A. Munsey (whose kind words Mitchell returned with interest compounded quarterly) but by the former governor of New York State, Martin H. Glynn, who in the course of his address digressed to state: "Into fiction even he has dipped and written short stories with the weirdness of Poe the humanity of O'Henry." With so many of America's leading editors in attendance, the coverage given the affair transcended any thing of comparable nature ever held in the United States.

It was somehow singularly appropriate that Mitchell should have been working for, and eulogized by, Frank A. Munsey, then the leading publisher of science fiction and fantasy in the world, running it regularly in ARGOSY–ALL STORY WEEKLY.

Mitchell had founded the town of Glen Ridge, New Jersey in the late nineties when he led a move for secession from Bloomfield. With his greater affluence he built a fourteen-room home in that community at 325 Ridgewood Avenue. There were books in every room for a total of six thousand, most predominantly on the subject of art. Dana Mitchell still remembers Garrett P. Serviss among their dinner guests in that house.

Though his children stayed behind, Mitchell left Glen Ridge for retirement at a farm called Watchady in Kenyon, Rhode

Island. On three sides for a circumference of forty or fifty miles there was an "enclosure of tree-tops, unbroken by human habitation." There was no electricity, no gas, and presumably no central heating. There, with his books and a few domestic animals, Mitchell, who had been at the crossroads of world events, retreated almost completely from them. With him was his second wife, Ada M. Burroughs, whom he had married on July 22, 1912, after the death of his first wife. One son, Burroughs Mitchell, resulted from the union and would become an editor of Scribner's.

Early in January 1927, possibly on the twentieth, Mitchell became ill from what appears to have been a heart attack. He was removed to the Mohican Hotel in New London, a skyscraper edifice that Frank A. Munsey had capriciously erected in a town of sixteen thousand initially to house the Mohican Food Store chain, which he had started. There he died on January 22, 1927. His body was taken to Glen Ridge, New Jersey, where he was buried.

An extraordinary two-full-page obituary ran in the February 12, 1927, LITERARY DIGEST, then the leading news magazine of its day. They featured him as the man who was "hardly known, even as a name, to the general public." They listed his many achievements (among one *not* included was his editorial drive, which resulted in the United States selecting Panama over Nicaragua for the location of the canal), and ended with notes on his fiction, including mention of *The Ablest Man in the World, The Tachypomp, The Man Without a Body,* and *The Balloon Tree.* They correctly termed the stories "scientific fantasies," but who, in a day when the world's first science fiction magazine, AMAZING STORIES, was not yet a year old attached much significance to such tales? So, with a final blast of rhetorical trumpets, was interred the name and literary reputation of one of the pivotal figures in the history of American science fiction—until now.

THE
CRYSTAL MAN

THE CRYSTAL MAN

Rapidly turning into the Fifth Avenue from one of the cross streets above the old reservoir, at quarter past eleven o'clock on the night of November 6, 1879, I ran plump into an individual coming the other way.

It was very dark on this corner. I could see nothing of the person with whom I had the honor to be in collision. Nevertheless, the quick habit of a mind accustomed to induction had furnished me with several well-defined facts regarding him before I fairly recovered from the shock of the encounter.

These were some of the facts: He was a heavier man than myself, and stiffer in the legs; but he lacked precisely three inches and a half of my stature. He wore a silk hat, a cape or cloak of heavy woolen material, and rubber overshoes or arctics. He was about thirty-five years old, born in America, educated at a German university, either Heidelberg or Freiburg, naturally of hasty temper, but considerate and courteous, in his demeanor to others. He was not entirely at peace with society: there was something in his life or in his present errand which he desired to conceal.

How did I know all this when I had not seen the stranger, and when only a single monosyllable had escaped his lips? Well, I knew that he was stouter than myself, and firmer on his foot, because it was I, not he, who recoiled. I knew that I was just three inches and a half taller than he, for the tip of my nose was still tingling from its contact with the stiff, sharp brim of his hat. My hand, involuntarily raised, had come under the edge of his cape. He wore rubber shoes, for I had not heard a footfall. To an observant ear, the indications of age are as plain in the tones of the voice as to the eye in the lines of the countenance. In the first moment of exasperation of my maladroitness, he had muttered "Ox!" a term that would occur to nobody except a German at such a time. The pronunciation of the guttural, however, told me that the speaker was an American German, not a German American, and that his German education had been derived south of the river Main. Moreover, the tone of the gentleman and scholar was manifest even in the utterance of wrath. That the gentleman was in no particular hurry, but for some reason anxious to remain unknown, was a conclusion drawn from the fact that, after listening in silence to my polite apology, he stooped to recover and restore to me my umbrella, and then passed on as noiselessly as he had approached.

I make it a point to verify my conclusions when possible. So I turned back into the cross street and followed the stranger toward a lamp part way down the block. Certainly, I was not more than five seconds behind him. There was no other road that he could have taken. No house door had opened and closed along the way. And yet, when we came into the light, the form that ought to have been directly in front of me did not appear. Neither man nor man's shadow was visible.

Hurrying on as fast as I could walk to the next gaslight, I paused under the lamp and listened. The street was apparently deserted. The rays from the yellow flame reached only a little way into the darkness. The steps and doorway, however, of the brownstone house facing the street lamp were sufficiently illuminated. The gilt figures above the door were distinct. I recognized the house: the number was a familiar one. While I stood under the gaslight, waiting, I heard a slight noise on these steps, and the click of a key in a lock. The vestibule door of the house was slowly opened, and then closed with a slam that echoed across the street. Almost immediately followed the sound of the opening and shutting of the inner door. Nobody had come out. As far as my eyes could be trusted to report an event hardly ten feet away and in broad light, nobody had gone in.

With a notion that here was scanty material for an exact application of the inductive process, I stood a long time wildly guessing at the philosophy of the strange occurrence. I felt that vague sense of the unexplainable which amounts almost to dread. It was a relief to hear steps on the sidewalk opposite, and turning, to see a policeman swinging his long black club and watching me.

II

This house of chocolate brown, whose front door opened and shut at midnight without indications of human agency, was, as I have said, well known to me. I had left it not more than ten minutes earlier, after spending the evening with my friend Bliss and his daughter Pandora. The house was of the sort in which each story constitutes a domicile complete in itself. The second floor, or flat, had been inhabited by Bliss since his return from abroad; that is to say, for a twelvemonth. I held Bliss in esteem for his excellent qualities of heart, while his deplorably illogical and unscientific mind commanded my profound pity. I adored Pandora.

Be good enough to understand that my admiration for Pandora Bliss was hopeless, and not only hopeless, but resigned to its hopelessness. In our circle of acquaintance there was a tacit covenant that the young lady's peculiar position as a flirt wedded to a memory should be at all times respected. We adored Pandora mildly, not passionately—just enough to feed her coquetry without excoriating the seared surface of her widowed heart. On her part, Pandora conducted herself with signal propriety. She did not sigh too obtrusively when she flirted: and she always kept her flirtations so well in hand that she could cut them short whenever the fond, sad recollections came.

It was considered proper for us to tell Pandora that she owed it to her youth and beauty to put aside the dead past like a closed book, and to urge her respectfully to come forth into the living present. It was not considered proper to press the subject after she had once replied that this was forever impossible.

The particulars of the tragic episode in Miss Pandora's European experience were not accurately known to us. It was understood, in a vague way, that she had loved while abroad, and trifled with her lover: that he had disappeared, leaving her in ignorance of his fate and in perpetual remorse for her capricious behavior. From Bliss I had gathered a few sporadic facts, not coherent enough to form a history of the case. There was no reason to believe that Pandora's lover had committed suicide. His name was Flack. He was a scientific man. In Bliss's opinion he was a fool. In Bliss's opinion Pandora was a fool to pine on his account. In Bliss's opinion all scientific men were more or less fools.

III

That year I ate Thanksgiving dinner with the Blisses. In the evening I sought to astonish the company by reciting the mysterious events on the night of my collision with the stranger. The story failed to produce the expected sensation. Two or three odious people exchanged glances. Pandora, who was unusually pensive, listened with seeming indifference. Her father, in his stupid inability to grasp anything outside the commonplace, laughed outright, and even went so far as to question my trustworthiness as an observer of phenomena.

Somewhat nettled, and perhaps a little shaken in my own faith in the marvel, I made an excuse to withdraw early. Pandora accompanied me to the threshold. "Your story," said she, "interested me strangely. I, too, could report occurrences in and about this house which would surprise you. I believe I am not wholly in the dark. The sorrowful past casts a glimmer of light—but let us not be hasty. For my sake probe the matter to the bottom."

The young woman sighed as she bade me good night. I thought I heard a second sigh, in a deeper tone than hers, and too distinct to be a reverberation.

I began to go downstairs. Before I had descended half a dozen steps I felt a man's hand laid rather heavily upon my shoulder from behind. My first idea was that Bliss had followed me into the hall to apologize for his rudeness. I turned around to meet his friendly overture. Nobody was in sight.

Again the hand touched my arm. I shuddered in spite of my philosophy.

This time the hand gently pulled at my coat sleeve, as if to invite me upstairs. I ascended a step or two, and the pressure on my arm was relaxed. I paused, and the silent invitation was repeated with an urgency that left no doubt as to what was wanted.

We mounted the stairs together, the presence leading the way, I following. What an extraordinary journey it was! The halls were bright with gaslight. By the testimony of my eyes there was no one but myself upon the stairway. Closing my eyes, the illusion, if illusion it could be called, was perfect. I could hear the creaking of the stairs ahead of me, the soft but distinctly audible footfalls synchronous with my own, even the regular breathing of my companion and guide. Extending my arm, I could touch and finger the skirt of his garment—a heavy woolen cloak lined with silk.

Suddenly I opened my eyes. They told me again that I was absolutely alone.

This problem then presented itself to mind: How to determine whether vision was playing me false, while the senses of hearing and feeling correctly informed me, or whether my ears and touch lied, while my eyes reported the truth. Who shall be arbiter when the senses contradict each other? The reasoning faculty? Reason was inclined to recognize the presence of an intelligent being, whose existence was flatly denied by the most trusted of the senses.

We reached the topmost floor of the house. The door leading out of the public hall opened for me, apparently of its own accord. A curtain within seemed to draw itself aside, and hold itself aside long enough to give me ingress to an apartment wherein every appointment spoke of good taste and scholarly habits. A wood fire was burning in the chimney place. The walls were covered with books and pictures. The lounging chairs were capacious and inviting. There was nothing in the room uncanny, nothing weird, nothing different from the furniture of everyday flesh and blood existence.

By this time I had cleared my mind of the last lingering suspicion of the supernatural. These phenomena were perhaps not inexplicable; all that I lacked was the key. The behavior of my unseen host argued his amicable disposition. I was able to watch with perfect calmness a series of manifestations of independent energy on the part of inanimate objects.

In the first place, a great Turkish easy chair wheeled itself out of a corner of the room and approached the hearth. Then a square-backed Queen Anne chair started from another corner, advancing until it was planted directly opposite the first. A little tripod table lifted itself a few inches above the floor and took a position between the two chairs. A thick octavo volume backed out of its place on the shelf and sailed tranquilly through the air at the height of three or four feet, landing neatly on top of the table. A finely painted porcelain pipe left a hook on the wall and joined the volume. A tobacco box jumped from the mantlepiece. The door of a cabinet swung open, and a decanter and wineglass made the journey in company, arriving simultaneously at the same destination. Everything in the room seemed instinct with the spirit of hospitality.

I seated myself in the easy chair, filled the wineglass, lighted the pipe, and examined the volume. It was the *Handbuch der Gewebelehre* of Bussius of Vienna. When I had replaced the book upon the table, it deliberately opened itself at the four hundred and forty-third page.

"You are not nervous?" demanded a voice, not four feet from my tympanum.

IV

This voice had a familiar sound. I recognized it as the voice that I heard in the street on the night of November 6, when it called me an ox.

"No," I said. "I am not nervous. I am a man of science, accustomed to regard all phenomena as explainable by natural laws, provided we can discover the laws. No, I am not frightened."

"So much the better. You are a man of science, like myself"— here the voice groaned—"a man of nerve, and a friend of Pandora's."

"Pardon me," I interposed. "Since a lady's name is introduced it would be well to know with whom or with what I am speaking."

"That is precisely what I desire to communicate," replied the voice, "before I ask you to render me a great service. My name is or was Stephen Flack. I am or have been a citizen of the United States. My exact status at present is as great a mystery to myself as it can possibly be to you. But I am, or was, an honest man and a gentleman, and I offer you my hand."

I saw no hand. I reached forth my own, however, and it met the pressure of warm, living fingers.

"Now," resumed the voice, after this silent pact of friendship, "be good enough to read the passage at which I have opened the book upon the table."

Here is a rough translation of what I read in German:

As the color of the organic tissues constituting the body depends upon the presence of certain proximate principles of the third class, all containing iron as one of the ultimate elements, it follows that the hue may vary according to well-defined chemico-physiological changes. An excess of hematin in the blood globules gives a ruddier tinge to every tissue. The melanin that colors the choroid of the eye, the iris, the hair, may be increased or diminished according to laws recently formulated by Schardt of Basel. In the epidermis the excess of melanin makes the Negro, the deficient supply the albino. The hematin and the melanin, together with the greenish-yellow biliverdine and the reddish-yellow urokacine, are the pigments which impart color character to tissues otherwise transparent, or nearly so. I deplore my inability to record the result of some highly interesting histological experiments conducted by that indefatigable investigator Fröliker in achieving success in the way of separating pink discoloration of the human body by chemical means.

"For five years," continued my unseen companion when I had finished reading, "I was Fröliker's student and laboratory assistant at Freiburg. Bussius only half guessed at the importance of our experiments. We reached results which were so astounding that public policy required they should not be published, even to the scientific world. Fröliker died a year ago last August.

"I had faith in the genius of this great thinker and admirable man. If he had rewarded my unquestioning loyalty with full confidence, I should not now be a miserable wretch. But his natural reserve, and the jealousy with which all savants guard their unverified results, kept me ignorant of the essential formulas governing our experiments. As his disciple I was familiar with the laboratory details of the work; the master alone possessed the radical secret. The consequence is that I have been led into a misfortune more appalling than has been the lot of any human being since the primal curse fell upon Cain.

"Our efforts were at first directed to the enlargement and variation of the quantity of pigmentary matter in the system. By increasing the proportion of melanin, for instance, conveyed in food to the blood, we were able to make a fair man dark, a dark man black as an African. There was scarcely a hue we could not impart to the skin by modifying and varying our combinations. The experiments were usually tried on me. At different times I have been copper-colored, violet blue, crimson, and chrome yellow. For one triumphant week I exhibited in my person all the colors of the rainbow. There still remains a witness to the interesting character of our work during this period."

The voice paused, and in a few seconds a hand bell upon the mantel was sounded. Presently an old man with a close-fitting skullcap shuffled into the room.

"Käspar," said the voice, in German, "show the gentleman your hair."

Without manifesting any surprise, and as if perfectly accustomed to receive commands addressed to him out of vacancy, the old domestic bowed and removed his cap. The scanty locks thus discovered were of a lustrous emerald green. I expressed my astonishment.

"The gentleman finds your hair very beautiful," said the voice, again in German. "That is all, Käspar."

Replacing his cap, the domestic withdrew, with a look of gratified vanity on his face.

"Old Käspar was Fröliker's servant, and is now mine. He was the subject of one of our first applications of the process. The worthy man was so pleased with the result that he would never permit us to restore his hair to its original red. He is a faithful soul, and my only intermediary and representative in the visible world.

"Now," continued Flack, "to the story of my undoing. The great histologist with whom it was my privilege to be associated, next turned his attention to another and still more interesting branch of the investigation. Hitherto he had sought merely to increase or to modify the pigments in the tissues. He now began a series of experiments as to the possibility of eliminating those pigments altogether from the system by absorption, exudation, and the use of the chlorides and other chemical agents acting on organic matter. He was only too successful!

"Again I was the subject of experiments which Fröliker super-vised, imparting to me only so much of the secret of this proc-ess as was unavoidable. For weeks at a time I remained in his private laboratory, seeing no one and seen by no one excepting the professor and the trustworthy Käspar. Herr Fröliker pro-ceeded with caution, closely watching the effect of each new test, and advancing by degrees. He never went so far in one experiment that he was unable to withdraw at discretion. He always kept open an easy road for retreat. For that reason I felt myself perfectly safe in his hands and submitted to whatever he required.

"Under the action of the etiolating drugs which the professor administered in connection with powerful detergents, I became at first pale, white, colorless as an albino, but without suffering in general health. My hair and beard looked like spun glass and my skin like marble. The professor was satisfied with his results, and went no further at this time. He restored to me my normal color.

"In the next experiment, and in those succeeding, he allowed his chemical agents to take firmer hold upon the tissues of my body. I became not only white, like a bleached man, but slightly translucent, like a porcelain figure. Then again he paused for a while, giving me back my color and allowing me to go forth into the world. Two months later I was more than translucent. You have seen floating those sea radiates, the medusa or jellyfish, their outlines almost invisible to the eye. Well, I became in the air like a jellyfish in the water. Almost perfectly transparent, it was only by close inspection that old Käspar could discover my whereabouts in the room when he came to bring me food. It was Käspar who ministered to my wants at times when I was cloistered."

"But your clothing?" I inquired, interrupting Flack's narrative. "That must have stood out in strong contrast with the dim aspect of your body."

"Ah, no," said Flack. "The spectacle of an apparently empty

suit of clothes moving about the laboratory was too grotesque even for the grave professor. For the protection of his gravity he was obliged to devise a way to apply his process to dead organic matter, such as the wool of my cloak, the cotton of my shirts, and the leather of my shoes. Thus I came to be equipped with the outfit which still serves me.

"It was at this stage of our progress, when we had almost attained perfect transparency, and therefore complete invisibility, that I met Pandora Bliss.

"A year ago last July, in one of the intervals of our experimenting, and at a time when I presented my natural appearance, I went into the Schwarzwald to recuperate. I first saw and admired Pandora at the little village of St. Blasien. They had come from the Falls of the Rhine, and were traveling north; I turned around and traveled north. At the Stern Inn I loved Pandora; at the summit of the Feldberg I madly worshiped her. In the Höllenpass I was ready to sacrifice my life for a gracious word from her lips. On Hornisgrinde I besought her permission to throw myself from the top of the mountain into the gloomy waters of the Mummelsee in order to prove my devotion. You know Pandora. Since you know her, there is no need to apologize for the rapid growth of my infatuation. She flirted with me, laughed with me, laughed at me, drove with me, walked with me through byways in the green woods, climbed with me up acclivities so steep that climbing together was one delicious, prolonged embrace; talked science with me, and sentiment; listened to my hopes and enthusiasm, snubbed me, froze me, maddened me—all at her sweet will, and all while her matter-of-fact papa dozed in the coffee rooms of the inns over the financial columns of the latest New York newspapers. But whether she loved me I know not to this day.

"When Pandora's father learned what my pursuits were, and what my prospects, he brought our little idyl to an abrupt termination. I think he classed me somewhere between the professional jugglers and the quack doctors. In vain I explained to him that I should be famous and probably rich. 'When you are famous and rich,' he remarked with a grin, 'I shall be pleased to see you at my office in Broad street.' He carried Pandora off to Paris, and I returned to Freiburg.

"A few weeks later, one bright afternoon in August, I stood in Fröliker's laboratory unseen by four persons who were almost within the radius of my arm's length. Käspar was behind me, washing some test tubes. Fröliker, with a proud smile upon his face, was gazing intently at the place where he knew I ought to be. Two brother professors, summoned on some pretext, were unconsciously almost jostling me with their elbows as they discussed I know not what trivial question. They could have heard my heart beat. 'By the way, Herr Professor,' one asked as he was about to depart, 'has your assistant, Herr Flack, returned from his vacation?' This test was perfect.

"As soon as we were alone, Professor Fröliker grasped my invisible hand, as you have grasped it tonight. He was in high spirits.

"'My dear fellow,' he said, 'tomorrow crowns our work. You shall appear—or rather not appear—before the assembled faculty of the university. I have telegraphed invitations to Heidelberg, to Bonn, to Berlin. Schrötter, Haeckel, Steinmetz, Lavallo, will be here. Our triumph will be in presence of the most eminent physicists of the age. I shall then disclose those secrets of our process which I have hitherto withheld even from you, my co-laborer and trusted friend. But you shall share the glory. What is this I hear about the forest bird that has flown? My boy, you shall be restocked with pigment and go to Paris to seek her with fame in your hands and the blessings of science on your head.'

"The next morning, the nineteenth of August, before I had arisen from my cot bed, Käspar hastily entered the laboratory.

"'Herr Flack! Herr Flack!' he gasped, 'the Herr Doctor Professor is dead of apoplexy.'"

V

The narrative had come to an end. I sat a long time thinking. What could I do? What could I say? In what shape could I offer consolation to this unhappy man?

Flack, the invisible, was sobbing bitterly.

He was the first to speak. "It is hard, hard, hard! For no crime in the eyes of man, for no sin in the sight of God, I have been condemned to a fate ten thousand times worse than hell. I must walk the earth, a man, living, seeing, loving, like other men, while between me and all that makes life worth having there is a barrier fixed forever. Even ghosts have shapes. My life is living death; my existence oblivion. No friend can look me in the face. Were I to clasp to my breast the woman I love, it would only be to inspire terror inexpressible. I see her almost every day. I brush against her skirts as I pass her on the stairs. Did she love me? Does she love me? Would not that knowledge make the curse still more cruel? Yet it was to learn the truth that I brought you here."

Then I made the greatest mistake of my life.

"Cheer up!" I said. "Pandora has always loved you."

By the sudden overturning of the table I knew with what vehemence Flack sprang to his feet. His two hands had my shoulders in a fierce grip.

"Yes," I continued; "Pandora has been faithful to your memory. There is no reason to despair. The secret of Fröliker's process died with him, but why should it not be rediscovered by experiment and induction *ab initio*, with the aid which you can render? Have courage and hope. She loves you. In five minutes you shall hear it from her own lips."

No wail of pain that I ever heard was half so pathetic as his wild cry of joy.

I hurried downstairs and summoned Miss Bliss into the hall. In a few words I explained the situation. To my surprise, she neither fainted nor went into hysterics. "Certainly, I will accompany you," she said, with a smile which I could not then interpret.

She followed me into Flack's room, calmly scrutinizing every corner of the apartment, with the set smile still upon her face. Had she been entering a ballroom she could not have shown greater self-possession. She manifested no astonishment, no terror, when her hand was seized by invisible hands and covered with kisses from invisible lips. She listened with composure to the torrent of loving and caressing words which my unfortunate friend poured into her ears.

Perplexed and uneasy, I watched the strange scene.

Presently Miss Bliss withdrew her hand.

"Really, Mr. Flack," she said with a light laugh, "you are sufficiently demonstrative. Did you acquire the habit on the Continent?"

"Pandora!" I heard him say, "I do not understand."

"Perhaps," she calmly went on, "you regard it as one of the privileges of your invisibility. Let me congratulate you on the success of your experiment. What a clever man your professor —what is his name?—must be. You can make a fortune by exhibiting yourself."

Was this the woman who for months had paraded her inconsolable sorrow for the loss of this very man? I was stupefied. Who shall undertake to analyze the motives of a coquette? What science is profound enough to unravel her unconscionable whims?

"Pandora!" he exclaimed again, in a bewildered voice. "What does it mean? Why do you receive me in this manner? Is that all you have to say to me?"

"I believe that is all," she coolly replied, moving toward the door. "You are a gentleman, and I need not ask you to spare me any further annoyance."

"Your heart is quartz," I whispered, as she passed me in going out. "You are unworthy of him."

Flack's despairing cry brought Käspar into the room. With the instinct acquired by long and faithful service, the old man went straight to the place where his master was. I saw him clutch at the air, as if struggling with and seeking to detain the invisible man. He was flung violently aside. He recovered himself and stood an instant listening, his neck distended, his face pale. Then he rushed out of the door and down the stairs. I followed him.

The street door of the house was open. On the sidewalk Käspar hesitated a few seconds. It was toward the west that he finally turned, running down the street with such speed that I had the utmost difficulty to keep at his side.

It was near midnight. We crossed avenue after avenue. An inarticulate murmur of satisfaction escaped old Käspar's lips. A little way ahead of us we saw a man, standing at one of the avenue corners, suddenly thrown to the ground. We sped on, never relaxing our pace. I now heard rapid footfalls a short distance in advance of us. I clutched Käspar's arm. He nodded.

Almost breathless, I was conscious that we were no longer treading upon pavement, but on boards and amid a confusion of lumber. In front of us were no more lights; only blank vacancy. Käspar gave one mighty spring. He clutched, missed, and fell back with a cry of horror.

There was a dull splash in the black waters of the river at our feet.

THE BALLOON TREE

The colonel said:

We rode for several hours straight from the shore toward the heart of the island. The sun was low in the western sky when we left the ship. Neither on the water nor on the land had we felt a breath of air stirring. The glare was upon everything. Over the low range of hills miles away in the interior hung a few copper-colored clouds. "Wind," said Briery. Kilooa shook his head.

Vegetation of all kinds showed the effects of the long continued drought. The eye wandered without relief from the sickly russet of the undergrowth, so dry in places that leaves and stems crackled under the horses' feet, to the yellowish-brown of the thirsty trees that skirted the bridle path. No growing thing was green except the bell-top cactus, fit to flourish in the crater of a living volcano.

Kilooa leaned over in the saddle and tore from one of these plants its top, as big as a California pear and bloated with juice. He crushed the bell in his fist, and, turning, flung into our hot faces a few grateful drops of water.

Then the guide began to talk rapidly in his language of vowels and liquids. Briery translated for my benefit.

The god Lalala loved a woman of the island. He came in the form of fire. She, accustomed to the ordinary temperature of the clime, only shivered before his approaches. Then he wooed her as a shower of rain and won her heart. Kakal was a divinity much more powerful than Lalala, but malicious to the last degree. He also coveted this woman, who was very beautiful. Kakal's importunities were in vain. In spite, he changed her to a cactus, and rooted her to the ground under the burning sun. The god Lalala was powerless to avert this vengeance; but he took up his abode with the cactus woman, still in the form of a rain shower, and never left her, even in the driest seasons. Thus it happens that the bell-top cactus is an unfailing reservoir of pure cool water.

Long after dark we reached the channel of a vanished stream, and Kilooa led us for several miles along its dry bed. We were exceedingly tired when the guide bade us dismount. He tethered the panting horses and then dashed into the dense thicket on the bank. A hundred yards of scrambling, and we came to a poor thatched hut. The savage raised both hands above his head and uttered a musical falsetto, not unlike the yodel peculiar to the Valais. This call brought out the occupant of the hut, upon whom Briery flashed the light of his lantern. It was an old woman, hideous beyond the imagination of a dyspeptic's dream.

"*Omanana gelaāl!*" exclaimed Kilooa.

"Hail, holy woman," translated Briery.

Between Kilooa and the holy hag there ensued a long colloquy, respectful on his part, sententious and impatient on hers. Briery listened with eager attention. Several times he clutched my arm, as if unable to repress his anxiety. The woman seemed to be persuaded by Kilooa's arguments, or won by his entreaties. At last she pointed toward the southeast, slowly pronouncing a few words that apparently satisfied my companions.

The direction indicated by the holy woman was still toward the hills, but twenty or thirty degrees to the left of the general course which we had pursued since leaving the shore.

"Push on! Push on!" cried Briery. "We can afford to lose no time."

II

We rode all night. At sunrise there was a pause of hardly ten minutes for the scanty breakfast supplied by our haversacks. Then we were again in the saddle, making our way through a thicket that grew more and more difficult, and under a sun that grew hotter.

"Perhaps," I remarked finally to my taciturn friend, "you have no objection to telling me now why two civilized beings and one amiable savage should be plunging through this infernal jungle, as if they were on an errand of life or death?"

"Yes," said he, "it is best you should know."

Briery produced from an inner breast pocket a letter which had been read and reread until it was worn in the creases. "This," he went on, "is from Professor Quakversuch of the University of Upsala. It reached me at Valparaiso."

Glancing cautiously around, as if he feared that every tree fern in that tropical wilderness was an eavesdropper, or that the hood-like spathes of the giant caladiums overhead were ears waiting to drink in some mighty secret of science, Briery read in a low voice from the letter of the great Swedish botanist:

"You will have in these islands," wrote the professor, "a rare opportunity to investigate certain extraordinary accounts given me years ago by the Jesuit missionary Buteaux concerning the Migratory Tree, the *cereus ragrans* of Jansenius and other speculative physiologists.

"The explorer Spohr claims to have beheld it; but there is reason, as you know, for accepting all of Spohr's statements with caution.

"That is not the case with the assertions of my late valued correspondent, the Jesuit missionary. Father Buteaux was a learned botanist, an accurate observer, and a most pious and conscientious man. He never saw the Migratory Tree; but during the long period of his labors in that part of the world he accumulated, from widely different sources, a mass of testimony as to its existence and habits.

"Is it quite inconceivable, my dear Briery, that somewhere in the range of nature there is a vegetable organization as far above the cabbage, let us say, in complexity and potentiality as the ape is above the polyp? Nature is continuous. In all her schemes we find no chasms, no gaps. There may be missing links in our books and classifications and cabinets, but there are none in the organic world. Is not all of lower nature struggling upward to arrive at the point of self-consciousness and volition? In the unceasing process of evolution, differentiation, improvement in special functions, why may not a plant arrive at this point and feel, will, act, in short, possess and exercise the characteristics of the true animal?"

Briery's voice trembled with enthusiasm as he read this.

"I have no doubt," continued Professor Quakversuch, "that if it shall be your great good fortune to encounter a specimen of the Migratory Tree described by Buteaux, you will find that it possesses a well-defined system of real nerves and ganglia, constituting, in fact, the seat of vegetable intelligence. I conjure you to be very thorough in your dissections.

"According to the indications furnished me by the Jesuit, this extraordinary tree should belong to the order of *Cactaceae*. It should be developed only in conditions of extreme heat and dryness. Its roots should be hardly more than rudimentary, affording a precarious attachment to the earth. This attachment it should be able to sever at will, soaring up into the air and away to another place selected by itself, as a bird shifts its habitation. I infer that these migrations are accomplished by means of the property of secreting hydrogen gas, with which it inflates at pleasure a bladder-like organ of highly elastic tissue, thus lifting itself out of the ground and off to a new abode.

"Buteaux added that the Migratory Tree was invariably worshiped by the natives as a supernatural being, and that the mystery thrown by them around its cult was the greatest obstacle in the path of the investigator."

"There!" exclaimed Briery, folding up Professor Quakversuch's letter. "Is not that a quest worthy the risk or sacrifice of life itself? To add to the recorded facts of vegetable morphology the proved existence of a tree that wanders, a tree that wills, a tree, perhaps, that thinks—this is glory to be won at any cost! The lamented Decandolle of Geneva—"

"Confound the lamented Decandolle of Geneva!" shouted I, for it was excessively hot, and I felt that we had come on a fool's errand.

III

It was near sunset on the second day of our journey, when Kilooa, who was riding several rods in advance of us, uttered a quick cry, leaped from his saddle, and stooped to the ground.

Briery was at his side in an instant. I followed with less agility; my joints were very stiff and I had no scientific enthusiasm to lubricate them. Briery was on his hands and knees, eagerly examining what seemed to be a recent disturbance of the soil. The savage was prostrate, rubbing his forehead in the dust, as if in a religious ecstasy, and warbling the same falsetto notes that we had heard at the holy woman's hut.

"What beast's trail have you struck?" I demanded.

"The trail of no beast," answered Briery, almost angrily. "Do you see this broad round abrasion of the surface, where a heavy weight has rested? Do you see these little troughs in the fresh earth, radiating from the center like the points of a star? They are the scars left by slender roots torn up from their shallow beds. Do you see Kilooa's hysterical performance? I tell you we are on the track of the Sacred Tree. It has been here, and not long ago."

Acting under Briery's excited instructions we continued the hunt on foot. Kilooa started toward the east, I toward the west, and Briery took the southward course.

To cover the ground thoroughly, we agreed to advance in gradually widening zigzags, communicating with each other at intervals by pistol shots. There could have been no more foolish arrangement. In a quarter of an hour I had lost my head and my bearings in a thicket. For another quarter of an hour I discharged my revolver repeatedly, without getting a single response from east or south. I spent the remainder of daylight in a blundering effort to make my way back to the place where the horses were; and then the sun went down, leaving me in sudden darkness, alone in a wilderness of the extent and character of which I had not the faintest idea.

I will spare you the history of my sufferings during the whole of that night, and the next day, and the next night, and another day. When it was dark I wandered about in blind despair, longing for daylight, not daring to sleep or even to stop, and in continual terror of the unknown dangers that surrounded me. In the daytime I longed for night, for the sun scorched its way through the thickest roof that the luxuriant foliage afforded, and drove me nearly mad. The provisions in my haversack were exhausted. My canteen was on my saddle; I should have died of thirst had it not been for the bell-top cactus, which I found twice. But in that horrible experience neither the torture of hunger and thirst nor the torture of heat equaled the misery of the thought that my life was to be sacrificed to the delusion of a crazy botanist, who had dreamed of the impossible.

The impossible?

On the second afternoon, still staggering aimlessly on through the jungle, I lost my last strength and fell to the ground. Despair and indifference had long since given way to an eager desire for the end. I closed my eyes with indescribable relief; the hot sun seemed pleasant on my face as consciousness departed.

Did a beautiful and gentle woman come to me while I lay unconscious, and take my head in her lap, and put her arms around me? Did she press her face to mine and in a whisper bid me have courage? That was the belief that filled my mind when it struggled back for a moment into consciousness; I clutched at the warm, soft arms, and swooned again.

Do not look at each other and smile, gentlemen; in that cruel wilderness, in my helpless condition, I found pity and benignant tenderness. The next time my senses returned I saw that Something *was* bending over me—something majestic if not beautiful, humane if not human, gracious if not woman. The arms that held me and drew me up were moist, and they throbbed with the pulsation of life. There was a faint, sweet odor, like the smell of a woman's perfumed hair. The touch was a caress, the clasp an embrace.

Can I describe its form? No, not with the definiteness that would satisfy the Quakversuches and the Brierys. I saw that the trunk was massive. The branches that lifted me from the ground and held me carefully and gently were flexible and symmetrically disposed. Above my head there was a wreath of strange foliage, and in the midst of it a dazzling sphere of scarlet. The scarlet globe grew while I watched it but the effort of watching was too much for me.

Remember, if you please, that at this time, physical exhaustion and mental torture had brought me to the point where I passed to and fro between consciousness and unconsciousness as easily and as frequently as one fluctuates between slumber and wakefulness during a night of fever. It seemed the most natural thing in the world that in my extreme weakness I should be beloved and cared for by a cactus. I did not seek an explanation of this good fortune, or try to analyze it; I simply accepted it as a matter of course, as a child accepts a benefit from an unexpected quarter. The one idea that possessed me was that I had found an unknown friend, instinct with womanly sympathy and immeasurably kind.

And as night came on it seemed to me that the scarlet bulb overhead became enormously distended, so that it almost filled the sky. Was I gently rocked by the supple arms that still held me? Were we floating off together into the air? I did not know, or care. Now I fancied that I was in my berth on board ship, cradled by the swell of the sea; now, that I was sharing the flight of some great bird; now, that I was borne on with prodigious speed through the darkness by my own volition. The sense of incessant motion affected all my dreams. Whenever I awoke I felt a cool breeze steadily beating against my face—the first breath of air since we had landed. I was vaguely happy, gentlemen. I had surrendered all responsibility for my own fate. I had gained the protection of a being of superior powers.

IV

"The brandy flask, Kilooa!"

It was daylight. I lay upon the ground and Briery was supporting my shoulders. In his face was a look of bewilderment that I shall never forget.

"My God!" he cried, "and how did you get here? We gave up the search two days ago."

The brandy pulled me together. I staggered to my feet and looked around. The cause of Briery's extreme amazement was apparent at a glance. We were not in the wilderness. We were at the shore. There was the bay, and the ship at anchor, half a mile off. They were already lowering a boat to send for us.

And there to the south was a bright red spot on the horizon, hardly larger than the morning star—the Balloon Tree returning to the wilderness. I saw it, Briery saw it, the savage Kilooa saw it. We watched it till it vanished. We watched it with very different emotions, Kilooa with superstitious reverence, Briery with scientific interest and intense disappointment, I with a heart full of wonder and gratitude.

I clasped my forehead with both hands. It was no dream, then. The Tree, the caress, the embrace, the scarlet bulb, the night journey through the air, were not creations and incidents of delirium. Call it tree, or call it plant-animal—there it was! Let men of science quarrel over the question of its existence in nature; this

I know: *It had found me dying and had brought me more than a hundred miles straight to the ship where I belonged.* Under Providence, gentlemen, that sentient and intelligent vegetable organism had saved my life.

At this point the colonel got up and left the club. He was very much moved. Pretty soon Briery came in, briskly as usual. He picked up an uncut copy of Lord Bragmuch's *Travels in Kerguellon's Land,* and settled himself in an easy chair at the corner of the fireplace.

Young Traddies timidly approached the veteran globetrotter. "Excuse me, Mr. Briery," said he, "but I should like to ask you a question about the Balloon Tree. Were there scientific reasons for believing that its sex was—"

"Ah," interrupted Briery, looking bored; "the colonel has been favoring you with that extraordinary narrative? Has he honored me again with a share in the adventure? Yes? Well, did we bag the game this time?"

"Why, no," said young Traddies. "You last saw the Tree as a scarlet spot against the horizon."

"By Jove, another miss!" said Briery, calmly beginning to cut the leaves of his book.

THE ABLEST MAN IN THE WORLD

It may or may not be remembered that in 1878 General Ignatieff spent several weeks of July at the Badischer Hof in Baden. The public journals gave out that he visited the watering-place for the benefit of his health, said to be much broken by protracted anxiety and responsibility in the service of the Czar. But everybody knew that Ignatieff was just then out of favor at St. Petersburg, and that his absence from the centers of active statecraft at a time when the peace of Europe fluttered like a shuttlecock in the air, between Salisbury and Shouvaloff, was nothing more or less than politely disguised exile.

I am indebted for the following facts to my friend Fisher, of New York, who arrived at Baden on the day after Ignatieff, and was duly announced in the official list of strangers as "Herr Doctor Professor Fischer, mit Frau Gattin und Bed. Nordamerika."

The scarcity of titles among the traveling aristocracy of North America is a standing grievance with the ingenious person who compiles the official list. Professional pride and the instincts of hospitality alike impel him to supply the lack whenever he can. He distributes governor, major-general, and doctor professor with tolerable impartiality, according as the arriving Americans wear a distinguished, a martial, or a studious air. Fisher owed his title to his spectacles.

It was still early in the season. The theatre had not yet opened.
The hotels were hardly half full, the concerts in the kiosk at the
Conversationshaus were heard by scattering audiences, and the
shopkeepers of the bazaar had no better business than to spend
their time in bewailing the degeneracy of Baden Baden since an
end was put to the play. Few excursionists disturbed the medita-
tions of the shriveled old custodian of the tower on the Mercuriusberg. Fisher found the place very stupid—as stupid as Saratoga
in June or Long Branch in September. He was impatient to get
to Switzerland, but his wife had contracted a table d'hôte intimacy with a Polish countess, and she positively refused to take
any step that would sever so advantageous a connection.

One afternoon Fisher was standing on one of the little bridges
that span the gutterwide Oosbach, idly gazing into the water
and wondering whether a good sized Rangely trout could swim
the stream without personal inconvenience, when the porter of
the Badischer Hof came to him on the run.

"Herr Doctor Professor!" cried the porter, touching his cap.
"I pray you pardon, but the highborn the Baron Savitch out of
Moscow, of the General Ignatieff's suite, suffers himself in a ter-
rible fit, and appears to die."

In vain Fisher assured the porter that it was a mistake to consider him a medical expert; that he professed no science save
that of draw poker; that if a false impression prevailed in the
hotel it was through a blunder for which he was in no way responsible; and that, much as he regretted the unfortunate condition of the highborn the baron out of Moscow, he did not feel
that his presence in the chamber of sickness would be of the
slightest benefit. It was impossible to eradicate the idea that possessed the porter's mind. Finding himself fairly dragged toward
the hotel, Fisher at length concluded to make a virtue of necessity and to render his explanations to the baron's friends.

The Russian's apartments were upon the second floor, not far
from those occupied by Fisher. A French valet, almost beside
himself with terror, came hurrying out of the room to meet the

porter and the doctor professor. Fisher again attempted to explain, but to no purpose. The valet also had explanations to make, and the superior fluency of his French enabled him to monopolize the conversation. No, there was nobody there—nobody but himself, the faithful Auguste of the baron. His Excellency, the General Ignatieff, His Highness, the Prince Koloff, Dr. Rapperschwyll, all the suite, all the world, had driven out that morning to Gernsbach. The baron, meanwhile, had been seized by an effraying malady, and he, Auguste, was desolate with apprehension. He entreated Monsieur to lose no time in parley, but to hasten to the bedside of the baron, who was already in the agonies of dissolution.

Fisher followed Auguste into the inner room. The Baron, in his boots, lay upon the bed, his body bent almost double by the unrelenting gripe of a distressful pain. His teeth were tightly clenched, and the rigid muscles around the mouth distorted the natural expression of his face. Every few seconds a prolonged groan escaped him. His fine eyes rolled piteously. Anon, he would press both hands upon his abdomen and shiver in every limb in the intensity of his suffering.

Fisher forgot his explanations. Had he been a doctor professor in fact, he could not have watched the symptoms of the baron's malady with greater interest.

"Can Monsieur preserve him?" whispered the terrified Auguste.

"Perhaps," said Monsieur, dryly.

Fisher scribbled a note to his wife on the back of a card and dispatched it in the care of the hotel porter. That functionary returned with great promptness, bringing a black bottle and a glass. The bottle had come in Fisher's trunk to Baden all the way from Liverpool, had crossed the sea to Liverpool from New York, and had journeyed to New York direct from Bourbon County, Kentucky. Fisher seized it eagerly but reverently, and held it up against the light. There were still three inches or three inches and a half in the bottom. He uttered a grunt of pleasure.

"There is some hope of saving the Baron," he remarked to Auguste.

Fully one half of the precious liquid was poured into the glass and administered without delay to the groaning, writhing patient. In a few minutes Fisher had the satisfaction of seeing the baron sit up in bed. The muscles around his mouth relaxed, and the agonized expression was superseded by a look of placid contentment.

Fisher now had an opportunity to observe the personal characteristics of the Russian baron. He was a young man of about thirty-five, with exceedingly handsome and clear-cut features, but a peculiar head. The peculiarity of his head was that it seemed to be perfectly round on top—that is, its diameter from ear to ear appeared quite equal to its anterior and posterior diameter. The curious effect of this unusual conformation was rendered more striking by the absence of all hair. There was nothing on the baron's head but a tightly fitting skullcap of black silk. A very deceptive wig hung upon one of the bed posts.

Being sufficiently recovered to recognize the presence of a stranger, Savitch made a courteous bow.

"How do you find yourself now?" inquired Fisher, in bad French.

"Very much better, thanks to Monsieur," replied the baron, in excellent English, spoken in a charming voice. "Very much better, though I feel a certain dizziness here." And he pressed his hand to his forehead.

The valet withdrew at a sign from his master, and was followed by the porter. Fisher advanced to the bedside and took the baron's wrist. Even his unpractised touch told him that the pulse was alarmingly high. He was much puzzled, and not a little uneasy at the turn which the affair had taken. "Have I got myself and the Russian into an infernal scrape?" he thought. "But no—he's well out of his teens, and half a tumbler of such whiskey as that ought not to go to a baby's head."

Nevertheless, the new symptoms developed themselves with

a rapidity and poignancy that made Fisher feel uncommonly anxious. Savitch's face became as white as marble—its paleness rendered startling by the sharp contrast of the black skull cap. His form reeled as he sat on the bed, and he clasped his head convulsively with both hands, as if in terror lest it burst.

"I had better call your valet," said Fisher, nervously.

"No, no!" gasped the baron. "You are a medical man, and I shall have to trust you. There is something—wrong—here." With a spasmodic gesture he vaguely indicated the top of his head.

"But I am not—" stammered Fisher.

"No words!" exclaimed the Russian, imperiously. "Act at once —there must be no delay. Unscrew the top of my head!"

Savitch tore off his skullcap and flung it aside. Fisher has no words to describe the bewilderment with which he beheld the actual fabric of the baron's cranium. The skullcap had concealed the fact that the entire top of Savitch's head was a dome of polished silver.

"Unscrew it!" said Savitch again.

Fisher reluctantly placed both hands upon the silver skull and exerted a gentle pressure toward the left. The top yielded, turning easily and truly in its threads.

"Faster!" said the baron, faintly. "I tell you no time must be lost." Then he swooned.

At this instant there was a sound of voices in the outer room, and the door leading into the baron's bed-chamber was violently flung open and as violently closed. The newcomer was a short, spare man of middle age, with a keen visage and piercing, deep-set little gray eyes. He stood for a few seconds scrutinizing Fisher with a sharp, almost fiercely jealous regard.

The baron recovered his consciousness and opened his eyes.

"Dr. Rapperschwyll!" he exclaimed.

Dr. Rapperschwyll, with a few rapid strides, approached the bed and confronted Fisher and Fisher's patient. "What is all this?" he angrily demanded.

Without waiting for a reply he laid his hand rudely upon Fisher's arm and pulled him away from the baron. Fisher, more and more astonished, made no resistance, but suffered himself to be led, or pushed, toward the door. Dr. Rapperschwyll opened the door wide enough to give the American exit, and then closed it with a vicious slam. A quick click informed Fisher that the key had been turned in the lock.

II

The next morning Fisher met Savitch coming from the Trinkhalle. The baron bowed with cold politeness and passed on. Later in the day a valet de place handed to Fisher a small parcel, with the message: "Dr. Rapperschwyll supposes that this will be sufficient." The parcel contained two gold pieces of twenty marks.

Fisher gritted his teeth. "He shall have back his forty marks," he muttered to himself, "but I will have his confounded secret in return."

Then Fisher discovered that even a Polish countess has her uses in the social economy.

Mrs. Fisher's table d'hôte friend was amiability itself, when approached by Fisher (through Fisher's wife) on the subject of the Baron Savitch of Moscow. Know anything about the Baron Savitch? Of course she did, and about everybody else worth knowing in Europe. Would she kindly communicate her knowledge? Of course she would, and be enchanted to gratify in the slightest degree the charming curiosity of her Americaine. It was quite refreshing for a *blasée* old woman, who had long since ceased to feel much interest in contemporary men, women, things and events, to encounter one so recently from the boundless prairies of the new world as to cherish a piquant inquisitiveness about the affairs of the grand monde. Ah! yes, she would very willingly communicate the history of the Baron Savitch of Moscow, if that would amuse her dear Americaine.

The Polish countess abundantly redeemed her promise, throwing in for good measure many choice bits of gossip and scandalous anecdotes about the Russian nobility, which are not relevant to the present narrative. Her story, as summarized by Fisher, was this:

The Baron Savitch was not of an old creation. There was a mystery about his origin that had never been satisfactorily solved in St. Petersburg or in Moscow. It was said by some that he was a foundling from the Vospitatelnoi Dom. Others believed him to be the unacknowledged son of a certain illustrious personage nearly related to the House of Romanoff. The latter theory was the more probable, since it accounted in a measure for the unexampled success of his career from the day that he was graduated at the University of Dorpat.

Rapid and brilliant beyond precedent this career had been. He entered the diplomatic service of the Czar, and for several years was attached to the legations at Vienna, London, and Paris. Created a Baron before his twenty-fifth birthday for the wonderful ability displayed in the conduct of negotiations of supreme importance and delicacy with the House of Hapsburg, he became a pet of Gortchakoff's, and was given every opportunity for the exercise of his genius in diplomacy. It was even said in well-informed circles at St. Petersburg that the guiding mind which directed Russia's course throughout the entire Eastern complication, which planned the campaign on the Danube, effected the combinations that gave victory to the Czar's soldiers, and which meanwhile held Austria aloof, neutralized the immense power of Germany, and exasperated England only to the point where wrath expends itself in harmless threats, was the brain of the young Baron Savitch. It was certain that he had been with Ignatieff at Constantinople when the trouble was first fomented, with Shouvaloff in England at the time of the secret conference agreement, with the Grand Duke Nicholas at Adrianople when the protocol of an armistice was signed, and would soon be in Berlin behind the scenes of the Congress, where it was expected that he would outwit the statesmen of all Europe, and play with

Bismarck and Disraeli as a strong man plays with two kicking babies.

But the countess had concerned herself very little with this handsome young man's achievements in politics. She had been more particularly interested in his social career. His success in that field had been not less remarkable. Although no one knew with positive certainty his father's name, he had conquered an absolute supremacy in the most exclusive circles surrounding the imperial court. His influence with the Czar himself was supposed to be unbounded. Birth apart, he was considered the best *parti* in Russia. From poverty and by the sheer force of intellect he had won for himself a colossal fortune. Report gave him forty million roubles, and doubtless report did not exceed the fact. Every speculative enterprise which he undertook, and they were many and various, was carried to sure success by the same qualities of cool, unerring judgment, far-reaching sagacity, and apparently superhuman power of organizing, combining, and controlling, which had made him in politics the phenomenon of the age.

About Dr. Rapperschwyll? Yes, the countess knew him by reputation and by sight. He was the medical man in constant attendance upon the Baron Savitch, whose high-strung mental organization rendered him susceptible to sudden and alarming attacks of illness. Dr. Rapperschwyll was a Swiss—had originally been a watchmaker or artisan of some kind, she had heard. For the rest, he was a commonplace little old man, devoted to his profession and to the baron, and evidently devoid of ambition, since he wholly neglected to turn the opportunities of his position and connections to the advancement of his personal fortunes.

Fortified with this information, Fisher felt better prepared to grapple with Rapperschwyll for the possession of the secret. For five days he lay in wait for the Swiss physician. On the sixth day the desired opportunity unexpectedly presented itself.

Half way up the Mercuriusberg, late in the afternoon, he encountered the custodian of the ruined tower, coming down. "No, the tower was not closed. A gentleman was up there, making observations of the country, and he, the custodian, would be back in an hour or two." So Fisher kept on his way.

The upper part of this tower is in a dilapidated condition. The lack of a stairway to the summit is supplied by a temporary wooden ladder. Fisher's head and shoulders were hardly through the trap that opens to the platform, before he discovered that the man already there was the man whom he sought. Dr. Rapperschwyll was studying the topography of the Black Forest through a pair of field glasses.

Fisher announced his arrival by an opportune stumble and a noisy effort to recover himself, at the same instant aiming a stealthy kick at the topmost round of the ladder, and scrambling ostentatiously over the edge of the trap. The ladder went down thirty or forty feet with a racket, clattering and banging against the walls of the tower.

Dr. Rapperschwyll at once appreciated the situation. He turned sharply around, and remarked with a sneer, "Monsieur is unaccountably awkward." Then he scowled and showed his teeth, for he recognized Fisher.

"It *is* rather unfortunate," said the New Yorker, with imperturbable coolness. "We shall be imprisoned here a couple of hours at the shortest. Let us congratulate ourselves that we each have intelligent company, besides a charming landscape to contemplate."

The Swiss coldly bowed, and resumed his topographical studies. Fisher lighted a cigar.

"I also desire," continued Fisher, puffing clouds of smoke in the direction of the Teufelmühle, "to avail myself of this opportunity to return forty marks of yours, which reached me, I presume, by a mistake."

"If Monsieur the American physician was not satisfied with his fee," rejoined Rapperschwyll, venomously, "he can without doubt have the affair adjusted by applying to the baron's valet."

Fisher paid no attention to this thrust, but calmly laid the gold pieces upon the parapet, directly under the nose of the Swiss.

"I could not think of accepting any fee," he said, with deliberate emphasis. "I was abundantly rewarded for my trifling services by the novelty and interest of the case."

The Swiss scanned the American's countenance long and steadily with his sharp little gray eyes. At length he said, carelessly:

"Monsieur is a man of science?"

"Yes," replied Fisher, with a mental reservation in favor of all sciences save that which illuminates and dignifies our national game.

"Then," continued Dr. Rapperschwyll, "Monsieur will perhaps acknowledge that a more beautiful or more extensive case of trephining has rarely come under his observation."

Fisher slightly raised his eyebrows.

"And Monsieur will also understand, being a physician," continued Dr. Rapperschwyll, "the sensitiveness of the baron himself, and of his friends upon the subject. He will therefore pardon my seeming rudeness at the time of his discovery."

"He is smarter than I supposed," thought Fisher. "He holds all the cards, while I have nothing—nothing, except a tolerably strong nerve when it comes to a game of bluff."

"I deeply regret that sensitiveness," he continued, aloud, "for it had occurred to me that an accurate account of what I saw, published in one of the scientific journals of England or America, would excite wide attention, and no doubt be received with interest on the Continent."

"What you saw?" cried the Swiss, sharply. "It is false. You saw nothing—when I entered you had not even removed the——"

Here he stopped short and muttered to himself, as if cursing his own impetuosity. Fisher celebrated his advantage by tossing away his half-burned cigar and lighting a fresh one.

"Since you compel me to be frank," Dr. Rapperschwyll went on, with visibly increasing nervousness, "I will inform you that the baron has assured me that you saw nothing. I interrupted you in the act of removing the silver cap."

"I will be equally frank," replied Fisher, stiffening his face for a final effort. "On that point, the baron is not a competent witness. He was in a state of unconsciousness for some time before you entered. Perhaps I was removing the silver cap when you interrupted me——"

Dr. Rapperschwyll turned pale.

"And, perhaps," said Fisher, coolly, "I was replacing it."

The suggestion of this possibility seemed to strike Rapperschwyll like a sudden thunderbolt from the clouds. His knees parted, and he almost sank to the floor. He put his hands before his eyes, and wept like a child, or, rather, like a broken old man.

"He will publish it! He will publish it to the court and to the world!" he cried, hysterically. "And at this crisis——"

Then, by a desperate effort, the Swiss appeared to recover to some extent his self-control. He paced the diameter of the platform for several minutes, with his head bent and his arms folded across the breast. Turning again to his companion, he said:

"If any sum you may name will——"

Fisher cut the proposition short with a laugh.

"Then," said Rapperschwyll, "if—if I throw myself on your generosity——"

"Well?" demanded Fisher.

"And ask a promise, on your honor, of absolute silence concerning what you have seen?"

"Silence until such time as the Baron Savitch shall have ceased to exist?"

"That will suffice," said Rapperschwyll. "For when he ceases to exist I die. And your conditions?"

"The whole story, here and now, and without reservation."

"It is a terrible price to ask me," said Rapperschwyll, "but larger interests than my pride are at stake. You shall hear the story.

"I was bred a watchmaker," he continued, after a long pause, "in the Canton of Zurich. It is not a matter of vanity when I say that I achieved a marvellous degree of skill in the craft. I developed a faculty of invention that led me into a series of experiments regarding the capabilities of purely mechanical combinations. I studied and improved upon the best automata ever constructed by human ingenuity. Babbage's calculating machine especially interested me. I saw in Babbage's idea the germ of something infinitely more important to the world.

"Then I threw up my business and went to Paris to study physiology. I spent three years at the Sorbonne and perfected myself in that branch of knowledge. Meanwhile, my pursuits had extended far beyond the purely physical sciences. Psychology engaged me for a time; and then I ascended into the domain of sociology, which, when adequately understood, is the summary and final application of all knowledge.

"It was after years of preparation, and as the outcome of all my studies, that the great idea of my life, which had vaguely haunted me ever since the Zurich days, assumed at last a well-defined and perfect form."

The manner of Dr. Rapperschwyll had changed from distrustful reluctance to frank enthusiasm. The man himself seemed transformed. Fisher listened attentively and without interrupting the relation. He could not help fancying that the necessity of yielding the secret, so long and so jealously guarded by the physician, was not entirely distasteful to the enthusiast.

"Now, attend, Monsieur," continued Dr. Rapperschwyll, "to several separate propositions which may seem at first to have no direct bearing on each other.

"My endeavors in mechanism had resulted in a machine which went far beyond Babbage's in its powers of calculation. Given the data, there was no limit to the possibilities in this direction. Babbage's cogwheels and pinions calculated logarithms, calculated an eclipse. It was fed with figures, and produced results in figures. Now, the relations of cause and effect are as fixed and unalterable as the laws of arithmetic. Logic is, or should be, as exact a science as mathematics. My new machine was fed with facts, and produced conclusions. In short, it *reasoned;* and the results of its reasoning were always true, while the results of human reasoning are often, if not always, false. The source of error in human logic is what the philosophers call the 'personal equation.' My machine eliminated the personal equation; it proceeded from cause to effect, from premise to conclusion, with steady precision. The human intellect is fallible; my machine was, and is, infallible in its processes.

"Again, physiology and anatomy had taught me the fallacy of the medical superstition which holds the gray matter of the brain and the vital principle to be inseparable. I had seen men living with pistol balls imbedded in the medulla oblongata. I had seen the hemispheres and the cerebellum removed from the crania of birds and small animals, and yet they did not die. I believed that, though the brain were to be removed from a human skull, the subject would not die, although he would certainly be divested of the intelligence which governed all save the purely involuntary actions of his body.

"Once more: a profound study of history from the sociological point of view, and a not inconsiderable practical experience of human nature, had convinced me that the greatest geniuses that ever existed were on a plane not so very far removed above the level of average intellect. The grandest peaks in my native country, those which all the world knows by name, tower only a few hundred feet above the countless unnamed peaks that surround them. Napoleon Bonaparte towered only a little over the ablest men around him. Yet that little was everything, and he overran Europe. A man who surpassed Napoleon, as Napoleon surpassed Murat, in the mental qualities which transmute thought into fact, would have made himself master of the whole world.

"Now, to fuse these three propositions into one: suppose that I take a man, and, by removing the brain that enshrines all the errors and failures of his ancestors away back to the origin of the race, remove all sources of weakness in his future career. Suppose, that in place of the fallible intellect which I have removed, I endow him with an artificial intellect that operates with the certainty of universal laws. Suppose that I launch this superior being, who reasons truly, into the hurly burly of his inferiors, who reason falsely, and await the inevitable result with the tranquillity of a philosopher.

"Monsieur, you have my secret. That is precisely what I have done. In Moscow, where my friend Dr. Duchat had charge of the new institution of St. Vasili for hopeless idiots, I found a boy of eleven whom they called Stépan Borovitch. Since he was born, he had not seen, heard, spoken or thought. Nature had granted him, it was believed, a fraction of the sense of smell, and perhaps a fraction of the sense of taste, but of even this there was no positive ascertainment. Nature had walled in his soul most effectually. Occasional inarticulate murmurings, and an incessant knitting and kneading of the fingers were his only manifestations of energy. On bright days they would place him in a little rocking-chair, in some spot where the sun fell warm, and he would rock to and fro for hours, working his slender fingers and mumbling forth his satisfaction at the warmth in the plaintive and unvarying refrain of idiocy. The boy was thus situated when I first saw him.

"I begged Stépan Borovitch of my good friend Dr. Duchat. If that excellent man had not long since died he should have shared in my triumph. I took Stépan to my home and plied the saw and the knife. I could operate on that poor, worthless, useless, hopeless travesty of humanity as fearlessly and as recklessly as upon a dog bought or caught for vivisection. That was a little more than twenty years ago. To-day Stépan Borovitch wields more power than any other man on the face of the earth. In ten years he will be the autocrat of Europe, the master of the world. He never errs; for the machine that reasons beneath his silver skull never makes a mistake."

Fisher pointed downward at the old custodian of the tower, who was seen toiling up the hill.

"Dreamers," continued Dr. Rapperschwyll, "have speculated on the possibility of finding among the ruins of the older civilizations some brief inscription which shall change the foundations of human knowledge. Wiser men deride the dream, and laugh at the idea of scientific kabbala. The wiser men are fools. Suppose that Aristotle had discovered on a cuneiform-covered tablet at Nineveh the few words, 'Survival of the Fittest.' Philosophy would have gained twenty-two hundred years. I will give you, in almost as few words, a truth equally pregnant. *The ultimate evolution of the creature is into the creator.* Perhaps it will be twenty-two hundred years before the truth finds general acceptance, yet it is not the less a truth. The Baron Savitch is my creature, and I am his creator—creator of the ablest man in Europe, the ablest man in the world.

"Here is our ladder, Monsieur. I have fulfilled my part of the agreement. Remember yours."

III

After a two months' tour of Switzerland and the Italian lakes, the Fishers found themselves at the Hotel Splendide in Paris, surrounded by people from the States. It was a relief to Fisher, after his somewhat bewildering experience at Baden, followed by a surfeit of stupendous and ghostly snow peaks, to be once more among those who discriminated between a straight flush and a crooked straight, and whose bosoms thrilled responsive to his own at the sight of the star-spangled banner. It was particularly agreeable for him to find at the Hotel Splendide, in a party of Easterners who had come over to see the Exposition, Miss Bella Ward, of Portland, a pretty and bright girl, affianced to his best friend in New York.

With much less pleasure, Fisher learned that the Baron Savitch was in Paris, fresh from the Berlin Congress, and that he was the lion of the hour with the select few who read between the written lines of politics and knew the dummies of diplomacy from the real players in the tremendous game. Dr. Rapperschwyll was not with the baron. He was detained in Switzerland, at the deathbed of his aged mother.

This last piece of information was welcome to Fisher. The more he reflected upon the interview on the Mercuriusberg, the more strongly he felt it to be his intellectual duty to persuade himself that the whole affair was an illusion, not a reality. He would have been glad, even at the sacrifice of his confidence in his own astuteness, to believe that the Swiss doctor had been amusing himself at the expense of his credulity. But the remembrance of the scene in the baron's bedroom at the Badischer Hof was too vivid to leave the slightest ground for this theory. He was obliged to be content with the thought that he should soon place the broad Atlantic between himself and a creature so unnatural, so dangerous, so monstrously impossible as the Baron Savitch.

Hardly a week had passed before he was thrown again into the society of that impossible person.

The ladies of the American party met the Russian baron at a ball in the New Continental Hotel. They were charmed with his handsome face, his refinement of manner, his intelligence and wit. They met him again at the American Minister's, and, to Fisher's unspeakable consternation, the acquaintance thus established began to make rapid progress in the direction of intimacy. Baron Savitch became a frequent visitor at the Hotel Splendide.

Fisher does not like to dwell upon this period. For a month his peace of mind was rent alternately by apprehension and disgust. He is compelled to admit that the baron's demeanor toward himself was most friendly, although no allusion was made on either side to the incident at Baden. But the knowledge that no good could come to his friends from this association with a being in whom the moral principle had no doubt been supplanted by a system of cog-gear, kept him continually in a state of distraction. He would gladly have explained to his American friends the true character of the Russian, that he was not a man of healthy mental organization, but merely a marvel of mechanical ingenuity, constructed upon a principle subversive of all society as at present constituted—in short, a monster whose very existence must ever be revolting to right-minded persons with brains of honest gray and white. But the solemn promise to Dr. Rapperschwyll sealed his lips.

A trifling incident suddenly opened his eyes to the alarming character of the situation, and filled his heart with a new horror.

One evening, a few days before the date designated for the departure of the American party from Havre for home, Fisher happened to enter the private parlor which was, by common consent, the headquarters of his set. At first he thought that the room was unoccupied. Soon he perceived, in the recess of a window, and partly obscured by the drapery of the curtain, the forms of the Baron Savitch and Miss Ward of Portland. They did not observe his entrance. Miss Ward's hand was in the baron's hand, and she was looking up into his handsome face with an expression which Fisher could not misinterpret.

Fisher coughed, and going to another window, pretended to be interested in affairs on the Boulevard. The couple emerged from the recess. Miss Ward's face was ruddy with confusion, and she immediately withdrew. Not a sign of embarrassment was visible on the baron's countenance. He greeted Fisher with perfect self-possession, and began to talk of the great balloon in the Place du Carrousel.

Fisher pitied but could not blame the young lady. He believed her still loyal at heart to her New York engagement. He knew that her loyalty could not be shaken by the blandishments of any man on earth. He recognized the fact that she was under the spell of a power more than human. Yet what would be the outcome? He could not tell her all; his promise bound him. It would be useless to appeal to the generosity of the baron; no human sentiments governed his exorable purposes. Must the affair drift on while he stood tied and helpless? Must this charming and innocent girl be sacrificed to the transient whim of an automaton? Allowing that the baron's intentions were of the most honorable character, was the situation any less horrible? Marry a Machine! His own loyalty to his friend in New York, his regard for Miss Ward, alike loudly called on him to act with promptness.

And, apart from all private interest, did he not owe a plain duty to society, to the liberties of the world? Was Savitch to be permitted to proceed in the career laid out for him by his creator, Dr. Rapperschwyll? He (Fisher) was the only man in the world in a position to thwart the ambitious programme. Was there ever greater need of a Brutus?

Between doubts and fears, the last days of Fisher's stay in Paris were wretched beyond description. On the morning of the steamer day he had almost made up his mind to act.

The train for Havre departed at noon, and at eleven o'clock the Baron Savitch made his appearance at the Hotel Splendide to bid farewell to his American friends. Fisher watched Miss Ward closely. There was a constraint in her manner which fortified his resolution. The baron incidentally remarked that he should make it his duty and pleasure to visit America within a very few months, and that he hoped then to renew the acquaintances now interrupted. As Savitch spoke, Fisher observed that his eyes met Miss Ward's, while the slightest possible blush colored her cheeks. Fisher knew that the case was desperate, and demanded a desperate remedy.

He now joined the ladies of the party in urging the baron to join them in the hasty lunch that was to precede the drive to the station. Savitch gladly accepted the cordial invitation. Wine he politely but firmly declined, pleading the absolute prohibition of his physician. Fisher left the room for an instant, and returned with the black bottle which had figured in the Baden episode.

"The Baron," he said, "has already expressed his approval of the noblest of our American products, and he knows that this beverage has good medical endorsement." So saying, he poured the remaining contents of the Kentucky bottle into a glass, and presented it to the Russian.

Savitch hesitated. His previous experience with the nectar was at the same time a temptation and a warning, yet he did not wish to seem discourteous. A chance remark from Miss Ward decided him.

"The baron," she said, with a smile, "will certainly not refuse to wish us *bon voyage* in the American fashion."

Savitch drained the glass and the conversation turned to other matters. The carriages were already below. The parting compliments were being made, when Savitch suddenly pressed his hands to his forehead and clutched at the back of a chair. The ladies gathered around him in alarm.

"It is nothing," he said faintly; "a temporary dizziness."

"There is no time to be lost," said Fisher, pressing forward. "The train leaves in twenty minutes. Get ready at once, and I will meanwhile attend to our friend."

Fisher hurriedly led the baron to his own bedroom. Savitch fell back upon the bed. The Baden symptoms repeated themselves. In two minutes the Russian was unconscious.

Fisher looked at his watch. He had three minutes to spare. He turned the key in the lock of the door and touched the knob of the electric annunciator.

Then, gaining the mastery of his nerves by one supreme effort for self-control, Fisher pulled the deceptive wig and the black skullcap from the baron's head. "Heaven forgive me if I am making a fearful mistake!" he thought. But I believe it to be best for ourselves and for the world." Rapidly, but with a steady hand, he unscrewed the silver dome. The Mechanism lay exposed before his eyes. The baron groaned. Ruthlessly Fisher tore out the wondrous machine. He had no time and no inclination to examine it. He caught up a newspaper and hastily enfolded it. He thrust the bundle into his open traveling bag. Then he screwed the silver top firmly upon the baron's head, and replaced the skullcap and the wig.

All this was done before the servant answered the bell. "The Baron Savitch is ill," said Fisher to the attendant, when he came. "There is no cause for alarm. Send at once to the Hotel de l'Athénée for his valet, Auguste." In twenty seconds Fisher was in a cab, whirling toward the Station St. Lazare.

When the steamship Pereire was well out at sea, with Ushant five hundred miles in her wake, and countless fathoms of water beneath her keel, Fisher took a newspaper parcel from his traveling bag. His teeth were firm set and his lips rigid. He carried the heavy parcel to the side of the ship and dropped it into the Atlantic. It made a little eddy in the smooth water, and sank out of sight. Fisher fancied that he heard a wild, despairing cry, and put his hands to his ears to shut out the sound. A gull came circling over the steamer—the cry may have been the gull's.

Fisher felt a light touch upon his arm. He turned quickly around. Miss Ward was standing at his side, close to the rail.

"Bless me, how white you are!" she said. "What in the world have you been doing?"

"I have been preserving the liberties of two continents," slowly replied Fisher, "and perhaps saving your own peace of mind."

"Indeed!" said she; "and how have you done that?"

"I have done it," was Fisher's grave answer, "by throwing overboard the Baron Savitch."

Miss Ward burst into a ringing laugh. "You are sometimes too droll, Mr. Fisher," she said.

THE TACHYPOMP
A Mathematical Demonstration

There was nothing mysterious about Professor Surd's dislike for me. I was the only poor mathematician in an exceptionally mathematical class. The old gentleman sought the lecture-room every morning with eagerness, and left it reluctantly. For was it not a thing of joy to find seventy young men who, individually and collectively, preferred x to XX; who had rather differentiate than dissipate; and for whom the limbs of the heavenly bodies had more attractions than those of earthly stars upon the spectacular stage?

So affairs went on swimmingly between the Professor of Mathematics and the Junior Class at Polyp University. In every man of the seventy the sage saw the logarithm of a possible La Place, of a Sturm, or of a Newton. It was a delightful task for him to lead them through the pleasant valleys of conic sections, and beside the still waters of the integral calculus. Figuratively speaking, his problem was not a hard one. He had only to manipulate, and eliminate, and to raise to a higher power, and the triumphant result of examination day was assured.

But I was a disturbing element, a perplexing unknown quantity, which had somehow crept into the work, and which seriously threatened to impair the accuracy of his calculations. It was a touching sight to behold the venerable mathematician as he

pleaded with me not so utterly to disregard precedent in the use
of cotangents; or as he urged, with eyes almost tearful, that ordi-
nates were dangerous things to trifle with. All in vain. More
theorems went on to my cuff than into my head. Never did chalk
do so much work to so little purpose. And, therefore, it came that
Furnace Second was reduced to zero in Professor Surd's estimation. He looked upon me with all the horror which an unalge-
braic nature could inspire. I have seen the professor walk around
an entire square rather than meet the man who had no mathematics in his soul.

For Furnace Second were no invitations to Professor Surd's
house. Seventy of the class supped in delegations around the
periphery of the professor's tea-table. The seventy-first knew
nothing of the charms of that perfect ellipse, with its twin
bunches of fuchsias and geraniums in gorgeous precision at the
two foci.

This, unfortunately enough, was no trifling deprivation. Not
that I longed especially for segments of Mrs. Surd's justly celebrated lemon pies; not that the spheroidal damsons of her excellent preserving had any marked allurements; not even that
I yearned to hear the professor's jocose tabletalk about binomials,
and chatty illustrations of abstruse paradoxes. The explanation
is far different. Professor Surd had a daughter. Twenty years before, he made a proposition of marriage to the present Mrs. S. He
added a little corollary to his proposition not long after. The
corollary was a girl.

Abscissa Surd was as perfectly symmetrical as Giotto's circle,
and as pure, withal, as the mathematics her father taught. It was
just when spring was coming to extract the roots of frozen-up
vegetation that I fell in love with the corollary. That she herself
was not indifferent I soon had reason to regard as a self-evident
truth.

The sagacious reader will already recognize nearly all the elements necessary to a well-ordered plot. We have introduced a
heroine, inferred a hero, and constructed a hostile parent after

the most approved model. A movement for the story, a *Deus ex machina*, is alone lacking. With considerable satisfaction I can promise a perfect novelty in this line, a *Deus ex machina* never before offered to the public.

It would be discounting ordinary intelligence to say that I sought with unwearying assiduity to figure my way into the stern father's good-will; that never did dullard apply himself to mathematics more patiently than I; that never did faithfulness achieve such meagre reward. Then I engaged a private tutor. His instructions met with no better success.

My tutor's name was Jean Marie Rivarol. He was a unique Alsatian—though Gallic in name, thoroughly Teuton in nature; by birth a Frenchman, by education a German. His age was thirty; his profession, omniscience; the wolf at his door, poverty; the skeleton in his closet, a consuming but unrequited passion. The most recondite principles of practical science were his toys; the deepest intricacies of abstract science his diversions. Problems which were foreordained mysteries to me were to him as clear as Tahoe water. Perhaps this very fact will explain our lack of success in the relation of tutor and pupil; perhaps the failure is alone due to my own unmitigated stupidity. Rivarol had hung about the skirts of the University for several years; supplying his few wants by writing for scientific journals, or by giving assistance to students who, like myself, were characterized by a plethora of purse and a paucity of ideas; cooking, studying and sleeping in his attic lodgings; and prosecuting queer experiments all by himself.

We were not long discovering that even this eccentric genius could not transplant brains into my deficient skull. I gave over the struggle in despair. An unhappy year dragged its slow length around. A gloomy year it was, brightened only by occasional interviews with Abscissa, the Abbie of my thoughts and dreams.

Commencement day was coming on apace. I was soon to go forth, with the rest of my class, to astonish and delight a waiting world. The professor seemed to avoid me more than ever. Nothing but the conventionalities, I think kept him from shaping his treatment of me on the basis of unconcealed disgust.

At last, in the very recklessness of despair, I resolved to see him, plead with him, threaten him if need be, and risk all my fortunes on one desperate chance. I wrote him a somewhat defiant letter, stating my aspirations, and, as I flattered myself, shrewdly giving him a week to get over the first shock of horrified surprise. Then I was to call and learn my fate.

During the week of suspense I nearly worried myself into a fever. It was first crazy hope, and then saner despair. On Friday evening, when I presented myself at the professor's door, I was such a haggard, sleepy, dragged-out spectre, that even Miss Jocasta, the harsh-favored maiden sister of the Surd's, admitted me with commiserate regard, and suggested pennyroyal tea.

Professor Surd was at a faculty meeting. Would I wait?

Yes, till all was blue, if need be. Miss Abbie?

Abscissa had gone to Wheelborough to visit a school friend. The aged maiden hoped I would make myself comfortable, and departed to the unknown haunts which knew Jocasta's daily walk.

Comfortable! But I settled myself in a great uneasy chair and waited, with the contradictory spirit common to such junctures, dreading every step lest it should herald the man whom, of all men, I wished to see.

I had been there at least an hour, and was growing right drowsy.

At length Professor Surd came in. He sat down in the dusk opposite me, and I thought his eyes glinted with malignant pleasure as he said, abruptly:

"So, young man, you think you are a fit husband for my girl?"

I stammered some inanity about making up in affection what I lacked in merit; about my expectations, family and the like. He quickly interrupted me.

"You misapprehend me, sir. Your nature is destitute of those mathematical perceptions and acquirements which are the only sure foundations of character. You have no mathematics in you.

You are fit for treason, stratagems, and spoils.—Shakespeare. Your narrow intellect cannot understand and appreciate a generous mind. There is all the difference between you and a Surd, if I may say it, which intervenes between an infinitesimal and an infinite. Why, I will even venture to say that you do not comprehend the Problem of the Couriers!"

I admitted that the Problem of the Couriers should be classed rather without my list of accomplishments than within it. I regretted this fault very deeply, and suggested amendment. I faintly hoped that my fortune would be such—

"Money!" he impatiently exclaimed. "Do you seek to bribe a Roman senator with a penny whistle? Why, boy, do you parade your paltry wealth, which, expressed in mills, will not cover ten decimal places, before the eyes of a man who measures the planets in their orbits, and close crowds infinity itself?"

I hastily disclaimed any intention of obtruding my foolish dollars, and he went on:

"Your letter surprised me not a little. I thought *you* would be the last person in the world to presume to an alliance here. But having a regard for you personally"—and again I saw malice twinkle in his small eyes—"and still more regard for Abscissa's happiness, I have decided that you shall have her—upon conditions. Upon conditions," he repeated, with a half-smothered sneer.

"What are they?" cried I, eagerly enough. "Only name them."

"Well, sir," he continued, and the deliberation of his speech seemed the very refinement of cruelty, "you have only to prove yourself worthy an alliance with a mathematical family. You have only to accomplish a task which I shall presently give you. Your eyes ask me what it is. I will tell you. Distinguish yourself in that noble branch of abstract science in which, you cannot but acknowledge, you are at present sadly deficient. I will place Abscissa's hand in yours whenever you shall come before me and square the circle to my satisfaction. No! That is too easy a condition. I should cheat myself. Say perpetual motion. How do you like that? Do you think it lies within the range of your mental capabilities? You don't smile. Perhaps your talents don't run in the way of perpetual motion. Several people have found that theirs didn't. I'll give you another chance. We were speaking of the Problem of the Couriers, and I think you expressed a desire to know more of that ingenious question. You shall have the opportunity. Sit down some day, when you have nothing else to do, and discover the principle of infinite speed. I mean the law of motion which shall accomplish an infinitely great distance in an infinitely short time. You may mix in a little practical mechanics, if you choose. Invent some method of taking the tardy Courier over his road at the rate of sixty miles a minute. Demonstrate me this discovery (when you have made it!) mathematically, and approximate it practically, and Abscissa is yours. Until you can, I will thank you to trouble neither myself nor her."

I could stand his mocking no longer. I stumbled mechanically out of the room, and out of the house. I even forgot my hat and gloves. For an hour I walked in the moonlight. Gradually I succeeded to a more hopeful frame of mind. This was due to my ignorance of mathematics. Had I understood the real meaning of what he asked, I should have been utterly despondent.

Perhaps this problem of sixty miles a minute was not so impossible after all. At any rate I could attempt, though I might not succeed. And Rivarol came to my mind. I would ask him. I would enlist his knowledge to accompany my own devoted perseverance. I sought his lodgings at once.

The man of science lived in the fourth story, back. I had never been in his room before. When I entered, he was in the act of filling a beer mug from a carboy labelled *aqua fortis*.

"Seat you," he said. "No, not in that chair. That is my Petty Cash Adjuster." But he was a second too late. I had carelessly thrown myself into a chair of seductive appearance. To my utter amazement it reached out two skeleton arms and clutched me with a grasp against which I struggled in vain. Then a skull stretched itself over my shoulder and grinned with ghastly familiarity close to my face.

Rivarol came to my aid with many apologies. He touched a spring somewhere and the Petty Cash Adjuster relaxed its horrid hold. I placed myself gingerly in a plain cane-bottomed rocking-chair, which Rivarol assured me was a safe location.

"That seat," he said, "is an arrangement upon which I much felicitate myself. I made it at Heidelberg. It has saved me a vast deal of small annoyance. I consign to its embraces the friends who bore, and the visitors who exasperate, me. But it is never so useful as when terrifying some tradesman with an insignificant account. Hence the pet name which I have facetiously given it. They are invariably too glad to purchase release at the price of a bill receipted. Do you well apprehend the idea?"

While the Alsation diluted his glass of *aqua fortis*, shook into it an infusion of bitters, and tossed off the bumper with apparent relish, I had time to look around the strange apartment.

The four corners of the room were occupied respectively by a turning lathe, a Rhumkorff Coil, a small steam engine and an orrery in stately motion. Tables, shelves, chairs and floor supported an odd aggregation of tools, retorts, chemicals, gas receivers, philosophical instruments, boots, flasks, paper-collar boxes, books diminutive and books of preposterous size. There were plaster busts of Aristotle, Archimedes, and Comte, while a great drowsy owl was blinking away, perched on the benign brow of Martin Farquhar Tupper. "He always roosts there when he proposes to slumber," explained my tutor. "You are a bird of no ordinary mind. *Schlafen Sie wohl.*"

Through a closet door, half open, I could see a humanlike form covered with a sheet. Rivarol caught my glance.

"That," said he, "will be my masterpiece. It is a Microcosm, an Android, as yet only partially complete. And why not? Albertus Magnus constructed an image perfect to talk metaphysics and confute the schools. So did Sylvester II; so did Robertus Greathead. Roger Bacon made a brazen head that held discourses. But the first named of these came to destruction. Thomas Aquinas got wrathful at some of its syllogisms and smashed its head. The idea is reasonable enough. Mental action will yet be reduced to laws as definite as those which govern the physical. Why should not I accomplish a manikin which shall preach as original discourses as the Reverend Dr. Allchin, or talk poetry as mechanically as Paul Anapest? My android can already work problems in vulgar fractions and compose sonnets. I hope to teach it the Positive Philosophy."

Out of the bewildering confusion of his effects Rivarol produced two pipes and filled them. He handed one to me.

"And here," he said, "I live and am tolerably comfortable. When my coat wears out at the elbows I seek the tailor and am measured for another. When I am hungry I promenade myself to the butcher's and bring home a pound or so of steak, which I cook very nicely in three seconds by this oxy-hydrogen flame. Thirsty, perhaps, I send for a carboy of *aqua fortis*. But I have it charged, all charged. My spirit is above any small pecuniary transaction. I loathe your dirty greenbacks, and never handle what they call scrip."

"But are you never pestered with bills?" I asked. "Don't the creditors worry your life out?"

"Creditors!" gasped Rivarol. "I have learned no such word in your very admirable language. He who will allow his soul to be vexed by creditors is a relic of an imperfect civilization. Of what use is science if it cannot avail a man who has accounts current? Listen. The moment you or any one else enters the outside door this little electric bell sounds me warning. Every successive step on Mrs. Grimler's staircase is a spy and informer vigilant for my benefit. The first step is trod upon. That trusty first step immediately telegraphs your weight. Nothing could be simpler. It is exactly like any platform scale. The weight is registered up here upon this dial. The second step records the size of my visitor's feet. The third his height, the fourth his complexion, and so on. By the time he reaches the top of the first flight I have a pretty accurate description of him right here at my elbow, and quite a margin of time for deliberation and action. Do you follow me? It is plain enough. Only the A B C of my science."

"I see all that," I said, "but I don't see how it helps you any. The knowledge that a creditor is coming won't pay his bill. You can't escape unless you jump out of the window."

Rivarol laughed softly. "I will tell you. You shall see what becomes of any poor devil who goes to demand money of me—of a man of science. Ha! ha! It pleases me. I was seven weeks perfecting my Dun Suppressor. Did you know"—he whispered exultingly—"did you know that there is a hole through the earth's center? Physicists have long suspected it; I was the first to find it. You have read how Rhuyghens, the Dutch navigator, discovered in Kerguellen's Land an abysmal pit which fourteen hundred fathoms of plumb-line failed to sound. Herr Tom, that hole has no bottom! It runs from one surface of the earth to the antipodal surface. It is diametric. But where is the antipodal spot? You stand upon it. I learned this by the merest chance. I was deep-digging in Mrs. Grimler's cellar, to bury a poor cat I had sacrificed in a galvanic experiment, when the earth under my spade crumbled, caved in, and wonder-stricken I stood upon the brink of a yawning shaft. I dropped a coal-hod in. It went down, down, down, bounding and rebounding. In two hours and a quarter that coal-hod came up again. I caught it and restored it to the angry Grimler. Just think a minute. The coal-hod went down, faster and faster, till it reached the center of the earth. There it would stop, were it not for acquired momentum. Beyond the center its journey was relatively upward, toward the opposite surface of the globe. So, losing velocity, it went slower and slower till it reached that surface. Here it came to rest for a second and then fell back again, eight thousand odd miles, into my hands. Had I not interfered with it, it would have repeated its journey, time after time, each trip of shorter extent, like the diminishing oscillations of a pendulum, till it finally came to eternal rest at the center of the sphere. I am not slow to give a practical application to any such grand discovery. My Dun Suppressor was born of it.

A trap, just outside my chamber door: a spring in here: a creditor on the trap: need I say more?"

"But isn't it a trifle inhuman?" I mildly suggested. "Plunging an unhappy being into a perpetual journey to and from Kerguellen's Land, without a moment's warning."

"I give them a chance. When they come up the first time I wait at the mouth of the shaft with a rope in hand. If they are reasonable and will come to terms, I fling them the line. If they perish, 'tis their own fault. Only," he added, with a melancholy smile, "the center is getting so plugged up with creditors that I am afraid there soon will be no choice whatever for 'em."

By this time I had conceived a high opinion of my tutor's ability. If anybody could send me waltzing through space at an infinite speed, Rivarol could do it. I filled my pipe and told him the story. He heard with grave and patient attention. Then, for full half an hour, he whiffed away in silence. Finally he spoke.

"The ancient cipher has overreached himself. He has given you a choice of two problems, both of which he deems insoluble. Neither of them is insoluble. The only gleam of intelligence Old Cotangent showed was when he said that squaring the circle was too easy. He was right. It would have given you your *Liebchen* in five minutes. I squared the circle before I discarded pantalets. I will show you the work—but it would be a digression, and you are in no mood for digressions. Our first chance, therefore, lies in perpetual motion. Now, my good friend, I will frankly tell you that, although I have compassed this interesting problem, I do not choose to use it in your behalf. I too, Herr Tom, have a heart. The loveliest of her sex frowns upon me. Her somewhat mature charms are not for Jean Marie Rivarol. She has cruelly said that her years demand of me filial rather than connubial regard. Is love a matter of years or of eternity? This question did I put to the cold, yet lovely Jocasta."

"Jocasta Surd!" I remarked in surprise, "Abscissa's aunt!"

"The same," he said, sadly. "I will not attempt to conceal that upon the maiden Jocasta my maiden heart has been bestowed. Give me your hand, my nephew in affliction as in affection!"

Rivarol dashed away a not discreditable tear, and resumed:

"My only hope lies in this discovery of perpetual motion. It will give me the fame, the wealth. Can Jocasta refuse these? If she can, there is only the trap-door and—Kerguellen's Land!"

I bashfully asked to see the perpetual-motion machine. My uncle in affliction shook his head.

"At another time," he said. "Suffice it at present to say, that it is something upon the principle of a woman's tongue. But you see now why we must turn in your case to the alternative condition—infinite speed. There are several ways in which this may be accomplished, theoretically. By the lever, for instance. Imagine a lever with a very long and a very short arm. Apply power to the shorter arm which will move it with great velocity. The end of the long arm will move much faster. Now keep shortening the short arm and lengthening the long one, and as you approach infinity in their difference of length, you approach infinity in the speed of the long arm. It would be difficult to demonstrate this practically to the professor. We must seek another solution. Jean Marie will meditate. Come to me in a fortnight. Good-night. But stop! Have you the money—*das Geld?*"

"Much more than I need."

"Good! Let us strike hands. Gold and Knowledge; Science and Love. What may not such a partnership achieve? We go to conquer thee, Abscissa. *Vorwärts!*"

When, at the end of a fortnight, I sought Rivarol's chamber, I passed with some little trepidation over the terminus of the Air Line to Kerguellen's Land, and evaded the extended arms of the Petty Cash Adjuster. Rivarol drew a mug of ale for me, and filled himself a retort of his own peculiar beverage.

"Come," he said at length. "Let us drink success to the TACHYPOMP."

"The TACHYPOMP?"

"Yes. Why not? *Tachu*, quickly, and *pempo, pepompa*, to send. May it send you quickly to your wedding-day. Abscissa is yours. It is done. When shall we start for the prairies?"

"Where is it?" I asked, looking in vain around the room for any contrivance which might seem calculated to advance matrimonial prospects.

"It is here," and he gave his forehead a significant tap. Then he held forth didactically.

"There is force enough in existence to yield us a speed of sixty miles a minute, or even more. All we need is the knowledge how to combine and apply it. The wise man will not attempt to make some great force yield some great speed. He will keep adding the little force to the little force, making each little force yield its little speed, until an aggregate of little forces shall be a great force, yielding an aggregate of little speeds, a great speed. The difficulty is not in aggregating the forces; it lies in the corresponding aggregation of the speeds. One musket ball will go, say a mile. It is not hard to increase the force of muskets to a thousand, yet the thousand musket balls will go no farther, and no faster, than the one. You see, then, where our trouble lies. We cannot readily add speed to speed, as we add force to force. My discovery is simply the utilization of a principle which extorts an increment of speed from each increment of power. But this is the metaphysics of physics. Let us be practical or nothing.

"When you have walked forward, on a moving train, from the rear car, toward the engine, did you ever think what you were really doing?"

"Why, yes, I have generally been going to the smoking car to have a cigar."

"Tut, tut—not that! I mean, did it ever occur to you on such an occasion, that absolutely you were moving faster than the train? The train passes the telegraph poles at the rate of thirty miles an hour, say. You walk toward the smoking car at the rate of four miles an hour. Then *you* pass the telegraph poles at the rate of thirty-four miles. Your absolute speed is the speed of the engine, plus the speed of your own locomotion. Do you follow me?"

I began to get an inkling of his meaning, and told him so.

"Very well. Let us advance a step. Your addition to the speed of the engine is trivial, and the space in which you can exercise it, limited. Now suppose two stations, A and B, two miles distant by the track. Imagine a train of platform cars, the last car resting at station A. The train is a mile long, say. The engine is therefore within a mile of station B. Say the train can move a mile in ten minutes. The last car, having two miles to go, would reach B in twenty minutes, but the engine, a mile ahead, would get there in ten. You jump on the last car, at A, in a prodigious hurry to reach Abscissa, who is at B. If you stay on the last car it will be twenty long minutes before you see her. But the engine reaches B and the fair lady in ten. You will be a stupid reasoner, and an indifferent lover, if you don't put for the engine over those platform cars, as fast as your legs will carry you. You can run a mile, the length of the train, in ten minutes. Therefore, you reach Abscissa when the engine does, or in ten minutes—ten minutes sooner than if you had lazily sat down upon the rear car and talked politics with the brakeman. You have diminished the time by one half. You have added your speed to that of the locomotive to some purpose. *Nicht wahr?*"

I saw it perfectly; much plainer, perhaps, for his putting in the clause about Abscissa.

He continued, "This illustration, though a slow one, leads up to a principle which may be carried to any extent. Our first anxiety will be to spare your legs and wind. Let us suppose that the two miles of track are perfectly straight, and make our train one platform car, a mile long, with parallel rails laid upon its top. Put a little dummy engine on these rails, and let it run to and fro along the platform car, while the platform car is pulled along the ground track. Catch the idea? The dummy takes your place. But it can run its mile much faster. Fancy that our locomotive is strong enough to pull the platform car over the two miles in two minutes. The dummy can attain the same speed. When the engine reaches B in one minute, the dummy, having gone a mile a-top the platform car, reaches B also. We have so combined the speeds of those two engines as to accomplish two miles in one minute. Is this all we can do? Prepare to exercise your imagination."

I lit my pipe.

"Still two miles of straight track, between A and B. On the track a long platform car, reaching from A to within a quarter of a mile of B. We will now discard ordinary locomotives and adopt as our motive power a series of compact magnetic engines, distributed underneath the platform car, all along its length."

"I don't understand those magnetic engines."

"Well, each of them consists of a great iron horseshoe, rendered alternately a magnet and not a magnet by an intermittent current of electricity from a battery, this current in its turn regulated by clock-work. When the horseshoe is in the circuit, it is a magnet, and it pulls its clapper toward it with enormous power. When it is out of the circuit, the next second, it is not a magnet, and it lets the clapper go. The clapper, oscillating to and fro, imparts a rotatory motion to a fly wheel, which transmits it to the drivers on the rails. Such are our motors. They are no novelty, for trial has proved them practicable.

"With a magnetic engine for every truck of wheels, we can reasonably expect to move our immense car, and to drive it along at a speed, say, of a mile a minute.

"The forward end, having but a quarter of a mile to go, will reach B in fifteen seconds. We will call this platform car number 1. On top of number 1 are laid rails on which another platform car, number 2, a quarter of a mile shorter than number 1, is moved in precisely the same way. Number 2, in its turn, is surmounted by number 3, moving independently of the tiers beneath, and a quarter of a mile shorter than number 2. Number 2 is a mile and a half long; number 3 a mile and a quarter. Above, on successive levels, are number 4, a mile long; number 5, three quarters of a mile; number 6, half a mile; number 7, a quarter of a mile, and number 8, a short passenger car, on top of all.

"Each car moves upon the car beneath it, independently of all the others, at the rate of a mile a minute. Each car has its own magnetic engines. Well, the train being drawn up with the latter end of each car resting against a lofty bumping-post at A, Tom Furnace, the gentlemanly conductor, and Jean Marie Rivarol, engineer, mount by a long ladder to the exalted number 8. The complicated mechanism is set in motion. What happens?

"Number 8 runs a quarter of a mile in fifteen seconds and reaches the end of number 7. Meanwhile number 7 has run a quarter of a mile in the same time and reached the end of number 6; number 6, a quarter of a mile in fifteen seconds, and reached the end of number 5; number 5, the end of number 4; number 4, of number 3; number 3, of number 2; number 2, of number 1. And number 1, in fifteen seconds, has gone its quarter of a mile along the ground track, and has reached station B. All this has been done in fifteen seconds. Wherefore, numbers 1, 2, 3, 4, 5, 6, 7, and 8 come to rest against the bumping-post at B, at precisely the same second. We, in number 8, reach B just when number 1 reaches it. In other words, we accomplish two miles in fifteen seconds. Each of the eight cars, moving at the rate of a mile a minute, has contributed a quarter of a mile to our journey, and has done its work in fifteen seconds. All the eight did their work at once, during the same fifteen seconds. Consequently we have been whizzed through the air at the somewhat startling speed of seven and a half seconds to the mile. This is the Tachypomp. Does it justify the name?"

Although a little bewildered by the complexity of cars, I apprehended the general principle of the machine. I made a diagram, and understood it much better. "You have merely improved on the idea of my moving faster than the train when I was going to the smoking car?"

"Precisely. So far we have kept within the bounds of the

practicable. To satisfy the professor, you can theorize in something after this fashion: If we double the number of cars, thus decreasing by one half the distance which each has to go, we shall attain twice the speed. Each of the sixteen cars will have but one eighth of a mile to go. At the uniform rate we have adopted, the two miles can be done in seven and a half instead of fifteen seconds. With thirty-two cars, and a sixteenth of a mile, or twenty rods difference in their length, we arrive at the speed of a mile in less than two seconds; with sixty-four cars, each travelling but ten rods, a mile under the second. More than sixty miles a minute! If this isn't rapid enough for the professor, tell him to go on, increasing the number of his cars and diminishing the distance each one has to run. If sixty-four cars yield a speed of a mile inside the second, let him fancy a Tachypomp of six hundred and forty cars, and amuse himself calculating the rate of car number 640. Just whisper to him that when he has an infinite number of cars with an infinitesimal difference in their lengths, he will have obtained that infinite speed for which he seems to yearn. Then demand Abscissa."

I wrung my friend's hand in silent and grateful admiration. I could say nothing.

"You have listened to the man of theory," he said proudly. "You shall now behold the practical engineer. We will go to the west of the Mississippi and find some suitably level locality. We will erect thereon a model Tachypomp. We will summon thereunto the professor, his daughter, and why not his fair sister Jocasta, as well? We will take them a journey which shall much astonish the venerable Surd. He shall place Abscissa's digits in yours and bless you both with an algebraic formula. Jocasta shall contemplate with wonder the genius of Rivarol. But we have much to do. We must ship to St. Joseph the vast amount of material to be employed in the construction of the Tachypomp. We must engage a small army of workmen to effect that construction, for we are to annihilate time and space. Perhaps you had better see your bankers."

I rushed impetuously to the door. There should be no delay. "Stop! stop! *Um Gottes Willen,* stop!" shrieked Rivarol. "I launched my butcher this morning and I haven't bolted the—"

But it was too late. I was upon the trap. It swung open with a crash, and I was plunged down, down, down! I felt as if I were falling through illimitable space. I remember wondering, as I rushed through the darkness, whether I should reach Kerguellen's Land or stop at the center. It seemed an eternity. Then my course was suddenly and painfully arrested.

I opened my eyes. Around me were the walls of Professor Surd's study. Under me was a hard, unyielding plane which I knew too well was Professor Surd's study floor. Behind me was the black, slippery, haircloth chair which had belched me forth, much as the whale served Jonah. In front of me stood Professor Surd himself, looking down with a not unpleasant smile.

"Good evening, Mr. Furnace. Let me help you up. You look tired, sir. No wonder you fell asleep when I kept you so long waiting. Shall I get you a glass of wine? No? By the way, since receiving your letter I find that you are a son of my old friend, Judge Furnace. I have made inquiries, and see no reason why you should not make Abscissa a good husband."

Still I can see no reason why the Tachypomp should not have succeeded. Can you?

THE MAN WITHOUT A BODY

On a shelf in the old Arsenal Museum, in the Central Park, in the midst of stuffed hummingbirds, ermines, silver foxes, and bright-colored parakeets, there is a ghastly row of human heads. I pass by the mummied Peruvian, the Maori chief, and the Flathead Indian to speak of a Caucasian head which has had a fascinating interest to me ever since it was added to the grim collection a little more than a year ago.

I was struck with the Head when I first saw it. The pensive intelligence of the features won me. The face is remarkable, although the nose is gone, and the nasal fossae are somewhat the worse for wear. The eyes are likewise wanting, but the empty orbs have an expression of their own. The parchmenty skin is so shriveled that the teeth show to their roots in the jaws. The mouth has been much affected by the ravages of decay, but what mouth there is displays character. It seems to say: "Barring certain deficiencies in my anatomy, you behold a man of parts!" The features of the Head are of the Teutonic cast, and the skull is the skull of a philosopher. What particularly attracted my attention, however, was the vague resemblance which this dilapidated countenance bore to some face which had at some time been familiar to me—some face which lingered in my memory, but which I could not place.

After all, I was not greatly surprised, when I had known the Head for nearly a year, to see it acknowledge our acquaintance and express its appreciation of friendly interest on my part by deliberately winking at me as I stood before its glass case.

This was on a Trustees' Day, and I was the only visitor in the hall. The faithful attendant had gone to enjoy a can of beer with his friend, the superintendent of the monkeys.

The Head winked a second time, and even more cordially than before. I gazed upon its efforts with the critical delight of an anatomist. I saw the masseter muscle flex beneath the leathery skin. I saw the play of the glutinators, and the beautiful lateral movement of the internal playtsyma. I knew the Head was trying to speak to me. I noted the convulsive twitchings of the risorius and the zygomatic major, and knew that it was endeavoring to smile.

"Here," I thought, "is either a case of vitality long after decapitation, or, an instance of reflex action where there is no diastaltic or excitor-motory system. In either case the phenomenon is unprecedented, and should be carefully observed. Besides, the Head is evidently well disposed toward me." I found a key on my bunch which opened the glass door.

"Thanks," said the Head. "A breath of fresh air is quite a treat."

"How do you feel?" I asked politely. "How does it seem without a body?"

The Head shook itself sadly and sighed. "I would give," it said, speaking through its ruined nose, and for obvious reasons using chest tones sparingly, "I would give both ears for a single leg. My ambition is principally ambulatory, and yet I cannot walk. I cannot even hop or waddle. I would fain travel, roam, promenade, circulate in the busy paths of men, but I am chained to this accursed shelf. I am no better off than these barbarian heads —I, a man of science! I am compelled to sit here on my neck and see sandpipers and storks all around me, with legs and to spare. Look at that infernal little Oedieneninus longpipes over there. Look at that miserable gray-headed porphyric. They have no brains, no ambition, no yearnings. Yet they have legs, legs, legs, in profusion." He cast an envious glance across the alcove at the tantalizing limbs of the birds in question and added gloomily, "There isn't even enough of me to make a hero for one of Wilkie Collins's novels."

I did not exactly know how to console him in so delicate a manner, but ventured to hint that perhaps his condition had its compensations in immunity from corns and the gout.

"And as to arms," he went on, "there's another misfortune for you! I am unable to brush away the flies that get in here—Lord knows how—in the summertime. I cannot reach over and cuff that confounded Chinook mummy that sits there grinning at me like a jack-in-the-box. I cannot scratch my head or even blow my nose (his nose!) decently when I get cold in this thundering draft. As to eating and drinking, I don't care. My soul is wrapped up in science. Science is my bride, my divinity. I worship her footsteps in the past and hail the prophecy of her future progress. I—"

I had heard these sentiments before. In a flash I had accounted for the familiar look which had haunted me ever since I first saw the Head. "Pardon me," I said, "you are the celebrated Professor Dummkopf?"

"That is, or was, my name," he replied, with dignity.

"And you formerly lived in Boston, where you carried on scientific experiments of startling originality. It was you who first discovered how to photograph smell, how to bottle music, how to freeze the aurora borealis. It was you who first applied spectrum analysis to Mind."

"Those were some of my minor achievements," said the Head, sadly nodding itself—"small when compared with my final invention, the grand discovery which was at the same time my greatest triumph and my ruin. I lost my Body in an experiment."

"How was that?" I asked. "I had not heard."

"No," said the Head. "I being alone and friendless, my disappearance was hardly noticed. I will tell you."

There was a sound upon the stairway. "Hush!" cried the Head. "Here comes somebody. We must not be discovered. You must dissemble."

I hastily closed the door of the glass case, locking it just in time to evade the vigilance of the returning keeper, and dissembled by pretending to examine, with great interest, a nearby exhibit.

On the next Trustees' Day I revisited the museum and gave the keeper of the Head a dollar on the pretense of purchasing information in regard to the curiosities in his charge. He made the circuit of the hall with me, talking volubly all the while.

"That there," he said, as we stood before the Head, "is a relic of morality presented to the museum fifteen months ago. The head of a notorious murderer guillotined at Paris in the last century, sir."

I fancied that I saw a slight twitching about the corners of Professor Dummkopf's mouth and an almost imperceptible depression of what was once his left eyelid, but he kept his face remarkably well under the circumstances. I dismissed my guide with many thanks for his intelligent services, and, as I had anticipated, he departed forthwith to invest his easily earned dollar in beer, leaving me to pursue my conversation with the Head.

"Think of putting a wooden-headed idiot like that," said the professor, after I had opened his glass prison, "in charge of a portion, however small, of a man of science—of the inventor of the Telepomp! Paris! Murderer! Last century, indeed!" and the Head shook with laughter until I feared that it would tumble off the shelf.

"You spoke of your invention, the Telepomp," I suggested.

"Ah, yes," said the Head, simultaneously recovering its gravity and its center of gravity; "I promised to tell you how I happen to be a Man without a Body. You see that some three or four years ago I discovered the principle of the transmission of sound by electricity. My telephone, as I called it, would have been an invention of great practical utility if I had been spared to introduce it to the public. But, alas—"

"Excuse the interruption," I said, "but I must inform you that somebody else has recently accomplished the same thing. The telephone is a realized fact."

"Have they gone any further?" he eagerly asked. "Have they discovered the great secret of the transmission of atoms? In other words, have they accomplished the Telepomp?"

"I have heard nothing of the kind," I hastened to assure him, "but what do you mean?"

"Listen," he said. "In the course of my experiments with the telephone I became convinced that the same principle was capable of indefinite expansion. Matter is made up of molecules, and molecules, in their turn, are made up of atoms. The atom, you know, is the unit of being. The molecules differ according to the number and the arrangement of their constituent atoms. Chemical changes are effected by the dissolution of the atoms in the molecules and their rearrangements into molecules of another kind. This dissolution may be accomplished by chemical affinity or by a sufficiently strong electric current. Do you follow me?"

"Perfectly."

"Well, then, following out this line of thought, I conceived a great idea. There was no reason why matter could not be telegraphed, or, to be etymologically accurate, 'telepomped.' It was only necessary to effect at one end of the line the disintegration of the molecules into atoms and to convey the vibrations of the chemical dissolution by electricity to the other pole, where a corresponding reconstruction could be effected from other atoms. As all atoms are alike, their arrangement into molecules of the same order, and the arrangement of those molecules into an organization similar to the original organization, would be practically a reproduction of the original. It would be a materialization —not in the sense of the spiritualists' cant, but in all the truth and logic of stern science. Do you still follow me?"

"It is a little misty," I said, "but I think I get the point. You would telegraph the Idea of the matter, to use the word Idea in Plato's sense."

"Precisely. A candle flame is the same candle flame although the burning gas is continually changing. A wave on the surface of water is the same wave, although the water composing it is shifting as it moves. A man is the same man although there is not an atom in his body which was there five years before. It is the form, the shape, the Idea, that is essential. The vibrations that give individuality to matter may be transmitted to a distance by wire just as readily as the vibrations that give individuality to sound. So I constructed an instrument by which I could pull down matter, so to speak, at the anode and build it up again on the same plan at the cathode. This was my Telepomp."

"But in practice—how did the Telepomp work?"

"To perfection! In my rooms on Joy Street, in Boston, I had about five miles of wire. I had no difficulty in sending simple compounds, such as quartz, starch, and water, from one room to another over this five-mile coil. I shall never forget the joy with which I disintegrated a three-cent postage stamp in one room and found it immediately reproduced at the receiving instrument in another. This success with inorganic matter emboldened me to attempt the same thing with a living organism. I caught a cat—a black and yellow cat—and I submitted him to a terrible current from my two-hundred-cup battery. The cat disappeared in a twinkling. I hastened to the next room and, to my immense satisfaction, found Thomas there, alive and purring, although somewhat astonished. It worked like a charm."

"This is certainly very remarkable."

"Isn't it? After my experiment with the cat, a gigantic idea took possession of me. If I could send a feline being, why not send a human being? If I could transmit a cat five miles by wire in an instant by electricity, why not transmit a man to London by Atlantic cable and with equal dispatch? I resolved to strengthen my already powerful battery and try the experiment. Like a thorough votary of science, I resolved to try the experiment on myself.

"I do not like to dwell upon this chapter of my experience," continued the Head, winking at a tear which had trickled down on to his cheek and which I gently wiped away for him with my own pocket handkerchief. "Suffice it that I trebled the cups in my battery, stretched my wire over housetops to my lodgings in Phillips Street, made everything ready, and with a solemn calmness born of my confidence in the theory, placed myself in the receiving instrument of the Telepomp at my Joy Street office. I was as sure that when I made the connection with the battery I would find myself in my rooms in Phillips Street as I was sure of my existence. Then I touched the key that let on the electricity. Alas!"

For some moments my friend was unable to speak. At last, with an effort, he resumed his narrative.

"I began to disintegrate at my feet and slowly disappeared under my own eyes. My legs melted away, and then my trunk and arms. That something was wrong, I knew from the exceeding slowness of my dissolution, but I was helpless. Then my head went and I lost all consciousness. According to my theory, my head, having been the last to disappear, should have been the first to materialize at the other end of the wire. The theory was confirmed in fact. I recovered consciousness. I opened my eyes in my Phillips Street apartments. My chin was materializing, and with great satisfaction I saw my neck slowly taking shape. Suddenly, and about at the third cervical vertebra, the process stopped. In a flash I knew the reason. I had forgotten to replenish the cups of my battery with fresh sulphuric acid, and there was not electricity enough to materialize the rest of me. I was a Head, but my body was Lord knows where."

I did not attempt to offer consolation. Words would have been mockery in the presence of Professor Dummkopf's grief.

"What matters it about the rest?" he sadly continued. The house in Phillips Street was full of medical students. I suppose that some of them found my head, and knowing nothing of me or of the Telepomp, appropriated it for purposes of anatomical study. I suppose that they attempted to preserve it by means of some arsenical preparation. How badly the work was done is shown by my defective nose. I suppose that I drifted from medical student to medical student and from anatomical cabinet to anatomical cabinet until some would-be humorist presented me to this collection as a French murderer of the last century. For some months I knew nothing, and when I recovered consciousness I found myself here.

"Such," added the Head, with a dry, harsh laugh, "is the irony of fate!"

"Is there nothing I can do for you?" I asked, after a pause.

"Thank you," the Head replied; "I am tolerably cheerful and resigned. I have lost pretty much all interest in experimental science. I sit here day after day and watch the objects of zoological, ichthyological, ethnological, and conchological interest with which this admirable museum abounds. I don't know of anything you can do for me.

"Stay," he added, as his gaze fell once more upon the exasperating legs of the Oedienenius longpipes opposite him. "If there is anything I do feel the need of, it is outdoor exercise. Couldn't you manage in some way to take me out for a walk?"

I confess that I was somewhat staggered by this request, but promised to do what I could. After some deliberation, I formed a plan, which was carried out in the following manner:

I returned to the museum that afternoon just before the closing hour, and hid myself behind the mammoth sea cow, or *Manatus Americanus*. The attendant, after a cursory glance through the hall, locked up the building and departed. Then I came boldly forth and removed my friend from his shelf. With a piece of stout twine, I lashed his one or two vertebrae to the headless vertebrae of a skeleton moa. This gigantic and extinct bird of New Zealand is heavy-legged, full-breasted, tall as a man, and has huge, sprawling feet. My friend, thus provided with legs and arms, manifested extraordinary glee. He walked about, stamped his big feet, swung his wings, and occasionally broke forth into a hilarious shuffle. I was obliged to remind him that he must support the dignity of the venerable bird whose skeleton he had borrowed. I despoiled the African lion of his glass eyes, and inserted them in the empty orbits of the Head. I gave Professor Dummkopf a Fiji war lance for a walking stick, covered him with a Sioux blanket, and then we issued forth from the old arsenal into the fresh night air and the moonlight, and wandered arm in arm along the shores of the quiet lake and through the mazy paths of the Ramble.

THE CLOCK THAT WENT BACKWARD

A row of Lombardy poplars stood in front of my great-aunt Gertrude's house, on the bank of the Sheepscot River. In personal appearance my aunt was surprisingly like one of those trees. She had the look of hopeless anemia that distinguishes them from fuller blooded sorts. She was tall, severe in outline, and extremely thin. Her habiliments clung to her. I am sure that had the gods found occasion to impose upon her the fate of Daphne she would have taken her place easily and naturally in the dismal row, as melancholy a poplar as the rest.

Some of my earliest recollections are of this venerable relative. Alive and dead she bore an important part in the events I am about to recount: events which I believe to be without parallel in the experience of mankind.

During our periodical visits of duty to Aunt Gertrude in Maine, my cousin Harry and myself were accustomed to speculate much on her age. Was she sixty, or was she six score? We had no precise information; she might have been either. The old lady was surrounded by old-fashioned things. She seemed to live altogether in the past. In her short half-hours of communicativeness, over her second cup of tea, or on the piazza where the poplars sent slim shadows directly toward the east, she used to tell us stories of her alleged ancestors. I say alleged, because we never fully believed that she had ancestors.

A genealogy is a stupid thing. Here is Aunt Gertrude's, reduced to its simplest forms:

Her great-great-grandmother (1599–1642) was a woman of Holland who married a Puritan refugee, and sailed from Leyden to Plymouth in the ship *Ann* in the year of our Lord 1632. This Pilgrim mother had a daughter, Aunt Gertrude's great-grandmother (1640–1718). She came to the Eastern District of Massachusetts in the early part of the last century, and was carried off by the Indians in the Penobscot wars. Her daughter (1680–1776) lived to see these colonies free and independent, and contributed to the population of the coming republic not less than nineteen stalwart sons and comely daughters. One of the latter (1735–1802) married a Wiscasset skipper engaged in the West India trade, with whom she sailed. She was twice wrecked at sea—once on what is now Seguin Island and once on San Salvador. It was on San Salvador that Aunt Gertrude was born.

We got to be very tired of hearing this family history. Perhaps it was the constant repetition and the merciless persistency with which the above dates were driven into our young ears that made us skeptics. As I have said, we took little stock in Aunt Gertrude's ancestors. They seemed highly improbable. In our private opinion the great-grandmothers and grandmothers and so forth were pure myths, and Aunt Gertrude herself was the principal in all the adventures attributed to them, having lasted from century to century while generations of contemporaries went the way of all flesh.

On the first landing of the square stairway of the mansion loomed a tall Dutch clock. The case was more than eight feet high, of a dark red wood, not mahogany, and it was curiously inlaid with silver. No common piece of furniture was this. About a hundred years ago there flourished in the town of Brunswick a horologist named Cary, an industrious and accomplished workman. Few well-to-do houses on that part of the coast lacked a Cary timepiece. But Aunt Gertrude's clock had marked the hours and minutes of two full centuries before the Brunswick artisan was born. It was running when William the Taciturn pierced the dikes to relieve Leyden. The name of the maker, Jan Lipperdam, and the date, 1572, were still legible in broad black letters and figures reaching quite across the dial. Cary's masterpieces were plebeian and recent beside this ancient aristocrat. The jolly Dutch moon, made to exhibit the phases over a landscape of windmills and polders, was cunningly painted. A skilled hand had carved the grim ornament at the top, a death's head transfixed by a two-edged sword. Like all timepieces of the sixteenth century, it had no pendulum. A simple Van Wyck escapement governed the descent of the weights to the bottom of the tall case.

But these weights never moved. Year after year, when Harry and I returned to Maine, we found the hands of the old clock pointing to the quarter past three, as they had pointed when we first saw them. The fat moon hung perpetually in the third quarter, as motionless as the death's head above. There was a mystery about the silenced movement and the paralyzed hands. Aunt Gertrude told us that the works had never performed their functions since a bolt of lightning entered the clock; and she showed us a black hole in the side of the case near the top, with a yawning rift that extended downward for several feet. This explanation failed to satisfy us. It did not account for the sharpness of her refusal when we proposed to bring over the watchmaker from the village, or for her singular agitation once when she found Harry on a stepladder, with a borrowed key in his hand, about to test for himself the clock's suspended vitality.

One August night, after we had grown out of boyhood, I was awakened by a noise in the hallway. I shook my cousin. "Somebody's in the house," I whispered.

We crept out of our room and on to the stairs. A dim light came from below. We held breath and noiselessly descended to the second landing. Harry clutched my arm. He pointed down over the banisters, at the same time drawing me back into the shadow.

We saw a strange thing.

Aunt Gertrude stood on a chair in front of the old clock, as spectral in her white nightgown and white nightcap as one of the poplars when covered with snow. It chanced that the floor creaked slightly under our feet. She turned with a sudden movement, peering intently into the darkness, and holding a candle high toward us, so that the light was full upon her pale face. She looked many years older than when I bade her good night. For a few minutes she was motionless, except in the trembling arm that held aloft the candle. Then, evidently reassured, she placed the light upon a shelf and turned again to the clock.

We now saw the old lady take a key from behind the face and proceed to wind up the weights. We could hear her breath, quick and short. She rested a hand on either side of the case and held her face close to the dial, as if subjecting it to anxious scrutiny. In this attitude she remained for a long time. We heard her utter a sigh of relief, and she half turned toward us for a moment. I shall never forget the expression of wild joy that transfigured her features then.

The hands of the clock were moving; they were moving backward.

Aunt Gertrude put both arms around the clock and pressed her withered cheek against it. She kissed it repeatedly. She caressed it in a hundred ways, as if it had been a living and beloved thing. She fondled it and talked to it, using words which we could hear but could not understand. The hands continued to move backward.

Then she started back with a sudden cry. The clock had stopped. We saw her tall body swaying for an instant on the chair. She stretched out her arms in a convulsive gesture of terror and despair, wrenched the minute hand to its old place at a quarter past three, and fell heavily to the floor.

Aunt Gertrude's will left me her bank and gas stocks, real estate, railroad bonds, and city sevens, and gave Harry the clock. We thought at the time that this was a very unequal division, the more surprising because my cousin had always seemed to be the favorite. Half in seriousness we made a thorough examination of the ancient timepiece, sounding its wooden case for secret drawers, and even probing the not complicated works with a knitting needle to ascertain if our whimsical relative had bestowed there some codicil or other document changing the aspect of affairs. We discovered nothing.

There was testamentary provision for our education at the University of Leyden. We left the military school in which we had learned a little of the theory of war, and a good deal of the art of standing with our noses over our heels, and took ship without delay. The clock went with us. Before many months it was established in a corner of a room in the Breede Straat.

The fabric of Jan Lipperdam's ingenuity, thus restored to its native air, continued to tell the hour of quarter past three with its old fidelity. The author of the clock had been under the sod for nearly three hundred years. The combined skill of his successors in the craft at Leyden could make it go neither forward nor backward.

We readily picked up enough Dutch to make ourselves understood by the townspeople, the professors, and such of our eight hundred and odd fellow students as came into intercourse. This language, which looks so hard at first, is only a sort of polarized English. Puzzle over it a little while and it jumps into your comprehension like one of those simple cryptograms made by running together all the words of a sentence and then dividing in the wrong places.

The language acquired and the newness of our surroundings worn off, we settled into tolerably regular pursuits. Harry devoted himself with some assiduity to the study of sociology, with especial reference to the round-faced and not unkind maidens of Leyden. I went in for the higher metaphysics.

Outside of our respective studies, we had a common ground of unfailing interest. To our astonishment, we found that not one in twenty of the faculty or students knew or cared a stiver about the glorious history of the town, or even about the circumstances under which the university itself was founded by the Prince of Orange. In marked contrast with the general indifference was the enthusiasm of Professor Van Stopp, my chosen guide through the cloudiness of speculative philosophy.

This distinguished Hegelian was a tobacco-dried little old man, with a skullcap over features that reminded me strangely of Aunt Gertrude's. Had he been her own brother the facial resemblance could not have been closer. I told him so once, when we were together in the Stadthuis looking at the portrait of the hero of the siege, the Burgomaster Van der Werf. The professor laughed. "I will show you what is even a more extraordinary coincidence," said he; and, leading the way across the hall to the great picture of the siege, by Wanners, he pointed out the figure of a burgher participating in the defense. It was true. Van Stopp might have been the burgher's son; the burgher might have been Aunt Gertrude's father.

The professor seemed to be fond of us. We often went to his rooms in an old house in the Rapenburg Straat, one of the few houses remaining that antedate 1574. He would walk with us through the beautiful suburbs of the city, over straight roads lined with poplars that carried us back to the bank of the Sheepscot in our minds. He took us to the top of the ruined Roman tower in the center of the town, and from the same battlements from which anxious eyes three centuries ago had watched the slow approach of Admiral Boisot's fleet over the submerged polders, he pointed out the great dike of the Landscheiding, which was cut that the oceans might bring Boisot's Zealanders to raise the leaguer and feed the starving. He showed us the headquarters of the Spaniard Valdez at Leyderdorp, and told us how heaven sent a violent northwest wind on the night of the first of October, piling up the water deep where it had been shallow and sweeping the fleet on between Zoeterwoude and Zwieten up to the very walls of the fort at Lammen, the last stronghold of the besiegers and the last obstacle in the way of succor to the famishing inhabitants. Then he showed us where, on the very night before the retreat of the besieging army, a huge breach was made in the wall of Leyden, near the Cow Gate, by the Walloons from Lammen.

"Why!" cried Harry, catching fire from the eloquence of the professor's narrative, "that was the decisive moment of the siege."

The professor said nothing. He stood with his arms folded, looking intently into my cousin's eyes.

"For," continued Harry, "had that point not been watched, or had defense failed and the breach been carried by the night assault from Lammen, the town would have been burned and the people massacred under the eyes of Admiral Boisot and the fleet of relief. Who defended the breach?"

Van Stopp replied very slowly, as if weighing every word:

"History records the explosion of the mine under the city wall on the last night of the siege; it does not tell the story of the defense or give the defender's name. Yet no man that ever lived had a more tremendous charge than fate entrusted to this unknown hero. Was it chance that sent him to meet that unexpected danger? Consider some of the consequences had he failed. The fall of Leyden would have destroyed the last hope of the Prince of Orange and of the free states. The tyranny of Philip would have been reestablished. The birth of religious liberty and of self-government by the people would have been postponed, who knows for how many centuries? Who knows that there would or could have been a republic of the United States of America had there been no United Netherlands? Our University, which has given to the world Grotius, Scaliger, Arminius, and Descartes, was founded upon this hero's successful defense of the breach. We owe to him our presence here today. Nay, you owe to him your very existence. Your ancestors were of Leyden; between their lives and the butchers outside the walls he stood that night."

The little professor towered before us, a giant of enthusiasm and patriotism. Harry's eyes glistened and his cheeks reddened.

"Go home, boys," said Van Stopp, "and thank God that while the burghers of Leyden were straining their gaze toward Zoeterwoude and the fleet, there was one pair of vigilant eyes and one stout heart at the town wall just beyond the Cow Gate!"

III

The rain was splashing against the windows one evening in the autumn of our third year at Leyden, when Professor Van Stopp honored us with a visit in the Breede Straat. Never had I seen the old gentleman in such spirits. He talked incessantly. The gossip of the town, the news of Europe, science, poetry, philosophy, were in turn touched upon and treated with the same high and good humor. I sought to draw him out on Hegel, with whose chapter on the complexity and interdependency of things I was just then struggling.

"You do not grasp the return of the Itself into Itself through its Otherself?" he said smiling. "Well, you will, sometime."

Harry was silent and preoccupied. His taciturnity gradually affected even the professor. The conversation flagged, and we sat a long while without a word. Now and then there was a flash of lightning succeeded by distant thunder.

"Your clock does not go," suddenly remarked the professor. "Does it ever go?"

"Never since we can remember," I replied. "That is, only once, and then it went backward. It was when Aunt Gertrude—"

Here I caught a warning glance from Harry. I laughed and stammered, "The clock is old and useless. It cannot be made to go."

"Only backward?" said the professor, calmly, and not appearing to notice my embarrassment. "Well, and why should not a clock go backward? Why should not Time itself turn and retrace its course?"

He seemed to be waiting for an answer. I had none to give.

"I thought you Hegelian enough," he continued, "to admit that every condition includes its own contradiction. Time is a condition, not an essential. Viewed from the Absolute, the sequence by which future follows present and present follows past is purely arbitrary. Yesterday, today, tomorrow; there is no reason in the nature of things why the order should not be tomorrow, today, yesterday."

A sharper peal of thunder interrupted the professor's speculations.

"The day is made by the planet's revolution on its axis from west to east. I fancy you can conceive conditions under which it might turn from east to west, unwinding, as it were, the revolutions of past ages. Is it so much more difficult to imagine Time unwinding itself; Time on the ebb, instead of on the flow; the past unfolding as the future recedes; the centuries countermarching; the course of events proceeding toward the Beginning and not, as now, toward the End?"

"But," I interposed, "we know that as far as we are concerned the—"

"We know!" exclaimed Van Stopp, with growing scorn. "Your intelligence has no wings. You follow in the trail of Compte and his slimy brood of creepers and crawlers. You speak with amazing assurance of your position in the universe. You seem to think that your wretched little individuality has a firm foothold in the Absolute. Yet you go to bed tonight and dream into existence men, women, children, beasts of the past or of the future. How do you know that at this moment you yourself, with all your conceit of nineteenth-century thought, are anything more than a creature of a dream of the future, dreamed, let us say, by some philosopher of the sixteenth century? How do you know that you are anything more than a creature of a dream of the past, dreamed by some Hegelian of the twenty-sixth century? How do you know, boy, that you will not vanish into the sixteenth century or 2060 the moment the dreamer awakes?"

There was no replying to this, for it was sound metaphysics. Harry yawned. I got up and went to the window. Professor Van Stopp approached the clock.

"Ah, my children," said he, "there is no fixed progress of human events. Past, present, and future are woven together in one inextricable mesh. Who shall say that this old clock is not right to go backward?"

A crash of thunder shook the house. The storm was over our heads.

When the blinding glare had passed away, Professor Van Stopp was standing upon a chair before the tall timepiece. His face looked more than ever like Aunt Gertrude's. He stood as she had stood in that last quarter of an hour when we saw her wind the clock.

The same thought struck Harry and myself.

"Hold!" we cried, as he began to wind the works. "It may be death if you—"

The professor's sallow features shone with the strange enthusiasm that had transformed Aunt Gertrude's.

"True," he said, "it may be death; but it may be the awakening. Past, present, future; all woven together! The shuttle goes to and fro, forward and back—"

He had wound the clock. The hands were whirling around the dial from right to left with inconceivable rapidity. In this whirl we ourselves seemed to be borne along. Eternities seemed to contract into minutes while lifetimes were thrown off at every tick. Van Stopp, both arms outstretched, was reeling in his chair. The house shook again under a tremendous peal of thunder. At the same instant a ball of fire, leaving a wake of sulphurous vapor and filling the room with dazzling light, passed over our heads and smote the clock. Van Stopp was prostrated. The hands ceased to revolve.

IV

The roar of the thunder sounded like heavy cannonading. The lightning's blaze appeared as the steady light of a conflagration. With our hands over our eyes, Harry and I rushed out into the night.

Under a red sky people were hurrying toward the Stadthuis. Flames in the direction of the Roman tower told us that the heart of the town was afire. The faces of those we saw were haggard and emaciated. From every side we caught disjointed phrases of complaint or despair. "Horseflesh at ten schillings the pound," said one, "and bread at sixteen schillings." "Bread indeed!" an old woman retorted: "It's eight weeks gone since I have seen a crumb." "My little grandchild, the lame one, went last night." "Do you know what Gekke Betje, the washerwoman, did? She was starving. Her babe died, and she and her man—"

A louder cannon burst cut short this revelation. We made our way on toward the citadel of the town, passing a few soldiers here and there and many burghers with grim faces under their broad-brimmed felt hats.

"There is bread plenty yonder where the gunpowder is, and full pardon, too. Valdez shot another amnesty over the walls this morning."

An excited crowd immediately surrounded the speaker. "But the fleet!" they cried.

"The fleet is grounded fast on the Greenway polder. Boisot may turn his one eye seaward for a wind till famine and pestilence have carried off every mother's son of ye, and his ark will not be a rope's length nearer. Death by plague, death by starvation, death by fire and musketry—that is what the burgomaster offers us in return for glory for himself and kingdom for Orange."

"He asks us," said a sturdy citizen, "to hold out only twenty-four hours longer, and to pray meanwhile for an ocean wind."

"Ah, yes!" sneered the first speaker. "Pray on. There is bread enough locked in Pieter Adriaanszoon van der Werf's cellar. I warrant you that is what gives him so wonderful a stomach for resisting the Most Catholic King."

A young girl, with braided yellow hair, pressed through the crowd and confronted the malcontent. "Good people," said the maiden, "do not listen to him. He is a traitor with a Spanish heart. I am Pieter's daughter. We have no bread. We ate malt cakes and rapeseed like the rest of you till that was gone. Then we stripped the green leaves from the lime trees and willows in our garden and ate them. We have eaten even the thistles and weeds that grew between the stones by the canal. The coward lies."

Nevertheless, the insinuation had its effect. The throng, now become a mob, surged off in the direction of the burgomaster's house. One ruffian raised his hand to strike the girl out of the way. In a wink the cur was under the feet of his fellows, and Harry, panting and glowing, stood at the maiden's side, shouting defiance in good English at the backs of the rapidly retreating crowd.

With the utmost frankness she put both her arms around Harry's neck and kissed him.

"Thank you," she said. "You are a hearty lad. My name is Gertruyd van der Wert."

Harry was fumbling in his vocabulary for the proper Dutch phrases, but the girl would not stay for compliments. "They mean mischief to my father"; and she hurried us through several exceedingly narrow streets into a three-cornered market place dominated by a church with two spires. "There he is," she exclaimed, "on the steps of St. Pancras."

There was a tumult in the market place. The conflagration raging beyond the church and the voices of the Spanish and Walloon cannon outside of the walls were less angry than the roar of this multitude of desperate men clamoring for the bread that a single word from their leader's lips would bring them. "Surrender to the King!" they cried, "or we will send your dead body to Lammen as Leyden's token of submission."

One tall man, taller by half a head than any of the burghers confronting him, and so dark of complexion that we wondered how he could be the father of Gertruyd, heard the threat in silence. When the burgomaster spoke, the mob listened in spite of themselves.

"What is it you ask, my friends? That we break our vow and surrender Leyden to the Spaniards? That is to devote ourselves to a fate far more horrible than starvation. I have to keep the oath! Kill me, if you will have it so. I can die only once, whether by your hands, by the enemy's, or by the hand of God. Let us starve, if we must, welcoming starvation because it comes before dishonor. Your menaces do not move me; my life is at your disposal. Here, take my sword, thrust it into my breast, and divide my flesh among you to appease your hunger. So long as I remain alive expect no surrender."

There was silence again while the mob wavered. Then there were mutterings around us. Above these rang out the clear voice of the girl whose hand Harry still held—unnecessarily, it seemed to me.

"Do you not feel the sea wind? It has come at last. To the tower! And the first man there will see by moonlight the full white sails of the prince's ships."

For several hours I scoured the streets of the town, seeking in vain my cousin and his companion; the sudden movement of the crowd toward the Roman tower had separated us. On every side I saw evidences of the terrible chastisement that had brought this stout-hearted people to the verge of despair. A man with hungry eyes chased a lean rat along the bank of the canal. A young mother, with two dead babes in her arms, sat in a doorway to which they bore the bodies of her husband and father, just killed at the walls. In the middle of a deserted street I passed unburied corpses in a pile twice as high as my head. The pestilence had been there—kinder than the Spaniard, because it held out no treacherous promises while it dealt its blows.

Toward morning the wind increased to a gale. There was no sleep in Leyden, no more talk of surrender, no longer any thought or care about defense. These words were on the lips of everybody I met: "Daylight will bring the fleet!"

Did daylight bring the fleet? History says so, but I was not a witness. I know only that before dawn the gale culminated in a violent thunderstorm, and that at the same time a muffled explosion, heavier than the thunder, shook the town. I was in the crowd that watched from the Roman Mound for the first signs of the approaching relief. The concussion shook hope out of every face. "Their mine has reached the wall!" But where? I pressed forward until I found the burgomaster, who was standing among the rest. "Quick!" I whispered. "It is beyond the Cow Gate, and this side of the Tower of Burgundy." He gave me a searching glance, and then strode away, without making any attempt to quiet the general panic. I followed close at his heels.

It was a tight run of nearly half a mile to the rampart in question. When we reached the Cow Gate this is what we saw:

A great gap, where the wall had been, opening to the swampy fields beyond: in the moat, outside and below, a confusion of up-turned faces, belonging to men who struggled like demons to achieve the breach, and who now gained a few feet and now were forced back; on the shattered rampart a handful of soldiers and burghers forming a living wall where masonry had failed; perhaps a double handful of women and girls, serving stones to the defenders and boiling water in buckets, besides pitch and oil and unslaked lime, and some of them quoiting tarred and burn-ing hoops over the necks of the Spaniards in the moat; my cousin Harry leading and directing the men; the burgomaster's daughter Gertruyd encouraging and inspiring the women.

But what attracted my attention more than anything else was the frantic activity of a little figure in black, who, with a huge ladle, was showering molten lead on the heads of the assailing party. As he turned to the bonfire and kettle which supplied him with ammunition, his features came into the full light. I gave a cry of surprise: the ladler of molten lead was Professor Van Stopp.

The burgomaster Van der Werf turned at my sudden exclamation. "Who is that?" I said. "The man at the kettle?"

"That," replied Van der Werf, "is the brother of my wife, the clockmaker Jan Lipperdam."

The affair at the breach was over almost before we had had time to grasp the situation. The Spaniards, who had overthrown the wall of brick and stone, found the living wall impregnable. They could not even maintain their position in the moat; they were driven off into the darkness. Now I felt a sharp pain in my left arm. Some stray missile must have hit me while we watched the fight.

"Who has done this thing?" demanded the burgomaster. "Who is it that has kept watch on today while the rest of us were straining fools' eyes toward tomorrow?"

Gertruyd van der Werf came forward proudly, leading my cousin. "My father," said the girl, "he has saved my life."

"That is much to me," said the burgomaster, "but it is not all. He has saved Leyden and he has saved Holland."

I was becoming dizzy. The faces around me seemed unreal. Why were we here with these people? Why did the thunder and lightning forever continue? Why did the clockmaker, Jan Lipperdam, turn always toward me the face of Professor Van Stopp? "Harry!" I said, "come back to our rooms."

But though he grasped my hand warmly his other hand still held that of the girl, and he did not move. Then nausea overcame me. My head swam, and the breach and its defenders faded from sight.

V

Three days later I sat with one arm bandaged in my accustomed seat in Van Stopp's lecture room. The place beside me was vacant.

"We hear much," said the Hegelian professor, reading from a notebook in his usual dry, hurried tone, "of the influence of the sixteenth century upon the nineteenth. No philosopher, as far as I am aware, has studied the influence of the nineteenth century upon the sixteenth. If cause produces effect, does effect never induce cause? Does the law of heredity, unlike all other laws of this universe of mind and matter, operate in one direction only? Does the descendant owe everything to the ancestor, and the ancestor nothing to the descendant? Does destiny, which may seize upon our existence, and for its own purposes bear us far into the future, never carry us back into the past?"

I went back to my rooms in the Breede Straat, where my only companion was the silent clock.

THE SENATOR'S DAUGHTER

On the evening of the fourth of March, year of grace nineteen hundred and thirty-seven, Mr. Daniel Webster Wanlee devoted several hours to the consummation of a rather elaborate toilet. That accomplished, he placed himself before a mirror and critically surveyed the results of his patient art.

The effect appeared to give him satisfaction. In the glass he beheld a comely young man of thirty, something under the medium stature, faultlessly attired in evening dress. The face was a perfect oval, the complexion delicate, the features refined. The high cheekbones and a slight elevation of the outer corners of the eyes, the short upper lip, from which drooped a slender but aristocratic mustache, the tapered fingers of the hand, and the remarkably small feet, confined tonight in dancing pumps of polished red morocco, were all unmistakable heirlooms of a pure Mongolian ancestry. The long, stiff, black hair, brushed straight back from the forehead, fell in profusion over the neck and shoulders. Several rich decorations shone on the breast of the black broadcloth coat. The knickerbocker breeches were tied at the knees with scarlet ribbons. The stockings were of a flowered silk. Mr. Wanlee's face sparked with intelligent good sense; his figure poised itself before the glass with easy grace.

A soft, distinct utterance, filling the room yet appearing to proceed from no particular quarter, now attracted Mr. Wanlee's attention. He at once recognized the voice of his friend, Mr. Walsingham Brown.

"How are we off for time, old fellow?"

"It's getting late," replied Mr. Wanlee, without turning his face from the mirror. "You had better come over directly."

In a very few minutes the curtains at the entrance to Mr. Wanlee's apartments were unceremoniously pulled open, and Mr. Walsingham Brown strode in. The two friends cordially shook hands.

"How is the honorable member from the Los Angeles district?" inquired the newcomer gaily. "And what is there new in Washington society? Prepared to conquer tonight, I see. What's all this? Red ribbons and flowered silk hose! Ah, Wanlee. I thought you had outgrown these frivolities!"

The faintest possible blush appeared on Mr. Daniel Webster Wanlee's cheeks. "It is cool tonight?" he asked, changing the subject.

"Infernally cold," replied his friend. "I wonder you have no snow here. It is snowing hard in New York. There were at least three inches on the ground just now when I took the Pneumatic."

"Pull an easy chair up to the thermo-electrode," said the Mongolian. "You must get the New York climate thawed out of your joints if you expect to waltz creditably. The Washington women are critical in that respect."

Mr. Walsingham Brown pushed a comfortable chair toward a sphere of shining platinum that stood on a crystal pedestal in the center of the room. He pressed a silver button at the base, and the metal globe began to glow incandescently. A genial warmth diffused itself through the apartment. "That feels good," said Mr. Walsingham Brown, extending both hands to catch the heat from the thermo-electrode.

"By the way," he continued, "you haven't accounted to me yet for the scarlet bows. What would your constituents say if they saw you thus—you, the impassioned young orator of the Pacific slope; the thoughtful student of progressive statesmanship; the mainstay and hope of the Extreme Left; the thorn in the side of conservative Vegetarianism; the *bête noire* of the whole Indo-European gang—you, in knee ribbons and florid extensions, like a club man at a fashionable Harlem hop, or a—"

Mr. Brown interrupted himself with a hearty but good-natured laugh.

Mr. Wanlee seemed ill at ease. He did not reply to his friend's raillery. He cast a stealthy glance at his knees in the mirror, and then went to one side of the room, where an endless strip of printed paper, about three feet wide, was slowly issuing from between noiseless rollers and falling in neat folds into a willow basket placed on the floor to receive it. Mr. Wanlee bent his head over the broad strip of paper and began to read attentively.

"You take the *Contemporaneous News*, I suppose," said the other.

"No, I prefer the *Interminable Intelligencer*," replied Mr. Wanlee. "The *Contemporaneous* is too much of my own way of thinking. Why should a sensible man ever read the organ of his own party? How much wiser it is to keep posted on what your political opponents think and say."

"Do you find anything about the event of the evening?"

"The ball has opened," said Mr. Wanlee, "and the floor of the Capitol is already crowded. Let me see," he continued, beginning to read aloud: "'The wealth, the beauty, the chivalry, and the brains of the nation combine to lend unprecedented luster to the Inauguration Ball, and the brilliant success of the new Administration is assured beyond all question.'"

"That is encouraging logic," Mr. Brown remarked.

"'President Trimbelly has just entered the rotunda, escorting his beautiful and stately wife, and accompanied by ex-President Riley, Mrs. Riley, and Miss Norah Riley. The illustrious group is of course the cynosure of all eyes. The utmost cordiality prevails among statesmen of all shades of opinion. For once, bitter political animosities seem to have been laid aside with the ordinary habiliments of everyday wear. Conspicuous among the guests are some of the most distinguished radicals of the opposition. Even General Quong, the defeated Mongol-Vegetarian candidate, is now proceeding across the rotunda, leaning on the arm of the Chinese ambassador, with the evident intention of paying his compliments to his successful rival. Not the slightest trace of resentment or hostility is visible upon his strongly marked Asiatic features.'

"The hero of the Battle of Cheyenne can afford to be magnanimous," remarked Mr. Wanlee, looking up from the paper.

"True," said Mr. Walsingham Brown, warmly. "The noble old hoodlum fighter has settled forever the question of the equality of your race. The presidency could have added nothing to his fame."

Mr. Wanlee went on reading: "'The toilets of the ladies are charming. Notable among those which attract the reportorial eye are the peacock feather train of the Princess Hushyida; the mauve—'"

"Cut that," suggested Mr. Brown. "We shall see for ourselves presently. And give me a dinner, like a good fellow. It occurs to me that I have eaten nothing for fifteen days."

The Honorable Mr. Wanlee drew from his waistcoat pocket a small gold box, oval in form. He pressed a spring and the lid flew open. Then he handed the box to his friend. It contained a number of little gray pastilles, hardly larger than peas. Mr. Brown took one between his thumb and forefinger and put it into his mouth. "Thus do I satisfy mine hunger," he said, "or, to borrow the language of the opposition orators, thus do I lend myself to the vile and degrading practice, subversive of society as at present constituted, and outraging the very laws of nature."

Mr. Wanlee was paying no attention. With eager gaze he was again scanning the columns of the *Interminable Intelligencer*. As if involuntarily, he read aloud: "'—Secretary Quimby and Mrs. Quimby, Count Schnecke, the Austrian ambassador, Mrs.

Hoyette and the Misses Hoyette of New York, Senator Newton
of Massachusetts, whose arrival with his lovely daughter is causing no small sensation—'"

He paused, stammering, for he became aware that his friend
was regarding him earnestly. Coloring to the roots of his hair, he
affected indifference and began to read again: "'Senator Newton of Massachusetts, whose arrival with his lovely—'"

"I think, my dear boy," said Mr. Walsingham Brown, with a
smile, "that it is high time for us to proceed to the Capitol."

II   THE BALL AT THE CAPITOL

Through a brilliant throng of happy men and charming women,
Mr. Wanlee and his friend made their way into the rotunda of
the Capitol. Accustomed as they both were to the spectacular
efforts which society arranged for its own delectation, the young
men were startled by the enchantment of the scene before them.
The dingy historical panorama that girds the rotunda was hidden
behind a wall of flowers. The heights of the dome were not visible, for beneath that was a temporary interior dome of red roses
and white lilies, which poured down from the concavity a continual and almost oppressive shower of fragrance. From the center of the floor ascended to the height of forty or fifty feet
a single jet of water, rendered intensely luminous by the newly
discovered hydrolectric process, and flooding the room with a
light ten times brighter than daylight, yet soft and grateful as the
light of the moon. The air pulsated with music, for every flower
in the dome overhead gave utterance to the notes which Rati-
bolial, in the conservatoire at Paris, was sending across the
Atlantic from the vibrant tip of his baton.

The friends had hardly reached the center of the rotunda,
where the hydrolectric fountain threw aloft its jet of blazing water, and where two opposite streams of promenaders from the
north and the south wings of the Capitol met and mingled in an
eddy of polite humanity, before Mr. Walsingham Brown was

seized and led off captive by some of his Washington acquaintances.

Wanlee pushed on, scarcely noticing his friend's defection. He directed his steps wherever the crowd seemed thickest, casting ahead and on either side of him quick glances of inquiry, now and then exchanging bows with people whom he recognized, but pausing only once to enter into conversation. That was when he was accosted by General Quong, the leader of the Mongol-Vegetarian party and the defeated candidate for President in the campaign of 1936. The veteran spoke familiarly to the young congressman and detained him only a moment. "You are looking for somebody, Wanlee," said General Quong, kindly. "I see it in your eyes. I grant you leave of absence."

Mr. Wanlee proceeded down the long corridor that leads to the Senate chamber, and continued there his eager search. Disappointed, he turned back, retraced his steps to the rotunda, and went to the other extremity of the Capitol. The Hall of Representatives was reserved for the dancers. From the great clock above the Speaker's desk issued the music of a waltz, to the rhythm of which several hundred couples were whirling over the polished floor.

Wanlee stood at the door, watching the couples as they moved before him in making the circuit of the hall. Presently his eyes began to sparkle. They were resting upon the beautiful face and supple figure of a girl in white satin, who waltzed in perfect form with a young man, apparently an Italian. Wanlee advanced a step or two, and at the same instant the lady became aware of his presence. She said a word to her partner, who immediately relinquished her waist.

"I have been expecting you this age," said the girl, holding out her hand to Wanlee. "I am delighted that you have come."

"Thank you, Miss Newton," said Wanlee.

"You may retire, Francesco," she continued, turning to the young man who had just been her partner. "I shall not need you again."

The young man addressed as Francesco bowed respectfully and departed without a word.

"Let us not lose this lovely waltz," said Miss Newton, putting her hand upon Wanlee's shoulder. "It will be my first this evening."

"Then you have not danced?" asked Wanlee, as they glided off together.

"No, Daniel," said Miss Newton, "I haven't danced with any gentlemen."

The Mongolian thanked her with a smile.

"I have made good use of Francesco, however," she went on. "What a blessing a competent protectional partner is! Only think, our grandmothers, and even our mothers, were obliged to sit dismally around the walls waiting the pleasure of their high and mighty—"

She paused suddenly, for a shade of annoyance had fallen upon her partner's face. "Forgive me," she whispered, her head almost upon his shoulder. "Forgive me if I have wounded you. You know, love, that I would not—"

"I know it," he interrupted. "You are too good and too noble to let that weigh a feather's weight in your estimation of the Man. You never pause to think that my mother and my grandmother were not accustomed to meet your mother and your grandmother in society—for the very excellent reason," he continued, with a little bitterness in his tone, "that my mother had her hands full in my father's laundry in San Francisco, while my grandmother's social ideas hardly extended beyond the cabin of our ancestral san-pan on the Yangtze Kiang. *You* do not care for that. But there are others—"

They waltzed on for some time in silence, he, thoughtful and moody, and she, sympathetically concerned.

"And the senator; where is he tonight?" asked Wanlee at last.

"Papa!" said the girl, with a frightened little glance over her shoulder. "Oh! Papa merely made his appearance here to bring me and because it was expected of him. He has gone home to work on his tiresome speech against the vegetables."

"Do you think," asked Wanlee, after a few minutes, whispering the words very slowly and very low, "that the senator has any suspicion?"

It was her turn now to manifest embarrassment. "I am very sure," she replied, "that Papa has not the least idea in the world of it all. And that is what worries me. I constantly feel that we are walking together on a volcano. I know that we are right, and that heaven means it to be just as it is; yet, I cannot help trembling in my happiness. You know as well as I do the antiquated and absurd notions that still prevail in Massachusetts, and that Papa is a conservative among the conservatives. He respects your ability, that I discovered long ago. Whenever you speak in the House, he reads your remarks with great attention. I think," she continued with a forced laugh, "that your arguments bother him a good deal."

"This must have an end, Clara," said the Chinaman, as the music ceased and the waltzers stopped. "I cannot allow you to remain a day longer in an equivocal position. My honor and your own peace of mind require that there shall be an explanation to your father. Have you the courage to stake all our happiness on one bold move?"

"I have courage," frankly replied the girl, "to go with you before my father and tell him all. And furthermore," she continued, slightly pressing his arm and looking into his face with a charming blush, "I have courage even beyond that."

"You beloved little Puritan!" was his reply.

As they passed out of the Hall of Representatives, they encountered Mr. Walsingham Brown with Miss Hoyette of New York. The New York lady spoke cordially to Miss Newton, but recognized Wanlee with a rather distant bow. Wanlee's eyes sought and met those of his friend. "I may need your counsel before morning," he said in a low voice.

"All right, my dear fellow," said Mr. Brown. "Depend on me." And the two couples separated.

The Mongolian and his Massachusetts sweetheart drifted with the tide into the supper room. Both were preoccupied with their own thoughts. Almost mechanically, Wanlee led his companion to a corner of the supper room and established her in a seat behind a screen of palmettos, sheltered from the observation of the throne.

"It is nice of you to bring me here," said the girl, "for I am hungry after our waltz."

Intimate as their souls had become, this was the first time that she had ever asked him for food. It was an innocent and natural request, yet Wanlee shuddered when he heard it, and bit his under lip to control his agitation. He looked from behind the palmettos at the tables heaped with delicate viands and surrounded by men, eagerly pressing forward to obtain refreshment for the ladies in their care. Wanlee shuddered again at the spectacle. After a momentary hesitation he returned to Miss Newton, seated himself beside her, and taking her hand in his, began to speak deliberately and earnestly.

"Clara," he said, "I am going to ask you for a final proof of your affection. Do not start and look alarmed, but hear me patiently. If, after hearing me, you still bid me bring you a *pâté*, or the wing of a fowl, or a salad, or even a plate of fruit, I will do so, though it wrench the heart in my bosom. But first listen to what I have to say."

"Certainly I will listen to all you have to say," she replied.

"You know enough of the political theories that divide parties," he went on, nervously examining the rings on her slender fingers, "to be aware that what I conscientiously believe to be true is very different from what you have been educated to believe."

"I know," said Miss Newton, "that you are a Vegetarian and do not approve the use of meat. I know that you have spoken eloquently in the House on the right of every living being to protection in its life, and that that is the theory of your party. Papa says that it is demagogy—that the opposition parade an absurd and sophistical theory in order to win votes and get themselves into office. Still, I know that a great many excellent people, friends of ours in Massachusetts, are coming to believe with you, and, of course, loving you as I do, I have the firmest faith in the honesty of your convictions. You are not a demagogue, Daniel. You are above pandering to the radicalism of the rabble. Neither my father nor all the world could make me think the contrary."

Mr. Daniel Webster Wanlee squeezed her hand and went on: "Living as you do in the most ultra-conservative of circles, dear Clara, you have had no opportunity to understand the tremendous significance and force of the movement that is now sweeping over the land, and of which I am a very humble representative. It is something more than a political agitation; it is an upheaval and reorganization of society on the basis of science and abstract right. It is fit and proper that I, belonging to a race that has only been emancipated and enfranchised by the march of time, should stand in the advance guard—in the forlorn hope, it may be—of the new revolution."

His flaming eyes were now looking directly into hers. Although a little troubled by his earnestness, she could not hide her proud satisfaction in his manly bearing.

"We believe that every animal is born free and equal," he said. "That the humblest polyp or the most insignificant mollusk has an equal right with you or me to life and the enjoyment of happiness. Why, are we not all brothers? Are we not all children of a common evolution? What are we human animals but the more favored members of the great family? Is Senator Newton of Massachusetts further removed in intelligence from the Australian bushman, than the Australian bushman or the Flathead Indian is removed from the ox which Senator Newton orders slain to yield food for his family? Have we a right to take the paltriest life that evolution has given? Is not the butchery of an ox or of a chicken murder—nay, fratricide—in the view of absolute justice? Is it not cannibalism of the most repulsive and cowardly sort to

prey upon the flesh of our defenseless brother animals, and to sacrifice their lives and rights to an unnatural appetite that has no
foundation save in the habit of long ages of barbarian selfishness?"

"I have never thought of these things," said Miss Clara, slowly.
"Would you elevate them to the suffrage—I mean the ox and
the chicken and the baboon?"

"There speaks the daughter of the senator from Massachusetts,"
cried Wanlee. "No, we would not give them the suffrage—at least,
not at present. The right to live and enjoy life is a natural, an in-
alienable right. The right to vote depends upon conditions of
society and of individual intelligence. The ox, the chicken, the
baboon are not yet prepared for the ballot. But they are voters in
embryo; they are struggling up through the same process that
our own ancestors underwent, and it is a crime, an unnatural,
horrible thing, to cut off their career, their future, for the sake of
a meal!"

"Those are noble sentiments, I must admit," said Miss Newton,
with considerable enthusiasm.

"They are the sentiments of the Mongol-Vegetarian party," said
Wanlee. "They will carry the country in 1940, and elect the next
President of the United States."

"I admire your earnestness," said Miss Newton after a pause,
"and I will not grieve you by asking you to bring me even so much
as a chicken wing. I do not think I could eat it now, with your
words still in my ears. A little fruit is all that I want."

"Once more," said Wanlee, taking the tall girl's hand again, "I
must request you to consider. The principles, my dearest, that
I have already enunciated are the principles of the great mass of
our party. They are held even by the respectable, easygoing, not
oversensitive voters such as constitute the bulk of every political
organization. But there are a few of us who stand on ground still
more advanced. We do not expect to bring the laggards up to our
line for years, perhaps in our lifetime. We simply carry the accepted theory to its logical conclusions and calmly await ultimate
results."

"And what is your ground, pray?" she inquired. "I cannot see how anything could be more dreadfully radical—that is, more bewildering and generally upsetting at first sight—than the ground which you just took."

"If what I have said is true, and I believe it to be true, then how can we escape including the Vegetable Kingdom in our proclamation of emancipation from man's tyranny? The tree, the plant, even the fungus, have they not individual life, and have they not also the right to live?"

"But how—"

"And indeed," continued the Chinaman, not noticing the interruption, "who can say where vegetable life ends and animal life begins? Science has tried in vain to draw the boundary line. I hold that to uproot a potato is to destroy an existence certainly, although perhaps remotely akin to ours. To pluck a grape is to maim the living vine; and to drink the juice of that grape is to outrage consanguinity. In this broad, elevated view of the matter it becomes a duty to refrain from vegetable food. Nothing less than the vital principal itself becomes the test and tie of universal brotherhood. 'All living things are born free and equal, and have a right to existence and the enjoyment of existence.' Is not that a beautiful thought?"

"It is a beautiful thought," said the maiden. "But—I know you will think me dreadfully cold, and practical, and unsympathetic —but how are *we* to live? Have *we* no right, too, to existence? Must we starve to death in order to establish the theoretical right of vegetables not to be eaten?"

"My dear love," said Wanlee, "that would be a serious and perplexing question, had not the latest discovery of science already solved it for us."

He took from his waistcoat pocket the small gold box, scarcely larger than a watch, and opened the cover. In the palm of her white hand he placed one of the little pastilles.

"Eat it," said he. "It will satisfy your hunger."

She put the morsel into her mouth. "I would do as you bade me," she said, "even if it were poison."

"It is not poison," he rejoined. "It is nourishment in the only rational form."

"But it is tasteless; almost without substance."

"Yet it will support life for from eighteen to twenty-five days. This little gold box holds food enough to afford all subsistence to the entire Seventy-sixth Congress for a month."

She took the box and curiously examined its contents.

"And how long would it support my life—for more than a year, perhaps?"

"Yes, for more than ten—more than twenty years."

"I will not bore you with chemical and physiological facts," continued Wanlee, "but you must know that the food which we take, in whatever form, resolves itself into what are called proximate principles—starch, sugar, oleine, flurin, albumen, and so on. These are selected and assimilated by the organs of the body, and go to build up the necessary tissues. But all these proximate principles, in their turn, are simply combinations of the ultimate chemical elements, chiefly carbon, nitrogen, hydrogen, and oxygen. It is upon these elements that we depend for sustenance. By the old plan we obtained them indirectly. They passed from the earth and the air into the grass; from the grass into the muscular tissues of the ox; and from the beef into our own persons, loaded down and encumbered by a mass of useless, irrelevant matter. The German chemists have discovered how to supply the needed elements in compact, undiluted form—here they are in this little box. Now shall mankind go direct to the fountainhead of nature for his aliment; now shall the old roundabout, cumbrous, inhuman method be at an end; now shall the evils of gluttony and the attendant vices cease; now shall the brutal murdering of fellow animals and brother vegetables forever stop—now shall all this be, since the new, holy cause has been consecrated by the lips I love!"

He bent and kissed those lips. Then he suddenly looked up and saw Mr. Walsingham Brown standing at his elbow.

"You are observed—compromised, I fear," said Mr. Brown, hurriedly. "That Italian dancer in your employ, Miss Newton, has been following you like a hound. I have been paying him the same gracious attention. He has just left the Capitol post haste. I fear there may be a scene."

The brave girl, with clear eyes, gave her Mongolian lover a look worth to him a year of life. "There shall be no scene," she said; "we will go at once to my father, Daniel, and bear ourselves the tale which Francesco would carry."

The three left the Capitol without delay. At the head of Pennsylvania Avenue they entered a great building, lighted up as brilliantly as the Capitol itself. An elevator took them down toward the bowels of the earth. At the fourth landing they passed from the elevator into a small carriage, luxuriously upholstered. Mr. Walsingham Brown touched an ivory knob at the end of the conveyance. A man in uniform presented himself at the door.

"To Boston," said Mr. Walsingham Brown.

III   THE FROZEN BRIDE

The senator from Massachusetts sat in the library of his mansion on North Street at two o'clock in the morning. An expression of astonishment and rage distorted his pale, cold features. The pen had dropped from his fingers, blotting the last sentences written upon the manuscript of his great speech—for Senator Newton still adhered to the ancient fashion of recording thought. The blotted sentences were these:

"The logic of events compels us to acknowledge the political equality of those Asiatic invaders—shall I say conquerors?—of our Indo-European institutions. But the logic of events is often repugnant to common sense, and its conclusions abhorrent to patriotism and right. The sword has opened for them the way to the ballot box; but, Mr. President, and I say it deliberately, no power under heaven can unlock for these aliens the sacred approaches to our homes and hearts!"

Beside the senator stood Francesco, the professional dancer. His face wore a smile of malicious triumph.

"With the Chinaman? Miss Newton—my daughter?" gasped the senator. "I do not believe you. It is a lie."

"Then come to the Capitol, Your Excellency, and see it with your own eyes," said the Italian.

The door was quickly opened and Clara Newton entered the room, followed by the Honorable Mr. Wanlee and his friend.

"There is no need of making that excursion, Papa," said the girl. "You can see it with your own eyes here and now. Francesco, leave the house!"

The senator bowed with forced politeness to Mr. Walsingham Brown. Of the presence of Wanlee he took not the slightest notice.

Senator Newton attempted to laugh. "This is a pleasantry, Clara," he said; "a practical jest, designed by yourself and Mr. Brown for my midnight diversion. It is a trifle unseasonable."

"It is no jest," replied his daughter, bravely. She then went up to Wanlee and took his hand in hers. "Papa," she said, "this is a gentleman of whom you already know something. He is our equal in station, in intellect, and in moral worth. He is in every way worthy of my friendship and your esteem. Will you listen to what he has to say to you? *Will* you, Papa?"

The senator laughed a short, hard laugh, and turned to Mr. Walsingham Brown. "I have no communication to make to the member of the lower branch," said he. "Why should he have any communication to make to me?"

Miss Newton put her arm around the waist of the young Chinaman and led him squarely in front of her father. "Because," she said, in a voice as firm and clear as the note of a silver bell "—because I love him."

In recalling with Wanlee the circumstances of this interview,

Mr. Walsingham Brown said long afterward, "She glowed for a moment like the platinum of your thermo-electrode."

"If the member from California," said Senator Newton, without changing the tone of his voice, and still continuing to address himself to Mr. Brown, "has worked upon the sentimentality of this foolish child, that is her misfortune, and mine. It cannot be helped now. But if the member from California presumes to hope to profit in the least by his sinister operations, or to enjoy further opportunities for pursuing them, the member from California deceives himself."

So saying he turned around in his chair and began to write on his great speech.

"I come," said Wanlee slowly, now speaking for the first time, "as an honorable man to ask of Senator Newton the hand of his daughter in honorable marriage. Her own consent has already been given."

"I have nothing further to say," said the Senator, once more turning his cold face toward Mr. Brown. Then he paused an instant, and added with a sting, "I am told that the member from California is a prophet and apostle of Vegetable Rights. Let him seek a cactus in marriage. He should wed on his own level."

Wanlee, coloring at the wanton insult, was about to leave the room. A quick sign from Miss Newton arrested him.

"But I have something further to say," she cried with spirit. "Listen, Father; it is this. If Mr. Wanlee goes out of the house without a word from you—a word such as is due him from you as a gentleman and as my father—I go with him to be his wife before the sun rises!"

"Go if you will, girl," the senator coldly replied. "But first consult with Mr. Walsingham Brown, who is a lawyer and a gentleman, as to the tenor and effect of the Suspended Animation Act."

Miss Newton looked inquiringly from one face to another. The words had no meaning to her. Her lover turned suddenly pale and clutched at the back of a chair for support. Mr. Brown's cheeks were also white. He stepped quickly forward, holding out his hands as if to avert some dreadful calamity.

"Surely you would not—" he began. "But no! That is an absolute low, an inhuman, outrageous enactment that has long been as dead as the partisan fury that prompted it. For a quarter of a century it has been a dead letter on the statute books."

"I was not aware," said the senator, from between firmly set teeth, "that the act had ever been repealed."

He took from the shelf a volume of statutes and opened the book. "I will read the text," he said. "It will form an appropriate part of the ritual of this marriage." He read as follows:

"Section 7.391. No male person of Caucasian descent, of or under the age of 25 years, shall marry, or promise or contract himself in marriage with any female person of Mongolian descent without the full written consent of his male parent or guardian, as provided by law; and no female person, either maid or widow, under the age of 30 years, of Caucasian parentage, shall give, promise, or contract herself in marriage with any male person of Mongolian descent without the full written and registered consent of her male and female parents or guardians, as provided by law. And any marriage obligations so contracted shall be null and void, and the Caucasian so contracting shall be guilty of a misdemeanor and liable to punishment at the discretion of his or her male parent or guardian as provided by law.

"Section 7.392. Such parents or guardians may, at their discretion and upon application to the authorities of the United States District Court for the district within which the offense is committed, deliver the offending person of Caucasian descent to the designated officers, and require that his or her consciousness, bodily activities, and vital functions be suspended by the frigorific process known as the Werkomer process, for a period equal to that which must elapse before the offending person will arrive at the age of 25 years, if a male, or 30 years, if a female; or for a shorter period at the discretion of the parent or guardian; said shorter period to be fixed in advance."

"What does it mean?" demanded Miss Newton, bewildered by the verbiage of the act, and alarmed by her lover's exclamation of despair.

Mr. Walsingham Brown shook his head, sadly. "It means," said he, "that the cruel sin of the fathers is to be visited upon the children."

"It means, Clara," said Wanlee with a great effort, "that we must part."

"Understand me, Mr. Brown," said the senator, rising and motioning impatiently with the hand that held the pen, as if to dismiss both the subject and the intruding party. "I do not employ the Suspended Animation Act as a bugaboo to frighten a silly girl out of her lamentable infatuation. As surely as the law stands, so surely will I put it to use."

Miss Newton gave her father a long, steady look which neither Wanlee nor Mr. Brown could interpret and then slowly led the way to the parlor. She closed the door and locked it. The clock on the mantel said four.

A complete change had come over the girl's manner. The spirit of defiance, of passionate appeal, of outspoken love, had gone. She was calm now, as cold and self-possessed as the senator himself. "Frozen!" she kept saying under her breath. "He has frozen me already with his frigid heart."

She quickly asked Mr. Walsingham Brown to explain clearly the force and bearings of the statute which her father had read from the book. When he had done so, she inquired, "Is there not also a law providing for voluntary suspension of animation?"

"The Twenty-seventh Amendment to the Constitution," replied the lawyer, "recognizes the right of any individual, not satisfied with the condition of his life, to suspend that life for a time, long or short, according to his pleasure. But it is rarely, as you know, that any one avails himself of the right—practically never, except as the only means to procure divorce from uncongenial marriage relations."

"Still," she persisted, "the right exists and the way is open?"
He bowed. She went to Wanlee and said:

"My darling, it must be so. I must leave you for a time, but as
your wife. We will arrange a wedding"—and she smiled sadly—
"within this hour. Mr. Brown will go with us to the clergyman.
Then we will proceed at once to the Refuge, and you yourself
shall lead me to the cloister that is to keep me safe till times are
better for us. No, do not be startled, my love! The resolution is
taken; you cannot alter it. And it will not be so very long, dear.
Once, by accident, in arranging my father's papers, I came across
his Life Probabilities, drawn up by the Vital Bureau at Washington. He has less than ten years to live. I never thought to calculate
in cold blood on the chances of my father's life, but it must be. In
ten years, Daniel, you may come to the Refuge again and claim
your bride. You will find me as you left me."

With tears streaming down his pale cheeks, the Mongolian
strove to dissuade the Caucasian from her purpose. Hardly less
affected, Mr. Walsingham Brown joined his entreaties and
arguments.

"Have you ever seen," he asked, "a woman who has undergone
what you propose to undergo? She went into the Refuge, perhaps,
as you will go, fresh, rosy, beautiful, full of life and energy. She
comes out a prematurely aged, withered, sallow, flaccid body, a
living corpse—a skeleton, a ghost of her former self. In spite of all
they say, there can be no absolute suspension of animation. Absolute suspension would be death. Even in the case of the most
perfect freezing there is still some activity of the vital functions,
and they gnaw and prey upon the existence of the unconscious
subject. Will you risk," he suddenly demanded, using the last
and most perfect argument that can be addressed to a woman
"—will you risk the effect your loss of beauty may have upon
Wanlee's love after ten years' separation?"

Clara Newton was smiling now. "For my poor beauty," she replied, "I care very little. Yet perhaps even that may be preserved."

She took from the bosom of her dress the little gold box which the Chinaman had given her in the supper room of the Capitol, and hastily swallowed its entire contents.

Wanlee now spoke with determination: "Since you have resolved to sacrifice ten years of your life my duty is with you. I shall share with you the sacrifice and share also the joy of awakening."

She gravely shook her head. "It is no sacrifice for me," she said. "But you must remain in life. You have a great and noble work to perform. Till the oppressed of the lower orders of being are emancipated from man's injustice and cruelty, you cannot abandon their cause. I think your duty is plain."

"You are right," he said, bowing his head to his breast.

In the gray dawn of the early morning the officials at the Frigorific Refuge in Cambridgeport were astonished by the arrival of a bridal party. The bridegroom's haggard countenance contrasted strangely with the elegance of his full evening toilet, and the bright scarlet bows at his knees seemed a mockery of grief. The bride, in white satin, wore a placid smile on her lovely face. The friend accompanying the two was grave and silent.

Without delay the necessary papers of admission were drawn up and signed and the proper registration was made upon the books of the establishment. For an instant husband and wife rested in each other's arms. Then she, still cheerful, followed the attendants toward the inner door, while he, pressing both hands upon his tearless eyes, turned away sobbing.

A moment later the intense cold of the congealing chamber caught the bride and wrapped her close in its icy embrace.

OLD SQUIDS AND LITTLE SPELLER

In the days of content, when wants were few and well supplied, when New England rum was pure and cheap, and while the older generation still wore the knee breeches and turkey-tailed coats of colonial days, and Bailey, who kept a tollgate on the Hartford and Providence turnpike, died. For forty years after the Revolution, Bailey lived in the solitary little tollhouse, near the bridge over the turbulent Quinnebaug, and in all that time had never failed to answer the call to come and take toll; but one night he responded not, and they found him sitting in his chair with an open Bible on his knees, and his spirit gone to the country of which he had been reading.

So it happened that a few days after, the big coach left a tall young man at the Quinnebaug tollhouse, who brought with him his possessions encased in a handkerchief. The driver of the stage informed the young man that here was the scene of his future activities for the turnpike company, and added as he saw the young fellow staring at the board beside the door on which, at a long distant time, the rates of toll had been painted, "See here, Old Squids, you'd better chalk up some new figures. The old ones is about washed out."

The driver called him Old Squids, but aside from the fact that such a surname, if such it was, had never been heard before in that country, it was strange that he should have been called old. He was, in fact, a young fellow, not more than two or three and twenty, seemingly. Though his skin was bronzed, it was smooth, and though his beard was tangled, each hair at cross purposes, it had never known the razor, and was, therefore, silky. He was sinewy, though his joints were protuberant, and his broad shoulders were not erect. Yet, perhaps, they called him old because he was moderate in his way, not so much because of laziness as by inborn disposition.

When the coach rolled away Squids was left standing there, gazing with a perplexed expression at the toll board and abstractedly tugging at his beard. No wonder he was perplexed. There appeared only fragments of words on the board, for the rains had washed the paint away with bewildering irregularity. He could make nothing of it. The very first thing that Squids did, therefore, was to tear down the board and take it into the little cottage. Then, without any examination of his new home, he threw his bundle upon the bed and began to repair the damage that time had done to the board. But age had done its inevitable work with it, and as Squids held it on his knees it crumbled in his strong grasp and broke into fragments, as though the rude change, after forty years of unmeddled security on the door, had been too much for it.

Squids sorrowfully looked at the fragments at his feet, then gathered them up carefully, and gave them a decent interment in an old chest. For a week Squids labored to make a new toll board. Not that the board itself needed so much time, but, alas, the announcement on it did. For, skillful as Squids was with the hammer and saw and nails, his fingers were clumsy with the pencil and paint brush. Hour after hour he worked, studying the printed card of rates which the company had given him, so that he might transfer those figures and letters intelligibly upon the board. One night he even dreamed how it should be done, and dreaming, awoke with delight, lighted his candle, and down on his knees he went, to transfer the dream to the board. But his fingers refused to respond to the picture in his mind, and, with a sigh, Squids returned to bed.

At last Squids gave it up. He simply painted upon the board something like this:

```
man ............................................ 1 ct.
horse .......................................... to ct.
critters ....................................... ask me.
```

The words and the spelling of them he slyly obtained from some passing stranger who wrote them out for Squids upon a shingle. This new board he hung up in the old place, and when he saw any one, man or beast, approaching the gate, he brought out his tariff card in case anybody should ask him the toll.

The manager of the company passing by in the stage, though he smiled at the board, comforted Squids by saying that he had done well, and then the manager told his companion that Squids was odd, but faithful, and had given proof of his integrity to one of the company's directors. "He doesn't know any name but Squids," said the manager, "and we suppose he is some whaler's waif cast ashore in New London, and left to look out for himself. But he is faithful."

But Squids, while pacified by the manager's approval, was by no means content. "Some day," said he to himself, as he gazed sadly at his rather abortive effort, "I'll put one up that'll be a credit."

Squids seemed happy enough in his lonely home. He made few friends, for the spot was remote from the farms of that town. The stage drivers liked him, for he always gave each of them a glass of cool milk. Squids's only possession, besides his clothes, was a cow.

One day one of the drivers said to him: "See here, old Squids. I've been a drinking your milk, off and on, a year or more for nothing. What can I get for you up to Hartford that will sorter square it up?"

"You might bring me a spelling book," said Squids. "If you'll buy it and bring it I'll pay what it costs: not more than a dollar, I guess."

On the next down trip the driver handed Squids a Webster's spelling book. His blue eyes sparkled as he received it, but he said nothing except to express his thanks. But when the stage rolled away, and Squids was alone, he opened the book haphazard, and then, standing before the billboard, said, with an accent of triumph in his tone and the gleam of victory in his eye. "By moy I can paint one and put it up that will be a credit."

Squids could spell two- and three-letter words, but beyond that he found himself mired in many difficulties very often. He struggled and wrestled manfully, but rather despairingly, with the two-syllabled words in the speller. "That's a B," he would say, "sure, and that's an A, and that spells Ba. But I don't quite get this 'ere yet. That's a K, that's an E, and that's an R. K is a K. E is an E. R is an R. Ker. That must be Keer. Bakeer. Now what kind of word is that?"

Thus Baker overthrew him and he was very despondent. One night, as he lay upon his bed, his eyes wide open and his brain throbbing with the misery of the mystery of Bakeer, a great light came to him. He arose, lighted a candle, and from his canvas bag drew forth ten copper pennies, which he placed conspicuously upon his table. Then he no sooner touched his pillow than he fell asleep.

In the morning the ten coppers were given to the driver, with the request that they should be exchanged at Hartford for ten peppermint bull's-eyes, streaked red and white. When Squids received the bull's-eyes he put them away on a plate in his cupboard and bided his time until the next Saturday afternoon. At that time, about an hour before sundown, he began to peer up the road toward the bend, for it was at such time that he knew that every Saturday a young lad came along with some good things from his father's farm for the minister's Sunday dinner at the parsonage, a mile away on the other side of the Quinnebaug.

At last Squids caught sight of the boy, who bore a basket on his arm seemingly heavily laden. Squids, with a slyness born of some sense of shame, concealed himself in the tollhouse. Soon the lad was at the gate calling upon Squids to come out and pass him.

"Hulloo! It's you, is it, Ebenezer, going to the minister's? That basket must be heavy. Should think you'd want to rest a bit."

"'T is heavy. There's a sparerib in it?"

"M'm. Want to know," said Squids, opening his eyes in surprise and sympathy well simulated. "Come in and sit down. Mebbe I can give you something kinder good."

"Now what's that air thing?" asked Squids, when he had Ebenezer in the house, holding up the monstrously tempting confection before the boy's eyes.

"Pepentink bull's-eyes," said the boy, delightedly.

"You like 'em. You shall have one." Here Squids seemed about to give Ebenezer the candy, but suddenly restrained himself.

"Hold on," he said. "You've got to earn it. Oh! You go to school?"

"Yes, in winter."

"H'm-m. How far have you got?"

"I've got to fractions and second reader."

"Sho! No! I wan't to know. Now let's see." Here Squids meditatively produced the Webster's speller from its place under his pillow, and opening it, said: "H'm-m. Let's see. Now, here, if you will read that colyumn down straight you shall have two bull's-eyes. Right here. Just to see how much you know."

"That's easy," said Ebenezer. "I will read some harder ones."

Squids seemed a little perplexed. At length he said, "Let's try the easy ones first. It'll be so much easier to earn the bull's-eyes. Don't you see?" And Squids placed the point of his jackknife blade upon Baker.

"That's Baker," said Ebenezer.

"Baker," replied Squids, with the queerest accent in his voice. "Baker. Sho! so 'tis." Here Squids abstractedly combed his beard with his jackknife.

"Of course it's Baker. Ker don't spell keer. Anybody but a fool might a' known that. Let me write it down, Ebenezer."

Then Squids, somewhat to the astonishment of Ebenezer, brought forth a shingle, and on the smooth white side, with a piece of charcoal, spelled out the word B-a-k-e-r.

"What do you write it down for, Squids?" asked the boy.

"What for? Oh, only to see how many you get right," replied the cunning Squids.

Thus Squids mastered some ten or twelve words, and the boy received two bull's-eyes, and Squids made a covenant with him that he should stop there every Saturday afternoon and show Squids whether he could read rightly such words in Webster's speller as Squids showed him, for which he was to receive two or more bull's-eyes.

Thus Squids, taught by a bribed and unconscious teacher, mastered the speller and began to make preparations to build a new toll board on which he purposed to paint the tariff of prices in a manner that would be a credit.

But something happened that made the new toll board and the credit that it was to be seem of petty consequence to him. One evening in March, when the line storm was raging without, Squids, with his speller on the table between two candles, and a shingle on his knee, was painting out with almost infinite pains the word cattle, so that he might be schooled in printing it correctly and as artistically as possible upon the toll board.

Suddenly Squids paused in his work and listened. There was surely a knock upon his door. The sound was not made by the beating of the oak branches on the roof. Squids took a candle and opened the door. A gust of wind blew the light out, as well as the other one on the table, but Squids had seen a woman's form on the doorstep, and he put forth his hand and drew her within. He bade her be patient until he relighted the candle, but before he could do so he heard her staggering step, and then he knew that she had fallen.

When Squids at last with nervous fingers coaxed a spark into the tinder and lighted a candle, he saw that the woman seemed to have sunk to the floor. Her face, over which her hair had fallen and was matted by the rain, was pale, and her eyes, half-opened with unconscious stare, seemed to him like the eyes of the dead. Her head, having fallen back, rested against the door. Squids held the candle to her parted lips and saw that she was not dead, but faint, and even before he could apply the simple remedies that he had she had somewhat recovered. She feebly rose, tottered to a chair, and then for the first time Squids saw that which startled him far more than her unconscious form had done. He saw in her arms the peaceful face of a sleeping infant.

She drank a glass of water, and Squids bustled about to prepare for her a cup of tea, for which he had made of great potency, so that, having taken it, she greatly revived.

"You're very wet," said Squids, and he threw some logs upon the hearth, urging her to draw near the fire. She did so, but with such manner of indifference that it seemed to Squids that she cared little whether she was wet or dry.

Though he had never touched the smooth, soft flesh of an infant before, Squids gently took this one from her unresisting arms and laid it upon his pillow. The child had not been wet by the storm, and Squids carefully tucked the quilt under the pillow. It did not even awaken under his unaccustomed touch, and as he looked upon the little sleeping one upon his pillow, with a chubby hand resting beside its cheek, Squids vowed that neither mother nor child should leave the house that night.

The woman watched him with the first sign of interest she had shown, and she said at length, "You are kind, very kind."

"That air's a cute little beauty," was all the reply Squids made.

The woman told him an incoherent, rambling story about missing the stage and losing her way, and she begged that she might rest there until the next stage came. Squids urged her to make herself comfortable, and he set milk and bread before her. Then, with cautions respecting the need of thorough drying, Squids went away to the little loft. He listened as he lay upon an extemporized bed, but all was silent below, and when he was assured that the stranger was in comfort he fell asleep.

In the morning Squids knocked at the door, but there was no response. "She is tired: let her sleep," said Squids to himself.

But by and by there being no sound within, Squids ventured to knock again, and still getting no response opened the door. The room was vacant.

"She went away before I awoke," reasoned Squids, and he set about getting his breakfast.

Soon he heard that which caused him to stop and stand in utter amazement. He did not stir until he heard the sound again.

"Ma! Ma!" It came to him once more, and then, gently raising the bedquilt, Squids's eyes met those of the baby.

The little thing put up its hands, chuckled, and bounced up and down upon the pillow.

"Mo! Mo!" it said.

"Mo! Mo!" said Squids. "That means moolly, moolly. It wants milk."

In an instant Squids was warming a basin of milk. "I calculate it'll like it sweet," he meditated. So he put in a heaping spoonful of sugar. Then, with the tenderness of a mother, Squids fed the little one, spoonful by spoonful, till at last it pushed the spoon away with its fat little hands, and, reaching up, clung with gentle yet firm grasp to Squids's long and silky beard, and then, tugging away, looked up into his eyes, and laughed and crowed.

"Seems as though it knowed me," said Squids. "I vum, the cute little rascal thinks it knows me," and two tears dropped from Squids' eyes right down upon the baby's cheek, and it lifted up one hand in sport, and as it felt of Squids's rough skin, it brushed away another tear or two with its frolicking. And Squids held his face down to it, and clucked and clucked, and spoke softly with all the instinct of paternity within him aroused. At last the little one's hands relaxed, and its eyelids drooped, and it fell asleep, and Squids stood there watching it, how long he knew not.

Thus Squids had a companion brought to him. He never knew why the mother, if such she was, left the baby there, or where she had gone, and as the days went by he began to have a secret terror lest she should sometime come and claim it. But she did not. No more thought had Squids for the new toll board, only as he set it before the child for a table whereon were gathered the marvelous toys that Squids whittled for it with his jackknife. Squids early discovered that the baby liked wheels above all things, and that it displayed wonderful cunning in the arrangement of them after he had whittled them out.

One day Squids found him gazing wonderingly at the Webster's speller, and though fearful of the lawlessness of those little hands, Squids bound the covers firmly together with cords and suffered him to play with the book. Then Squids called the baby Little Speller, and never by any other name. The little one tried hard to say Squids, but could only lisp "Thid," so that Squids came to like this diminutive as spoken by the child better than all other sounds.

"Some day you and me will rastle with this book, and I calculate we'll get the best of it, won't we, sir?" Squids would say to the child when it grew old enough to understand, and the little one would reply, "Yes we will, Thid."

Thus they lived, day by day, Little Speller content, while Squids—his happiness was a revelation of delight of which he had had no conception. By and by, when the little one was older, Squids would take him on his knee, and with the Webster speller and a new slate brought from Hartford, they would take up their tasks.

"That's A, sir. See how I make it. One line down, so, and another down, so, and one across, and that makes A." And Little Speller, with faltering fingers, would draw the lines and say, "That's A, Thid," and Squids would laugh and say, "We'll have a toll board by and by that will be a credit, and no mistake."

One day Squids spelled out horse on the slate, and Little Speller took the pencil and sketched a horse with very rectangular head and body and very wavy legs, and he said, "No, that's horse, Thid."

Squids roared, and got a shingle and made Little Speller spell horse in that way on it with a crayon. Then Squids nailed the shingle on the wall over the fireplace, and when anybody came in he would point proudly to it, saying, "See how Little Speller spells horse. He's a cute one!"

But before many months went by Squids found that the boy and he were exchanging places, for the teacher was becoming the taught and the scholar becoming the teacher. So Squids sent to Hartford and bought a first reader and an arithmetic, and great was their delight in pondering over the mysteries of these books and solving them.

"Little Speller," said Squids, one day, "you took to spelling natural, but you take to 'rithmetic more natural. But it's beyond me. After this you'll have to do the figgering and the spelling for me."

That the child had a talent for mathematics and mechanics Squids understood fully, though he could not express it in any other way than by saying: "He's mighty sharp at figgers and mighty cute with the jackknife."

One morning, as Squids was opening the tollgate, he astonished the traveler who waited to pass through by suddenly stopping and staring at the house. The stranger feared he had gone mad, or was carrying too much New England rum, till Squids, with triumphant utterance, said, "Look at that air. That's a credit at last," and he pointed to a new toll board neatly painted and accurately lettered. Then he rushed into the house and brought forth the lad.

"This is the boy that done it," said Squids, "unbeknown to me, and nailed her up unbeknown. Ain't that a credit? It is Little Speller, it is."

Then, when Little Speller grew older, he builded, with Squids's help, a marvelous tollgate that opened and shut automatically by the touching of a lever; and the fame of it spread, so that the manager even came, and wondered, too, and praised the lad, saying: "Squids, that boy is a genius, sure."

And Squids would watch Little Speller, when the lad knew it not, as an enthusiast studies a painting, and many and many a time did Squids in the night quietly arise from the bed, light a candle, and look, with something like awe in his glance, upon the face of the sleeping boy.

One day there came to the Quinnebaug tollgate some men, and they drove stakes and dug ditches, and builded a great dam across the river, half a mile above. Then they put up a building, larger than any Little Speller ever saw, and placed within it curious machines, and they put a huge wheel outside the building. Little Speller seemed entranced as he watched them day by day, and he caused the men to deal with him with great respect, because at a critical time in setting up the wheel, when it seemed as though something had gone wrong, they heard a little voice shouting peremptorily, "Loose your ropes, quick," and they did so, and the wheel settled properly in place. The men wondered how it was that that little fellow standing there on a rock could have shouted so commandingly that they trusted him. But they said: "He's got some gumption, sure."

When the big wheel was set agoing and the machines in the mill began to make a frightful clatter, then it was that Little Speller's enthusiasm and delight seemed to be greater even than such a little body as his could contain. He spent hours and hours in the mill watching the machines as they wove the threads of wool into cloth.

By and by Squids saw that Little Speller was silent, dreaming abstracted, and Squids became alarmed. "It's that air dreadful noise in the mill that's confusing his little head," reasoned Squids: and he urged the boy to go there less frequently, but Little Speller went as was his wont. At length, Squids saw that the boy was busying himself day and night with the jackknife and such other tools as were there, and Squids was pleased, though he could not comprehend what this strange thing was that Little

Speller was building. The boy seemed absorbed by his work. When he ate, his great dreamy eyes were fixed abstractedly upon his plate; but he slept soundly, and Squids was not greatly alarmed.

"There's something in him that's working out," reasoned Squids, and when he saw the fierce energy and enthusiasm with which Little Speller cut and shaped and planed and fashioned the bits of wood, Squids was sure that whatever it was that was working out of him was working out well.

One day Little Speller said, as he put his hand on the thing he had made, "There, it's done, and it's all right. It's better than the ones they've got in the mill, only it's wood."

"What might it be, Little Speller?" asked Squids.

"It's a weaving machine."

"It's worked out of you. Part of you is in that thing, Little Speller, and it's a greater credit than the toll board or the gate."

Then Squids in great glee went and fetched the superintendent of the mill. "See," said he, when he had brought the man, "that air is worked out of Little Speller. Part of him is in it, and it's a credit."

The superintendent glanced with some interest at the model, more to please the lad and Squids than for any other reason.

"Show him how it works," said Squids.

Little Speller did so. It was rude, clumsy; but as the boy explained the working of it, the superintendent became excited. He fingered it himself. He worked at it. Great beads of sweat stood on his forehead, for he was intensely interested. At last he said: "That will revolutionize woolen mills. The thing's built wrong, but the idea is there. Where did you get that idea, Squids?"

"Me!" exclaimed Squids. "Me! 'Taint me. It worked out of Little Speller. It's been working out of him ever since the mill was built. Ain't it a credit?"

"Credit!" and the superintendent smiled. "What do you want for it?" he asked.

"I want to see one built and set to working in the mill," said Little Speller.

"Will you let me build it?"

"Oh, if you only will," begged Little Speller.

"Put that down in writing, and I'll promise you I'll fit the mill with them; yes, and a hundred mills."

Squids and Little Speller seemed dazed by this unexpected glory.

"He's going to put what's worked out of you into a hundred mills, Little Speller," said Squids, as he looked almost reverentially upon the boy.

It was as the superintendent had said. Seizing Little Speller's idea, he had properly handled it, builded machines, obtained patents, therefore, and had revolutionized the woolen mills that were then springing up throughout eastern New England, and had he opened a mine of gold there on the banks of the Quinnebaug, the superintendent could hardly have had more riches.

But Squids and Little Speller were content. They would go up to the mill and watch the new machine, weaving yards and yards of cloth, Little Speller with the most ecstatic delight, and Squids with a sense of awe. "That's you, Little Speller. That's you working. It ain't the machine. That's only wood and iron."

By and by Little Speller began to appear abstracted again, and he spent many hours watching the transmission of power from the water wheel to the machinery. "Something more is working out," reasoned Squids, but he held his peace.

One day Squids heard someone coming down the road. He went to open the gate. There were four or five men, and they were bearing a burden. When they were near, Squids saw that they moved gently and bore their burden tenderly and that their faces were very grave. They did not try to pass the gate, but instead entered Squids's little house and laid their burden upon his bed. Then Squids saw Little Speller's pale face, and a little red thread that was vividly tracing its way on the white cheek down from the temple, and the eyes were closed and the hand hung limp. Squids stood there motionless a long time, then, turning to the men, he said, with dull, phlegmatic speech and a veiled appearance of his eyes,

"Was he working it out?"

"He was," said one, "and he forgot himself and got too near the shafting and it—"

"Yes, yes. He was a-working it out," said Squids mechanically, and with no intelligence in his eyes. Then suddenly he darted fiercely to the bedside. Little Speller had opened his eyes. He saw Squids and knew him.

"Thid," he said.

Squids bent over him, but could not speak.

"Thid, I shall never work it out," he whispered.

Then he turned his eyes longingly to the old model across the room, and then looked imploringly at Squids. The gatekeeper read his wishes. He pushed the old model up to the bedside. Then Little Speller put one hand upon it, and with the other outstretched till the palm rested gently upon Squids's face, he looked up with one peaceful glance and the flicker of a faint smile, and then the light passed out of Little Speller's eyes forever.

The men saw what had happened and went quietly away, leaving Squids alone with Little Speller.

In the afterdays, Squids would sit by the old model, gently speaking to it, and affectionately causing its mechanism to be put in operation, and he would say, "Little Speller is in there. He is in a hundred mills. You can hear him, but I, when I look at this, I can see him, too."

THE FACTS IN THE RATCLIFF CASE

I first met Miss Borgier at a tea party in the town of R——, where I was attending medical lectures. She was a tall girl, not pretty; her face would have been insipid but for the peculiar restlessness of her eyes. They were neither bright nor expressive, yet she kept them so constantly in motion that they seemed to catch and reflect light from a thousand sources. Whenever, as rarely happened, she fixed them even for a few seconds upon one object, the factitious brilliancy disappeared, and they became dull and somnolent. I am unable to say what was the color of Miss Borgier's eyes.

After tea, I was one of a group of people whom our host, the Reverend Mr. Tinker, sought to entertain with a portfolio of photographs of places in the Holy Land. While endeavoring to appear interested in his descriptions and explanations, all of which I had heard before, I became aware that Miss Borgier was honoring me with steady regard. My gaze encountered hers and I found that I could not, for the life of me, withdraw my own eyes from the encounter. Then I had a singular experience, the phenomena of which I noted with professional accuracy. I felt the slight constriction of the muscles of my face, the numbness of the nerves that precedes physical stupor induced by narcotic agency. Although I was obliged to struggle against the physical sense of drowsiness, my mental faculties were more than ordinarily active. Her eyes seemed to torpify my body while they stimulated my mind, as opium does. Entirely conscious of my present surroundings, and particularly alert to the Reverend Mr. Tinker's narrative of the ride from Joppa, I accompanied him on that journey, not as one who listens to a traveler's tale, but as one who himself travels the road. When, finally, we reached the point where the Reverend Mr. Tinker's donkey makes the last sharp turn around the rock that has been cutting off the view ahead, and the Reverend Mr. Tinker beholds with amazement and joy the glorious panorama of Jerusalem spread out before him, I saw it all with remarkable vividness. I saw Jerusalem in Miss Borgier's eyes.

I tacitly thanked fortune when her eyes resumed their habitual dance around the room, releasing me from what had become a rather humiliating captivity. Once free from their strange influence, I laughed at my weakness. "Pshaw!" I said to myself. "You are a fine subject for a young woman of mesmeric talents to practice upon."

"Who is Miss Borgier?" I demanded of the Reverend Mr. Tinker's wife, at the first opportunity.

"Why, she is Deacon Borgier's daughter," replied that good person, with some surprise.

"And who is Deacon Borgier?"

"A most excellent man; one of the pillars of my husband's congregation. The young people laugh at what they call his torpidity, and say that he has been walking about town in his sleep for twenty years; but I assure you that there is not a sincerer, more fervent Chris—"

I turned abruptly around, leaving Mrs. Tinker more astonished than ever, for I knew that the subject of my inquiries was looking at me again. She sat in one corner of the room, apart from the rest of the company. I straightway went and seated myself at her side.

"That is right," she said. "I wished you to come. Did you enjoy your journey to Jerusalem?"

"Yes, thanks to you."

"Perhaps. But you can repay the obligation. I am told that you are Dr. Mack's assistant in surgery at the college. There is a clinic tomorrow. I want to attend it."

"As a patient?" I inquired.

She laughed. "No, as a spectator. You must find a way to gratify my curiosity."

I expressed, as politely as possible, my astonishment at so extraordinary a fancy on the part of a young lady, and hinted at the scandal which her appearance in the amphitheater would create. She immediately offered to disguise herself in male attire. I explained that the nature of the relations between the medical college and the patients who consented to submit to surgical treatment before the class were such that it would be a dishonorable thing for me to connive at the admission of any outsider, male or female. That argument made no impression upon her mind. I was forced to decline peremptorily to serve her in the affair. "Very well," she said. "I must find some other way."

At the clinic the next day I took pains to satisfy myself that Miss Borgier had not surreptitiously intruded. The students of the class came in at the hour, noisy and careless as usual, and seated themselves in the lower tiers of chairs around the operating table. They produced their notebooks and began to sharpen lead pencils. Miss Borgier was certainly not among them. Every face in the lecture room was familiar to me. I locked the door that opened into the hallway, and then searched the anteroom on the other side of the amphitheater. There were a dozen or more patients, nervous and dejected, waiting for treatment and attended by friends hardly less frightened than themselves. But neither Miss Borgier nor anybody resembling Miss Borgier was of the number.

Dr. Mack now briskly entered by his private door. He glanced sharply at the table on which his instruments were arranged, ready for use, and, having assured himself that everything was in its place, began the clinical lecture. There were the usual minor operations—two or three for strabismus, one for cataract, the excision of several cysts and tumors, large and small, the amputation of a railway brakeman's crushed thumb. As the cases were disposed of, I attended the patients back to the anteroom and placed them in the care of their friends.

Last came a poor old lady named Wilson, whose leg had been drawn up for years by a rheumatic affection, so that the joint of the knee had ossified. It was one of those cases where the necessary treatment is almost brutal in its simplicity. The limb had to be straightened by the application of main force. Mrs. Wilson obstinately refused to take advantage of anesthesia. She was placed on her back upon the operating table, with a pillow beneath her head. The geniculated limb showed a deflection of twenty or twenty-five degrees from a right line. As already remarked, this deflection had to be corrected by direct, forcible pressure downward upon the knee.

With the assistance of a young surgeon of great physical strength, Dr. Mack proceeded to apply this pressure. The operation is one of the most excruciating that can be imagined. I was stationed at the head of the patient, in order to hold her shoulders should she struggle. But I observed that a marked change had come over her since we established her upon the table. Very much agitated at first, she had become perfectly calm. As she passively lay there, her eyes directed upward with a fixed gaze, the eyelids heavy as if with approaching slumber, the face tranquil, it was hard to realize that this woman had already crossed the threshold of an experience of cruel pain.

I had no time, however, to give more than a thought to her wonderful courage. The harsh operation had begun. The surgeon and his assistant were steadily and with increasing force bearing down upon the rigid knee. Perhaps the Spanish Inquisition never devised a method of inflicting physical torture more intense than that which this woman was now undergoing, yet not a muscle of her face quivered. She breathed easily and regularly, her features retained their placid expression, and, at the moment when her sufferings must have been the most agonizing, I saw her eyes close, as if in peaceful sleep.

At the same instant the tremendous force exerted upon the knee produced its natural effect. The ossified joint yielded, and, with a sickening noise—the indescribable sound of the crunching and gritting of the bones of a living person, a sound so frightful that I have seen old surgeons, with sensibilities hardened by long experience, turn pale at hearing it—the crooked limb became as straight as its mate.

Closely following this horrible sound, I heard a ringing peal of laughter.

The operating table, in the middle of the pit of the amphitheater, was lighted from overhead. Directly above the table, a shaft, five or six feet square, and closely boarded on its four sides, led up through the attic story of the building to a skylight in the roof. The shaft was so deep and so narrow that its upper orifice was visible from no part of the room except a limited space immediately around the table. The laughter which startled me seemed to come from overhead. If heard by any other person present, it was probably ascribed to a hysterical utterance on the part of the patient. I was in a position to know better. Instinctively I glanced upward, in the direction in which the eyes of Mrs. Wilson had been so fixedly bent.

There, framed in a quadrangle of blue sky, I saw the head and neck of Miss Borgier. The sash of the skylight had been removed, to afford ventilation. The young woman was evidently lying at full length upon the flat roof. She commanded a perfect view of all that was done upon the operating table. Her face was flushed with eager interest and wore an expression of innocent wonder, not unmingled with delight. She nodded merrily to me when I looked up and laid a finger against her lips, as if to warn me to silence. Disgusted, I withdrew my eyes hastily from hers. Indeed, after my experience of the previous evening, I did not care to trust my self-control under the influence of her gaze.

As Dr. Mack with his sharp scissors cut the end of a linen bandage, he whispered to me: "This is without a parallel. Not a sign of syncope, no trace of functional disorder. She has dropped quietly into healthy sleep during an infliction of pain that would drive a strong man mad."

As soon as released from my duties in the lecture room, I made my way to the roof of the building. As I emerged through the scuttle-way, Miss Borgier scrambled to her feet and advanced to meet me without manifesting the slightest discomposure. Her face fairly beamed with pleasure.

"Wasn't it beautiful?" she asked with a smile, extending her hand. "I heard the bones slowly grinding and crushing!"

I did not take her hand. "How came you here?" I demanded, avoiding her glance.

"Oh!" said she, with a silvery laugh. "I came early, about sunrise. The janitor left the door ajar and I slipped in while he was in the cellar. All the morning I spent in the place where they dissect; and when the students began to come in downstairs I escaped here to the roof."

"Are you aware, Miss Borgier," I asked, very gravely, "that you have committed a serious indiscretion, and must be gotten out of the building as quickly and privately as possible?"

She did not appear to understand. "Very well," she said. "I suppose there is nothing more to see. I may as well go."

I led her down through the garret, cumbered with boxes and barrels of unarticulated human bones; through the medical library, unoccupied at that hour; by a back stairway into and across the great vacant chemical lecture room; through the anatomical cabinet, full of objects appalling to the imagination of her sex. I was silent and she said nothing; but her eyes were everywhere, drinking in the strange surroundings with an avidity which I could feel without once looking at her. Finally we came to a basement corridor, at the end of which a door, not often used, gave egress by an alleyway to the street. It was through this door that subjects for dissection were brought into the building. I took a bunch of keys from my pocket and turned the lock. "Your way is clear now," I said.

To my immense astonishment, Miss Borgier, as we stood together at the end of the dark corridor, threw both arms around my neck and kissed me.

"Good-by," she said, as she disappeared through the half-opened door.

When I awoke the next morning, after sleeping for more than fifteen hours, I found that I could not raise my head from the pillow without nausea. The symptoms were exactly like those which mark the effects of an overdose of laudanum.

II

I have thought it due to myself and to my professional reputation to recount these facts before briefly speaking of my recent testimony as an expert, in the Ratcliff murder trial, the character of my relations with the accused having been persistently misrepresented.

The circumstances of that celebrated case are no doubt still fresh in the recollection of the public. Mr. John L. Ratcliff, a wealthy, middle-aged merchant of Boston, came to St. Louis with his young bride, on their wedding journey. His sudden death at the Planters' Hotel, followed by the arrest of his wife, who was entirely without friends or acquaintances in the city, her indictment for murder by poisoning, the conflict of medical testimony at the trial, and the purely circumstantial nature of the evidence against the prisoner, attracted general attention and excited public interest to a degree that was quite extraordinary.

It will be remembered that the state proved that the relations of Mr. and Mrs. Ratcliff, as observed by the guests and servants of the hotel, were not felicitous; that he rarely spoke to her at table, habitually averting his face in her presence; that he wandered aimlessly about the hotel for several days previous to his illness, apparently half stupefied, as if by the oppression of some heavy mental burden, and that when accosted by anyone connected with the house he started as if from a dream, and answered incoherently if at all.

It was also shown that, by her husband's death, Mrs. Ratcliff became the sole mistress of a large fortune.

The evidence bearing directly upon the circumstances of Mr. Ratcliff's death was very clear. For twenty-four hours before a physician was summoned, no one had access to him save his wife. At dinner that day, in response to the polite inquiry of a lady neighbor at table, Mrs. Ratcliff announced, with great self-possession, that her husband was seriously indisposed. Soon after eleven o'clock at night, Mrs. Ratcliff rang her bell, and, without the least agitation of manner, remarked that her husband appeared to be dying, and that it might be well to send for a physician. Dr. Culbert, who arrived within a very few minutes, found Mr. Ratcliff in a profound stupor, breathing stertorously. He swore at the trial that when he first entered the room the prisoner, pointing to the bed, coolly said, "I suppose that I have killed him."

Dr. Culbert's testimony seemed to point unmistakably to poisoning by laudanum or morphine. The unconscious man's pulse was full but slow; his skin cold and pallid; the expression of his countenance placid, yet ghastly pale; lips livid. Coma had already supervened, and it was impossible to rouse him. The ordinary expedients were tried in vain. Flagellation of the palms of his hands and the soles of his feet, electricity applied to the head and spine, failed to make any impression on his lethargy. The eyelids being forcibly opened, the pupils were seen to be contracted to the size of pinheads, and violently turned inward. Later, the stertorous breathing developed into the ominously loud rattle of mucous in the trachea; there were convulsions, attended by copious frothings at the mouth; the under jaw fell upon the breast; and paralysis and death followed, four hours after Dr. Culbert's arrival.

Several of the most eminent practitioners of the city, put upon the stand by the prosecution, swore that, in their opinion, the symptoms noted by Dr. Culbert not only indicated opium poisoning, but could have resulted from no other cause.

On the other hand, the state absolutely failed to show either that opium in any form had been purchased by Mrs. Ratcliff in St. Louis, or that traces of opium in any form were found in the room after the event. It is true that the prosecuting attorney, in his closing argument, sought to make the latter circumstance tell against the prisoner. He argued that the disappearance of any vessel containing or having contained laudanum, in view of the positive evidence that laudanum had been employed, served to establish a deliberate intention of murder and to demolish any theory of accidental poisoning that the defense might attempt to build; and he propounded half a dozen hypothetical methods by which Mrs. Ratcliff might have disposed, in advance, of this evidence of her crime. The court, of course, in summing up, cautioned the jury against attaching weight to these hypotheses of the prosecuting attorney.

The court, however, put much emphasis on the medical testimony for the prosecution, and on the calm declaration of Mrs. Ratcliff to Dr. Culbert, "I suppose that I have killed him."

Having conducted the autopsy, and afterward made a qualitative analysis of the contents of the dead man's stomach, I was put upon the stand as a witness for the defense.

Then I saw the prisoner for the first time in more than five years. When I had taken the oath and answered the preliminary questions, Mrs. Ratcliff raised the veil which she had worn since the trial began, and looked me in the face with the well-remembered eyes of Miss Borgier.

I confess that my behavior during the first few moments of surprise afforded some ground for the reports that were afterward current concerning my relations with the prisoner. Her eyes chained not only mine, but my tongue also. I saw Jerusalem again, and the face framed in blue sky peering down into the amphitheater of the old medical college. It was only after a struggle which attracted the attention of judge, jury, bar, and spectators that I was able to proceed with my testimony.

That testimony was strong for the accused. My knowledge of the case was wholly post-mortem. It began with the autopsy. Nothing had been found that indicated poisoning by laudanum or by any other agent. There was no morbid appearance of the intestinal canal; no fullness of the cerebral vessels, no serous effusion. Every appearance that would have resulted from death by poison was wanting in the subject. That, of course, was merely negative evidence. But, furthermore, my chemical analysis had proved the absence of the poison in the system. The opium odor could not be detected. I had tested for morphine with nitric acid, permuriate of iron, chromate of potash, and, most important of all, iodic acid. I had tested again for meconic acid with the permuriate of iron. I had tested by Lassaigne's process, by Dublane's, and by Flandin's. As far as the resources of organic chemistry could avail, I had proved that, notwithstanding the symptoms of Mr. Ratcliff's case before death, death had not resulted from laudanum or any other poison known to science.

The questions by the prosecuting counsel as to my previous acquaintance with the prisoner, I was able to answer truthfully in a manner that did not shake the force of my medical testimony. And it was chiefly on the strength of this testimony that the jury, after a short deliberation, returned a verdict of not guilty.

Did I swear falsely? No; for science bore me out in every assertion. I knew that not a drop of laudanum or a grain of morphine had passed Ratcliff's lips. Ought I to have declared my belief regarding the true cause of the man's death, and told the story of my previous observations of Miss Borgier's case? No; for no court of justice would have listened to that story for a single moment. I knew that the woman did not murder her husband. Yet I believed and knew—as surely as we can know anything where the basis of ascertained fact is slender and the laws obscure—that she poisoned him, *poisoned him to death with her eyes.*

I think that it will be generally conceded by the profession that I am neither a sensationalist nor prone to lose my self-command in the mazes of physico-psychologic speculation. I make the foregoing assertion deliberately, fully conscious of all that it implies.

What was the mystery of the noxious influence which this woman exerted through her eyes? What was the record of her ancestry, the secret of predisposition in her case? By what occult process of evolution did her glance derive the toxical effect of the *papaver somniferum?* How did she come to be a Woman-Poppy? I cannot yet answer these questions. Perhaps I shall never be able to answer them.

But if there is need of further proof of the sincerity of my denial of any sentiment on my part which might have led me to shield Mrs. Ratcliff by perjury, I may say that I have now in my possession a letter from her, written after her acquittal, proposing to endow me with her fortune and herself; as well as a copy of my reply, respectfully declining the offer.

THE STORY OF THE DELUGE

Interesting Particulars Respecting the Translations of the Assyrian Tablets in the British Museum—Newly Discovered Facts About the Flood and Noah, Together with Some Light on the History of the Senator from Maine and the Settlement of Brooklyn.

Boston, April 26—Mr. Jacob Rounds of London, one of the assistant curators of the British Museum, in a private letter to a distinguished Orientalist of this city, gives some interesting particulars regarding the progress which has been made in the arrangement and translation of the sculptured tablets and *lateres coctiles* brought from Assyria and Chaldea by Mr. George Smith. The results of the past three or four months are gratifying in the extreme. The work, which was begun three quarters of a century ago by Grotefend, and pursued by archaeologists such as Rask, St. Martin, Klaproth, Oppert, and the indefatigable Rawlinson, each of whom was satisfied if he carried it forward a single step, has been pushed far and fast by Mr. George Smith and his scholarly associates. The Assyrio-Babylonian cuneiforms, the third and most complicated branch of the trilogy, may fairly be said to have found their Oedipus.

The riddles of Accad and of Sumir are read at last. The epigraphs on tablets dug from the earth and rubbish of the Ninevite mounds are now translated by Mr. George Smith as readily as Professor Whitney translates Greek, or a fifth-term schoolboy, the fable of the man and the viper.

It is not many years since the learned Witte declared that these sphenographic characters, arranged so neatly upon the slabs of gray alabaster, or the carefully prepared surface of clay—like specimen arrowheads in the museum of some ancient war department—were entirely without alphabetic significance, mere whimsical ornaments, or perhaps the trail of worms! But their exegesis has been perfected. The mounds of Nimroud, and Kouyunjik, and Khorsabad, and Nebbi Yunus have yielded up their precious treasures, and are now revealing, page by page, the early history of our globe.

Mr. Smith and Mr. Rounds are both confirmed in the belief, first entertained by Westergaarde, that the cuneiform character is closely akin to the Egyptian demotic; and also that its alphabet—which contains over four hundred signs, some syllable, some phonetic, and some ideographic—is of the most complicated and arbitrary nature. As already intimated, the inscriptions which Mr. Smith and his colaborers have deciphered are in the primitive or Babylonian character, which is much more obscure than either of its successors and modifications, the so-called Persian and Median cunei.

The slabs of the greatest interest and importance were those found buried in the famous Kouyunjik mound, first opened in 1843 by M. Paul Émile Botta, and subsequently explored by Layard himself.

The inscriptions are mostly upon clay, and seem to have constituted the walls of the great library of Assurbanipal in Sennacherib's palace. Sennacherib was probably a monarch of a nautical turn of mind, for a large portion of the inscriptions

illustrate the history of the flood and the voyage of Noah, or of
Nyab, his Assyrian counterpart, who also corresponds, in some
particulars, with the Deucalion of the Grecian myths. Piece by
piece and fragment by fragment the diluvian narrative has been
worked out, until it stands complete, a distinct episode in the
vast epic which Mr. George Smith is engaged in reconstructing.
Mr. Rounds may certainly be pardoned for the naturally enthusiastic terms in which he speaks of these labors.

And well may he be proud. These men in the British Museum
are successfully compiling, brick by brick, what they claim to be
a complete encyclopedia of sacred and profane history, beginning with the conception of matter and the birth of mind. Their
extraordinary researches have placed them upon a pedestal of
authority, from which they now gravely pronounce their approval of the Holy Scriptures, and even stoop to pat Moses on
the head and to tell him that his inspired version was very nearly
correct.

So graphic is the account of the adventures of Nyab, or Noah
as he may more conveniently be called; so clear is the synopsis
of his method of navigation; so startling are the newly discovered facts regarding the Ark and its passengers, that I am
tempted to avail myself of the kind permission of the Boston
savant who has the honor to be Mr. Rounds's esteemed correspondent, and to transcribe somewhat in detail, for the benefit
of your readers, the extraordinary story of the flood as told by the
Assyrian cuneiforms—cryptograms for four thousand years until
the genius of a Smith unveiled the mystery of their meaning.

THE RISING OF THE WATERS

Mr. Smith ascertains from these inscriptions that when Noah
began to build his Ark and prophesy a deluge, the prevailing
opinion was that he was either a lunatic or a shrewd speculator
who proposed, by his glowing predictions and appearance of

perfect sincerity, so to depreciate real estate that he might buy, through his brokers, to any extent at prices merely nominal.

Even after the lowlands were submerged, and it was apparent that there was to be a more than usually wet season, Noah's wicked neighbors were accustomed to gather for no other purpose than to deride the ungainly architecture of the Ark and to question its sailing qualities. They were not wanting who asserted that the Thing would roll over at the first puff of wind like a too heavily freighted tub. So people came from far and near to witness and laugh at the discomfiture of the aged patriarch.

But there was no occasion for ridicule. The Ark floated like a cork. Noah dropped his center board and stood at the helm waving graceful adieus to his wicked contemporaries, while the good vessel caught a fresh southerly breeze and moved on like a thing of life. There is nothing whatever in the Assyrian account to confirm the tradition that Noah accelerated the motion of the Ark by raising his own coattails. This would have been an unnecessary as well as undignified proceeding. The tall house on deck afforded sufficient resistance to the wind to drive the Ark along at a very respectable rate of speed.

NOAH AS A NAVIGATOR

After the first novelty of the situation had worn off, and there was no longer the satisfaction of kindly but firmly refusing applications for passage, and seeing the lately derisive people scrambling for high land, only to be eventually caught by and swallowed up in the roaring waters, the voyage was a vexatious and disagreeable one. The Ark at the best was an unwieldy craft. She fell off from the wind frightfully, and almost invariably missed stays. Every choppy sea hammered roughly upon her flat bottom, making all on board so seasick as to wish that they too had been wicked, and sunk with the crowd.

Inside the miserable shanty which served for a cabin, birds, beasts, and human beings were huddled promiscuously together.

One of the deluge tablets says, not without a touch of pathos: "It was extremely uncomfortable [*amakharsyar*] to sleep with a Bengal tiger glaring at one from a corner, and a hedgehog nestled up close against one's bare legs. But it was positively dangerous when the elephant became restless, or the polar bear took offense at some fancied slight."

I will not anticipate Mr. Smith's detailed account of the cruise of the Ark. He has gathered data for a complete chart of Noah's course during the many months of the voyage. The tortuous nature of the route pursued and the eccentricity of Noah's great circle sailing are proof that the venerable navigator, under the depressing influence of his surroundings, had frequent recourse to ardent spirits, an infirmity over which we, his descendants, should drop the veil of charity and of silence.

EXTRACT FROM NOAH'S LOG

The most astounding discovery of all, however, is a batch of tablets giving an actual and literal transcript from Noah's logbook. The journal of the voyage—which Noah, as a prudent navigator, doubtless kept with considerable care—was probably bequeathed to Shem, eldest born and executive officer of the Ark. Portions of the log, it may be, were handed down from generation to generation among the Semitic tribes; and Mr. Rounds does not hesitate to express his opinion that these tablets in the British Museum were copied directly from the original entries made in the ship's book by Noah or Shem.

He sends to his Boston correspondent early proofs of some of the lithographic facsimiles which are to illustrate Mr. Smith's forthcoming work, *An Exhaustive History of the Flood and of the Noachic Voyage*. They should bear in mind that the inscription reads from left to right, and not, like Arabic and numerous other Semitic languages, from right to left.

Expressed in the English character, this inscription would read as follows:

. . . dahyarva saka ormudzi . . . fraharram athura uvatish . . .
kia rish thyar avalna nyasadayram okanaus mana frabara . . .
gathava Hambi Humin khaysathryam nam Buhmi . . . pasara ki
hi baga Jethyths paruvnam oazarka . . . Rhsayarsha . . .

Such progress has been made in the interpretation of the Aramaic dialects that it is comparatively an easy matter for Mr. Rounds to put this into our vernacular, which he does as follows, supplying certain hiatuses to the inscription where the connection is obvious:

SCOW "AHK," LATITUDE 44° 15', LONGITUDE . . . Water falling rapidly. Ate our last pterodactyl yesterday . . . Hambl Hamin [Hannibal Hamlin!] down with scurvy. Must put him ashore . . . THURS. 7TH. Bitter ale and mastodons all gone. Mrs. Japheth's had another pair of twins. All well.

The importance of this scrap of diluvian history can hardly be overestimated. It throws light on three or four points which have been little understood hitherto. Having viewed the subject in all its bearings, and having compared the extract here quoted with numberless other passages which I have not time to give, Mr. Smith and Mr. Rounds arrive at the following

IMPORTANT CONCLUSIONS

I. When this entry was made in the logbook by Noah (or Shem) the Ark was somewhere off the coast of Maine. The latitude warrants this inference; the longitude is unfortunately wanting. Parallel proof that Noah visited the shores of North America is to be found in the old ballad, founded on a Habbinical tradition, where mention is made of Barnegat. The singular error which locates Ararat just three miles south of Barnegat is doubtless due to some confusion in Noah's logarithms—the natural result of his unfortunate personal habits.

II. "Ate our last pterodactyl yesterday . . . Bitter ale and mastodons all gone." There we have a simple solution of a problem

which has long puzzled science. The provisions stowed away in
the Ark did not prove sufficient for the unexpectedly protracted
voyage. Hard-pressed for food, Noah and his family were obliged
to fall back on the livestock. They devoured the larger and more
esculent animals in the collection. The only living specimens of
the icthyosaurus, the dodo, the silurian, the pleisosaurus, the
mastodon, were eaten up by the hungry excursionists. We can
therefore explain the extinction of certain species, which, as ge-
ology teaches us, existed in antediluvian times. Were this
revelation the only result of Mr. Smith's researches he would not
have dug in vain. Mr. Rounds justly observes that the allusion
to bitter ale affords strong presumptive evidence that this entry
in the log was made by the hand of no other than Noah himself!

III. The allusion to the interesting increase of Japheth's family
shows that woman—noble woman, who always rises to the occasion—was doing her utmost to repair the breaches made in the
earth's population by the whelming waters. The phrase *hibaga*
may possibly signify triplets; but Mr. Smith, with that conserva-
tism and repugnance to sensation which ever characterize the
true archaeologist, prefers to be on the safe side and call it twins.

HANNIBAL HAMLIN THE ORIGINAL HAM

IV. We now come to a conclusion which is as startling as it is
inevitable. It connects the Honorable Hannibal Hamlin with the
diluvian epoch, and thus with the other long-lived patriarchs
who flourished before the flood. Antiquarians have long suspected
that the similarity between the names Ham and Hamlin was
something more than a coincidence. The industry of a Smith has
discovered among the Assyrian ruins the medial link which
makes the connection perfectly apparent. Ham, the second son of
Noah, is spoken of in these records from Kouyunjik as Hambl
Hamin; and no candid mind can fail to see that the extreme an-

tiquity of the senator from Maine is thus very clearly established!

"Hambl Hamin down with the scurvy. Must put him ashore."
Buhmi literally signifies earth, dirt: and the phrase *nam Buhmi*
is often used in these inscriptions in the sense of to put in the
earth, or bury. This can hardly be the meaning here, however,
for the Ark was still afloat. *Nam Buhmi* can therefore hardly be
construed otherwise than "put ashore."

Note the significance. The Ark is beating up and down, off
the coast of Maine, waiting for a nor'west wind. Poor Ham, or
Hambl Hamin, as he should properly be called, has reason to
regret his weakness for maritime excursions and naval junketing
parties. The lack of fresh vegetables, and a steady diet of corned
mastodon, have told upon his system. Poor Hambl! When he was
collector of a Mediterranean port just before the flood, he was
accustomed to have green peas and asparagus franked him daily
from the Garden of Eden. But now the franking privilege has
been abrogated, and the Garden of Eden is full forty fathoms
under the brine. Everything is salt. His swarthy face grows pale
and haggard. His claw-hammer coat droops upon an attenuated
frame. He chews his cherrot moodily as he stands upon the hurricane deck of the Ark with his thumbs in his vest pocket, and
thinks that he can hold office on this earth but little longer. His
gums begin to soften. He shows the ravages of the scurvy. And
Noah, therefore, after considerable argument—for Hambl is reluctant to get out of any place he has once got into—*nam Buhmi's* him—puts him ashore.

We have no further record of Hambl Hamin, but it is perfectly
reasonable to assume that after being landed on the rocky coast
of Maine he subsisted upon huckleberries until sufficiently recovered from the scurvy, then sailed up the Penobscot upon a
log, founded the ancient village of Ham-den, which he named
after himself, and was immediately elected to some public position.

AN OPPOSITION ARK

In Mr. Rounds's long and profoundly interesting communication I have, I fear, an *embarras de richesses*. From the many curious legends which Mr. Smith has deciphered, I shall select only one more, and shall deal briefly with that. It is the story of an opposition ark.

At the time of the flood there lived a certain merchant named Brith, who had achieved a competence in the retail grocery business. In fact, he was an antediluvian millionaire. Brith had been converted from heathenism by the exceedingly effective preaching of Noah, but had subsequently backslidden. When it began to thunder and lighten, however, and to grow black in the northeast, Brith professed recurring symptoms of piety. He came down to the gangway plank and applied for passage for himself and family. Noah, who was checking off the animals on the back of an old tax bill, sternly refused to entertain any such idea. Brith had recently defeated him for the Common Council.

The worthy grocer's money now stood him in good stead. He did the most sensible thing possible under the circumstances. He built an ark for himself, painted in big letters along the side the words: "The Only Safe Plan of Universal Navigation!" and named it the *Toad*. The *Toad* was fashioned after the model of the Ark, and there being no copyright in those days, Noah could only hope that it might prove unseaworthy.

In the *Toad*, Brith embarked his wife Briatha, his two daughters, Phessar and Barran, his sons-in-law, Lampra and Pinnyish, and a select assortment of beasts hardly inferior to that collected by Noah himself. Lampra and Pinnyish, sly dogs, persuaded fifty of the most beautiful women they could find to come along with them.

Brith was not so good a sailor as Noah. He put to sea full forty days too soon. He lost his dead reckoning and beat around the ocean for the space of seven years and a quarter, living mostly upon the rats that infested the *Toad*. Brith had foolishly neglected to provision his craft for a long voyage.

After this protracted sailing, the passengers and crew of the *Toad* managed to make a landing one rainy evening and took ashore, with themselves, their baggage and a coon and dromedary, the sole surviving relics of their proud menagerie. Once on terra firma, the three men separated, having drawn up a tripartite covenant of perpetual amity and divided up the stock of wives. Brith took eighteen, Lampra took eighteen, and Pinnyish, who seems to have been an easygoing sort of fellow, too lazy to quarrel, had to be satisfied with the seventeen that remained.

Tablets from Nebbi Yunus throw some light on the interesting question as to the landing place of this party. *Khayarta* certainly means island, and *Dyinim* undeniably signifies long. Perhaps, therefore, Mr. Rounds is justified in his opinion that the *Toad* dropped anchor in Wallabout Bay, and that Brooklyn and the Plymouth society owe their origin to this singular expedition.

THE PROFESSOR'S EXPERIMENT

The red wine of Affenthal has this quality, that one half-bottle makes you kind but firm, two make you talkative and obstinate, and three, recklessly unreasonable.

If the waiter at the Prinz Carl in Heidelberg had possessed a soul above drink-money, he might have calculated accurately the effect of the six half-bottles of Affenthaler which he fetched to the apartment of the Reverend Dr. Bellglory at the six o'clock dinner for three. That is to say, he might have deduced this story in advance by observation of the fact that of the six half-bottles one was consumed by Miss Blanche Bellglory, two went to the Reverend Doctor, her father, while the remaining moiety fell to the share of young Strout, remotely of New York and immediately of Professor Schwank's psycho-neurological section in the university.

So when in the course of the evening the doctor fell asleep in his chair, and young Strout took opportunity to put to Miss Blanche a question which he had already asked her twice, once at Saratoga Springs and once in New York city, she returned the answer he had heard on two former occasions, but in terms even more firm, while not less kind than before. She declared her unalterable determination to abide by her parent's wishes.

This was not exactly pleasing to young Strout. He knew better than anybody else that, while approving him socially and humanly, the doctor abhorred his opinions. "No man," the doctor had repeatedly said, "who denies the objective verity of knowledge derived from intuition or otherwise by subjective methods—no man who pushes noumena aside in his impetuous pursuit of phenomena can make a safe husband for my child."

He said the same thing again in a great many words and with much emphasis, after he awoke from his nap, Miss Blanche having discreetly withdrawn.

"But, my dear Doctor," urged Strout, "this is an affair of the heart, not of metaphysics; and you leave for Nuremberg tomorrow, and now is my last chance."

"You are an excellent young man in several respects," rejoined the doctor. "Abjure your gross materialism and Blanche is yours with all my heart. Your antecedents are unexceptionable, but you are intellectually impregnated with the most dangerous heresy of this or any other age. If I should countenance it by giving you my daughter, I could never look the Princeton faculty in the face."

"It appears to me that this doesn't concern the Princeton faculty in the least," persisted Strout. "It concerns Blanche and me."

Here, then, were three people, two of them young and in love with each other, divided by a question of metaphysics, the most abstract and useless question that ever wasted human effort. But that same question divided the schools of Europe for centuries and contributed largely to the list of martyrs for opinion's sake. The famous old controversy was now taken up by the six half-bottles of Affenthaler, three of them stoutly holding ground against the other three.

"No argument in the world," said the doctor's two half-bottles, "can shake my decision"; and off he went to sleep again.

"No amount of coaxing," said Miss Blanche's half-bottle, two hours later in the evening, "can make me act contrary to Papa's wishes. But," continued the half-bottle in a whisper, "I am sorry he is so stubborn."

"I don't believe it," retorted Strout's three half-bottles. "You have no more heart than one of your father's non-individualized ideas. You are not real flesh and blood like other women. You are simply Extension, made up of an aggregate of concepts, and assuming to be Entity, and imposing your unreal existence upon a poor Devil like me. You are unreal, I say. A flaw in logic, an error of the senses, a fallacy in reasoning, a misplaced premise, and what becomes of you? Puff! Away you go into all. If it were otherwise, you would care for me. What a fool I am to love you! I might as well love a memory, a thought, a dream, a mathematical formula, a rule of syntax, or anything else that lacks objective existence."

She said nothing, but the tears came into her eyes.

"Good-by, Blanche," he continued at the door, pulling his hat over his eyes and not observing the look of pain and bewilderment that clouded her fair face—"Heaven bless you when your father finally marries you to a syllogism!"

II

Strout went whistling from the Prinz Carl Hotel toward his rooms in the Plöckstrasse. He reviewed his parting with Blanche. "So much the better, perhaps," he said to himself. "One dream less in life, and more room for realities." By the clock in the market place he saw that it was half-past nine, for the full moon hanging high above the Königstuhle flooded the town and valley with light. Up on the side of the hill the gigantic ruin of the old castle stood boldly out from among the trees.

He stopped whistling and gritted his teeth.

"Pshaw!" he said aloud, "one can't take off his convictions like a pair of uncomfortable boots. After all, love is nothing more nor less than the disintegration and recombination of certain molecules of the brain or marrow, the exact laws governing which have not yet been ascertained." So saying, he ran plump into a portly individual coming down the street.

"Hallo! Herr Strout," said the jolly voice of Professor Schwank. "Whither are you going so fast, and what kind of physiology talk you to the moon?"

"I am walking off three half-bottles of your cursed Affenthaler, which have gone to my feet, Herr Professor," replied Strout, "and I am making love to the moon. It's an old affair between us."

"And your lovely American friend?" demanded the fat professor, with a chuckle.

"Departs by the morning train," replied Strout gravely.

"*Himmelshitzen!*" exclaimed the professor. "And grief has blinded you so that you plunge into the abdomens of your elders? But come with me to my room, and smoke yourself into a philosophic frame of mind."

Professor Schwank's apartments faced the university buildings in the Ludwig-platz. Established in a comfortable armchair, with a pipe of excellent tobacco in his mouth, Strout felt more at peace with his environment. He was now in an atmosphere of healthful, practical, scientific activity that calmed his soul. Professor Schwank had gone further than the most eminent of his contemporaries in demonstrating the purely physiological basis of mind and thought. He had gotten nearer than any other man in Europe to the secrets of the nerve aura, the penetralia of the brain, the memory scars of the ganglia. His position in philosophy was the antipodes of that occupied by the Reverend Dr. Bellglory, for example. The study reflected the occupations of the man. In one corner stood an enormous Ruhmkorff coil. Books were scattered everywhere—on shelves, on tables, on chairs, on the floor. A plaster bust of Aristotle looked across the room into the face of a plaster bust of Leibnitz. Prints of Gall, of Pappenheim, of Leeuwenhoek, hung upon the walls. Varnished dissections and wet preparations abounded. In a glass vessel on the table at Strout's elbow, the brain of a positivist philosopher floated in yellow alcohol: near it, also suspended in spirits, swung the medulla oblongata of a celebrated thief.

The appearance of the professor himself, as he sat in his armchair opposite Strout, serenely drawing clouds of smoke from the amber mouthpiece of his long porcelain pipe, was of the sort which, by promising sympathy beforehand, seduces reserve into confidential utterances. Not only his rosy face, with its fringe of yellow beard, but his whole mountainous body seemed to beam on Strout with friendly good will. He looked like the refuge of a broken heart. Drawn out in spite of himself by the professor's kindly, attentive smile and discreet questions, Strout found satisfaction in unbosoming his troubles. The professor, smoking in silence, listened patiently to the long story. If Strout had been less preoccupied with his own woes he might, perhaps, have discovered that behind the friendly interest that glimmered on the glasses of the professor's gold-bowed spectacles, a pair of small, steel-gray eyes were observing him with the keen, unrelenting coldness of scientific scrutiny.

"You have seen, Herr Professor," said Strout in conclusion, "that the case is hopeless."

"My dear fellow," replied the professor, "I see nothing of the kind."

"But it is a matter of conviction," explained Strout. "One cannot renounce the truth even to gain a wife. She herself would despise me if I did."

"In this world everything is true and nothing is true," replied the professor sententiously. "You must change your convictions."

"That is impossible!"

The professor blew a great cloud of smoke and regarded the young man with an expression of pity and surprise. It seemed to Strout that Aristotle and Leibnitz, Leeuwenhoek, Pappenheim, and Gall were all looking down upon him with pity and surprise.

"Impossible did you say?" remarked Professor Schwank. "On the contrary, my dear boy, nothing is easier than to change one's convictions. In the present advanced condition of surgery, it is a matter of little difficulty."

Strout looked at his respected instructor in blank amazement.

"What you call your convictions," continued the savant, "are matters of mental constitution, depending on adventitious circumstances. You are a positivist, an idealist, a skeptic, a mystic, a what-not, why? Because nature, predisposition, the assimilation of bony elements, have made your skull thicker in one place, thinner in another. The cranial wall presses too close upon the brain in one spot; you sneer at the opinions of your friend, Dr. Bellglory. It cramps the development of the tissues in another spot; you deny faith a place in philosophy. I assure you, Herr Strout, we have discovered and classified already the greater part of the physical causes determining and limiting belief, and are fast reducing the system to the certainty of science."

"Granting all that," interposed Strout, whose head was swimming under the combined influence of Affenthaler, tobacco smoke, and startling new ideas, "I fail to see how it helps my case. Unfortunately, the bone of my skull is no longer cartilage, like an infant's. You cannot mold my intellect by means of compresses and bandages."

"Ah! there you touch my professional pride," cried Schwank. "If you would only put yourself into my hands!"

"And what then?"

"Then," replied the professor with enthusiasm, "I should remodel your intellect to suit the emergency. How, you ask? If a blow on the head had driven a splinter of bone down upon the gray matter overlaying the cerebrum, depriving you of memory, the power of language, or some other special faculty, as the case might be, how should I proceed? I should raise a section of the bone and remove the pressure. Just so when the physical conformation of the cranium limits your capacity to understand and credit the philosophy which your American theologian insists upon in his son-in-law. I remove the pressure. I give you a charming wife, while science gains a beautiful and valuable fact. That is what I offer you, Herr Strout!"

"In other words—" began Strout.

"In other words, I should trephine you," shouted the professor, jumping from his chair and no longer attempting to conceal his eagerness.

"Well, Herr Professor," said Strout slowly, after a long pause, during which he had endeavored to make out why the pictured face of Gall seemed to wear a look of triumph "—Well, Herr Professor, I consent to the operation. Trephine me at once—to-night."

The professor feebly demurred to the precipitateness of this course. "The necessary preparations," he urged. "Need not occupy five minutes," replied Strout. "Tomorrow I shall have changed my mind."

This suggestion was enough to impel the professor to immediate action. "You will allow me," asked he, "to send for my esteemed colleague in the university, the Herr Dr. Anton Diggelmann?" Strout assented. "Do anything that you think needful to the success of the experiment."

Professor Schwank rang. "Fritz," said he to the stupid-faced Black Forester who answered the bell, "run across the square and ask Dr. Diggelmann to come to me immediately. Request him to bring his surgical case and sulphuric ether. If you find the doctor, you need not return."

Acting on a sudden impulse, Strout seized a sheet of paper that lay on the professor's table and hastily wrote a few words. "Here!" he said, tossing the servant a gold piece of ten marks. "Deliver this note at the Prince Carl in the morning—mind you, in the morning."

The note which he had written was this:

Blanche: When you receive this I shall have solved the problem in one way or another. I am about to be trephined under the superintendence of my friend Professor Schwank. If the intellectual obstacle to our union is removed by the operation, I shall follow you to Bavaria and Switzerland. If the operation results otherwise, think sometimes kindly of your unfortunate

G.S.

Ludwig-platz; 10:30 P.M.

Fritz faithfully delivered the message to Dr. Diggelmann, and then hied toward the nearest wine shop. His gold piece dazed him. "A nice, liberal gentleman that!" he thought. "Ten marks for carrying the letter to the Prinz Carl in the morning—ten marks, a thousand pfennige; beer at five pfennige the glass, two hundred glasses!" The immensity of the prospect filled him with joy. How might he manifest his gratitude? He reflected, and an idea struck him. "I will not wait till morning," he thought. "I will deliver the gentleman's letter tonight, at once. He will say, 'Fritz, you are a prompt fellow. You do even better than you are told.'"

III

Strout was stretched upon a reclining chair, his coat and waistcoat off. Professor Schwank stood over him. In his hand was a hollow cone, rolled from a newspaper. He held the cone by the apex: the broad aperture at the base was closely pressed against Strout's face, covering all but his eyes and forehead.

"By long, steady, regular inspiration," said the professor, in a soothing, monotonous voice. "That is right; that is right; that—is—right—there—there—there!"

With every inhalation Strout drew in the pleasant, tingling coldness of the ether fumes. At first his breathing was forced: at the end of each inspiration he experienced for an instant a sensation as if mighty waters were rushing through his brain. Gradually the period of the rushing sensation extended itself, until it began with the beginning of each breath. Then the ether seemed to seize possession of his breathing, and to control the expansions and contractions of his chest independently of his own will. The ether breathed for him. He surrendered himself to its influence with a feeling of delight. The rushings became rhythmic, and the intervals shorter and shorter. His individuality seemed to be wrapped up in the rushings, and to be borne to and fro in their tremendous flux and reflux. "I shall be gone in one second more," he thought, and his consciousness sank in the whirling flood.

Professor Schwank nodded to Dr. Diggelmann. The doctor nodded back to the professor.

Dr. Diggelmann was a dry little old man, who weighed hardly more than a hundred pounds. He wore a black wig, too large for his head. His eyes were deep set under corrugated brows, while strongly marked lines running from the corners of his nostrils to the corners of his mouth gave his face a lean, sardonic expression, in striking contrast with the jolly rotundity of Professor Schwank's visage. Dr. Diggelmann was taciturn but observant. At the professor's nod, he opened his case of surgical instruments and selected a scalpel with a keen curved blade, and also a glittering piece of steel which looked like an exaggerated auger bit with a gimlet handle. Having satisfied himself that these instruments were in good condition, he deliberately rolled up the sleeves of his coat and approached the unconscious Strout.

"About on the median line, just behind the junction of the coronal and sagittal sutures," whispered Professor Schwank eagerly.

"Yes. I know—I know," replied Diggelmann.

He was on the point of cutting away with his scalpel some of the brown hair that encumbered operations on the top of Strout's head, when the door was quickly opened from the outside and a young lady, attended by a maid, entered without ceremony.

"I am Blanche Bellglory," the young lady announced to the astonished savants, as soon as she had recovered her breath. "I have come to—"

At this moment she perceived the motionless form of Strout upon the reclining chair, while the gleaming steel in Dr. Diggelmann's hand caught her alert eyes. She uttered a little shriek and ran toward the group.

"Oh, this is terrible!" she cried. "I am too late, and you have already killed him."

"Calm yourself, I beg you," said the polite professor. "No circumstance is terrible to which we are indebted for a visit from so charming a young lady."

"So great an honor!" added Dr. Diggelmann, grinning diabolically and rubbing his hands.

"And Herr Strout," continued the professor, "is unfortunately not yet trephined. As you entered, we were about beginning the operation."

Miss Bellglory gave a sob of relief and sank into a chair.

In a few well-chosen words the professor explained the theory of his experiment, dwelling especially upon the effect it was expected to have on the fortunes of the young people. When he finished, the American girl's eyes were full of tears, but the firm lines of her mouth showed that she had already resolved upon her own course.

"How noble in him," she exclaimed, "to submit to be trephined for my sake! But that must not be. I can't consent to have his poor, dear head mutilated. I should never forgive myself. The trouble all originates from my decision not to marry him without Papa's approval. With my present views of duty, I cannot alter that decision. But don't you think," she continued, dropping her voice to a whisper, "that if you should trephine me, I might see my duty in a different light?"

"It is extremely probable, my dear young lady," replied the professor, throwing a significant glance at Dr. Diggelmann, who responded with the faintest wink imaginable.

"Then," said Miss Blanche, arising and beginning to remove her bonnet, "please proceed to trephine me immediately. I insist on it."

"What's all this?" demanded the deep voice of the Reverend Dr. Bellglory, who had entered the room unnoticed, piloted by Fritz. "I came as rapidly as I could, Blanche, but not early enough, it appears, to learn the first principles of your singular actions."

"My papa, gentlemen," said Miss Bellglory.

The two Germans bowed courteously. Dr. Bellglory affably returned their salutation.

"These gentlemen, Papa," Miss Blanche explained, "have kindly undertaken to reconcile the difference of opinion between poor George and ourselves by means of a surgical operation. I don't at all understand it, but George does, for you see that he has thought best to submit to the operation, which they were about to begin when I arrived. Now, I cannot allow him to suffer for my obstinacy; and, therefore, dear Papa, I have requested the gentlemen to trephine me instead of him."

Professor Schwank repeated for Dr. Bellglory's information the explanation which he had already made to the young lady. On learning of Strout's course in the matter, Dr. Bellglory was greatly affected.

"No, Blanche!" he said, "our young friend must not be trephined. Although I cannot conscientiously accept him as a son-in-law while our views on the verity of subjective knowledge differ so widely, I can at least emulate his generous willingness to open his intellect to conviction. It is I who will be trephined, provided these gentlemen will courteously substitute me for the patient now in their hands."

"We shall be most happy," said Professor Schwank and Dr. Diggelman in the same breath.

"Thanks! Thanks!" cried Dr. Bellglory, with genuine emotion.

"But I shall not permit you to sacrifice your lifelong convictions to my happiness, Papa," interposed Blanche. The doctor insisted that he was only doing his duty as a parent. The amiable dispute went on for some time, the Germans listening with indifference. Sure of a subject for their experiment at any rate, they cared little which one of the three Americans finally came under the knife. Meanwhile Strout opened his eyes, slowly raised himself upon one elbow, vacantly gazed about the room for a few seconds, and then sank back, relapsing temporarily into unconsciousness.

Professor Schwank, who perceived that father and daughter were equally fixed in their determination, and each unlikely to yield to the other, was on the point of suggesting that the question be settled by trephining both of them, when Strout again regained his senses. He sat bolt upright, staring fixedly at the glass jar which contained the positivist's brain. Then he pressed both hands to his head, muttering a few incoherent words. Gradually, as he recovered from the clutch of the ether one after another of his faculties, his eyes brightened and he appeared to recognize the faces around him. After some time he opened his lips and spoke.

"Marvelous!" he exclaimed.

Miss Bellglory ran to him and took his hand. The doctor hurried forward, intending to announce his own resolution to be trephined. Strout pressed Blanche's hand to his lips for an instant, gave the doctor's hand a cordial grasp, and then seized the hand of Professor Schwank, which he wrung with all the warmth of respectful gratitude.

"My dear Herr Professor," he said, "how can I ever repay you? The experiment is a perfect success."

"But—" began the astounded professor.

"Don't try to depreciate your own share in my good fortune," interrupted Strout. "The theory was yours, and all the triumph of the practical success belongs to you and Dr. Diggelmann's skill."

Strout, still holding Blanche's hand, now turned to her father.

"There is now no obstacle to our union, Doctor," he said. "Thanks to Professor Schwank's operation, I see the blind folly of my late attitude toward the subjective. I recant. I am no longer a positivist. My intellect has leaped the narrow limits that hedged it in. I know now that there is more in our philosophy than can be measured with a metric ruler or weighed in a coulomb balance. Ever since I passed under the influence of the ether, I have been floating in the infinite. I have been freed from conditions of time and space. I have lost my own individuality in the immensity of the All. A dozen times I have been absorbed in Brahma; a dozen times I have emanated from Brahma, a new being, forgetful of my old self. I have stood face to face with the mystic and awful Om; my world-soul, descending to the finite, has floated calmly over an ocean of Affenthaler. My consciousness leaped back as far as the thirtieth century before Christ and

forward as far as the fortieth century yet to come. There is no
time; there is no space; there is no individual existence; there is
nothing save the All, and the faith that guides reason through the
changeless night. For more than one million years my identity
was that of the positivist in the glass jar yonder. Pardon me,
Professor Schwank, but for the same period of time yours was
that of the celebrated thief in the other jar. Great heavens!
How mistaken I have been up to the night when you, Herr Professor, took charge of my intellectual destiny."

He paused for want of breath, but the glow of the mystic's
rapture still lighted up his handsome features. There was an awkward silence in the room for considerable time. Then it was
broken by the dry, harsh voice of Dr. Diggelmann.

"You labor under a somewhat ridiculous delusion, young
gentleman. You haven't been trephined yet."

Strout looked in amazement from one to another of his friends;
but their faces confirmed the surgeon's statement.

"What was it then?" he gasped.

"Sulphuric ether," replied the surgeon, laconically.

"But after all," interposed Dr. Bellglory, "it makes little difference what agent has opened our friend's mind to a perception
of the truth. It is a matter for congratulation that the surgical
operation becomes no longer necessary."

The two Germans exchanged glances of dismay. "We shall lose
the opportunity for our experiment," the professor whispered to
Diggelmann. Then he continued aloud, addressing Strout: "I
should advise you to submit to the operation, nevertheless. There
can be no permanent intellectual cure without it. These effects
of the ether will pass away."

"Thank you," returned Strout, who at last read correctly the
cold, calculating expression that lurked behind the scientist's
spectacles. "Thank you, I am very well as I am."

"But you might, for the sake of science, consent—" persisted
Schwank.

"Yes, for the sake of science," echoed Diggelmann.

"Hang science!" replied Strout, fiercely. "Don't you know that I no longer believe in science?"

Blanche also began to understand the true motives which had led the German professor to interfere in her love affair. She cast an approving glance at Strout and arose to depart. The three Americans moved toward the door. Professor Schwank and Dr. Diggelmann fairly gnashed their teeth with rage. Miss Bellglory turned and made them a low curtsey.

"If you must trephine somebody for the sake of science, gentlemen," she remarked with her sweetest smile, "you might draw lots to see which of you shall trephine the other."

THE SOUL SPECTROSCOPE
The Singular Materialism of a
Progressive Thinker

PROFESSOR TYNDALL'S VIEWS MORE THAN JUSTIFIED
BY THE EXPERIMENTS OF THE CELEBRATED
PROFESSOR DUMMKOPF OF BOSTON, MASS.

BOSTON, December 13—Professor Dummkopf, a German gentleman of education and ingenuity, at present residing in this city, is engaged on experiments which, if successful, will work a great change both in metaphysical science and in the practical relationships of life.

The professor is firm in the conviction that modern science has narrowed down to almost nothing the border territory between the material and the immaterial. It may be some time, he admits, before any man shall be able to point his finger and say with authority, "Here mind begins; here matter ends." It may be found that the boundary line between mind and matter is as purely imaginary as the equator that divides the northern from the southern hemisphere. It may be found that mind is essentially objective as is matter, or that matter is as entirely subjective as is mind. It may be that there is no matter except as conditioned in mind. It may be that there is no mind except as conditioned in matter. Professor Dummkopf's views upon this broad topic are interesting, although somewhat bewildering. I can cordially recommend the great work in nine volumes, *Koerperliehegelswissenschaft,* to any reader who may be inclined to follow up the subject. The work can undoubtedly be obtained in the original Leipzig edition through any responsible importer of foreign books.

Great as is the problem suggested above, Professor Dummkopf has no doubt whatever that it will be solved, and at no distant day. He himself has taken a masterly stride toward a solution by the brilliant series of experiments I am about to describe. He not only believes with Tyndall that matter contains the promise and potency of all life, but he believes that every force, physical, intellectual, and moral, may be resolved into matter, formulated in terms of matter, and analyzed into its constituent forms of matter; that motion is matter, mind is matter, law is matter, and even that abstract relations of mathematical abstractions are purely material.

PHOTOGRAPHING SMELL

In accordance with an invitation extended to me at the last meeting of the Radical Club—an organization, by the way, which is doing a noble work in extending our knowledge of the Unknowable—I dallied yesterday at Professor Dummkopf's rooms in Joy Street, at the West End. I found the professor in his apartment on the upper floor, busily engaged in an attempt to photograph smell.

"You see," he said, as he stirred up a beaker from which strongly marked fumes of sulphuretied hydrogen were arising and filling the room, "you see that, having demonstrated the objectiveness of sensation, it has now become my privilege and easy task to show that the phenomena of sensation are equally material. Hence I am attempting to photograph smell."

The professor then darted behind a camera which was leveled upon the vessel in which the suffocating fumes were generated and busied himself awhile with the plate.

A disappointed look stole over his face as he brought the negative to the light and examined it anxiously. "Not yet, not yet!" he said sadly, "but patience and improved appliances will finally bring it. The trouble is in my tools, you see, and not in my theory. I did fancy the other day that I obtained a distinctly marked negative from the odor of a hot onion stew, and the thought has cheered me ever since. But it's bound to come. I tell you, my worthy friend, the actinic ray wasn't made for nothing. Could you accommodate me with a dollar and a quarter to buy some more collodion?"

THE BOTTLE THEORY OF SOUND

I expressed my cheerful readiness to be banker to genius.

"Thanks," said the professor, pocketing the scrip and resuming his position at the camera. "When I have pictorially captured smell, the most palpable of the senses, the next thing will be to imprison sound—vulgarly speaking, to bottle it. Just think a moment. Force is as imperishable as matter; indeed, as I have been somewhat successful in showing, it is matter. Now, when a sound wave is once started, it is only lost through an indefinite extension of its circumference. Catch that sound wave, sir! Catch it in a bottle, then its circumference cannot extend. You may keep the sound wave forever if you will only keep it corked up tight. The only difficulty is in bottling it in the first place. I shall attend to the details of that operation just as soon as I have managed to photograph the confounded rotten-egg smell of sulphydric acid."

The professor stirred up the offensive mixture with a glass rod, and continued:

"While my object in bottling sound is mainly scientific, I must confess that I see in success in that direction a prospect of considerable pecuniary profit. I shall be prepared at no distant day to put operas in quart bottles, labeled and assorted, and contemplate a series of light and popular airs in ounce vials at prices to suit the times. You know very well that it costs a ten-dollar bill now to take a lady to hear *Martha* or *Mignon*, rendered in first-class style. By the bottle system, the same notes may be heard in one's own parlor at a comparatively trifling expense. I could put the operas into the market at from eighty cents to a dollar a bottle. For oratorios and symphonies I should use demijohns, and the cost would of course be greater. I don't think that ordinary bottles would hold Wagner's music. It might be necessary to employ carboys. Sir, if I were of the sanguine habit of you Americans, I should say that there were millions in it. Being a phlegmatic Teuton, accustomed to the precision and moderation of scientific language, I will merely say that in the success of my experiments with sound I see a comfortable income, as well as great renown.

A SCIENTIFIC MARVEL

By this time the professor had another negative, but an eager examination of it yielded nothing more satisfactory than before. He sighed and continued:

"Having photographed smell and bottled sound, I shall proceed to a project as much higher than this as the reflective faculties are higher than the perceptive, as the brain is more exalted than the ear or nose.

"I am perfectly satisfied that elements of mind are just as susceptible of detection and analysis as elements of matter. Why, mind is matter.

"The soul spectroscope, or, as it will better be known, Dummkopf's duplex self-registering soul spectroscope, is based on the broad fact that whatever is material may be analyzed and determined by the position of the Frauenhofer lines upon the spectrum. If soul is matter, soul may thus be analyzed and determined. Place a subject under the light, and the minute exhalations or emanations proceeding from his soul—and these exhalations or emanations are, of course, matter—will be represented by their appropriate symbols upon the face of a properly arranged spectroscope.

"This, in short, is my discovery. How I shall arrange the spectroscope, and how I shall locate the subject with reference to the light is of course my secret. I have applied for a patent. I shall exploit the instrument and its practical workings at the Centennial. Till then I must decline to enter into any more explicit description of the invention."

THE IMPORTANCE OF THE DISCOVERY

"What will be the bearing of your great discovery in its practical workings?"

"I can go so far as to give you some idea of what those practical workings are. The effect of the soul spectroscope upon everyday affairs will be prodigious, simply prodigious. All lying, deceit, double dealing, hypocrisy, will be abrogated under its operation. It will bring about a millennium of truth and sincerity.

"A few practical illustrations. No more bell punches on the horse railroad. The superintendent, with a smattering of scientific knowledge and one of my soul spectroscopes in his office, will examine with the eye of infallible science every applicant for the position of conductor and will determine by the markings on his spectrum whether there is dishonesty in his soul, and this as readily as the chemist decides whether there is iron in a meteorolite or hydrogen in Saturn's ring.

"No more courts, judges, or juries. Hereafter justice will be represented with both eyes wide open and with one of my duplex self-registering soul spectroscopes in her right hand. The inmost nature of the accused will be read at a glance and he will be acquitted, imprisoned for thirty days, or hung, just as the Frauenhofer lines which lay bare his soul may determine.

"No more official corruption or politicians' lies. The important element in every campaign will be one of my soul spectroscopes, and it will effect the most radical, and, at the same time, the most practicable of civil service reforms.

"No more young stool pigeons in tall towers. No man will subscribe for a daily newspaper until a personal inspection of its editor's soul by means of one of my spectroscopes has convinced him that he is paying for truth, honest conviction, and uncompromising independence, rather than for the false utterances of a hired conscience and a bought judgment.

"No more unhappy marriages. The maiden will bring her glibly promising lover to me before she accepts or rejects his proposal, and I shall tell her whether his spectrum exhibits the markings of pure love, constancy, and tenderness, or of sordid avarice, vacillating affections, and post-nuptial cruelty. I shall be the angel with shining sword [or rather spectroscope] who shall attend Hymen and guard the entrance to his paradise.

"No more shame. If anything be wanting in the character of a man, no amount of brazen pretension on his part can place the missing line in his spectrum. If anything is lacking in him, it will be lacking there. I found by a long series of experiments upon the imperfectly constituted minds of the patients in the lunatic asylum at Taunton—"

"Then you have been at Taunton?"

"Yes. For two years I pursued my studies among the unfortunate inmates of that institution. Not exactly as a patient myself, you understand, but as a student of the phenomena of morbid intellectual developments. But I see I am wearying you, and I must resume my photography before this stuff stops smelling. Come again."

Having bid the professor farewell and wished him abundant success in his very interesting experiments, I went home and read again for the thirty-ninth time Professor Tyndall's address at Belfast.

THE INSIDE OF THE EARTH
A Big Hole Through the Planet
from Pole to Pole

HOW CLALTUS TREATS THE THEORY OF THE OPEN
POLAR SEA—WHAT HE SAYS ABOUT THE GULF
STREAM—LIFE OF A BROOKLYN DISCOVERER

He was an elderly man with a beard of grizzled gray unkempt hair, light eyes that shot quick, furtive glances, pale lips that trembled often with weak, uneasy smiles, and hands that restlessly rubbed each other, or else groped unconsciously for some missing tool. His clothes were coarse and in rags, and as he sat on a low upturned box, close before a half-warm stove, he shivered sometimes when a fierce gust of freezing wind rattled the patched and dingy windows. Behind him was a carpenter's bench, with a rack of neatly kept woodworking tools above it; a lathe and a small stock of very handsomely finished library stepladders. A great pile of black walnut chips and lathe dust lay on the floor, and the air was full of the clean, fresh smell of the wood. The room in which he sat was a garret, at the top of two eroded flights of steep and rickety stairs, in a building within three blocks of the southernmost extremity of that Lilliputian railway on which Saratoga trunks, fitted up as horse cars, are run from Fulton ferry to Hamilton ferry.

"Don't mention my name at all, sir," said he to the SUN reporter, who perched upon an unsteady box before him, "nor don't give them the exact place, please, for there are lots about who know me, and who'd be bothering me, and maybe laughing at me. Call me John Claltus. That's the name I was known by down in Charleston and all down South, and it did very well while I was working there, so you can put it in that."

"But why, having a grand scientific idea, and being the originator of novel and bold theories, do you shrink so modestly from public recognition and admiration?"

"I don't want any glory. I've thought out what I have because I felt I had a mission to do it, and maybe mightn't be let live if I didn't; but I'm done now. I can't last much longer. I'm old and poor, and I don't care to have folks bothering me and maybe laughing at me; and you see my brother, my cousins, and sometimes some sailor friends come to see me, and I'd rather you'd let it go as Claltus, sir."

"And as Claltus it shall go. But about your discovery. Was it not Symmes's theory of a hole through the globe that first gave you the idea?"

REMARKABLE VISIONS

"Oh, not at all! I was shown it all in a vision years before I ever heard of him. It was more than thirty-eight years ago. I was only a twelve-year-old boy. I was greatly afraid when I saw it; it was so terrible to me. I really think, from what I saw, that the earth was all in a sort of mist or fog once. I felt that I must go to sea and try to find out what I could about it as a poor man; so as a sailor I went for years, always thinking about it and inquiring when I could of them that might have had a chance to know something. About two years ago I went South and tried to establish myself there, and then I saw the vision again, not so terrible as before, and I could understand it better. It came to me like a globe, about two feet through, and a hole through it one third of its diameter in bigness. I told it to people there and they said I was crazy. I told it to two men I was working for—brothers they were and Frenchmen. I built an extension table and raised the roof of their house for them, and they said, 'How can it be that you do our work so well and yet are not in your right mind?' So I quit saying anything about it. This is a model of like what I saw in the vision."

The model of the vision as produced is a ball of black walnut wood, four and a half inches in diameter, traversed by a round aperture whose diameter seemed to be about one third the diameter of the ball or globe. Around the exterior, lines have been traced by a lathe tool, the spaces between them representing ten degrees each. A chalk mark on one side represents New York. This ball is mounted between the points of an inverted U of strong wire, so based upon a little board as to admit of being tipped to change the angle at which the ball is poised. The points of the wire are fastened near the edges of the ends of the hole at opposite sides of the little globe, so as to admit of its turning, and thus alternately raising and depressing, with reference to the false poles, the ends of the hole. As the thing stood on a little stand, where he placed it very carefully, the sunlight poured through the hole, and as he turned it the area covered in the interior of the ball by the sun's direct rays was gradually narrowed, shortened, and finally so diminished as to extend inward only a very little way; then, as he continued turning it, the patch of light once more widened and lengthened until the sun again shone all the way through.

THE LESSON OF THE MODEL

"There," said he, "that represents a day and a night for the people in the inside of the earth. I'm perfectly satisfied in my own mind that the turn is made on about ten degrees, and about ten degrees from the outside rim of it; them that goes there would get to the flat part on the inside. When they get to the ninetieth degree that's the pole they've always been trying to make. They'll be turning into the inside. Eighty degrees is the furthest they've ever got yet, at least that's the furthest for anyone that has come back to tell about it. Perry's Point is the furthest land northward on this continent that has ever been reached, and Spitsbergen is about as far on the other side. The furtherst they have gone south is Victoria Island, opposite Cape Horn, maybe a thousand miles away from the Cape, and that's only about eighty degrees. I've got a bit of stone here that came from Victoria Island that a sailor man gave me, thinkin', maybe, I might find out something about it from somebody that knew."

The discoverer arose and walked slowly to the further end of his garret, where he took from a shelf a little piece of stone, about three inches in length, two in width, and three quarters in thickness, soft as rotten stone almost, light brown and looking like a bit of petrified wood.

"I don't know what it is. There isn't much curious about it. I've seen bits of stone from the Central Park that looked much like it, but not just the same. I tried to make a whetstone of it, but it was too soft; it wouldn't take any polish."

"In your long sea service did you ever get far enough toward the poles to find anything corroborative of your theories?"

"Not myself, though I've noticed things that confirmed me. Now, there's the Gulf Stream, for instance. They say there's a current from the Gulf of Mexico that goes across to Europe; but I've seen enough myself, in the Indian Ocean, that I've crossed many a time and often, and round to Cape Horn, that I'm convinced it's the polar stream and the action of the sun on the narrow part of the rim there causes it. I studied it in the Gulf of Mexico. They thought the pressure of them big rivers flowing into the gulf made it. Now if that was so it would make a great pressure where it rushes through the narrow place between Florida and the West Indies that would set the stream going away to the other side of the ocean, but I couldn't see any such pressure greater there than anywhere else. Them rivers has no more effect there than a bucket of water poured into the bay down beyond. It's the great heat of the sun at the narrow rim melting the ice, and the current pouring out of that hole, that makes what they call the Gulf Stream in the part of it they've observed."

WHAT A SAILOR SAID HE SAW

"Have you ever met any sailors who knew anything more about it than you did yourself?"

"Yes," the discoverer answered quickly, ceasing to bore bits from the soft stone with his thick thumbnail and looking up with an eager smile, "I met a sailor man in Charleston—Tola or Toland his name was—and he said he had been far enough to see a great, bright arch that rose out of the water like, and I said, 'That's my arch; that's the rim of the hole to the inside of the earth.' He was there in Charleston waiting for a ship, and I was making patterns. We used to meet every night to talk about the thing, for he was a knowledgeable man, and took an interest in it, the same as I did. He saw that arch every night for two weeks while the privateer he was on was in them waters, and all that was with him saw it, but they couldn't make it out. Then they got frightened of it, beating about in strange waters, and at last they got back to parts of the ocean they knew, and so came away as fast as they could. Well," sighing as he spoke, "sailors sometimes make a heap of brag about what they've seen and possibly there's nothing in it, but there may be. I know it's there all the same, for I've seen it in the vision and it stands to reason. I asked him if he could see anything in the daytime, and he said no—nothing, only clouds and mists about him. And that stands to reason, for in the night, you see, the reflected light would shine up the arch and show it, but in daytime it would be so high and so far off that it could not be seen. I had some hopes that he might have got the color of land, but he didn't."

"What do you suppose is the character of the country in there?"

"Oh! I don't know, but it's likely there are mountains and rivers in there. I think it's most likely they have most water in there, but maybe a good deal of land, too; and maybe gold and various kinds of things that's scarce on the outside."

"And people, too?"

"I shouldn't wonder at all if there was people there, driven in there by the storms, and that couldn't find their way out again."

"And how do you suppose they support life?"

"Why shouldn't they the same as people on the outside? Haven't they got air and light and heat and the change of seasons, and water and soil, the same as there is outside? It's a big place in there. The open polar circle, I calculate, is in circumference about the diameter of the earth, and that would give one third of the earth open inside. They get light and heat from the sun, and maybe a good deal of reflected light and heat all the way through from the south end of the hole. That's where it all goes in at."

THE MEN WHO LIVE INSIDE

"And what sort of folks do you suppose are in there?"

"Ah! I don't know. There may be Irishmen there, and there may be Dutch there, and there may be Malays there, and other kinds of people, and there may be Danes there, too—they were good smart sailor people, too, in their time, always beating about the waters and they might have got drifted in there and couldn't get out."

"How do you mean 'couldn't get out'?"

"Couldn't find their way. There's no charts of them waters, and maybe the needle won't work the same there, and the place is so big they may go on sailing there and never going straight or finding their way back. Maybe they've been wrecked, and had no means of coming away. Sure there must be mighty storms in there. Great storms come out of that hole in the south. 'Great storms come out of the South,' the Scriptures say. You'll find that in the Book of Job, that and lots more about the earth. He talks about it as if he knew all about it. He knew all about that hole in the inside of the earth, and as he wasn't with the Creator when He made it, he must have seen it to know so much about it as he shows he did.

"And yet—" he murmured in a lower voice, meditatively digging off little bits from a piece of chalk with his fingernails, and touching up the spot representing New York on the wooden ball —"you'll find a good many things in the Scriptures if you search them, about the interior of the earth."

"Have you ever tried to enlist government or private enterprise to prosecute an investigation of the correctness of your theories?"

"No. What could I do? I was always only a poor, hard-working, ignorant man, but I seen it in a vision and I felt it my duty to study on it and make it known. But I think if a good steamship was laid on her course proper from New York, set in the way I know she would have to be, and provided for rightly, in about ten weeks she would get there and into the inside of the earth. Her wheels would never stop until she got there, for there's more than human thought about it. It's God's will it should be known, and her machinist couldn't stop her wheels if she was going the right way for it. But she would have to be provided with a good shower bath to keep her wet all the time, for on the rim there, on the narrow part, it will be five times as hot as at the equator. If they get up an expedition to go there, it will have to be well armed, too. If they find them Irish and Danes in there, there will be fighting, for they are hostile people. Yes, and them Malays, too. They know how to navigate ships, too, and they're warlike chaps and they'll give them some trouble. Yes, the expedition will have to be well armed."

OF LIGHT

"Do the inhabitants of the hole see the moon and the stars?"

"Partly, I conceive. They get the good of the moon about nine days in the month, and can see such parts of the heavens as are visible out of the ends of the hole. That's all; but it would never be real night there, for even when the sun would be off on one side its light would be reflected from the walls of the other side. You see the earth is moving about the sun all the time. Not that I think it goes round in the form them astronomers say it does. I think it goes round on the high and low orbit, that is, one side of the circle is raised in coming down from the sun—and always at the same distance from the sun. Any globe working about the sun must have the same force and the same balance all the time to keep face. The theory of the astronomers is that it goes out many millions of miles at certain times of the year and comes back. Now, there would be no order or regularity about that. It isn't reason. It would make a regular hurly-burly of everything if the earth was allowed to run around in that wild way. And there's another thing that goes to show the world is hollow inside. A solid globe you can't make roll of itself in the sunlight but a hollow one will. You go to work and make a globe of fine silk and fill it with gas, or make it of cork and hollow, and put it into a glass jar in the sun, and pump the air out, and raise it up to a certain temperature—about 180 degrees or maybe 200, I think—and it'll roll in the sun, but a solid one won't do it. So it stands to reason the earth is hollow, so it will roll in the sun. I've tried that experiment in my shop during the war. I made it up nice, but I haven't got it now, for my shop was robbed three years ago, and I lost that and a lot more things, and all my tools. The model I had for the Patent Office was carried away, too."

"But let us get back to our hole. Beyond what the sailor told you, you have nothing more than theory?"

"Not altogether. There are signs of life from further to the south than anybody has ever gone yet that we know of. I read in a paper last August that an English captain went far enough south to get into warm water; and there he picked up a log drifting from still further south, with nails in it and marks of an ax on it, and that log he brought back with him to England, and it's there now. Anyway, I read that in the paper—but," speaking in a tone of regretful sadness, "these newspapers start so many curious things and ideas that you can't always be certain about what they say. But other sailor men than that captain have found the water growing warmer, and had reason to know of open seas at the poles. Besides, there's another thing that goes to show that there's life inside the earth, and that is the great bones and tusks of animals, so big that no animals on the earth now can carry them or have such things, that they find away up in Siberia. Them came from the inside of the earth, I've no doubt, drifted out in the ice that was parted there when the sun cracked the floes and set them drifting out in a polar current."

SURELY HOLLOW

"You are, of course, aware that many people have a theory that the interior of the earth is in a state of fusion, and others that there are vast internal seas, whose waves act upon chemical substances in the earth, and produce spontaneous combustion and earthquakes and volcanoes?"

"Yes, and what's to hinder. The crust of the earth, between the hole inside and the outside surface, is nearly three thousand miles thick, and surely in all that there's a heap of room for many strange things. But as sure as you live and I live the earth is hollow inside, and there's a great country there where people can live, and where I've no doubt they do live, and some day it will all be found out about it."

AN UNCOMMON SORT OF SPECTRE

I

The ancient castle of Weinstein, on the upper Rhine, was, as everybody knows, inhabited in the autumn of 1352 by the powerful Baron Kalbsbraten, better known in those parts as Old Twenty Flasks, a sobriquet derived from his reputed daily capacity for the product of the vineyard. The baron had many other admirable qualities. He was a genial, whole-souled, public-spirited gentleman, and robbed, murdered, burned, pillaged, and drove up the steep sides of the Weinstein his neighbors' cattle, wives, and sisters, with a hearty bonhomie that won for him the unaffected esteem of his contemporaries.

One evening the good baron sat alone in the great hall of Weinstein, in a particularly happy mood. He had dined well, as was his habit, and twenty empty bottles stood before him in a row upon the table, like a train of delightful memories of the recent past. But the baron had another reason to be satisfied with himself and with the world. The consciousness that he had that day become a parent lit up his countenance with a tender glow that mere wine cannot impart.

"What ho! Without! Hi! Seneschal!" he presently shouted, in a tone that made the twenty empty bottles ring as if they were musical glasses, while a score of suits of his ancestors' armor hanging around the walls gave out in accompaniment a deep metallic bass. The seneschal was speedily at his side.

"Seneschal," said Old Twenty Flasks, "you gave me to understand that the baroness was doing finely?"

"I am told," replied the seneschal, "that her ladyship is doing as well as could be expected."

The baron mused in silence for a moment, absently regarding the empty bottles. "You also gave me to understand," he continued, "that there were—"

"Four," said the seneschal, gravely. "I am credibly informed that there are four, all boys."

"That," exclaimed the baron, with a glow of honest pride, bringing a brawny fist down upon the table—"That, in these days, when the abominable doctrines of Malthus are gaining ground among the upper classes, is what I call creditable—creditable, by Saint Christopher. If I do say it!" His eyes rested again upon the empty bottles. "I think, Seneschal," he added, after a brief pause, "that under the circumstances we may venture—"

"Nothing could be more eminently proper," rejoined the seneschal. "I will fetch another flask forthwith, and of the best. What says Your Excellency to the vintage of 1304, the year of the comet?"

"But," hesitated the baron, toying with his mustache, "I understood you to say that there were four of 'em—four boys?"

"True, my lord," replied the seneschal, snatching the idea with the readiness of a well-trained domestic. "I will fetch four more flasks."

As the excellent retainer deposited four fresh bottles upon the table within the radius of the baron's reach, he casually remarked, "A pious old man, a traveler, is in the castle yard, my lord, seeking shelter and a supper. He comes from beyond the Alps, and fares toward Cologne."

"I presume," said the baron, with an air of indifference, "that he has been duly searched for plunder."

"He passed this morning," replied the retainer, "through the

domain of your well-born cousin, Count Conrad of Schwinkenfels. Your lordship will readily understand that he has nothing
now save a few beggarly Swiss coins of copper."

"My worthy cousin Conrad!" exclaimed the baron, affectionately. "It is the one great misfortune of my life that I live to the
leeward of Schwinkenfels. But you relieved the pious man of his
copper?"

"My lord," said the seneschal, with an apologetic smile, "it was
not worth the taking."

"Now by my soul," roared the baron, "you exasperate me! Coin,
and not worth the taking! Perhaps not for its intrinsic value,
but you should have cleaned him out as a matter of principle, you
fool!"

The seneschal hung his head and muttered an explanation. At
the same time he opened the twenty-first bottle.

"Never," continued the baron, less violently but still severely,
"if you value my esteem and your own paltry skin, suffer yourself to be swerved a hair's breadth from principle by the apparent
insignificance of the loot. A conscientious attention to details is
one of the fundamental elements of a prosperous career—in fact,
it underlies all political economy."

The withdrawal of the cork from the twenty-second bottle
emphasized this statement.

"However," the baron went on, somewhat mollified, "this is
not a day on which I can consistently make a fuss over a trifle.
Four, and all boys! This is a glorious day for Weinstein. Open
the two remaining flasks, Seneschal, and show the pious stranger
in. I fain would amuse myself with him."

II

Viewed through the baron's twenty-odd bottles, the stranger
appeared to be an aged man—eighty years, if a day. He wore a
shabby gray cloak and carried a palmer's staff, and seemed an
innocuous old fellow, cast in too commonplace a mold to furnish

even a few minutes' diversion. The baron regretted sending for him, but being a person of unfailing politeness, when not upon the rampage, he bade his guest be seated and filled him a beaker of the comet wine.

After an obeisance, profound yet not servile, the pilgrim took the glass and critically tasted the wine. He held the beaker up athwart the light with trembling hand, and then tasted again. The trial seemed to afford him great satisfaction, and he stroked his long white beard.

"Perhaps you are a connoisseur. It pleases your palate, eh?" said the baron, winking at the full-length portrait of one of his ancestors.

"Proper well," replied the pilgrim, "though it is a trifle syrupy from too long keeping. By the bouquet and the tint, I should pronounce it of the vintage of 1304, grown on the steep slope south southeast of the castle, in the fork of the two pathways that lead to under the hill. The sun's rays reflected from the turret give a peculiar excellence to the growth of that particular spot. But your rascally varlets have shelved the bottle on the wrong side of the cellar. It should have been put on the dry side, near where your doughty grandsire Sigismund von Weinstein, the Hairy Handed, walled up his third wife in preparation for a fourth."

The baron regarded his guest with a look of amazement. "Upon my life!" said he, "but you appear to be familiar with the ins and outs of this establishment."

"If I do," rejoined the stranger, composedly sipping his wine, "'tis no more than natural, for I lived more than sixty years under this roof and know its every leak. I happen to be a Von Weinstein myself."

The baron crossed himself and pulled his chair a little further away from the bottles and the stranger.

"Oh no," said the pilgrim, laughing; "quiet your fears. I am aware that every well-regulated castle has an ancestral ghost, but my flesh and blood are honest. I was lord of Weinstein till I went, twelve years ago, to study metaphysics in the Arabic schools, and the cursed scriveners wrote me out of the estate. Why, I know this hall from infancy! Yonder is the fireplace at which I used to warm my baby toes. There is the identical suit of armor into which I crawled when a boy of six and hid till my sainted mother —heaven rest her!—nigh died of fright. It seems but yesterday. There on the wall hangs the sharp two-handed sword of our ancestor, Franz, the One-Eared, with which I cut off the mustaches of my tipsy sire as he sat muddled over his twentieth bottle. There is the very casque—but perhaps these reminiscences weary you. You must pardon the garrulity of an old man who has come to revisit the home of his childhood and prime."

The baron pressed his hand to his forehead. "I have lived in this castle myself for half a century," said he, "and am tolerably familiar with the history of my immediate progenitors. But I can't say that I ever had the pleasure of your acquaintance. However, permit me to fill your glass."

"It is good wine," said the pilgrim, holding out his glass. "Except, perhaps, the vintage of 1392, when the grapes—"

The baron stared at his guest. "The grapes of 1392," said he dryly, "lack forty years of ripening. You are aged, my friend, and your mind wanders."

"Excuse me, worthy host," calmly replied the pilgrim. "The vintage of 1392 has been forty years cellared. You have no memory for dates."

"What call you this year?" demanded the baron.

"By the almanacs, and the stars, and precedent, and common consent, it is the year of grace 1433."

"By my soul and hope of salvation," ejaculated the baron, "it is the year of grace 1352."

"There is evidently a misunderstanding somewhere," remarked the venerable stranger. "I was born here in the year 1352, the year the Turks invaded Europe."

"No Turk has invaded Europe, thanks be to heaven," replied Old Twenty Flasks, recovering his self-control. "You are either a magician or an imposter. In either case I shall order you drawn

and quartered as soon as we have finished this bottle. Pray proceed with your very interesting reminiscences, and do not spare
the wine."

"I never practice magic," quietly replied the pilgrim, "and as
to being an imposter, scan well my face. Don't you recognize
the family nose, thick, short, and generously colored? How about
the three lateral and two diagonal wrinkles on my brow? I see
them there on yours. Are not my chaps Weinstein chaps? Look
closely. I court investigation."

"You do look damnably like us," the baron admitted.

"I was the youngest," the stranger went on, "of quadruplets.
My three brothers were puny, sickly things, and did not long sur-
vive their birth. As a child I was the idol of my poor father, who
had some traits worthy of respectful mention, guzzing old toper
and unconscionable thief though he was."

The baron winced.

"They used to call him Old Twenty Flasks. It is my candid opinion, based on memory, that Old Forty Flasks would have been
nearer the truth."

"It's a lie!" shouted the baron, "I rarely exceeded twenty
bottles."

"And as for his standing in the community," the pilgrim went
on, without taking heed of the interruption, "it must be confessed
that nothing could be worse. He was the terror of honest folk for
miles around. Property rights were extremely insecure in this
neighborhood, for the rapacity of my lamented parent knew no
bounds. Yet nobody dared to complain aloud, for lives were not
much safer than sheep or ducats. How the people hated his
shadow, and roundly cursed him behind his back! I remember
well that, when I was about fourteen—it must have been in '66,
the year the Grand Turk occupied Adrianople—tall Hugo, the
miller, called me up to him, and said: 'Boy, thou has a right pretty
nose.' 'It is a pretty nose, Hugo,' said I, straightening up. 'Is it on
firm and strong?' asked Hugo, with a sneer. 'Firm enough, and
strong enough, I dare say,' I answered; 'but why ask such a fool's

question?' 'Well, well, boy,' said Hugo, turning away, 'look sharp with thine eyes after thy nose when thy father is unoccupied, for he has just that conscience to steal the nose off his son's face in lack of better plunder.'"

"By St. Christopher!" roared the baron, "tall Hugo, the miller, shall pay for this. I always suspected him. By St. Christopher's burden, I'll break every bone in his villainous body."

"'Twould be an ignoble vengeance," replied the pilgrim, quietly, "for tall Hugo has been in his grave these sixty years."

"True," said the baron, putting both hands to his head, and gazing at his guest with a look of utter helplessness. "I forget that it is now next century—that is to say, if you be not a spectre."

"You will excuse me, my respected parent," returned the pilgrim, "if I subject your hypothesis to the test of logic, for it touches me upon a very tender spot, impugning, as it does, my physical verity and my status as an actual individualized ego. Now, what is our relative position? You acknowledge the date of my birth to have been the year of grace 1352. That is a matter in which your memory is not likely to be at fault. On the other hand, with a strange inconsistency, you maintain, in the face of almanacs, chronologies, and the march of events, that it is still the year of grace 1352. Were you one of the seven sleepers, your hallucination [to use no harsher term] might be pardoned, but you are neither a sleeper nor a saint. Now, every one of the eighty years that are packed away in the carpet bag of my experience protests against your extraordinary error. It is I who have a prima facie right to question your physical existence, not you mine. Did you ever hear of a ghost, spectre, wraith, apparition, eldolon, or spook coming out of the future to haunt, annoy, or frighten individuals of an earlier generation?"

The baron was obliged to admit that he never had.

"But you have heard of instances where apparitions, ghosts, spooks, call them what you will, have invaded the present from out the limbo of the past?"

The baron crossed himself a second time and peered anxiously into the dark corners of the apartment. "If you are a genuine Von Weinstein," he whispered, "you already know that this castle is overrun with spectres of that sort. It is difficult to move about after nightfall without tumbling over half a dozen of them."

"Then," said the placid logician, "you surrender your case. You commit what, my revered preceptor in dialectics, the learned Arabian Ben Dusty, used to style syllogistic suicide. For you allow that, while ghosts out of the future are unheard of, ghosts from the past are not infrequently encountered. Now I submit to you as a man, this proposition: That it is infinitely more probable that you are a ghost than that I am one!"

The baron turned very red. "Is this filial," he demanded, "to deny the flesh and blood of your own father?"

"Is it paternal," retorted the pilgrim, not losing his composure, "to insinuate the unrealness of the son of your own begetting?"

"By all the saints!" growled the baron, growing still redder, "this question shall be settled, and speedily. Halloo, there, Seneschal!" He called again and again, but in vain.

"Spare your lungs," calmly suggested the pilgrim. "The best-trained domestic in the world will not stir from beneath the sod for all your shouting."

Twenty Flasks sank back helplessly in his chair. He tried to speak, but his tongue and throat repudiated their functions. They only gurgled.

"That is right," said his guest, approvingly. "Conduct yourself as befits a venerable and respectable ghost from the last century. A well-behaved apparition neither blusters nor is violent. You can well afford to be peaceable in your deportment now; you were turbulent enough before your death."

"My death?" gasped the baron.

"Excuse me," apologized the pilgrim, "for referring to that unpleasant event."

"My death!" stammered the baron, his hair standing on end. "I should like to hear the particulars."

"I was hardly more than fifteen at the time," said the pilgrim musingly; "but I shall never forget the most trifling circumstances of the great popular arising that put an end to my worthy sire's career. Exasperated beyond endurance by your outrageous crimes, the people for miles around at last rose in a body, and, led by my old friend tall Hugo, the miller, flocked to Schwinkenfels and appealed to your cousin, Count Conrad, for protection against yourself, their natural protector. Von Schwinkenfels heard their complaints with great gravity. He replied that he had long watched your abominable actions with distress and consternation; that he had frequently remonstrated with you, but in vain; that he regarded you as the scourge of the neighborhood; that your castle was full of blood-stained treasure and shamefully acquired booty; and that he now regarded it as the personal duty of himself, the conservator of lawful order and good morals, to march against Weinstein and exterminate you for the common good."

"The hypocritical pirate!" exclaimed Twenty Flasks.

"Which he proceeded to do," continued the pilgrim, "supported not only by his retainers but by your own. I must say that you made a sturdy defense. Had not your rascally seneschal sold you out to Schwinkenfels and let down the drawbridge one evening when you were as usual fuddling your brains with your twenty bottles, perhaps Conrad never would have gained an entrance, and my young eyes would have been spared the horrid task of watching the body of my venerated parent dangling at the end of a rope from the topmost turret of the northwest tower."

The baron buried his face in his hands and began to cry like a baby. "They hanged me, did they?" he faltered.

"I am afraid no other construction can be put on it," said the pilgrim. "It was the inevitable termination of such a career as yours had been. They hanged you, they strangled you, they choked you to death with a rope; and the unanimous verdict of the community was Justifiable Homicide. You weep! Behold,

Father, I also weep for the shame of the house of Von Weinstein!
Come to my arms."

Father and son clasped each other in a long, affectionate embrace and mingled their tears over the disgrace of Weinstein.
When the baron recovered from his emotion he found himself
alone with his conscience and twenty-four empty bottles. The
pilgrim had disappeared.

III

Meanwhile, in the apartments consecrated to the offices of
maternity, all had been confusion, turmoil, and distress. In four
huge armchairs sat four experienced matrons, each holding in
her lap a pillow of swan's-down. On each pillow had reposed an
infinitesimal fraction of humanity, recently added to the sum total
of Von Weinstein. One experienced matron had dozed over her
charge; when she awoke the pillow in her lap was unoccupied.
An immediate census taken by the alarmed attendants disclosed
the startling fact that, although there were still four armchairs,
and four sage women, and four pillows of swan's-down, there
were but three infants. The seneschal, as an expert in mathematics and accounts, was hastily summoned from below. His
reckoning merely confirmed the appalling suspicion. One of the
quadruplets was gone.

Prompt measures were taken in this fearful emergency. The
corners of the rooms were ransacked in vain. Piles of bedclothing
and baskets of linen were searched through and through. The
hunt extended to other parts of the castle. The seneschal even
sent out trusted and discreet retainers on horseback to scour the
surrounding country. They returned with downcast countenances;
no trace of the lost Von Weinstein had been found.

During one terrible hour the wails of the three neglected infants mingled with the screams of the hysterical mother, to whom
the attention of the four sage women was exclusively directed.
At the end of the hour her ladyship had sufficiently recovered to

implore her attendants to make a last, though hopeless count. On three pillows lay three babies howling lustily in unison. On the fourth pillow reposed a fourth infant, with a mysterious smile upon his face, but cheeks that bore traces of recent tears.

THE CAVE OF THE SPLURGLES

One October afternoon, as I was scrambling through the woods on my way to the best of the trout brooks that abound in the neighborhood of Canaan, Vermont, I nearly broke my left leg in a deep hole in the ground.

The first thought was for my rod, which had become involved in certain complications with the underbrush; the second was for my left leg, which, fortunately, had sustained no serious damage; and the third for the pitfall into which I had stumbled. The hole was directly under the branches of a big red oak that grew on the slope of a hill, or ledge, of metamorphic limestone. Juniper bushes and brambles almost hid the orifice. Pulling these aside, I got on all fours and peered down into the black hole, for what purpose I do not know. My left leg was no longer there, and I certainly had no interest in the inhabitants of the burrow, whatever they might be—undoubtedly either snakes, woodchucks, or skunks, with the weight of probability in favor of the last-mentioned species. So I did not crawl in to explore the cavity, although by a tight squeeze I could have done so, but pursued my way across Rodney Prince's pasture to Rodney Prince's brook, and brought home at sundown a string which weighed so many pounds that, out of consideration for Rodney Prince's feelings, I shall say nothing about it. The hospitable Granger had assured me with friendly earnestness the evening before that there had never been any trout in his brook, that the boys had long since fished them out, and that if there were anything there now they were miserable little finger-long specimens, unworthy of the attention of a city man with a fifteen-dollar rod and a book full of flies.

After supper I joined as usual the small circle of choice spirits who gather every evening in the back part of Deacon Plympton's grocery to smoke their pipes and to profit by the oracular wisdom of the proprietor of the store. In a humble attempt to contribute to the conversational interest of the occasion, I casually remarked that I had stepped into a deep hole that afternoon while going a fishing. I was flattered to find that my insignificant adventure was treated with respect by the company, and that even the taciturn deacon, from his seat on the pork barrel, condescended to lend an attentive ear.

"Sho!" said he. "In Rodney's paster?"

"Yes."

"Under red oak?"

"Yes."

"Humph!" he grunted, blowing out a cloud of smoke, "narrer escape."

"Why?" I asked, resolved to be no less laconic than he. "Skunks?"

"No—Splurgles!"

And Andrew Hinckley, from a barrel of the deacon's highest-priced flour, whispered "Splurgles." And his brother John, from a box of washing soap, echoed the mysterious word. And Squire Trull on the platform scales, and old Orrison Ripley on a barrel of the sweetened bar, which the honest deacon sold as powdered sugar at a shilling the pound, took up the refrain, and solemnly remarked in concert, "Yes, the Splurgles!"

I knew that to ask a question would be to put myself at a disadvantage with these worthy citizens, so I merely said, "Ah,

Splurgles," and nodded my head, as if to escape the Splurgles were a matter of common experience with me.

"It's providence," said Squire Trull, after a few moments' silence, "that they didn't pull ye in."

"Ain't ben no closer shave sence Fuller stumbled in when he was drunk and had the boot drawed clean off his fut. Has there, Deacon?"

The deacon, thus appealed to, descended from the pork barrel, walked to the other end of the store, returned with a sulphur match in his hand, relit his pipe, and gravely shook his head.

From the rambling conversation which ensued and lasted till the nine o'clock bell inspired the deacon to take in his designatory hams and put up shutters, I gathered the following facts and allegations:

For many years, indeed ever since the infancy of the venerable Orrison Ripley, the people of Canaan had regarded the hole in the side of the hill under the red oak tree with superstitious awe. There were few who would venture near the spot in broad daylight; none after dark. The popular opinion of the hole seemed to be well grounded. Sounds as of demoniac laughter were frequently heard issuing from the cavern—indescribable sounds, guttural and gurgling. As far as I could learn, this circumstance was the only explanation of the etymology of the name Splurgles, applied by tradition and usage to the inhabitants of the cave. These supernatural beings were believed to be malevolent, not only from the peculiar harshness of their laughter, which had been heard by many at different times during the last half century, but also on the testimony of a few who claimed to have seen diabolical heads protruding from the hole as if demons had come up from below to get a breath of fresh air. Moreover, there was the horrible fate of Jeremiah Stackpole, a reckless, atheistical young man, who, on the twenty-first of October 1858, had boasted of his intention to gather acorns under the red oak by the hill, and whose hat, discovered afterward beside the hole, was the only trace of him that could ever be found. There was also the experience of Jack Fuller, the brother of the town clerk. Fuller, in a maudlin condition, had wandered into Rodney Prince's pasture about four years ago, and had come home perfectly sobered and minus one boot. He declared that while rambling about in search of boxberry plums, he had stumbled into the Splurgle hole. His leg had been grasped from below by fiery hands—fingers that burned his foot through leather and woolen—and it was only by an almost superhuman effort on his part that he escaped being pulled bodily into the hole. Fortunately, being afflicted with corns, he wore very loose boots, and to this circumstance he owed his deliverance from the awful grip of the Splurgles. Fuller solemnly affirmed that long after he had pulled out his stocking foot and fled to a place of safety, he felt the burning reminder of the red-hot fingers and thumb that had clasped his instep.

The laconic deacon's summing up of the various stories about the Splurgle hole with which I had been regaled, was concise, comprehensive, and startling. "It's the back door of hell," he said.

"Fuller," said I the next day to the hero of the demon-snatched boot, "how much rum would it take to work up your courage to the point of visiting the Splurgle hole with me this afternoon?"

"Nigh onto a quart, I guess," replied Fuller, after an inspection of my features had satisfied him that I was not quizzing. "Best to be on the safe side and call it a full quart. I calculate I should have to be pooty drunk."

"Will you go with me first," I then inquired, "and take the quart of rum afterward, and a five-dollar bill into the bargain?"

Fuller balanced the risk against the gain. You could almost watch through his skin the temptation wrestling with the fear. Rum conquered, as it will. At three o'clock, Mr. Fuller, carrying a rope, a dark lantern, and a perfectly sober head, accompanied me across Rodney Prince's pasture to the red oak on the side of the hill.

A close examination of the hole convinced me that it was not the burrow of any animal. Exploring it with a long stick, I found that beyond the dirt lining, near the orifice, its walls were of solid rock. It was, in fact, a tunnel into the ledge—a natural tunnel, old as the hills of Vermont, and therefore, dating back to the Lower Bilurian period. Beyond the mouth of the tunnel, where the debris and soil from the surface had partially choked it up, the passage was as large as a Croton main. For about ten feet the shaft trended downward at an angle of sixty or seventy degrees. Thence its course, as far as I could determine with my pole, was nearly horizontal, and directly toward the heart of the hill.

I stepped down and shouted into the mouth of the cave. There came back the confused and rambling echoes of my voice and then, when they had ceased, I distinctly heard a low, strange laugh, intelligent, yet not human, close to my ear and yet of another and unknown world.

Fuller heard it too. He turned pale and ran a rod or two away. I called to him sharply, and he came back trembling.

"That laugh we heard," said I, "is half in the peculiar echoes of the hole and half in our imaginations. I am going to crawl in."

By Fuller's earnest advice, I decided to enter the cave backward, so that, in an emergency, I might scramble out with the more expedition. I lit the dark lantern and tied one end of our rope under my arms. The other end I gave to Fuller. "If I call out," I said, "pull with all your might, and if necessary take a double turn around the oak." Then I backed slowly and cautiously down into the cave of the Splurgles.

Before my head and shoulders had left the daylight I felt both ankles grasped from below with a powerful grip, and knew that I was being drawn with superhuman strength down into the bowels of the hill. I shouted to Fuller in desperation, but my cry was almost drowned by a ringing peal of terrible, triumphant laughter. I saw my companion jump toward the trunk of a big tree. He did his best to save me, but his foot caught in the juniper bushes, and he fell to the ground, the rope slipping from his fear-benumbed fingers. My own fingers caught in vain at the loose dirt at the mouth of the hole. The power that dragged me downward was irresistible. My eyes met his, and his were full of horror. "God help you!" he cried, as the darkness closed around me.

As I was pulled down and down with constantly increasing speed, I lost my terror in the strange exhilaration of the motion. I fancied that I was a flying express train tearing through the night. I knew not, cared not whither. There I was, a light boat towed in the hissing wake of a swift steamer. The roar of the water took the rhythm of the singing, rushing sensation that precedes a swoon, and consciousness left me.

The first of my senses to return, after an indefinite lapse of time, was that of taste. The taste was that of incomparably good brandy.

"He is reviving. You need attend no longer," said a voice, harsh, yet not unkind.

I opened my eyes and looked around me. I lay in a small apartment upon a comfortable couch. On every side heavy curtains limited the field of vision. The one striking peculiarity of the place is difficult to describe, for it involves a quality which has no exact equivalent in any of the languages which men speak. Every object was self-luminous, radiating light, so to speak, instead of reflecting it. The crimson drapery shone with a crimson glow, and yet it was opaque—not even translucent. A couch was apparently wrought in copper, and yet the copper glowed as if copper were a source of light. The tall person who stood over me, looking down into my face with friendly and compassionate regard, was also self-luminous. His features radiated light; even his boots, which bore an immaculate polish, shone with an indescribable sort of radiant blackness. I believed that I could have read a newspaper by the light of his boots alone.

The effect of this singular phenomenon was so grotesque that I was impolite enough to laugh aloud.

"Pardon me," I said, "but you look so deucedly like a Chinese lantern that I can't help it."

"I see nothing to excite mirth," he gravely replied. "Do you refer to my luster?"

His sublime unconsciousness set me off again. Afterward, when I had become accustomed to the phenomenon of universally diffused light, each luminous color seemed perfectly natural, and I saw no more reason for mirth than he did.

"My friend," I remarked, to turn the conversation, seeing that he was a little piqued, "that was admirable brandy you were kind enough to give me just now. Perhaps you have no objection to telling me where I am."

"I can assure you that you are among those who are well disposed toward you, notwithstanding your sinful follies and weaknesses. We shall try to make you cease to regret the frivolous world which you have left forever."

"You are altogether too hospitable," I said. "I shall get back to Canaan as soon as possible."

"You will never get back to Canaan. The road by which you came is traveled in one direction only."

"And you intend to keep me here in this infernal cave?"

"For your own good."

"It strikes me," I rejoined, with some heat, "that you are too much interested in my moral welfare."

It must have been for full a week—although I had no means of measuring time, my watch obstinately refusing to go—that I was kept a close prisoner inside the luminous curtains. At regular intervals my jack-o'-lantern guardian visited me, bringing food which shone as if it were phosphorescent, but which, nevertheless, I ate with infinite relish, finding it very good. He seemed disinclined to converse, but always kind and courteous, and invariably greeted and left me with a calm, superior smile that came to be at last in the highest degree exasperating.

"Look here," I said one day, finally losing all patience, "you know very well that I don't lack the disposition to strangle you and kick my way out of this place back to honest daylight. Still, I am weak and human enough to say that you will oblige me exceedingly by stating who you are, why you always smile on me in that superior manner, and what you propose to do with me. Who the devil are you, anyway?"

"All that you will speedily learn," he replied with unlimited politeness, "for I am directed to conduct you at once to my lord."

"The lord of the Splurgles?"

"Splurgles, if you choose. I believe that that is the name given us in the wretched world which you are fortunate enough to have escaped. Accompany me, if you please, to the audience chamber of my lord."

The lord of the Splurgles was a personage of severe gravity of countenance. Like my guardian and the counselors and courtiers (with one exception) who surrounded him in the comfortably appointed apartment, he was self-luminous. The exception was an individual who seemed to be present in a menial capacity. This person, apparently a human being like myself, had done his best to remedy his natural deficiency in this respect. He had rubbed his face, his hands, and his habiliments with phosphorus, and shone artificially with a poor imitation of the genuine illuminating principle of the Splurgle world. That this imitation was in his case the sincerest form of flattery was evident from his actions and looks. His bearing toward the Splurgles was subservient in the extreme. He ran at their beck and call, rejoiced under their approving notice, and seemed to swell with conscious importance whenever the lord of these strange beings deigned to give him a patronizing word or look.

"Worm of the earth!" said the principal Splurgle. "Are you disposed to embrace a great opportunity?"

"I am disposed," I replied, "to crawl back to my groveling life at the first chance."

"Poor fool," said the lord Splurgle, without the least sign of impatience.

"Thank you," I replied, with a bow that was intended to be ironical, "and what shall I call your lordship?"

"Oh, I am Ahriman," he returned, "the great Ahriman, the powerful devil Ahriman. Mortals tremble at the thought of me, and my name they dare not speak. I ruled over a vast empire of Devs and Archdevs in my time, and wrought a great deal of mischief in Persia and thereabouts. I am a tremendous fiend, I assure you. I inspire much terror."

"Pardon me, Uncle Ahriman," I remarked, "but are you sure you are quite as terrible as you used to be?"

An expression of mortified vanity stole over his countenance. "Perhaps," he answered, hesitating a little, "perhaps I am a little out of practice. Years and circumstances have limited my field of action. But I am still very terrible. Beelzebub, am I not very terrible?"

"My lord Ahriman," said a familiar voice behind me, "you are inexpressibly terrible." I looked around and saw that this opinion proceeded from my old acquaintance and custodian.

"You hear Beelzebub," continued Ahriman; "he says that I am inexpressibly terrible. You may believe Beelzebub, he is one of the most truthful and conscientious devils in our community. He takes rather a low view of human nature, but in matters like this his opinion is as good as anybody's. Yes, I'm undeniably awful. Isn't that so, Stackpole?"

The fellow whom I had previously noted as a mortal like myself, and a base truckler withal to the ways and whims of the Splurgles, stepped forward from the throng, raised his eyes from the ground until they met those of Ahriman, and forthwith began to shake and shiver as if stricken speechless with terror. I believed at the time that the rascal simulated it all. I even thought he gave me a sly wink as he retired when he had got through trembling.

"You see," said Ahriman, turning proudly to me, "what a marked effect my presence has on our worthy friend Jeremiah Stackpole, though he has been accustomed to the sight of me for nearly twenty years."

This mortal, then, was the atheistical young man of Canaan, of whose mysterious disappearance in 1858 I had been informed in Deacon Plympton's grocery. I afterward learned that the manner of his introduction to the cave of the Splurgles was identical with my own. Unlike me, he had speedily become reconciled to the situation. The society of the retired devils in the bowels of the earth exactly suited his tastes. Assured of a comfortable subsistence as long as he lived, he made no attempt to escape from the cave and found it to his interest to earn the good will of his captors by toadying to their harmless vanity.

"Now, mortal," resumed Ahriman with a lofty air, "you may think it strange that evil spirits, so powerful and terrible as we are, should contemplate any other disposition of your worthless body and totally depraved nature than to wipe you out of existence altogether. To tell the truth, however, we find it convenient to have a mortal or two on hand to do the hard work of the community—to assist in the development of the immense natural resources of the cave. Not that we are lazy," he added, "but in our honorable retirement we are perhaps less active and energetic than we used to be. It is for this reason that you are offered the opportunity to enjoy the remarkable advantages of perpetual companionship with beings so great as we are. Dear, dear," continued this awe-inspiring demon, fanning himself with a barbed tail, which I had not previously noticed, "it is rather warm! Moloch, take this mortal away. I find it very fatiguing to talk so much."

I confess that I felt a trifle uneasy at the mention of a name which had been awful to the ears of men for centuries. There was something ghoulish in the idea of being turned over to the cruel and bloodthirsty Moloch, at whose red altars thousands of human lives had been sacrificed. The appearance of my new custodian, however, was reassuring. Moloch came up with a friendly smile, patted me on the head, and offered to show me over the cave. He was a fat demon, good-natured, and apparently lazy, with a grotesque face and a merry twinkle in his eyes. I liked Moloch from the first.

"I'll tell you a good one," he whispered in my ear. "What were the silliest nations that ever lived on the face of the earth? Ha, ha! It's a good one, I assure you."

"I give it up," I said.

"Why," he said, beginning to shake like a jellyfish with suppressed mirth, "the silliest nations were the Ass-yrians and the Ninny-vites and the Babble-onians. D'ye see?" And Moloch went off into a convulsion of merriment.

I laughed heartily, and he seemed to be much gratified at my appreciation of his humor. "I'll tell you a better one than that," he said confidentially, "as soon as I think of the answer. I've quite forgotten how the answer comes in. It's something about a frisky rogue and a risky frog—no, I'm not certain that's just it. But it's one of the best jokes you've ever heard when it's put properly.

"Those devils over there," said Moloch, as we walked out of the audience chamber into a field, under the overhanging roof of the cave, where sundry rather innocuous-looking demons were hoeing corn, "are the asuras and goblin Pretas and terrible rakshashas of the Hindoca. They used to range the earth with bloody tongues and ogre teeth and cannibal appetites. Now they are strictly graminivorous devils. Oh, I tell you there has been a vast improvement in our race since we retired from active business. You might call it the march of civilization," he added, with violent symptoms of inward laughter.

We came upon a gigantic demon sitting unsteadily on a rock, his huge right fist clasping a wicker flask. "It's Typhon," whispered Moloch, "the Set of the ancient Egyptians. Set used to breathe smoke and pelt his enemies with red-hot boulders. He frightened all the gods once, if you remember, and drove them out of the country. He won't hurt you. He's very peaceable now, even when he's fuddled. Set has a great gullet for liquor and he is the worse for it now, as you observe. Set has declined, you see," added Moloch chuckling, "Set, sat, sot."

"You are a mad wag, Moloch," said I.

"It's only my joking way," he replied. "I do enjoy a good joke. Sometimes they get me up by the Canaan outlet and set me laughing to scare the countrymen outside. Do you notice my peculiarly merry eyes?"

In the course of my walk with Moloch through the Splurgle community I came to understand how harmless and even simple-minded these ancient bugaboos really were. If they were ever malevolent, they had discarded their malevolence when superstition discarded them. Like decayed gentlemen in other branches of industry, some of them retained a certain pride in their whilom fiendishness, but the shadow was ludicrously unlike the substance. One by one, as the friendly Moloch told me with many brilliant *jeux d'esprit*, which I regret that I am unable to remember, the devils of antiquity, superseded in dogma and creed by newer and more fashionable devils, had withdrawn from the face of the earth and gone into retirement in this cavern under the roots of the three-pronged mountain. Here the played-out fiends of forty centuries had gradually rusted into the condition in which I found them when dragged by the heels into their community.

"Ahriman has kept his head better than the rest of us," explained my guide, the cheerful Moloch, "and therefore he bosses us, but privately, between you and me, I don't believe he is more formidable or devilish than any man of the lot."

I saw and talked with Baal. He seemed a little weak in his head, and was employed in the kitchen of the establishment, dealing out rations of phosphorescent soup. "Your soup shines today," I remarked, for the want of anything better to say.

"Yes, it shines, it shines," replied the superannuated fiend, apparently struck with the force of my remark. Then he paused, as if unable to grasp the immensity of the idea, and put his ladle hand to his forehead, spilling a stream of soup down over his clothes. "It shines, it shines," he repeated, not noticing his mishap, "and there's something in my head that buzzes and buzzes." Then he went on ladling out soup and muttering to himself the feeble analogy, "It shines, it shines; it buzzes, it buzzes."

"Some of us are farther gone than Baal is," said Moloch. "There is a houseful of 'em in the institution over there—poor devils who sit and moon and hardly know enough to eat and drink. You ought to see Abaddon. He's a sad sight. So far gone that he can't appreciate a good conundrum."

Afterward I had the honor of an introduction to Lilith, the mistress of Adam, and by him the mother of a pernicious brood of devils. She was a sweet-tempered, grandmotherly old lady, and, when I saw her, was knitting a pair of warm woolen socks for Belial, a shiftless ne'er-do-well sort of fiend. I saw Asmodeus; he was reading, with evident enjoyment, Timothy Titcomb's *Letters to Young Men.* I met Leviathan, Nergal, and Belphegor; they would have cowed and trembled had I said a harsh word. I talked with Rimnon, Dagon, Kohai, Behemoth, and Antichrist; they were as staid and respectable as the honest citizens who met nightly in Deacon Plympton's grocery.

During a residence of several weeks with the Splurgles, I was somewhat mortified to find that their moral standards put to shame the common practices of mankind. Harmless fellows, vain of their reputation for diabolical malignity, their private lives were above reproach. They neither lied nor stole. They held every trust to be sacred. Of their hospitality, I bear willing testimony. The only form of vice which I discovered among them was drunkenness, and that was confined to Typhon and one or two others. Yet, while I credit them with virtues unfortunately rare on earth, candor compels me to add that the Splurgles were rather tedious companions, and I was glad when, having learned the secret of the outlet through the good nature of my friend Moloch, I stood once more under the red oak in Rodney Prince's pasture.

Black and dead as every color looked after the self-luminous hues of the Splurgle cave, the contrast was not so great as that which oppressed me when I began to associate again with mankind. The venality of trade, the petty malice of society, the degradation of humanity, assumed a new and repulsive aspect. I shared the pity of Beelzebub for mortal imperfection.

THE DEVIL'S FUNERAL

I felt myself lifted up from my bed by hands invisible and swiftly borne down the ever-narrowing avenue of Time. Each moment I passed a century and encountered new empires, new peoples, strange ideas, and unknown faiths. So at last I found myself at the end of the avenue, at the end of Time, under a blood-red sky more awful than the deepest black.

Men and women hurried to and fro, their pale faces reflecting the accursed complexion of the heavens. A desolate silence rested upon all things. Then I heard afar a low wail, indescribably grievous, swelling and falling again and blending with the notes of the storm that began to rage. The wailing was answered by a groan, and the groaning grew into thunder. The people wrung their hands and tore their hair, and a voice, piercing and persistent, shrieked above the turmoil, "Our lord and master, the Devil, is no more! Our lord and master is no more!" Then I, too, joined the mourners who bewailed the Devil's death.

An old man came to me and took me by the hand. "You also loved and served him?" he asked. I made no reply, for I knew not wherefore I lamented. He gazed steadfastly into my eyes. "There are no sorrows," he said, meaningly, "that are beyond utterance." "Not, then, like your sorrow," I retorted, "for your eyes are dry, and there is no grief behind their pupils." He placed his finger on my lips and whispered, "Wait!"

The old man led the way to a vast and lofty hall, filled to the farthest corner with a weeping crowd. The multitude was, indeed, a mighty one, for all the people of every age of the world who had worshiped and served the Devil were assembled there to do for him the last offices for the dead. I saw there men of my own day and recognized others of earlier ages, whose faces and fame had been brought down to me by art and by history; and I saw many others who belonged to the later centuries through which I had passed in my night progress down the avenue of Time. But as I was about to inquire concerning these, the old man checked me. "Hush," he said, "and listen." And the multitude cried with one voice, "Hark and hear the report of the autopsy!"

From another apartment there came forth surgeons and physicians and philosophers and learned faculties of all times charged to examine the Devil's body and to discover, if they could, the mystery of his existence. "For," the people had said, "if these men of science can tell us wherein the Devil was the Devil, if they can separate from his mortal parts the immortal principle which distinguished him from ourselves, we may still worship that immortal principle to our own continued profit and to the unending glory of our late lord and master."

With grave looks upon their countenances, and with reluctant steps, three delegates advanced from among the other sages. The old man beside me raised his hand to command perfect silence. Every sound of woe was at the instant suppressed. I saw that one was Galen, Paracelsus another, and Corneilus Agrippa the third.

"Ye who have faithfully served the master," said Agrippa in a loud voice, "must listen in vain for the secret which our scalpels have disclosed. We have lain bare both the heart and the soul of him who lies yonder. His heart was like our own hearts, fitly formed to throb with hot passions, to shrink with hatred, and to swell with rage. But the mystery of his soul would blast the lips that uttered it."

The old man hurriedly drew me a little way apart, out of the throng. The multitude began to surge and sway with furious wrath. It sought to seize and rend to pieces the learned and venerable men who had dissected the Devil, yet refused to publish the mystery of his existence. "What rubbish is this you tell us, you charlatan hackers and hewers of corpses?" exclaimed one. "You have discovered no mystery; you lie to our faces." "Put them to death!" screamed others. "They wish to hoard the secret for their own advantage. We shall presently have a triumvirate of quacks setting themselves up above us, in place of him whom we have worshiped for the dignity of his teachings, the ingenuity of his intellect, the exalted character of his morality. To death with these upstart philosophers who would usurp the Devil's soul."

"We have sought only the Truth," replied the men of science, soberly, "but we cannot give you the Truth as we found it. Our functions go not further." And thereupon they withdrew.

"Let us see for ourselves," shouted the foremost in the angry crowd. So they made their way into the inner apartment where the Devil's body lay in state. Thousands pressed after them and struggled in vain to enter the presence of death that they, too, might discover the true essential quality of the departed. Those who gained entrance reverently but eagerly approached the massive bier of solid gold, studded with glistening stones, and resplendent with the mingled lustre of the emerald, the chrysolite, and jasper. Dazzled, they shrank back with wild faces and bewildered looks. Not a man among them dared stretch forth his hand to tear away the bandages and coverings with which the surgeons had veiled their work.

Then the old man who with me had silently witnessed the tumultuous scene drew himself up to a grand height and said aloud: "Worshipers of the Devil, whose majesty even in death holds you subject! It is well that you have not seized the mystery before the time. A variety of signs combine to inspire me with hope that that which has sealed the lips of the men of science may yet be revealed through faith. Let us forthwith pay the last sad tribute to our departed lord. Let us make to his memory a sacrifice worthy of our devotion. My art can kindle a fire which consumes weighty ingots of gold as readily as it burns tinsel paper, and which leaves behind no ashes and no regrets. Let every man bring hither all the gold, whether in coin, or in plate, or in trinkets, that he has earned in serving the Devil, and every woman the gold that she has earned, and cast it into the consuming fire. Then will the funeral pyre be worthy of him whom we mourn."

"Well said, old man!" cried the Devil worshipers. "Thus we will prove that our worship has not been base. Build you the pyre while we go to fetch our gold."

My eyes were fixed upon the face of my companion, but I could not read the thoughts that occupied his brain. When I turned again the vast hall was empty of all save him and me.

Slowly and laboriously we built the funeral pile in the centre of the apartment. We built it of the costly woods that were at hand, already sprinkled by devout mourners with the choicest spices. We built the pile broad and high, and draped it with gorgeous stuffs. The old man smiled as he prepared the magic fire that was to consume the gold which the Devil worshipers had gone to fetch. Within the pyre he left an ample space for their sacrifice.

Together we brought forth the Devil's body and placed it carefully in position at the top of the pile. Thunders rolled in the lofty space above our heads, and the whole building shook so terribly that I expected it to fall, crushing us between roof and pavement. Crash came after crash of thunder, nearer and nearer to the pyre. Lightnings played close around us—around the old man, the Devil's corpse, and me. Still we waited for the multitude, but the multitude returned not.

"Behold the obsequies!" said the old man at last, thrusting his lighted torch into the midst of the pile. "You and I are the only mourners, and we have not a single ounce of gold to offer. Go you now forth and bid all the Devil worshipers to the reading of the last will and testament. They will come."

I hastened forth to obey the old man's command, and speedily the funeral hall was thronged again. This time the Devil worshipers brought their gold, and every man sought to make excuse for his tardiness at the pyre. The air was thick with explanations. "I tarried only," said one, "to be sure that I had gathered all—all to the very last piece of gold in my possession." "I have fetched," said another, "the laborious accumulations of fifty years, but I cheerfully sacrifice it all to the memory of our dear lord." A third said, "See, I bring all of mine, even to the wedding ring of my dead wife."

There was a contention among the Devil worshipers to be first to cast treasure into the fire. The charmed flames caught up the gold, and streamed high above the corpse, casting upon every eager face in the vast room a fierce yellow glare. Still the fire was fed by hands innumerable, and still the old man stood beside the pyre, smiling strangely.

The Devil worshipers now cried out with hoarse voices: "The will! The will! Let us hear the last testament of our dead lord!"

The old man opened a roll of asbestos paper and began to read aloud, while the hubbub of the great throng died away into silence and the angry roar of the consuming flames subsided into a dull murmur. What the old man read was this:

" 'To my well-beloved subjects, the whole world, my faithful worshipers and loyal servitors, greeting, and the Devil's only blessing, a perpetual curse!

" 'For as much as I am conscious of the approach of the Change that hunts every active existence, yet being of sound mind and firm purpose, I do declare this to be my last will, pleasure, and command as to the disposal of my kingdom and effects.

"'To the wise I bequeath folly, and to the fools, pain. To the rich I leave the wretchedness of the earth, and to the poor the anguish of the unattainable; to the just, ingratitude, and to the unjust, remorse; and to the theologians I bequeath the ashes of my bones.

"'I decree that the place called hell be closed forever.

"'I decree that the torments, in fee simple, be divided among all my faithful subjects, according to their merit, that the pleasure and the treasure shall also be divided equitably among my subjects.'"

Thereupon the Devil worshipers shrieked with one accord: "There is no God but the Lord Devil, and he is dead! Now let us enter into our inheritance."

But the old man replied, "Ye wretched! The Devil is dead, and with the Devil died the world. The world is dead."

Then they stood aghast, looking at the pyre. All at once the gold-laden flames leaped into a blazing column to the roof and expired. And forth from the red embers of the Devil's heart there crept a small snake, hissing hideously. The old man clutched at the snake to crush it, but it slipped through his hands and made its way into the midst of the crowd. Judas Iscariot caught up the snake and placed it in his bosom. And when he did so, the earth beneath us began to quiver as if in the convulsion of death. The lofty pillars of the funeral chamber reeled like giants seized with dizziness. The Devil worshipers fell flat upon their faces; the old man and I stood alone. Crash followed quick on crash on every side of us, but it was not this time the concussions of thunder. It was the hopeless sound of the tumbling of man's structures and fabrics and the echo from the other worlds of this world's crack of doom. Then the stars began to fall, and the fainter lights of heaven came down upon us like a driving sleet of frozen fire. And children died of terror, and mothers clasped their dead babes to their own cold breasts and hurried this way and that for shelter that was never found. Light became black, fire lost its heat in the utter disorganization of Nature, and a whelming flood of chaos surged from the womb of the universe and swallowed up the Devil worshipers and their dead world.

Then I said to the old man as we stood in the void, "Now there is surely no evil and no good; no world and no God."

But he smiled and shook his head, and left me to wander back unguided through the centuries. Yet as he disappeared I saw that high over the ruins of the world a rainbow of infinite brightness stretched its arch.

THE WONDERFUL COROT

On the twentieth of May, 1881 (said John Nicholas, in the smoking room of the Gallia), I spent the day and part of the night at the house of my good friend Scott Jordan, President of the Bloomsburgh and Lycoming Railroad. Jordan has a place in one of the charming suburban neighborhoods a few miles out of Philadelphia. His character deserves a word.

He is an intensely superstitious, intensely practical man—a type of a class much more numerous than people will readily believe. Half a dozen railroads, conceived, built, equipped, and run to the profit of their legitimate owners, bear witness to his honesty and sound business sense. If further evidence of his worldly judgment is wanted, it may be found in a safe full of marketable securities. In his power of managing men and handling complicated enterprises, Scott Jordan comes nearer to my idea of Thomas Brassey than does any other capitalist-contractor I know. His name on a Board of Direction is a guarantee of conservative, prudent, yet never timid management. I wish he would undertake the comptrollership of my modest finances, to the last dollar I possess. He is a companionable old gentleman, and likes to be considered as a man of taste. He is in the full sense a man of the world while concerned with the affairs of this world, yet he spends nearly half his life in another—a strange world where banjos play and bells ring without human hands, where ghostly arms are stretched forth from behind the curtains of the unknown, and dim forms belonging to every age of history meet face to face.

Jordan's house is the happy hunting ground of all the professional charlatans in the spirit-raising line. They fasten to him like leeches—the rappers, the test mediums, the healing mediums, the physical-manifestation people and the rope tiers, the clairvoyants, the controlled of every sort, male and female, young and old, prosperous and shabby.

Jordan has told me that these gentry cost him twelve or fifteen thousand dollars a year. When they come to his door he welcomes them as aids in his tireless investigation of truth. They live like princes in his establishment; every morning brings its honorarium for the performance of the night before. Jordan royally entertains his Egyptians and Greeks until he detects them in some piece of imposture cruder than usual. Then he talks to them like a grieved parent, ships them off with a free pass over one of his railroads, and is all ready to go through the same process with the next comer.

You will understand now, gentlemen, that I had looked forward with considerable interest to my visit to Jordan's house.

Although the family was entertaining several professionals, I found that I was the only social guest. I make this distinction, but Jordan never does. You can hardly help liking the old fellow the better for the magnificent old-school courtesy with which he treats the seediest humbug of the lot.

"It is they who condescend," he is accustomed to say, somewhat pompously, "when they honor me with their company; for do they not bring with them the kings and great poets and artists and the wisest and best of every century?"

And if Jordan's testimony is accorded the same weight in this matter as it would have in any railroad suit in any court in Pennsylvania, the wisest and best of every century, from Socrates down to George Washington, have, in fact, visited his private cabinet.

At the dinner table I had the pleasure of meeting Mr. John Roberts and his brother William, the celebrated cabinet mediums; fellows with villainous faces. I was also presented in due form to Mr. Helder, a gentleman of consumptive appearance, who is said to possess remarkable developing powers; a fat lady whose name I have forgotten, but who practices medicine under inspiration of the eminent Dr. Rush; Mrs. Blackwell, the materializing medium, and her daughter, introduced as Mrs. Work, a young lady with black eyes, said to be a flower and modeling medium of rare promise. At no time did I see any Mr. Work.

I thought the flower and modeling medium looked at me with not unkind eyes during dinner. The behavior of the other professionals indicated suspicious reserve. They furtively watched me, as if trying to guess the depth of my penetration. I contrived to drop a few remarks that seemed to encourage them. Jordan was jovial, and wholly unconscious of all this byplay.

In my friend's library after dinner, there was the usual jugglery, with the gas turned halfway down. A small extension room, separated by a portiere from the library, served as a cabinet. William Roberts suffered me to tie him with a clothesline. He produced some of the commoner manifestations, and then declared that the conditions were unfavorable. At Jordan's urgent request, Mrs. Blackwell went into the cabinet. Hands and vague white faces were shown between the curtains. The lights were turned still lower. Mrs. Work touched the piano, singing in a very musical voice, "Scots wha hae" and "Coming through the Rye." The persistent repetition of these airs finally elicited a full-length figure in a cloud of white, and the apparition was pronounced to be Mary, Queen of Scots. Mary withdrew and reappeared several times. At last, as if gaining courage, she ventured forth from the cabinet, advanced a yard or more into the room, and curtsied. Jordan called my attention in a whisper to the supernal beauty of her face and apparel. In a reverent voice he inquired if she would permit a stranger to approach. A slight inclination of Mary's head granted the boon. I stood face to face with the Queen; she allowed my hand to rest lightly for a second upon one of the folds of mull that draped her form. Her face was so near mine that even in the dim light I could see her eyes shining through the eye holes of her absurd papier-mâché mask.

The impulse to seize Mary and expose the ridiculous imposture was almost irresistible. I must have raised my hands unconsciously, for the Queen took fright and disappeared behind the portiere. Mrs. Work hastily left the piano and turned up the gas. In the glance that she gave me I read a piteous appeal.

Jordan's face was beaming with satisfaction. "So beautiful," he murmured, "and so gracious!"

"Yes, beautiful," I repeated, still looking at the flower and modeling medium; "beautiful and uncommonly gracious!"

"Thanks!" she whispered. "You are generous."

Half ashamed of myself as the voluntary accomplice of vulgar tricksters, I listened with growing impatience to Jordan's ecstatic account of other materializations not less marvelous and convincing than this of Mary, Queen of Scots. The mediums had returned to the ordinary occupations of evening leisure. The younger Roberts and Mr. Helder were playing backgammon, conversing at the same time in low voices. The fat representative of Dr. Rush was asleep in her chair. Mrs. Work was crocheting. Her mother was sipping brandy and water—a necessary restorative, Jordan was careful to tell me, after the draft made upon her vital forces by the recent materialization of Mary. The situation would have been thoroughly commonplace had it not been for occasional rattling detonations, or successions of sharp raps, apparently in the ceiling, in the partition walls, all over the furniture, and underneath the floor.

"They are playful tonight," said Roberts, looking up from his backgammon board.

"Yes," said Mrs. Work's mother, as she stirred her brandy and water. "They are very fond of Mr. Jordan. They hover around him always. Sometimes, when my inner vision is clearer, I see the air full of their beautiful forms, following him wherever he goes. They love and reward him for his great interest in them and us."

"Mr. Jordan," said I, "do you never find yourself imposed on?"

"Oh, often," he replied. "Frequently by wicked spirits; frequently by fraudulent mediums."

"There are frauds in every profession, you know," said Mrs. Blackwell.

"There would be no paste diamonds," suggested Helder, "if there were no real diamonds."

"And your repeated discoveries of imposture," I persisted, "have not shaken your faith?"

"Why should they?" replied the railroad president. "Nine hundred and ninety-nine experiments with negative results prove nothing; but the one-thousandth case, if established, proves everything. Demonstrated once, the possibility of communication with disembodied spirits is demonstrated forever."

A fusillade of raps in every part of the room greeted this proposition.

"I grant that," said I. "Prove one instance of the interference of spirits in the affairs of men and you have established the whole case."

"But you believe," he rejoined, with a smile, "that the thousandth and absolutely authentic instance will never be proved; and meanwhile you reserve the right to explain away all such things as you have seen tonight by the hypothesis of jugglery."

"I'm sure the gentleman doesn't think that," insinuated Mrs. Blackwell, who had now finished her brandy and water.

"Nevertheless," continued Jordan, "the one-thousandth instance may happen, may happen at any time, and may happen to you. Come and see my pictures."

I tried to keep a grave face while my host did the honors of a score or more of Raphaels, Titians, Correggios, Guidos, and what not, all painted in his own house by mediums under inspiration. Jordan's old masters make a collection probably unlike any other on earth. When he demanded what I thought of the internal evidence of their authenticity, I was able to reply with perfect truthfulness that nobody could mistake them.

From this amazing trash I turned with feelings of relief to a landscape hanging in the hallway. "I moved it out here," said Jordan, "to make room for that superb Carracci, 'Daniel in the Lion's Den'—the large canvas you particularly admired."

I looked at the old gentleman to see if he was in earnest. Then I looked again at the glorious landscape.

Here was no painted fiction, but truth itself: A clump of rounded willows, seen by early morning light and seen again in the perfectly calm water of the canal or sluggish stream which they overhung; a skiff, resting partly on the water and partly on the wet grass of the nearer bank; beyond, an indistinct distance and the outline of a château tower with the conical Burgundian peak; a marvelous humid atmosphere of blue and mist, a soft light enveloping everything and caressing everything. No painted fiction, I say, but a window through which anyone having eyes might survey nature in her eternal truth.

I said: "That comes nearer to the supernatural than anything I have ever seen. It is worth all your old masters together."

"You like it?" said he. "It is well enough, I suppose, though of a school for which I have no particular fancy. It was painted here about a year ago by a spirit who did not choose to identify himself."

"Nonsense," said I, for this passed all endurance, "Corot has been dead six years."

Jordan led the way back into the library. "Mrs. Work," said he, "do you remember the circumstances under which the large landscape in the hall—the hazy green one—was painted?"

"Certainly," replied the young lady, looking up from her needles; "I recollect very well. It was painted through me."

In claiming the authorship of this wonderful work of genius, she used the matter-of-fact tone in which she would have acknowledged a stork and sunflower in crewel, or a sleeping pussy cat in Berlin wools.

"And you are an artist yourself—that is to say, when not in the trance state?"

"Oh, yes," she replied, returning my gaze with unflinching eyes; and thereupon she produced from one of Mr. Jordan's portfolios a preposterous bunch of lilacs in water color. Meanwhile, Jordan had been rummaging in his desk. He now brought forth an account book. "Here we have it," he said, "all set down in black and white." In the middle of a page of similar memoranda I read this item:

1880, May 13—Pd. M. A. Work for painting done under control; large view (trees, stream, boat, etc.) . . . $25.00

"All I can say, madam," I exclaimed, turning to Mrs. Work, "is that Knoedler or Avery would have been most happy to pay you ten thousand dollars for that Corot, for Corot it is, and a masterpiece at that."

"Good night," said Jordan, a little later, when I rose to retire. "After what you have already experienced I need hardly warn you not to be disturbed by any noises you may hear in your bedroom." A hailstorm of raps punctuated his sentence. "They hover, hover around," Mrs. Blackwell was saying, as I left the library; "but in this house it is as guardian—"

I went to bed thoroughly bewildered. Was there, after all, behind this wretched jack-in-the-box jugglery something incomprehensible, unexplainable, unspeakable—something which the jugglers themselves understood no better than their dupes? When I thought of Mary, Queen of Scots, ogling me through her pasteboard mask, and of Jordan's rhapsody over her unearthly beauty, the problem seemed too ignoble to engage an intelligent man's attention for a single minute; but there was the Corot. The whole machinery of raps, hands, ropes, apparitions, guitars, Raphaels, Correggios, and Carraccis was almost childish in its simplicity;

but there again was the Corot. Every train of logical thought, every analytical process led me back to the marvelous Corot.

One of three things must be true: The picture was a commonplace daub, like the old masters, and I was laboring under a strange delusion or hallucination in regard to its merits. Or, Mrs. Work and her accomplices had procured a Corot unknown to connoisseurs and had sold it for one five-hundredth part of its market value, to bolster up a petty deception. Or, the landscape was a marvel and the manner of its production a miracle. The first supposition was the most plausible, yet I was not disposed to accept it at the expense of my self-possession and judgment; no doubt daylight would confirm my estimate of the picture. The second supposition involved a degree of folly—disinterested and expensive folly—on the part of these precious mediums that did not tally with my observations of their character. To accept the third supposition was, of course, to accept the theory of the spiritualists. Thus reasoning I fell asleep, and was awakened, about half-past two o'clock, by a muffled hammering directly beneath my bed.

Now, gentlemen, what followed passed very rapidly, but every incident is distinct in my memory, and I ask you to reserve judgment until you have heard me through.

The noise came from the room under mine. As nearly as I could judge, this was the library. Notwithstanding Jordan's advice, I determined to see what was the matter. I jumped into my trousers and cautiously proceeded toward the stairway. At the head of the stairs a door opened as I passed and a hand was laid upon my shoulder.

"Don't go down!" was eagerly whispered into my ear. "Don't go down! Return to your chamber!"

A white figure stood before me. It was the flower and modeling medium in her nightdress, her black hair all loose.

"Why should I not go down?" I demanded. "Are you afraid that I shall embarrass the spirits in their carpenter work?"

She spoke hurriedly and with evident excitement: "You believe it all a fraud, but it isn't. There's fraud enough, Lord knows, for mediums must live; but, then, there are things—once in a while, not often—that stun us."

"Tell me the truth about the Corot."

"As truly as I stand here, it was produced in the way we said —on my easel, with my brush held in my hand, yet not by me. I can tell you no more, for I know no more." The noise of pounding downstairs increased.

"And if I go down, shall I encounter one of the mysteries that you speak of!"

"No, but you will run into great danger. It is for your own sake I ask you not to go." By this time I was in the lower hall.

Downstairs I discovered the Roberts brothers holding a séance at Jordan's plate closet, while the developing medium, Mr. Helder, with a dark lantern in his hand, was developing the combination lock of Jordan's safe.

In my brief and not victorious struggle with the three rascals I must have received some hurt upon the head. My eyes were half blinded with blood. With a vague idea of shouting for help at the foot of the stairs, I staggered back into the lower hall, closely pushed by two of the mediums. I heard one of them whisper, "Hit hard! It's got to be done," and saw a heavy iron bar raised and aimed at my head.

At this moment I stood directly in front of the Corot. Even in the imperfect light, that wonderful glimpse of nature opened beside me like a window in the wall. In another instant the crowbar would have buried itself in my skull. Then there reached my ears a cry from the head of the stairs, where I had left the flower medium standing, "Jump! Jump into the picture! For God's sake, jump!"

Resting one hand upon the frame, as upon a window sill, I launched myself against the canvas. The weapon descended, but I was already beyond its range. I fell, fell, fell, as if falling through infinite space, yet partially borne up by invisible hands. Then I found myself upon the wet grass of the canal bank. I jumped into the skiff and hurriedly poled it across the stream; and then, having reached the other bank, I fainted dead away under the willows.

When I came to my senses I was lying in snowy linen in the Hôtel Dieu at Dijon, with a good sister to take care of me. Here is a translation of the entry in the hospital books:

1881, May 21—Received from Monsieur the Mayor of Flavigny an Unknown, found early this morning, unconscious, and only partially clad, on the bank of the canal of Burgundy, near the limits of the arrondissement. Injuries—Severe scalp wound and slight fracture of the right parietal bone. Property—One pair of trousers, one nightshirt, pair slippers. Means of identification—None.

Gentlemen, that is the end of my statement of facts. I am now on my way back to America. I shall establish the interference of spirits in human affairs by affording conclusive evidence that a wonderful picture was painted by a dead artist; that this picture was used by the spirits in my behalf as a way of escape out of mortal danger, and that, by the most extraordinary instance of levitation on record, I was borne bodily more than three thousand miles in a few seconds.

Do not laugh just yet. To the scientific world and to all fair-minded investigators of the truth of spiritualism, I shall soon offer in the way of evidence:

1. The register of the Continental Hotel in Philadelphia for May 19, 1881. I stopped there on my way to visit Jordan. My name will be found under that date.

2. The testimony of Mr. Jordan and his family that I was with them at Bryn Mawr on May 20, 1881, up to eleven o'clock at night.

3. The duly attested record of my admission to the hospital at Dijon, France, on May 21, 1881.

4. The wonderful picture now in the possession of Jordan.

II

Dear Sir: In reply to your note of inquiry, I beg leave to say that our common friend, Mr. John Nicholas, has been under my care for more than a year, with the exception of two months spent in the Côte d'Or in charge of another medical attendant.

The facts in his unfortunate case are accurately set forth (up to a certain point) in his own narrative, as outlined by you. Mr. Nicholas' recollection is not trustworthy in regard to events happening after he had suffered a severe blow on the head in his encounter with thieves.

As to the value of his estimate of the merits of the picture upon which his delusion is founded, I cannot speak. I have never seen it. It may be well to say, however, that prior to his departure for France, Mr. Nicholas was in the habit of attributing the picture to an American artist, some years ago deceased. As he used to tell the story, it was not to Burgundy but to Wissahickon Valley that he was transported by levitation.

I also beg leave to say that this mania does not affect his sanity in all other respects; nor do I see reason to despair of his entire recovery.

Yours respectfully,
HORACE F. DANIELS, M.D.

THE TERRIBLE VOYAGE OF
THE *TOAD*

It was not owing to any lack of enterprise or courage that Captain Peter Crum of Mackerel Cove, Maine, did not visit the Paris Exposition in his own sloop yacht, the *Toad*. Nor was the failure of his famous expedition due to any demerit in the craft which he commanded. Ever since Captain Crum sailed his sloop by dead reckoning to Boston, in spite of unpropitious weather, including a heavy sou'east blow off Cape Elizabeth, and returned in safety with a cargo of Medford rum to discomfit the critics who had predicted certain disaster, there had been no question as to the seagoing qualities of the *Toad*. It is generally conceded at Mackerel Cove that Captain Peter Crum would have reached Paris in triumph but for the malignant hostility of a power justly abhorred and dreaded by all serious-minded men.

"Oh, the *Toad* sails, she does!" Captain Crum carelessly remarked to his neighbor, Deacon Silsbee, in the deacon's store one day early in June.

"The *Toad* does sail," allowed the deacon.

The captain gazed significantly at the deacon, whose face put on a receptive expression, as if to say the court awaits further communications.

"An ef you kin diskiver any rashn'l reason," continued Captain Crum, lowering his voice to a confidential whisper, "why

she shouldn't carry you and me and Andrew Jackson's son Tobias
to the big show over yonder, it's more'n I'kin, Deacon."

The deacon bore the reputation of being, when sober, the sub-
tlest logician, both in theological and secular matters, on that
section of the coast. He sympathized heartily in the captain's
project, but felt it due to himself to proceed deliberately, analy-
tically, and cautiously.

"Hum!" said he, wagging his head; "the *Toad's* a toler'b'l old
boat."

"She is," assented the captain. "Old an' thurowly seasoned."

"Without intendin' to disperidge," continued the deacon, "her
bottom's more putty'n timber."

"Putty or no putty," rejoined the owner of the *Toad*, "she sails
afore the wind like a thing of life and minds her hellum like a
lady."

"It's a long tack to Paris," suggested the deacon, shifting his
ground, "and them that go down upon the sea in ships [so to
speak of the *Toad*] take their lives in the palms of their hands."

"Deacon!" said the captain, solemnly; "you ain't actin' up fer to
deny an overrulin' Providence, or the efficacy of prayer? Won't
you be along?"

"True," said the deacon, mollified by the compliment to his
powers of intercession. "The godly man feareth neither the hurricane's fury nor the leviathan's rage. Are you certain you kin lay
the course?"

"Unless the geographics lie like Anernias," continued the captain, growing more earnest as the details of the adventurous
scheme presented themselves to his mind, "it's as plain a course
to Havy-de-Grass as it is to Bangor. You take a short hitch round
Cape Sable and then you're practically thar. Who says the *Toad*
won't sail? Gimme a sou'east or sou'west wind, Andrew Jackson's
old compass out of the schooner *Parida P.*, a good stock of pervi-
sions, two or three of them twenty-gallon kags of rum, and the
benefit of your petitions mornin' and evenin', and I'll allow I'll

lay the *Toad* 'longside the city landin' in Paris in sixty days, spite of blows or Beelzebub!"

The captain brought his fist down upon the cover of Deacon Silsbee's pork barrel with a vigor that denoted fixed determination. Several neighbors who had dropped into the store while he was speaking and had gathered around him, attracted by the energy of his utterances, applauded the daring vow. "In spite," he repeated, "of blows or Beelzebub!"

"Cap'n! Cap'n!" said the deacon, coming round from behind his counter and holding up both hands in protest, "say nothing thet's rash. While I hold that prayerful navigators, sailing so seaworthy and serious a craft as the *Toad,* hev little or nothin' to fear from Satan's wiles, I hold it likewise that a willful and froward sperrit of defiance at sech a mement is onnecessary and foolish. And I would also remark that if it's a question in your mind between two and three of them kags of rum for so long a v'yage, it's a dooty and a vartue to be on the safe side, Cap'n Crum!"

It is as well authenticated a fact as any in the history of Mackerel Cove that on the morning of Monday, June 17, 1878, the sloop *Toad,* of 8,825–10,000 registered tonnage, Crum master, cleared for Havre with a cargo consisting of Deacon Silsbee, Andrew Jackson's son Tobias, and nearly eighty gallons of Medford rum. Deacon Silsbee and Tobias Jackson are advisedly classed with the cargo rather than with the working crew of the vessel. In order to be on hand for an early departure they had thought it prudent to embark the night before. In accordance with a suggestion of the deacon's, namely, that any surplus of rum left over from the outward voyage could be profitably disposed of in Paris for such articles of merchandise as the natives might have to offer in exchange, the captain had added a fourth keg to the stock already on board. When the captain took command of the craft in the morning, he found his younger passenger curled up in the cuddy, utterly insensible to the momentous character of the occasion. By comparison with Tobias Jackson, Deacon Silsbee was very sober, but judged by any other standard he was very drunk. The deacon sat on the heel of the bowsprit, his chin resting heavily on both hands, singing in a dismal voice hymn after hymn of various metres, but to one unvarying tune. An invitation from the captain to lend a hand at the jib halyard met with no response. The deacon did not stir, but sat with his bleary eyes glued on the rum kegs in the standing room aft and began, "The voice of free grace cries escape to the mountain!" in a louder and more melancholy intonation than before.

The entire population of the cove had come down to the shore to witness the departure of the *Toad*. Many were the weather prophecies and the arguments of dissuasion shouted at the bold skipper. Even those of his neighbors who had been friendliest to the undertaking urged him to postpone his start until a more favorable day. They pointed to the long fog bank that lined the horizon to the seaward and had already shut in Damiscove Island and was hurrying toward Bald Head light and the main shore. "I calkilate to hev considerable fog more or less till I fetch beyond the Banks," returned the captain, cheerfully. "Guess I mought as well overhaul thet air compass of Andrew Jackson now ez later on."

Under these discouraging circumstances, with prophecies of evil sounding behind him and a thick fog dead ahead, with one of his companions helplessly drunk below deck and the other uncomfortably noisy above, Captain Peter Crum began his memorable voyage. Standing erect at the stern sheets, he poured out for himself a brimming tumblerful of rum as a sort of first line of fortifications against the fog. Then, alone and unaided, he ran up his mainsail and his jib and resumed his position at the helm. He had sworn in the presence of all Mackerel Cove to sail the *Toad* across the Atlantic in spite of Beelzebub. He would do it or perish in the attempt, along with Deacon Silsbee and Andrew Jackson's son Tobias. Captain Crum drank another tumblerful of rum. The mainsail fluttered in the first flurry of the fog breeze. Waving a graceful adieu to the assembled multitude on shore, and throwing an affectionate kiss to his weeping wife, who already considered herself in effect his widow, and whom he could readily distinguish in the distance by her pocket handkerchief, he grasped the tiller and brought the *Toad* round into the wind. The sails filled and the gallant though rather aged craft bounded off toward the open sea, while loud above the splash of the waves and the shouts of the crowd on shore rang out the deep voice of Deacon Silsbee, as he sang at the top of his lungs:

> "My willing soul wo-o-od shtay
>   In slusha framer zish;
>   An' sit an' sing her shellaway
>   To efferlash [hic] blish."

The first news of the *Toad's* progress was brought to Mackerel Cove twenty-eight hours after her departure, by the crew of a Halifax lumberman which put in on account of the fog. The lumberman reported it very thick outside—thicker than anything he remembered at that time of year. He had narrowly escaped running on to the Clamshell, a well-known rock in the shelter of Pumpkin Island, twenty miles out. As he sheered off he had perceived a small sloop, apparently fast hung on the ledge. To his hailing there had come the answer, in a voice as thick, if not thicker than the fog and much more unsteady, that the stranded sloop was the *Toad* of Mackerel Cove, bound for the Paris Exposition with a cargo of rum. The captain of the *Toad* confidently expected to get off at the next flood tide. Offers of assistance were received by the *Toad's* crew with derisive howls, and with some insulting reference to Beelzebub, which the lumberman could not distinctly understand.

"As I had no call to stand thar and be sarsed," concluded the lumberman's captain, "I put round agin and left the critter on the Clamshell. It's my private opinion that all hands on board had been splicin' the main brace a good many times too often."

For the next three weeks the anxious population of Mackerel Cove heard nothing further of the fortunes of their adventurous townsmen. The fog clung to the coast relentlessly for all that time. At last a northwest wind drove it off the shore, and on the second clear day the little steamer *Moonbeam*, engaged in the porgy fishery, came up to the cove with a small sloop in tow and three dejected, exhausted, and thoroughly disgusted navigators on board. This sloop was the *Toad*.

The master of the porgy boat reported that he had found the *Toad* aground on the Clamshell. At first he had seen no signs of life on board, but upon running as near to the rock as the draft of his steamer would allow, he discovered three human beings lying unconscious in the cuddy, together with several empty kegs that still smelled strong of rum. He took off the men, and by attaching a rope to the sloop, succeeded in dragging her into deep water. The rescued sailors partially recovered their senses under the influence of hot coffee, dry clothing, and kind treatment, but they still appeared to be in a state of semi-stupefaction, and the story they told was so deliriously incoherent that he could make neither head nor tail of it.

Of course the first inference drawn by the people of the Mackerel Cove was that the *Toad*, seen aground on the Clamshell June 19 by the Halifax lumberman, and found aground on the same ledge July 11 by the porgy steamer, had remained aground uninterruptedly between those two dates, the crew, meanwhile, consuming the four kegs of rum. This theory implied so inglorious a termination to an adventure begun with so much bravado that for several weeks Captain Crum, Deacon Silsbee, and Tobias Jackson were subject to a great deal of ridicule on the part of their neighbors and friends, and even the *Toad* itself became an object of derision in the cove.

The returned voyagers bore all this with extraordinary meekness for a while. At last, however, they began to hint that the reproach was unmerited: that there was a marvelous and mysterious history behind their apparent failure; and that if the whole truth were known, they would figure for all time as the heroes of one of the most protracted and terrific encounters with diabolical agencies in this or any other age.

Little by little the story came out: partly in conversations at Deacon Silsbee's store, partly in Tobias Jackson's communications to boon companions in convivial hours, and partly in allusions made by the deacon himself in prayer and exhortation in the vestry of the Baptist meetinghouse. When the whole story became known, it was so consistent and conclusive that it carried conviction at the first recital.

The hostility of a malign power had confronted the voyagers at the outset and driven them upon the Clamshell, in spite of Captain Crum's positive knowledge that he was at least seventeen miles to the southward of that rock at the moment when the *Toad* struck it. Once aground and waiting for the tide to flow, it became necessary, as a precaution against the chilling fog, to use a good deal of the rum medicinally. The voyagers did not remember being hailed by any Halifax lumberman. They did remember, however, that a huge black craft sailing without sails in the very teeth of the wind, yet not propelled by steam, and manned by no earthly crew, loomed up in the fog close to the Clamshell. There came to the rail of this apparitional vessel a monster with a head four times as big as a rum keg, and eyes that shone like coals of green fire, who demanded, in a supernally awful voice, who it was that proposed to cross the sea in spite of Beelzebub. Upon their shouting back defiance and the deacon's repeating a text from Job, the phantom (for phantom they believed it to be) vanished as suddenly as it had appeared.

That, however, was only an unimportant episode, and one that had almost escaped their memories in the press of later and more terrible experiences. It was Tobias Jackson, who, when they found that the *Toad* did not float at flood tide, suggested that the only way to get off was to lighten the cargo. They, therefore, went to work industriously on the contents of one of the rum kegs, and by nightfall, to their unspeakable satisfaction, felt the *Toad* rising and falling beneath them with the motion of the water. Captain

Crum then laid a course for Havre, as straight as he could, allowing always for the hitch round Cape Sable.

From the moment when the *Toad* got fairly afloat the voyage was like a continuous succession of nightmares. After they had cleared the fog the atmosphere became hot and heavy and mysteriously oppressive to the lungs, though the sun was shining brightly and there was, to all appearances, a fine fresh breeze. Sometimes even at noonday the heavens would suddenly turn as dark as pitch while strange phosphorescent lights played around the mast of the *Toad* and the bungholes of the rum kegs. The air seemed to be charged with electricity. One day the compass acted as if possessed with the Devil. As an aid to navigation it was very much worse than useless. The needle swung round and round without any obvious cause, with a rapidity which no one could contemplate without becoming dizzy and bewildered. Captain Crum at last wedged the needle so that it could not move in the box. But as soon as the compass stood still the *Toad* itself began to spin round so viciously that they hastened to release the needle.

On the fourth or fifth day out the wind freshened, and the sloop went bounding over the billows. The deacon and Tobias Jackson were seriously affected by the motion, and retired to the cuddy. Even the captain himself, an old sailor who had weathered many storms, was obliged to succumb to the nausea; but though deadly sick, he held his post at the helm, and kept the bowsprit pointed straight for Havre. The breeze increased to a gale, the waves seemed animated with a merciless desire to overwhelm and swallow up the frail *Toad*, appalling thunders filled the sky, lightnings darted from every square inch of the heavens, and the sloop labored fearfully. In this emergency it became necessary, as a matter of self-preservation, to lighten the cargo still further. The captain, after some trouble, succeeded in arousing his sick and discouraged companions, and all hands went to work on the second keg with an energy born of desperation. Thus the *Toad* outrode the storm.

According to the best recollection of the sorely tried navigators, who about this time lost all reckoning of days and hours and began to measure events by another chronology, it was either in the last quarter of the second keg or the first quarter of the third keg that the sea suddenly became populous with reptiles of vast dimensions and manifestly hostile disposition. Captain Crum, Deacon Silsbee, and Tobias Jackson are agreed in affirming most positively that it was neither whales nor porpoises that they saw. The monsters which crowded the water around the *Toad,* and fairly tumbled over each other in their malignant eagerness to get at and annihilate that little craft, were far larger than any whale, far livelier than any porpoise. They were gigantic, antediluvian creatures of hideous shape, with eyes that shone with malevolent purpose, and voices that bellowed loud enough to strike you dumb with fear. They swam round and round the *Toad,* glaring with hungry eyes upon her unfortunate crew, and lashing the sea with their huge tails until it was foam white as far as sight could reach. In the largest of all these alarming monsters Deacon Silsbee was confident that he identified the terrible beast with seven heads and ten horns mentioned in Revelations.

"It is Beelzebub," whispered the deacon to the captain, as soon as horror allowed him the use of his tongue. "It is the old horned beast himself!"

As if to confirm the deacon's recognition, the air rang with a diabolical laugh, and the principal beast reared its seven heads high out of the water, and bore down directly upon the *Toad,* while all the other beasts gave way.

"The critter come right on," said the deacon afterward in describing the crisis, "and the cap'n and Tobias Jackson flopped down among the kags, limp ez dead flounders. I knew the righteous need not fear, so I stood firm and looked the sarpint squar in the eyes. At this he begun to show symptoms of oneasiness. He hitched an' backed an' sheered off a bit, glarin' at me ez fierce ez ever. I felt encouraged, but bein' a little shaky in the legs, reached down for the tin dipper and began fumblin' at the plug in the bung of one of the kags. This giv him a minnit's advantage, and he swum up close alongside; but I cotched his eye agin, and he stopped short ez if shot. 'Beelzebub, begone!' sez I. 'You are known, and you'd better begone!' 'Ho! Ho!' sez he, in an aggravatin' tone, 'you're known likewise, Deacon Silsbee, an' you'd better put round for Mackerel Cove, if you valley your health. Crost the Atlantic in spite of me, ho! ho!' With that he roars an onearthly roar, and I could feel Tobias Jackson, who was lyin' agin my right leg, shake like a jellyfish."

"How about the cap'n?" asked one of the deacon's audience.

"The cap'n," continued the deacon, "had crawled into the cuddy. It's no discredit to him ez a sailor or ez a man, for the critter's roar was powerful skeerin'. But I, you see, bein' varsed in Scripter and familiar with doctrine, knew the beast's weak pints. 'Beelzebub!' sez I, looking him squar in the eye, 'you may roar and lash, but you can't intimidate me. Resist the Devil and he will flee from you. You old serpent, you adversary, you tormenter, you prince of unholiness, begone! Now git!'"

"And did he git?" inquired one of the deacon's neighbors.

"Not at wunst," said the deacon. "The old liar is dreadf'l subtile. He swam off a few hundred rods in a hesitatin' uncertain fashion and then turned round agin. 'Look here, Deacon Silsbee,' sez he in an insinuatin' voice, 'I come in a friendly, neighborly sperrit, and it's onnecessary fer you to speak so ha'sh. Ez long ez you're bound to crost, and won't be balked of it, I mought ez well give ye a lift an' save ye a sight of trouble. Jest turn your eyes the tother way a jiffy till I git alongside the *Toad*. Then take a double hitch with your tow line round one of my horns and I'll snake ye over to the French coast in less than it takes a cable despatch to crost. That's solid!' 'It's solid,' replied I, waxin' very wrothy, 'that I know you and your lyin' ways. The *Toad* wants none of your unholy towin', Beelzebub. Now git!'

"That time," added the deacon, "he did git. He and all of his ten thousand lesser devils sot up a howl of baffled rage so loud that I thought it would shake the sun out of the sky down on to our heads, and then of a suddin they all dove under. The sea was smooth, the weather fair, with a good, fav'able sou'wester, and the *Toad* seemed to be bowlin' along to the Exposishun. We were so delighted at havin' escaped Satan's wiles that we forgot the commercial featur of the enterprise, and went straight through the third kag, plum into the fourth."

Captain Crum's version of this encounter with the demon monster in mid-ocean agreed substantially with the deacon's, except in one unimportant particular. According to the captain's recollection, it was Deacon Silsbee who sought shelter in the cuddy when Beelzebub began to roar, and he, the captain, who repulsed the arch enemy by the firmness of his demeanor. On being questioned as to the relative accuracy of those two versions, Tobias Jackson privately confessed that the memory of both the captain and the deacon was at fault, and that it was he, Tobias, that had saved the *Toad*. The diabolical fish had swum up to the sloop and seized hold of the gunwale with its huge, talon-like fins, the captain and the deacon had taken refuge below deck, and the destruction of all on board seemed imminent, when Tobias, who alone preserved his presence of mind, grasped a belaying pin that happened to be within reach and beat Beelzebub so lustily about the head and claws that he was glad to relinquish his infernal clutch. This trifling discrepancy in the narratives of the three navigators need not distract attention from the main facts, namely, that Beelzebub did appear, was boldly met, and was put to flight.

As to the remainder of the voyage, there was no disagreement. The navigators again found that they were no match for Beelzebub, who, though defeated in the face to face encounter, was a wily and persevering foe and possessed a great advantage by reason of his unfair and unscrupulous employment of supernatural agencies. If Captain Crum attempted to take an observation of the sun to determine the latitude and longitude of the *Toad*, the sun would not stand still, but at Satan's instigation bobbed and wobbled around the heavens in a manner that made nautical reckoning an impossibility. Nor did the stars at night afford any better data for calculation. They danced about through each other's constellations with utter recklessness of consequences, and all three of the *Toad*'s crew testify that four moons often appeared simultaneously, and the dipper frequently rose in the west and set in the southeast. At times the wind would blow from all points of the compass and the *Toad* would remain stationary for hours, buffeted by conflicting breezes.

Notwithstanding these impediments to a prosperous passage, Captain Crum believes that he finally would have made the coast of France had not Beelzebub resorted to an unexpected and insuperable trick. It was a foul blow to navigation—a blow beneath the belt.

For day after day the *Toad*, to all appearances, had been making good progress and the *Toad*'s crew were well along in the last half of the fourth and last keg. The wind blew steadily abaft, the jib and mainsail drew finely, the water rippled about the bows, and the captain had begun to look sharp ahead for signs of land. By his rough reckoning the *Toad* ought to have been in west longitude 5°40', somewhere off Ushant. At length land appeared—a faint blue line of land—but, to their complete bewilderment, it was neither ahead nor on either beam. It was directly behind the *Toad*, and although by the wind, by the compass, by the swash of waves, and by every other indication known to navigators they were sailing directly away from it, its outlines every moment became more distinct. Captain Crum caught up an empty rum keg (they were all empty now) and threw it overboard. The keg rapidly passed by the *Toad* from stern to stem, disappeared for a second under the bowsprit, and was soon lost in the horizon to the eastward.

The three bold sailors looked at each other with despairing eyes. By this infallible test they knew that the *Toad* was sailing, and had for days been sailing, directly backward, in the teeth of the wind and in the face of all natural laws. It was no use contending against an enemy who had such diabolical resources at his command. Discouraged and sick at heart, they sank down under the weight of their terrible disappointment and knew nothing more until they found themselves on board the porgy steamer *Moonbeam,* steaming up Mackerel Cove. Of the *Toad*'s second grounding upon the Clamshell they knew nothing. It was a singular coincidence, but what event could surprise them now?

Such was the story told of the *Toad*'s voyage to France by the courageous navigators who had fought hard against unearthly odds. The inhabitants of Mackerel Cove, after hearing it attentively, weighing it judicially, and cross-examining closely, are unanimously agreed on three points:

1. That the voyage, although unsuccessful, is highly creditable to the *Toad,* to the *Toad*'s crew, and, by reflex glory, to Mackerel Cove.

2. That Beelzebub, when actuated by motives of spite, is a hard fellow to beat; yet

3. That if the rum had held out long enough, the three navigators would finally have got across and viewed the splendors of the Exhibition in spite of him.

THE DEVILISH RAT

You know that when a man lives in a deserted castle on the top of a great mountain by the side of the river Rhine, he is liable to misrepresentation. Half the good people of the village of Schwinkenschwank, including the burgomaster and the burgomaster's nephew, believed that I was a fugitive from American justice. The other half were just as firmly convinced that I was crazy, and this theory had the support of the notary's profound knowledge of human character and acute logic. The two parties to the interesting controversy were so equally matched that they spent all their time in confronting each other's arguments, and I was left pretty much to myself.

As everybody with the slightest pretension to cosmopolitan knowledge is already aware, the old Schloss Schwinkenschwank is haunted by the ghosts of twenty-nine medieval barons and baronesses. The behavior of these ancient spectres was very considerate. They annoyed me, on the whole, far less than the rats, which swarmed in great numbers in every part of the castle. When I first took possession of my quarters, I was obliged to keep a lantern burning all night, and continually to beat about me with a wooden club in order to escape the fate of Bishop Hatto. Afterward I sent to Frankfort and had made for me a wire cage in which I was able to sleep with comfort and safety as soon as

I became accustomed to the sharp gritting of the rats' teeth as they gnawed the iron in their impotent attempts to get in and eat me.

Barring the spectres and the rats, and now and then a transient bat or owl, I was the first tenant of the Schloss Schwinkenschwank for three or four centuries. After leaving Bonn, where I had greatly profited by the learned and ingenious lectures of the famous Calcarius, Herr Professor of Metaphysical Science in that admirable university, I had selected this ruin as the best possible place for the trial of a certain experiment in psychology. The hereditary *landgraf* Von Toplitz, who owned Schloss Schwinkenschwank, showed no signs of surprise when I went to him and offered six thalers a month for the privilege of lodging in his ramshackle castle. The clerk of a Broadway hotel could not have taken my application more coolly or my money in a more businesslike spirit.

"It will be necessary to pay the first month's rent in advance," said he.

"That I am fortunately prepared to do, my well-born hereditary *landgraf*," I replied, counting out six dollars. He pocketed them and gave me a receipt for the same. I wonder whether he ever tried to collect rent from his ghosts.

The most inhabitable room in the castle was that in the northwest tower, but it was already occupied by the Lady Adelaide Maria, eldest daughter of the Baron von Schotten, and starved to death in the thirteenth century by her affectionate papa for refusing to wed a one-legged freebooter from over the river. As I could not think of intruding upon a lady, I took up my quarters at the head of the south turret stairway, where there was nobody in possession except a sentimental monk, who was out a good deal nights and gave me no trouble at any time.

In such calm seclusion as I enjoyed in the Schloss it is possible to reduce physical and mental activity to the lowest degree consistent with life. St. Pedro of Alcantara, who passed forty years in a convent cell, schooled himself to sleep only an hour and a half a day, and to take food but once in three days. While diminishing the functions of his body to such an extent he must also, I firmly believe, have reduced his soul almost to the negative character of an unconscious infant's. It is exercise, thought, friction, activity, that bring out the individuality of a man's nature. Professor Calcarius' pregnant words remained burned into my memory:

"What is the mysterious link that binds soul to the living body? Why am I Calcarius, or rather why does the soul called Calcarius inhabit this particular organism? [Here the learned professor slapped his enormous thigh with his pudgy hand.] Might not I as well be another, and might not another be I? Loosen the individualized ego from the fleshy surroundings to which it coheres by force of habit and by reason of long contact, and who shall say that it may not be expelled by an act of volition, leaving the living body receptive, to be occupied by some non-individualized ego, worthier and better than the old?"

This profound suggestion made a lasting impression upon my mind. While perfectly satisfied with my body, which is sound, healthy, and reasonably beautiful, I had long been discontented with my soul, and constant contemplation of its weakness, its grossness, its inadequacy, had intensified discontentment to disgust. Could I, indeed, escape myself, could I tear this paste diamond from its fine casket and replace it with a genuine jewel, what sacrifices would I not consent to, and how fervently would I bless Calcarius and the hour that took me to Bonn!

It was to try this untried experiment that I shut myself up in the Schloss Schwinkenschwank.

Excepting little Hans, the innkeeper's son, who climbed the mountain three times a week from the village to bring me bread and cheese and white wine, and afterward Hans's sister, my only visitor during the period of my retirement was Professor Calcarius. He came over from Bonn twice to cheer and encourage me.

On the occasion of his first visit night fell while we were still talking of Pythagoras and metempsychosis. The profound meta-physicist was a corpulent man and very short-sighted.

"I can never get down the hill alive," he cried, wringing his hands anxiously. "I should stumble, and, *Gott in Himmel*, precipitate myself peradventure upon some jagged rock."

"You must stay all night, Professor," said I, "and sleep with me in my wire cage. I should like you to meet my roommate, the monk."

"Subjective entirely, my dear young friend," he said. "Your apparition is a creature of the optic nerve and I shall contemplate it without alarm, as becomes a philosopher."

I put my herr professor to bed in the wire cage and with extreme difficulty crowded myself in by his side. At his especial request I left the lantern burning. "Not that I have any apprehension of your subjective spectres," he explained. "Mere figments of the brain they are. But in the dark I might roll over and crush you."

"How progresses the self-suppression," he asked at length, "the subordination of the individual soul? Eh! What was that?"

"A rat, trying to get in at us," I replied. "Be calm: you are in no peril. My experiment proceeds satisfactorily. I have quite eliminated all interest in the outside world. Love, gratitude, friendship, care for my own welfare and the welfare of my friends have nearly disappeared. Soon, I hope, memory will also fade away, and with my memory my individual past."

"You are doing splendidly!" he exclaimed with enthusiasm, "and rendering to psychologic science an inestimable service. Soon your psychic nature will be a blank, a vacuum, ready to receive—God preserve me! What was that?"

"Only the screech of an owl," said I, reassuringly, as the great gray bird with which I had become familiar fluttered noisily down through an aperture in the roof and lit upon the top of our wire cage.

Calcarius regarded the owl with interest, and the owl blinked gravely at Calcarius.

"Who knows," said the herr professor, "but what that owl is animated by the soul of some great dead philosopher? Perhaps Pythagoras, perhaps Plotinus, perhaps the spirit of Socrates himself abides temporarily beneath those feathers."

I confessed that some such idea had already occurred to me.

"And in that case," continued the professor, "you have only to negative your own nature, to nullify your own individuality, in order to receive into your body this great soul, which, as my intuitions tell me, is that of Socrates, and is hovering around your physical organization, hoping to effect an entrance. Persist, my worthy young student, in your most laudable experiment, and metaphysical science— Merciful heaven! Is that the Devil?"

It was the huge gray rat, my nightly visitor. This hideous creature had grown in his life, perhaps of a century, to the size of a small terrier. His whiskers were perfectly white and very thick. His immense tushes had become so long that they curved over till the points almost impaled his skull. His eyes were big and blood red. The corners of his upper lip were so shriveled and drawn up that his countenance wore an expression of diabolical malignity, rarely seen except in some human faces. He was too old and knowing to gnaw at the wires; but he sat outside on his haunches, and gazed in at us with an indescribable look of hatred. My companion shivered. After a while the rat turned away, rattled his callous tail across the wire netting, and disappeared in the darkness. Professor Calcarius breathed a deep sigh of relief, and soon was snoring so profoundly that neither owls, rats, nor spectres ventured near us till morning.

I had so far succeeded in merging my intellectual and moral qualities in the routine of mere animal existence that when it was time for Calcarius to come again, as he had promised, I felt little interest in his approaching visit. Hansel, who constituted my commissariat, had been taken sick of the measles, and I was dependent for my food and wine upon the coming of his pretty sister Emma, a flaxen-haired maiden of eighteen, who climbed the steep path with the grace and agility of a gazelle. She was an artless little thing, and told me of her own accord the story of her simple love. Fritz was a soldier in the Emperor Wilhelm's army. He was now in garrison at Cologne. They hoped that he would soon get a lieutenancy, for he was brave and faithful, and then he would come home and marry her. She had saved up her dairy money till it amounted to quite a little purse, which she had sent him that it might help purchase his commission. Had I ever seen Fritz? No? He was handsome and good, and she loved him more than she could tell.

I listened to this prattle with the same amount of romantic interest that a proposition in Euclid would excite and congratulated myself that my old soul had so nearly disappeared. Every night the gray owl perched above me. I knew that Socrates was waiting to take possession of my body, and I yearned to open my bosom and receive that grand soul. Every night the detestable rat came and peered through the wires. His cool, contemptuous malice exasperated me strangely. I longed to reach out from beneath my cage and seize and throttle him, but I was afraid of the venom of his bite.

My own soul had by this time nearly wasted away, so to speak, through disciplined disuse. The owl looked down lovingly at me with his great placid eyes. A noble spirit seemed to shine through them and to say, "I will come when you are ready." And I would look back into their lustrous depths and exclaim with infinite yearning, "Come soon, oh Socrates, for I am almost ready!" Then I would turn and meet the devilish gaze of the monstrous rat, whose sneering malevolence dragged me back to earth and to earth's hatreds.

My detestation of the abominable beast was the sole lingering trace of the old nature. When he was not by, my soul seemed to hover around and above my body, ready to take wing and leave it free forever. At his appearance, an unconquerable disgust and loathing undid in a second all that had been accomplished, and I was still myself. To succeed in my experiment I felt that the hateful creature whose presence barred out the grand old philosopher's soul must be dispatched at any cost of sacrifice or danger.

"I will kill you, you loathsome animal!" I shouted to the rat; "and then to my emancipated body will come the soul of Socrates which awaits me yonder."

The rat turned on me his leering eyes and grinned more sardonically than ever. His scorn was more than I could bear. I threw up the side of the wire cage and clutched desperately at my enemy. I caught him by the tail. I drew him close to me. I crunched the bones of his slimy legs, felt blindly for his head, and when I got both hands to his neck, fastened upon his life with a terrible grip. With all the strength at my command, and with all the recklessness of a desperate purpose, I tore and twisted the flesh of my loathsome victim. He gasped, uttered a horrible cry of wild pain, and at last lay limp and quiet in my clutch. Hate was satisfied, my last passion was at an end, and I was free to welcome Socrates.

When I awoke from a long and dreamless sleep, the events of the night before and, indeed, of my whole previous life were as the dimly remembered incidents in a story read years ago.

The owl was gone but the mangled carcass of the rat lay by my side. Even in death his face wore its horrible grin. It now looked like a Satanic smile of triumph.

I arose and shook off my drowsiness. A new life seemed to tingle in my veins. I was no longer indifferent and negative. I took a lively interest in my surroundings and wanted to be out in the world among men, to plunge into affairs and exult in action.

Pretty Emma came up the hill bringing her basket. "I am going to leave you," said I. "I shall seek better quarters than the Schloss Schwinkenschwank."

"And shall you go to Cologne," she eagerly asked, "to the garrison where the Emperor's soldiers are?"

"Perhaps so—on my way to the world."

"And will you go for me to Fritz?" she continued, blushing. "I have good news to send him. His uncle, the mean old notary, died last night. Fritz now has a small fortune and he must come home to me at once."

"The notary," said I slowly, "died last night?"

"Yes, sir; and they say he is black in the face this morning. But it is good news for Fritz and me."

"Perhaps—" continued I, still more slowly "—perhaps Fritz would not believe me. I am a stranger, and men who know the world, like your young soldier, are given to suspicion."

"Carry this ring," she quickly replied, taking from her finger a worthless trinket. "Fritz gave it to me and he will know by it that I trust you."

My next visitor was the learned Calcarius. He was quite out of breath when he reached the apartment I was preparing to leave.

"How goes our metempsychosis, my worthy pupil?" he asked. "I arrived last evening from Bonn, but rather than spend another night with your horrible rodents, I submitted my purse to the extortion of the village innkeeper. The rogue swindled me," he continued, taking out his purse and counting over a small treasure of silver. "He charged me forty groschen for a bed and breakfast."

The sight of the silver, and the sweet clink of the pieces as they came in contact in Professor Calcarius' palm, thrilled my new soul with an emotion it had not yet experienced. Silver seemed the brightest thing in the world to me at that moment, and the acquisition of silver, by whatever means, the noblest exercise of human energy. With a sudden impulse that I was unable to resist, I sprang upon my friend and instructor and wrenched the purse from his hands. He uttered a cry of surprise and dismay.

"Cry away!" I shouted; "it will do no good. Your miserly screams will be heard only by rats and owls and ghosts. The money is mine."

"What's this?" he exclaimed. "You rob your guest, your friend, your guide and mentor in the sublime walks of metaphysical science? What perfidy has taken possession of your soul?"

I seized the herr professor by the legs and threw him violently to the floor. He struggled as the gray rat had struggled. I tore pieces of wire from my cage, and bound him hand and foot so tightly that the wire cut deep into his fat flesh.

"Ho! Ho!" said I, standing over him; "what a feast for the rats your corpulent carcass will make," and I turned to go.

"Good *Gott!*" he cried. "You do not intend to leave me: No one ever comes here."

"All the better," I replied, gritting my teeth and shaking my fist in his face; "the rats will have uninterrupted opportunity to relieve you of your superfluous flesh. Oh, they are very hungry, I assure you, Herr Metaphysician, and they will speedily help you to sever the mysterious link that binds soul to living body. They well know how to loosen the individualized ego from the fleshly surroundings. I congratulate you on the prospect of a rare experiment."

The cries of Professor Calcarius grew fainter and fainter as I made my way down the hill. Once out of hearing I stopped to count my gains. Over and over again, with extraordinary joy, I told the thalers in his purse, and always with the same result. There were just thirty pieces of silver.

My way into the world of barter and profit led me through Cologne. At the barracks I sought out Fritz Schneider of Schwinkenschwank.

"My friend," said I, putting my hand upon his shoulder, "I am going to do you the greatest service which one man may do another. You love little Emma, the innkeeper's daughter?"

"I do indeed," he said. "You bring news of her?"

"I have just now torn myself away from her too ardent embrace."

"It is a lie!" he shouted. "The little girl is as true as gold."

"She is as false as the metal in this trinket," said I with composure, tossing him Emma's ring. "She gave it to me yesterday when we parted."

He looked at the ring and then put both hands to his forehead.

"It is true," he groaned. "Our betrothal ring!" I watched his anguish with philosophical interest.

"See here," he continued, taking a neatly knitted purse from his bosom. "Here is the money she sent to help me buy promotion. Perhaps that belongs to you?"

"Quite likely," I replied, very coolly. "The pieces have a familiar look."

Without another word the soldier flung the purse at my feet and turned away. I heard him sobbing, and the sound was music. Then I picked up the purse and hastened to the nearest café to count the silver. There were just thirty pieces again.

To acquire silver, that is the chief joy possible to my new nature. It is a glorious pleasure, is it not? How fortunate that the soul, which took possession of my body in the Schloss, was not Socrates', which would have made me, at best, a dismal ruminator like Calcarius; but the soul that had dwelt in the gray rat till I strangled him. At one time I thought that my new soul came to me from the dead notary in the village. I know, now, that I inherited it from the rat, and I believe it to be the soul that once animated Judas Iscariot, that prince of men of action.

EXCHANGING THEIR SOULS
Prince Michalskovich and Dr. Harwood's Wonderful Cure

THE STRANGE CONFESSION OF A NEW YORK PHYSICIAN—
A CASE THAT HAS PUZZLED THE MEDICAL
FRATERNITY FOR MANY YEARS PAST

Dr. James Harwood, who died last week, stood for more than twenty years very near the head of the medical profession. His fame extended also to the other side of the water, and when traveling in Europe other celebrated physicians availed themselves of the opportunity of consulting him. On one of his Continental tours, Dr. James Harwood effected a most marvelous cure which soon made the rounds of the papers and helped materially in establishing his world-wide reputation. He succeeded in curing the Russian Prince Michalskovich of an almost hopeless form of monomania. What made the case of such interest to the medical profession was the extraordinary and strange means which the doctor had employed to effect the cure. Dr. James Harwood maintained, verbally and in print, that he had restored the prince to a sound mind by means of mesmerizing him. This occurred about twenty or thirty years ago, and mesmerism was then all the rage, and there were many intelligent persons who fully believed in all the wonderful things told of its power. Naturally, the case formed for a long time a fertile subject for discussion in medical circles and periodicals, and after a while, in view of the high respectability of the practitioner and the testimony corroborating it, the prince's strange case of insanity and Dr. James Harwood's wonderful cure was entered as a fact into the various medical annals and finally found also a place in the textbooks used in our medical schools and colleges.

But scientific men are always somewhat skeptical, and to this day some members of the medical profession continue to look with suspicion upon the doctor's account of the cure.

Six or seven years ago the prince himself paid a visit to this city. He had scarcely looked at his new quarters in the hotel when he was told that two celebrated New York physicians, father and son, begged the favor of an interview. When admitted, the older explained that he was a professor of medicine, and now engaged on an elaborate work on physiology, and that he would feel obliged if the prince would give him a detailed account of his own famous case, to be incorporated in the chapter on insanity. The prince graciously complied and, entering upon every particular connected with his cure, he ascribed it again to the effects of mesmerism. The aged professor thereupon ventured on letting an incredulous smile flit across his face. But the moment the prince had seen and interpreted this treacherous smile, the medical gentleman became aware of having been seized by the coat collar and deposited on the soft carpet of the corridor outside of the prince's door, where his son soon came rushing after him, followed by his hat and cane. There is a rumor in medical circles that this is the reason why the prince's curious case is not mentioned in a recently published great American work on physiology.

The original account of the marvelous cure of the insane prince as Dr. James Harwood first gave it reads as follows:

"I was called to St. Petersburg to examine the case of Prince Michalskovich, who was suffering from a very curious mental affection. I found him raving in a language wholly unknown, at least to the attending physicians and several linguists who had

been invited to his bedside. After having succeeded in allaying
his brain fever, I was in hopes of hearing him resume the use of
Russian, French, or English, in which he was in the habit of conversing, but he persisted in using his unintelligible gibberish.
Otherwise he was quiet and inoffensive. His deportment toward
his numerous serfs and servants was, in fact, wondrously gentle
and courteous while, when sane, he exhibited always to them the
most irascible temper, and treated them habitually brutally and
cruelly. He began to show also an extraordinary preference for
coarse clothing and frugal meats. One day he showed a desire
to leave the palace. I instructed his attendants to give him as
much liberty as possible, and to follow him only at a distance. In
the evening these men reported that the prince had been at work
all day in the shop of a carriage maker. He had gone into the shop
and, without saying a word, had taken hammer and hatchet and
assisted the workmen in making a carriage. The wheelwright
said that he had let the prince have his way because he saw at
once that he was a very skilled laborer. Early in the morning, the
prince was at work again in the wheelwright's shop, and continued there until evening. In a week or two it became perfectly
plain that the prince had the monomania of being nothing but a
simple carriage maker. I tried at first to prevent him from going to
the shop, but seeing that it distracted his mind only more, I consented to let him go on, trusting that something would occur
which would lead his mind back into its proper channels.

"I was very near fixing a day for my return to New York, and
about to decide that the prince was an incurable lunatic, when
my eyes fell on a paragraph in a medical journal speaking of the
case of an insane journeyman in Tiflis, who imagined himself
to be a powerful and wealthy prince. I read the account through
a second time, feeling peculiarly impressed by the singular coin-
cidences that this poor fellow was a carriage maker by trade, and
that, while he had never been heard to speak anything but an
obscure Georgian dialect of Mingrolia, and had always been
known as a low and ignorant peasant, he was now heard in his

ravings to make a fluent and cultured use of Russian, German, French, and English. It was this unexpected talking in foreign languages which had caused this journeyman's case to make the rounds of the papers. I could not help observing that it was exactly the same case as that of Prince Michalskovich, only inverted. The prince wanted to be a wheelwright; the wheelwright wanted to be a prince. The one had given up talking in civilized languages, and talked gibberish; the other had given up his gibberish, and talked Russian, English, and other tongues. Naturally enough I took at once the necessary steps to have the man removed from the Tiflis to the St. Petersburg insane asylum. I claimed him there and found that the correspondence between his case and that of the prince was most surprising. After consulting the family of Prince Michalskovich, I had the fellow taken to the palace with all the pomp and ceremony that was due a prince, just out of sheer curiosity to see what the development would be. He confounded everybody. He took possession of the prince's private apartments as if he had occupied them all of his life. He greeted the parents, relatives, and friends of the prince by name, used the wardrobe, and ordered the servants, as if he were really the prince himself. The grace of his manners and the elegance with which he expressed himself in various languages were most astonishing, and withal he had the build, the hands, and features of a rough artisan. I put him to another test. I confronted him with the veritable prince in the carriage factory. He spoke to the prince patronizingly, even somewhat familiarly, but still preserving always a certain distance and showing at times unmistakable haughtiness. He did not seem to notice the fact that the prince gave him no answer in return to anything he said.

"Thus another week or two passed by, and I had made no progress in the case of the prince, except that instead of one insane man I had now two on my hands. I was again on the point of abandoning the prince when one day a seedy-looking individual paid me a visit and offered to cure the prince instantly if I guaranteed that he should be paid well for his services. A thousand rubles was his price. I made the bargain with him, but put in the condition that I was to be present at every step of the operation.

"At the appointed time I had the prince and the artisan in the palace. The mysterious stranger made me order them to sit side by side as closely as possible. Then he passed his hands over their faces, moving them continually to and fro as if mesmerizing the two men, who soon fell into a state of the most complete unconsciousness which I have ever witnessed. Thereupon he stripped them of every garment on their bodies, continuing all the time his mesmerizing manipulations. Suddenly the prince and the artisan felt simultaneously a heavy shock, after which their bodies lay as rigid as in death.

"'I have caused their spirits to depart from them,' said the stranger, in an explanatory tone. 'Now I shall order the spirit of this one to enter the body of the other, and shall make the spirit of the other come into this body.'

"He stretched out his hands and commanded, 'Now!'

"The very instant he uttered the word the two bodies shook and trembled.

"The stranger then came up to me and said, 'Have you the money ready for me? Take it out, if you please, and hold it in your hand. The moment I order the bodies to move, and you hear the prince talk Russian and see him act like a prince, while the journeyman looks around bewildered and abashed as a peasant would, you will know that I have performed the cure, and you must slip the thousand rubles into my hand. I have not the time to wait another moment. Are you ready? All right, then. Now!'

"Instantly the prince jumped up in full possession of his mind, called in Russian for his servants, and stepped up to me and demanded an explanation of the strange condition in which he had been placed—he was still naked. The Tiflis artisan looked as stupid and terrified as he could. To make the matter short, the stranger had indeed effected a perfect cure; both men were again of a sound mind.

"I turned to the stranger and handed him his thousand rubles, adding that I should like to see him at my hotel and converse with him about the strange methods of his cure. But he shook his head and stole quietly out of the room.

"Mesmerism or no mesmerism," said Dr. James Harwood, in conclusion, "this is the way Prince Michalskovich was cured, and this is all that I have to state in regard to it."

Such was the great sensation of about twenty years ago. The papers were full of it, everybody was full of it, and nobody knew what to make of it. Spiritualists and mesmerizers, of course, were proud of it, and felt triumphant. There was, in fact, no possibility of denying the case. Prince Michalskovich was a well-known character, and his prolonged sickness and final monomania of believing himself a simple carriage maker were well-authenticated facts. Also the Tiflis artisan's sudden and wonderful gift of tongues was attested to by several eminent physicians who had examined and treated him in the early stages of his insanity.

Several years ago, when the doctor was still residing in this city, he was urged by a colleague to come forward with the real facts of the case, and thereby save the honor of the profession as well as his own. The doctor acceded in so far to the demand that he deposited with a friend a full account of the case, taking a solemn promise that the same should not be published before the prince and he himself were dead and buried. This confession is now laid before the world, and though rather strange and unexpected, yet it cannot be said of the doctor that the course he pursued was entirely unjustifiable. He says:

"The medical world will not be very much surprised when they read that I acknowledge the stranger's cure of the prince and the artisan to have been a deception, and that I knew it at the time to have been such, because the whole scene was of my own devising. From the first I have always felt confident that the better class of physicians would not fail to perceive that my making use of a magician to cure an insane man was one of those tricks to which a physician has sometimes to resort in the treatment of the insane, especially of those who are laboring under a great self-deception. But the great credulity of the masses took me by surprise. In a fortnight all the papers had copied the nonsensical account of the prince's cure, and I was at once besieged with thousands of letters from medical men and associations, and everybody I met wanted me to tell him the story over again. I could not do otherwise than give the same version of the case to all inquirers, for in cures of insanity effected by deception it is of the utmost importance that the patient does never discover that his physician only deceived him. Here is a case in point: A merchant once imagined that he had a watch in his head, and that the never-ceasing ticking prevented him from thinking and sleeping. When placed in an asylum, he was told that he had to submit to the very dangerous operation of having the watch got out of his head. He was chloroformed, a deep cut was made into a safe spot, and when he awoke a small blood-stained mechanism was shown and given him with the assurance that it had been taken out of his head. He believed it, and was cured. He resumed his commercial pursuits and made a great fortune.

"But now comes the terrible sequel. One day, after ten or twenty years, he met in the street the physician who had cured him of his insanity. The doctor, attempting to joke with him about the former monomania, said laughingly, 'What a funny fancy that was of yours to think that you carried a watch in your brain. Don't you now sometimes laugh at yourself when you recollect it?'

"The merchant looked at him in surprise. 'Then you did not cut it out of my head! I thought so. I always thought so. I never believed it. I heard it tick all the time just the same. Now put your ear right here. How it ticks! Don't you hear it tick? Tick, tick, tick!'

"The man was insane again. Nothing could cure him now, for nobody could deceive him again.

"I determined to manage my own case better. I resolved to tell my secret to nobody in order to be sure that nobody would tell it again. If a single word of it had at any time crept out, it would have reached the prince by some means or other, sooner or later. Luckily, the mystery was deepened by the strange coincidence of the Tiflis carriage maker, and whenever I could, I drew the attention of medical men away from my trick with the magician to the real and well-authenticated fact of the wonderful similarity and simultaneousness of the insanity of the artisan and the prince. It cannot be denied that the case is one of the most wonderful occurrences in medical practice, and I shall proceed to present it, shorn of everything but what actually happened.

"Prince Michalskovich's nurse was a beautiful Georgian woman whose own child was made his playfellow, and shared his tuition until he was about fourteen years of age. Then the prince went on his travels, and his foster brother returned with his mother to the district of Mingrolia, in Russian Georgia, where he learned the trade of a carriage maker. The prince loved the nurse and his foster brother dearly, and he spent many a season in the Transcaucasian mountains in order to be near them. He was a very active youth, fond of hunting and fishing, and taking delight in mechanical employments, he spent many a day in the wheelwright's shop working at the side of his foster brother.

"Unfortunately the prince fell in love with the same young peasant woman whom his foster brother was about to marry. When the young artisan discovered the unfaithfulness of his betrothed he had a violent scene with the prince and the very day, as misfortune would have it, the young woman died, suddenly and unexpectedly. Her two lovers were then equally wretched. Both left Mingrolia. The wheelwright went to Tiflis and worked there under an assumed name to prevent the prince from finding him again. The prince returned to St. Petersburg and it was soon discovered that he was subject to abnormal fits of melancholia. His yearning for his foster brother, coupled with the unfortunate termination of his love affair, finally developed the peculiar form of insanity already described.

"The young artisan continued at work in Tiflis. He spoke to no one of his past history and formed no friendships among his fellow workmen. The day's work done, he returned at night to his hovel where he spent the remainder of the day in strict seclusion. He became insane, too, imagining on a sudden to be his own foster brother, Prince Michalskovich. This considering one's self to be some great and powerful person is quite a common form of monomania, and hence the artisan's case would hardly have attracted attention if it had not been coupled with his surprising use of foreign languages. He had never been known to speak anything but his peasant dialect, and nobody suspected to think that he was a man of education and refinement. The physician who attended him at once pronounced his case the great marvel of the age. The story of the sudden gift of tongues traveled over the world, and at last reached me also. You know how I sent for the young man and finally took him into the palace. He was instantly recognized as the foster brother of the prince. One day he startled me by inquiring for his brother Paul. I perceived at once that his reason was dawning again, and by careful treatment I succeeded in restoring him to his senses.

When I told him of the prince's mental malady and of the wonderful coincidence of his own, the young man's affection for the prince revived and he was full of ardor to assist me to set up the situation by which I hoped to bring about a cure. In the course of a conversation he told me one day some anecdotes illustrative of the gross superstition of the prince. He mentioned, among other things, the prince's strong faith in the transmigration of souls, and his firm belief in the pretensions of persons like Cagliostro or Joseph Balsamo. I saw at once an opportunity for another experiment, and I quickly concocted the scene with the magician which I described. When the prince came to his senses again, he listened to my account of his wonderful cure by the mysterious stranger in perfect good faith, and when he saw his foster brother and heard him say that he had also been cured that very moment, he was perfectly satisfied, and acted again the sane man.

"The notoriety which the prince attained through the widespread accounts of his wonderful cure flattered him very much, and if anybody had insinuated to him that he had been duped, he would have regarded it as a great insult. It is rumored that some New York physician was made to feel his wrath when he called on the prince and wished him to understand that he believed that I had only deceived him. Of course, if somebody had told the prince that he had heard me say that his cure was effected simply by a medical trick, the consequences would have been of a very serious nature."

Such is Dr. James Harwood's confession. Does it justify him?

THE CASE OF THE DOW TWINS

"My notions about soul's influence on soul," said Dr. Richards of Saturday Cove to me one day last September, "are a little peculiar. I don't make a practice of giving 'em away to the folks around here. The cove people hold that when a doctor gets beyond jalap and rhubarb he's trespassing on the parson's property. Now it's a long road from jalap to soul, but I don't see why one man mightn't travel as well as another. Will you oblige me with a clam?"

I obliged him with a clam. We were sitting together on the rocks, fishing for tomcod. Saturday Cove is a small watering place a few miles below Belfast, on the west shore of Penobscot bay. It apparently derives its name from a belief, generally entertained by the covers, that this spot was the final and crowning achievement of the Creator before resting on the seventh day. The cove village consists of a hotel, two churches, several stores, and a graveyard containing former generations of Saturdarians. It is a favorite gibe among outsiders, who envy the placid quiet of the place, that if the population of the graveyard should be dug up and distributed through the village, and the present inhabitants laid away beneath the sod, there would be no perceptible diminution in the liveliness of the settlement. The cove proper abounds with tomcod, which may be caught with clams.

"Yes," continued Dr. Richards, as he forced the barb of his jig hook into the tender organism of the clam, "my theory is that a strong soul may crowd a weak soul out of the body which belongs to the weak soul and operate through that body, even though miles away and involuntarily. I believe, moreover, that a man may have two souls, one his own by right and the other an intruder. In fact I know that this is so and it being so what becomes of your moral responsibility? What, I ask, becomes of your moral responsibility?"

I replied that I could not imagine.

"Your doctrine of moral responsibility," said the doctor sternly, as if it were my doctrine and I were responsible for moral responsibility, "isn't worth this tomcod." And he took a small fish off his hook and contemptuously tossed it back into the cove. "Did you ever hear of the case of the Dow twins?"

I had never heard of the case of the Dow twins.

"Well," resumed the doctor, "they were born into the family of Hiram Dow, thirty years or more ago, in the red farmhouse just over the hill back of us. My predecessor, old Dr. Gookin, superintended their birth, and has often told me the circumstances. The Dow twins came into the world bound back to back by a fleshy ligature which extended half the length of the spinal processes. They would probably have traveled through life in an intimate juxtaposition had the matter depended on your great city surgeons—your surgeons who were afraid to disconnect Chang and Eng, and who discussed the operation till the poor fellows died without parting company. Old Dr. Gookin, however, who hadn't attempted anything for years in the surgical line, more than to pull a tooth or to cut out an occasional wen, calmly went to work and sharpened up his rusty old operating knife and slashed and gashed the twins apart before they had been three hours breathing. This promptitude of Gookin's saved the Dow twins a good deal of inconvenience."

"I should think so."

"And yet," added the doctor, reflectively, "perhaps it might have been better for 'em both if they hadn't been separated. Better for Jehiel, especially, since he wouldn't have been put in a false position. Then, on the other hand, my theory would have lacked the confirmation of an illustrative example. Do you want the story?"

"By all means."

"Well, Jacob and Jehiel grew up healthy, strapping boys, like as two peas physically, but not mentally and morally. Jehiel was all Dow—slow, slow-witted, melancholy inclined, and disposed to respect the Ten Commandments. Jake, he had his mother's git-up-and-git—she was a Fox of Fox Island—and was into mischief from the time he was tall enough to poke burdock burrs down his grandmother's back. Dr. Gookin watched the development of the twins with great interest. He used to say that there was an invisible nerve telegraph between Jake and Jehiel. Jehiel seemed to sense whenever Jacob was up to any of his pranks. One night, for instance, when Jake was off robbing a hen roost, Jehiel sat up in bed in his sleep and crowed like a frightened cock until the whole family was aroused.

"I came here and opened my office about ten years ago. At that time Jehiel had grown into a steady, tolerably industrious young man, prominent in the Congregational Church, and so sober and decorous that the village people had trusted him with the driving of the town hearse. When I first knew him he was courting a young woman by the name of Giles, who lived about seven miles out in the country. Jehiel was a tin knocker by trade, and a more pious, respectable, reliable tin knocker you never saw.

"Jake had turned out very differently. By the time he was twenty-one he had made Saturday Cove too hot to hold him, and everybody, including his twin Jehiel, was glad when he enlisted in a Maine regiment. I never saw Jake in my life, for I came here after he had departed, but I had a pretty good notion of what a reckless, loud-mouthed, harum-scarum reprobate he must have been. After the war he drifted into the western country, and we heard of him occasionally, first as a steamboat runner at St. Louis, then in jail at Jefferson for swindling a blind Dutchman, then as a gambler and rough in Cheyenne, and finally as a debt beat in Frisco. You could tell pretty well when Jake was in deviltry by watching the actions of Jehiel. At such times, Jehiel was restless. Knocked tin with an uneasy impatience that wasn't natural with him, was as solemn and glum as an undertaker.

He was impatient and short to the people of Saturday Cove, and evidently had to struggle hard to be good. It seemed as if Dr. Gookin's knife had severed the physical bond but not the mental one.

"The strangest thing of all was in regard to Jehiel's attentions to the young woman named Giles. She was a sober, demure, church-going person, whom Jacob had never been able to interest, but who, as everybody said, would make an excellent helpmate for Jehiel. He seemed to care a good deal for her in his steady, slow way and made a point twice a week of driving over to bring her to prayer-meeting at the cove. But when one of his odd spells was on him he forsook her altogether, and weeks would go by, to her great distress, without his appearing at the Giles gate. As Jake went from bad to worse these periods of indifference became more frequent and prolonged, and occasioned the young woman named Giles much misery and a good many tears.

"One fine afternoon in the summer of 1871, Jacob Dow, as we afterward learned, was shot through the heart by a Mexican in a drunken row at San Diego. He sprang high into the air and fell upon his face, and when they laid him away a good Catholic priest said mass for the repose of his soul.

"That same afternoon, as it happened, old Dr. Gookin was to have been buried in the graveyard yonder. He had died a day or two before, at an extreme age, but in the full possession of his faculties, and one of the last remarks he made was to express regret that he would be unable to follow the career of the Dow twins any further.

"It became Jehiel's melancholy duty to harness up his hearse on account of old Dr. Gookin's funeral, and as he dusted the plumes and polished the ebony panels of the vehicle, his thoughts naturally recurred to the great service which that excellent physician had rendered him in early youth. Then he thought of his twin brother Jacob, and wondered where he was and how he prospered. Then his eyes wandered over the hearse, and he felt a dull pride in its creditable appearance. It looked so bright and shiny in the sun that he resolved, as it still wanted a couple of hours of the time appointed for the funeral, to drive it over to the Giles farm and fetch his sweetheart to the village on the box with him. The young woman named Giles had frequently ridden with Jehiel on the hearse, her demure features and sober apparel detracting nothing from the respectable solemnity of the equipage.

"Jehiel drew up in state to the door of his betrothed, and she, not at all reluctant to enjoy the mild excitement of a funeral, mounted to the box and settled herself comfortably beside him. Then they started for Saturday Cove, and jogged along on the hearse, discoursing affectionately as they went.

"Miss Giles affirms that it was at the third apple tree next the stone wall of Hosea Getchell's orchard, just opposite the bars leading to Mr. Lord's private road, that a sudden and most extraordinary change came over Jehiel. He jumped, she says, high into the air and landed sprawling in the sandy road alongside the hearse, yelling so hideously that it was with difficulty that she held the frightened horses. Picking himself up and uttering a round oath (something that had never before passed the virtuous lips of Jehiel), he turned his attention to the horses, kicking and beating them until they stood quiet. He next proceeded to cut and trim a willow switch at the roadside, and putting his decent silk hat down over one eye, and darting from the other a surly glance at the astonished Miss Giles, he climbed to his seat on the hearse.

"'Jehiel Dow!' said she, 'what does this mean?'

"'It means,' he replied, giving the horses a vicious cut with his switch, 'that I have been goin' slow these thirty year, and now I'm goin' to put a little ginger in my gait. Gelang!'

"The hearse horses jumped under the unaccustomed lash and broke into a gallop. Jehiel applied the switch again and again, and the dismal vehicle was soon bumping over the road at a tremendous pace, Jehiel shouting all the time like a circus rider, and Miss Giles clinging to his side in an agony of terror. The people in the farmhouses along the way rushed to doors and windows and gazed in amazement at the unprecedented spectacle. Jehiel had a word for each—a shout of derision for one, a blast of blasphemy for another, and an invitation to ride for a third—but he reined in for nobody, and in a twinkling the five miles between Hosea Getchell's farm at Duck Trap at the village at Saturday Cove had been accomplished. I think I am safe in saying that never before did hearse rattle over five miles of hard road so rapidly.

"'Oh, Jehiel, Jehiel!' said Miss Giles, as the hearse entered the village, 'are you took crazy of a sudden?'

"'No,' said Jehiel curtly, 'but my eyes are open now. Gelang, you beasts! You get out here; I'm going to Belfast.'

"'But, Jehiel, dear,' she protested, with many sobs, 'remember Dr. Gookin.'

"'Dang Gookin!' said Jehiel.

"'And for my sake,' she continued. 'Dear Jehiel, for my sake.'

"'Dang you, too!' said Jehiel.

"Drawing up his team in magnificent style before the village hotel, he compelled the weeping Miss Giles to alight, and then, with an admirable imitation of the war whoop of a Sioux brave, started his melancholy vehicle for Belfast, and was gone in a flash, leaving the entire population of Saturday Cove in a state of bewilderment that approached coma.

"The remains of the worthy Dr. Gookin were borne to the graveyard that afternoon upon the shoulders of half a dozen of the stoutest farmers in the neighborhood. Jehiel came home long after midnight, uproariously intoxicated. The revolution in his character had been as complete as it was sudden. From the moment of Jacob's death, he was a dissipated, dishonest scoundrel, the scandal of Saturday Cove, and the terror of quiet respectable folks for miles around. After that day he never could be persuaded to speak to or even to recognize the young woman named Giles. She, to her credit, remained faithful to the memory of the lost Jehiel. His downward course was rapid. He gambled, drank, quarreled, and stole; and he is now in state prison at Thomaston, serving out a sentence for an attempt to rob the Northport Bank. Miss Giles goes down every year in the hopes that he will see her, but he always refuses. He is in for ten years."

"And he, does he feel no remorse for what he did?" I asked.

"See here," said Dr. Richards, turning suddenly and looking me square in the face. "Do you think of what you are saying? Now I hold that he is as innocent as you or I. I believe that the souls of the twins were bound by a bond which Dr. Gookin's knife could not dissect. When Jacob died, his soul, with all its depravity, returned to its twin soul in Jehiel's body. Being stronger than the Jehiel soul it mastered and overwhelmed it. Poor Jehiel is not responsible; he is suffering the penalty of a crime that was clearly Jake's."

My friend spoke with a good deal of earnestness and some heat, and concluding that Jehiel's personality was submerged. I did not press the discussion. That evening, in conversation with the village clergyman, I remarked:

"Strange case that of the Dow twins."

"Ah," said the parson, "you have heard the story. Which way did the doctor end it?"

"Why, with Jehiel in jail, of course. What do you mean?"

"Nothing," replied the parson with a faint smile. "Sometimes when he feels well disposed toward humanity, the doctor lets Jehiel's soul take possession of Jacob and reform him into a pious, respectable Christian. In his pessimistic moods, the story is just as you heard it. So this is one of his Jacob days. He should take a little vacation."

AN EXTRAORDINARY WEDDING

Professor Daniel Dean Moody of Edinburgh, a gentleman equally well known as a profound psychologist and as an honest and keen-eyed investigator of the phenomena sometimes called spiritualistic, visited this country not many months ago and was entertained in Boston by Dr. Thomas Fullerton at his delightful home on Mount Vernon Street. One evening when there were present in Dr. Fullerton's parlors, besides himself and his Scotch guest, Dr. Curtis of the medical school of the Boston University, the Reverend Dr. Amos Cutler of the Lynde Street Church, Mr. Magnus of West Newton, three ladies, and the writer, the conversation turned to subjects of an occult character.

"There once lived in Aberdeen," said Professor Moody, "a medium named Jenny McGraw, of slender intellectuality, but of remarkable psychic strength. Two hundred years ago you good people of Boston would have hanged Jenny for a witch. I have seen in her cottage materialization for which I could not and cannot account by any hypothesis of deception or of hallucination. I have seen forms come forth, not from any cabinet or trick closet, but extruded before my eyes from the person of Jenny herself, hanging nebulous in the air for a moment and then slowly taking corporate shape. That there was no vulgar trick about this I am willing to stake my scientific reputation. One night Plato himself, or an eidolon claiming to be Plato, emerged from Jenny McGraw's bosom and conversed with me for full fifteen minutes upon the duality of the idea, the medium, in the meanwhile, remaining entranced."

Dr. Fullerton exchanged a significant glance with his wife. Their guest intercepted it and said:

"You don't believe me? No wonder."

"Not that," rejoined Dr. Fullerton. "Your testimony as a scientific observer is worthy of all possible respect. But what became of Jenny McGraw?"

"She was a dull, unsympathetic young woman, hardly to be classed as a rational being. So far from becoming interested in these wonderful manifestations exhibited through her organization, she was excessively annoyed by them, and I believe she finally left Scotland to escape the troublesome spirits and the still more troublesome mortals who flocked to her cottage and sadly interfered with her washing, ironing, and baking."

"A Yankee girl," said Mr. Magnus, "would have turned such powers to account and have made her fortune."

"Jenny McGraw," replied Professor Moody, "whom I believe to be the only medium in the world capable of producing materializations in the broad light and independently of her surroundings, was thrifty enough, like all Scotchwomen, but she hadn't the intelligence to recognize the opportunity. She was frequently advised to go before the public. Advice is wasted on the Scotch. I don't know where she is at present."

Dr. Fullerton again glanced at his wife. Mrs. Fullerton arose and touched a bell.

The door soon opened, and there appeared a lumpy, red-haired domestic, who curtsied awkwardly as she entered the room.

"Did ye rang, ma'am?" she asked.

"Jenny," said Mrs. Fullerton, "here is an old friend of yours from Scotland."

The girl showed no sign of surprise. Scarcely a shade of recognition passed over her stupid countenance as she walked sullenly up to the professor and sullenly took his extended hand.

"I didna ken ye was cam to America, Maister Moody," she said, and looked around as if she would be glad to escape the learned company.

"Now, with your permission, Mrs. Fullerton," said the professor, looking over Jenny McGraw's shoulder toward his hostess, "we will ask the young woman if she will kindly assist us in an investigation which we purpose to make."

Jenny looked up suspiciously and turned her small, dull eyes from her master to her mistress, and from her mistress to the door.

"I'm na ower fond of sic investigatin'," she stolidly remarked, "an' it gies me a pain in the breast to brang oot the auld ghaists, as ye na doot remember wull, Maister Moody."

For a long time the girl stubbornly refused to renew her relations with the mysterious yonder. I have forgotten what argument or plea it was that at last won her to a reluctant consent. I have not forgotten what followed.

The room was as light as the full blaze of five gas jets could make it. Under this blaze, and surrounded by the partly amused, partly skeptical company, Jenny was seated in a Turkish easy chair. She did not form an attractive picture, short, squat, sandy, freckled, and peevish-eyed as she was. "Good Lord!" I whispered to a neighbor. "Do glorified spirits choose such a channel as that when they wish to come back to us?"

"Hush!" said Professor Moody. "The girl is passing into a trance."

The swinish eyes opened and closed. A sluggish convulsion fluttered across the flabby cheeks. A sigh or two, a nervous twitching of her chair, breathing heavily.

"Ineffectively simulated coma," whispered Dr. Curtis to me, "and *not* the work of an artist. This is a farce."

For fifteen or twenty minutes we sat in patience, the stillness broken only by the rough respiration of the girl. Then one or two of the party began to yawn, and the hostess, fearing that the experiment was becoming a bore, moved as if to break up the circle. But Professor Moody raised his hand in protest. Before he dropped it he made a rapid gesture which directed all our eyes toward Jenny McGraw.

Her head and bust seemed to be enveloped in a dim, thin film of opalescent vapor, which floated free about her, yet was fixed at one point, as a wreath of blue smoke hangs at the end of a good cigar. The point of attachment appeared to be in the neighborhood of Jenny's heart. She had stopped breathing loudly, and was as pale as the dead; but her face was no whiter than that of Dr. Curtis. I felt his hand groping for mine. He found it and clutched it till it was numb.

While we watched, the vapor that proceeded from Jenny's bosom grew in volume and became opaque. It was like a dark, well-defined cloud, floating before our eyes, here gathering itself in and extending itself there, till at last the shape was perfect.

You have seen a dim, meaningless object under a lens gradually define itself as it was brought into focus, and suddenly stand out clear and sharp. Or, better, you have seen at a shadow pantomime a vague, amorphous cloudiness intensify and take shape as the person approached the screen, until it became a perfect silhouette. Now, imagine the silhouette stepping forth into your presence a solidified fact, and you get some idea of the marvelous transition by which this shadow from a world we know not of stepped forth into the midst of our little company.

I looked across the room at the Reverend Dr. Cutler. He was clasping his forehead with both hands. I have never seen a more striking picture of mingled horror, terror, and perplexity.

The newcomer was a man of twenty-eight or thirty, of fine features and dignified bearing. He made a courteous bow to the assemblage, but when he saw that Professor Moody was about to speak put his finger to his lips and glanced back uneasily at the medium. I fancied that an expression of disgust stole over his handsome countenance when he perceived how unlovely was the gateway through which he had returned to earth. Nevertheless, he kept his eyes fixed upon Jenny McGraw's pallid face and folded his arms as if waiting.

We were now thoroughly under the spell of this mysterious happening. With eager expectation, but without surprise, we saw again the phenomena of the cloud, the shadow, the concentration, and the presence.

Slowly out of the white mist and nebulous shadow there took form the most beautiful woman that mortal eyes ever beheld. It *was* a woman—a living, breathing woman, her magnificent lips slightly parted, her bosom rising and falling beneath a garment of wonderfully woven texture, her glorious black eyes shining upon us till our heads swam and our thoughts reeled. It would be easier to fathom the secret of her being than to describe the unearthly beauty that startled and awed us.

The first comer unfolded his arms, and with the tenderness of a lover and the deference due a queen, took the shapely white hand of the marvelous lady and led her forth to the middle of the room. She said no word, but suffered herself to be guided by his hand, and stood like an empress scanning our faces and habiliments with a puzzled curiosity in which it was possible to detect the slightest trace of disdain. He spoke at last in a low voice.

"Friends," he slowly said, "a great love carried one who was lately a mortal into the presence of a goddess. A greater good fortune befell him than his small sacrifices had earned. I cannot speak more plainly. Hear our entreaty and grant it without questioning. There is here a servant of the church, duly qualified to pronounce the only words that can crown a love like mine. That love reached back over centuries to meet its object, and was sealed by a willing death. We come from another world to ask to be joined in wedlock according to the forms of this world."

Strange as it may seem, the preceding events had so attuned our consciousness to the spirit of the surroundings that we heard this extraordinary speech without amazement. And when Mr.

Magnus of West Newton, who would preserve his cool, matter-of-fact manner in the company of archangels, audibly whispered, "Eloped, by Jove, from the spirit land!" His words jarred harshly in our ears.

The Reverend Dr. Amos Cutler displayed most strikingly the effect of the glamor that had been thrown over our nineteenth-century common sense. That pious man rose from his chair with a dazed and helpless look in his face, and, like one walking in his sleep, advanced toward the couple.

Raising his hand to command silence, he solemnly and deliberately asked the questions that by usage of the church are preliminary to the marriage rite. The man responded in a clear, triumphant tone. The bride answered only by a slight inclination of her beautiful head.

"Then," continued Dr. Cutler, "in the presence of these witnesses, I pronounce you man and wife. And God forgive me," he added, "for lending myself to the Devil's works by the sacrilege of this act."

One by one we passed up to take the bridegroom's hand and salute the bride. His hand was like the hand of a marble statue, but a radiant smile brightened his face. At a whispered suggestion from him, she bent her regal head, and allowed each one of us to kiss her cheek. It was soft and blood-warm.

When Dr. Cutler saluted her she smiled for the first time and, with a rapid, graceful movement detached from her black hair a great pearl and put it in his hand. He gazed at it a moment and, then on a sudden impulse, flung it into the open grate. In the hot blaze, Dr. Cutler's wedding fee whitened, calcined, crumbled, and disappeared.

Then the bridegroom led his wife back to the chair where the medium still sat entranced. He clasped her close in his arms. Their melting forms interblended in shadowy vapor, and, fading slowly away, this newly married couple found their nuptial pillow in the bosom of Jenny McGraw.

II

One day after Professor Moody had left Boston, I went to the Athaeneum Library in search of certain facts and dates regarding the Franco-Prussian war. While turning over the leaves of a bound file of the London DAILY NEWS for 1871 my eyes happened to fall upon the following paragraph:

The Vienna FREIE PRESSE says that at four o'clock in the afternoon of July 12 a young man of good appearance shot himself through the heart in the east corridor of the Imperial Gallery. It was at the hour of closing the gallery, and the young man had been warned by an attendant that he must depart. He was standing motionless before Herr Hans Makart's fine picture of "Cleopatra's Barge," and paid no heed to the admonition. When it was repeated more emphatically he pointed in an absent manner to the painting, and having remarked, "Is not that a woman worth dying for!" drew a pistol and fired with fatal effect.

There is no clue to the suicide's individuality except that afforded at the Golden Lamb Hotel, where he was registered simply as "Cotton." He had been in Vienna several weeks, had spent money freely, and had frequently been observed at the Imperial Gallery, always before this picture of Cleopatra. The unfortunate youth is believed to have been insane.

I made a careful copy of this brief story, and sent it, without comment, to the Reverend Dr. Cutler. A day or two later he returned it with a note.

"The events of that night at Dr. Fullerton's," he wrote, "are to me as the events of a dimly remembered dream. Pardon me if I say that it will be a kindness to let me forget them altogether."

BACK FROM THAT BOURNE
Practical Working of Materialization in Maine

A STRANGE STORY FROM POCOCK ISLAND—
A MATERIALIZED SPIRIT THAT WILL NOT GO BACK—
THE FIRST GLIMPSE OF WHAT MAY YET CAUSE
VERY EXTENSIVE TROUBLE IN THE WORLD

We are permitted to make extracts from a private letter which bears the signature of a gentleman well known in business circles, and whose veracity we have never heard called in question. His statements are startling and well nigh incredible, but, if true, they are susceptible of easy verification. Yet the thoughtful mind will hesitate about accepting them without the fullest proof, for they spring upon the world a social problem of stupendous importance. The dangers apprehended by Mr. Malthus and his followers become remote and commonplace by the side of this new and terrible issue.

The letter is dated at Pocock Island, a small township in Washington County, Maine, about seventeen miles from the mainland, and nearly midway between Mt. Desert and the Grand Manan. The last state census accords to Pocock Island a population of 311, mostly engaged in the porgy fisheries. At the presidential election of 1872 the island gave Grant a majority of three. These two facts are all that we are able to learn of the locality from sources outside of the letter already referred to.

The letter, omitting certain passages which refer solely to private matters, reads as follows:

"But enough of the disagreeable business that brought me here to this bleak island in the month of November. I have a singular story to tell you. After our experience together at Chittenden I know you will not reject statements because they are startling.

"My friend, there is upon Pocock Island a materialized spirit which [or who] refuses to be dematerialized. At this moment and within a quarter of a mile from me as I write, a man who died and was buried four years ago, and who has exploited the mysteries beyond the grave, walks, talks, and holds intercourse with the inhabitants of the island, and is, to all appearances, determined to remain permanently upon this side of the river. I will relate the circumstances as briefly as I can.

JOHN NEWBEGIN

"In April 1870, John Newbegin died and was buried in the little cemetery on the landward side of the island. Newbegin was a man of about forty-eight, without family or near connections, and eccentric to a degree that sometimes inspired questions as to his sanity. What money he had earned by many seasons' fishing upon the banks was invested in quarters of two small mackerel schooners, the remainder of which belonged to John Hodgdon, the richest man on Pocock, who was estimated by good authorities to be worth thirteen or fourteen thousand dollars.

"Newbegin was not without a certain kind of culture. He had read a good deal of the odds and ends of literature, and, as a simple-minded islander expressed it in my hearing, 'knew more bookfuls than anybody else on Pocock.' He was naturally an intelligent man; and he might have attained influence in the community had it not been for his utter aimlessness of character, his indifference to fortune, and his consuming thirst for rum.

"Many yachtsmen, who have had occasion to stop at Pocock for water or for harbor shelter during eastern cruises, will remember a long, listless figure, astonishingly attired in blue army pants, rubber boots, loose toga made of some bright chintz material, and very bad hat, staggering through the little settlement, followed by a rabble of jeering brats, and pausing to strike uncertain blows at those within reach of the dead sculpin which he usually carried around by the tail. This was John Newbegin."

HIS SUDDEN DEATH

"As I have already remarked, he died four years ago last April. The *Mary Emmeline*, one of the little schooners in which he owned, had returned from the eastward, and had smuggled, or 'run in,' a quantity of St. John brandy. Newbegin had a solitary and protracted debauch. He was missed from his accustomed walks for several days, and when the islanders broke into the hovel where he lived, close down to the seaweed, and almost within reach of the incoming tide, they found him dead on the floor, with an emptied demijohn hard by his head.

"After the primitive custom of the island, they interred John Newbegin's remains without coroner's inquest, burial certificate, or funeral services, and, in the excitement of a large catch of porgies that summer, soon forgot him and his friendless life. His interest in the *Mary Emmeline* and the *Puttyboat* recurred to John Hodgdon; and as nobody came forward to demand an administration of the estate, it was never administered. The forms of the law are but loosely followed in some of these marginal localities."

HIS REAPPEARANCE AT POCOCK

"Well, my dear ——, four years and four months had brought their quota of varying seasons to Pocock Island, when John Newbegin reappeared, under the following circumstances:

"In the latter part of last August, as you may remember, there was a heavy gale all along our Atlantic coast. During this storm the squadron of the Naugatuck Yacht Club, which was returning from a summer cruise as far as Campobello, was forced to take shelter in the harbor to the leeward of Pocock Island. The gentlemen of the club spent three days at the little settlement ashore. Among the party was Mr. R.——E.——, in which name you will recognize a medium of celebrity, and one who has been particularly successful in materializations. At the desire of his companions, and to relieve the tedium of their detention, Mr. E.—— improvised a cabinet in the little schoolhouse at Pocock, and gave a séance, to the delight of his fellow yachtsmen and the utter bewilderment of such natives as were permitted to witness the manifestations.

"The conditions seemed unusually favorable to spirit appearances, and the séance was, upon the whole, perhaps the most remarkable that Mr. E.—— ever held. It was all the more remarkable because the surroundings were such that the most prejudiced skeptic could discover no possibility of trickery.

"The first form to issue from the wood closet which constituted the cabinet, when Mr. E.—— had been tied therein by a committee of old sailors from the yachts, was that of an Indian chief who announced himself as Hock-a-mock, and who retired after dancing a 'Harvest moon' *pas seul* and declaring himself, in very emphatic terms, opposed to the present Indian policy of the Administration. Hock-a-mock was succeeded by the aunt of one of the yachtsmen, who identified herself beyond question by allusion to family matters and by displaying the scar of a burn upon her left arm, received while making tomato catsup upon earth. Then came successively a child whom no one present recognized, a French-Canadian who could not talk English, and a portly gentleman who introduced himself as William King, first governor of Maine. These in turn re-entered the cabinet, and were seen no more.

"It was some time before another spirit manifested itself, and

Mr. E.—— gave directions that the light be turned down still further. Then the door of the wood closet was slowly opened and a singular figure in rubber boots and a species of Dolly Varden garment emerged, bringing a dead fish in his right hand."

HIS DETERMINATION TO REMAIN

"The city men who were present, I am told, thought that the medium was masquerading in grotesque habiliments for the more complete astonishment of the islanders, but these latter rose from their seats and exclaimed with one consent: 'It is John Newbegin! It is Johnny for sartain!' And then, in not unnatural terror at the apparition, they turned and fled from the schoolroom, uttering dismal cries.

"John Newbegin came calmly forward and turned up the solitary kerosene lamp that shed uncertain light over the proceedings. He then sat down in the teacher's chair, folded his arms, and looked complacently around him.

"'You might as well untie the medium,' he at length remarked. 'I propose to remain in the materialized condition.'

"And he did remain. When the party left the schoolhouse among them walked John Newbegin, as truly a being of flesh and blood as any man of them. From that day to this he has been a living inhabitant of Pocock Island, eating, drinking (water only), and sleeping after the manner of men. The yachtsmen, who made sail for Bar Harbor the very next morning, probably believe that he was a fraud hired for the occasion by Mr. E.——. But the people of Pocock, who laid him out, dug his grave, and put him into it four years ago, know that John Newbegin has come back to them from a land they know not of."

A SINGULAR MEMBER OF SOCIETY

"The idea of having a ghost—somewhat more condensed, it is true, than the traditional ghost—as a member was not at first over-pleasing to the 311 inhabitants of Pocock Island. To this day they are a little sensitive upon the subject, feeling evidently that if the matter got abroad, it might injure the sale of the really excellent porgy oil which is the product of their sole manufacturing interest. This reluctance to advertise the skeleton in their closet, superadded to the slowness of these obtuse, fishy, matter-of-fact people to recognize the transcendent importance of the case, must be accepted as an explanation of the fact that John Newbegin's spirit has been on earth between three and four months, and yet the singular circumstance is not known to the whole country.

"But the Pocockians have at last come to see that a spirit is not necessarily a malevolent spirit, and, accepting his presence as a fact in their stolid, unreasoning way, they are quite neighborly and sociable with Mr. Newbegin.

"I know that your first question will be: 'Is there sufficient proof of his ever having been dead?' To this I answer unhesitatingly, 'Yes.' He was too well known a character and too many people saw the corpse to admit of any mistake on this point. I may here add that it was at one time proposed to disinter the original remains, but that the project was abandoned in deference to the wishes of Mr. Newbegin, who feels a natural delicacy about having his first set of bones disturbed from motives of mere curiosity."

AN INTERVIEW WITH A DEAD MAN

"You will readily believe that I took occasion to see and converse with John Newbegin. I found him affable and even communicative. He is perfectly well aware of his doubtful status as a being, but is in hopes that at some future time there may be legislation which shall correctly define his position and the position of any spirit who may follow him into the material world. The only point upon which he is reticent is his experience during the four years that elapsed between his death and his reappearance at Pocock. It is to be presumed that the memory is not a pleasant one; at least he never speaks of this period. He candidly admits, however, that he is glad to get back to earth, and that he embraced the very first opportunity to be materialized.

"Mr. Newbegin says that he is consumed with remorse for the wasted years of his previous existence. Indeed, his course during the past three months would show that this regret is genuine. He has discarded his eccentric costume, and dresses like a reasonable spirit. He has not touched liquor since his reappearance. He has embarked in the porgy oil business, and his operations already rival those of Hodgdon, his old partner in the *Mary Emmeline* and the *Puttyboat*. By the way, Newbegin threatens to sue Hodgdon for his undivided quarter in each of these vessels, and this interesting case therefore bids fair to be thoroughly investigated in the courts.

"As a businessman he is generally esteemed on the island, although there is a noticeable reluctance to discount his paper at long dates. In short, Mr. John Newbegin is a most respectable citizen [if a dead man can be a citizen], and has announced his intention of running for the next legislature!"

IN CONCLUSION

"And now, my dear ——. I have told you the substance of all I know respecting this strange, strange case. Yet, after all, why so strange? We accepted materialization at Chittenden. Is this any more than the logical issue of that admission? If the spirit may return to earth, clothed in flesh and blood and all the physical attributes of humanity, why may it not remain on earth as long as it sees fit?

"Thinking of it from whatever standpoint, I cannot but regard John Newbegin as the pioneer of a possibly large immigration from the spirit world. The bars once down, a whole flock will come trooping back to earth. Death will lose its significance altogether. And when I think of the disturbance which will result in our social relations, of the overthrow of all accepted institutions, and of the nullification of all principles of political economy, law, and religion, I am lost in perplexity and apprehension."

THE LAST CRUISE OF THE
JUDAS ISCARIOT

"She formerly showed the name *Flying Sprite* on her starn moldin'," said Captain Trumbull Cram, "but I had thet gouged out and planed off, and *Judas Iscariot* in gilt sot thar instid."

"That was an extraordinary name," said I.

" 'Strornary craft," replied the captain, as he absorbed another inch and a half of niggerhead. "I'm neither a profane man or an irreverend; but sink my jig if I don't believe the sperrit of Judas possessed thet schooner. Hey, Ammi?"

The young man addressed as Ammi was seated upon a mackerel barrel. He deliberately removed from his lips a black brierwood and shook his head with great gravity.

"The cap'n, " said Ammi, "is neither a profane or an irreverend. What he says he mostly knows; but when he sinks his jig he's allers to be depended on."

Fortified with this neighborly estimate of character, Captain Cram proceeded. "You larf at the idea of a schooner's soul? Perhaps you hev sailed 'em forty-odd year up and down this here coast, an' 'quainted yourself with their dispositions an' habits of mind. Hey, Ammi?"

"The cap'n," explained the gentleman on the mackerel keg, "hez coasted an' hez fished for forty-six year. He's lumbered and he's iced. When the cap'n sees fit for to talk about schooners he understands the subjeck."

"My friend," said the captain, "a schooner has a soul like a human being, but considerably broader of beam, whether for good or for evil. I ain't a goin' to deny thet I prayed for the *Judas* in Tuesday 'n' Thursday evenin' meetin', week arter week an' month arter month. I ain't a goin' to deny thet I interested Deacon Plympton in the 'rastle for her redemption. It was no use, my friend; even the deacon's powerful p'titions were clear waste."

I ventured to inquire in what manner this vessel had manifested its depravity. The narrative which I heard was the story of a demon of treachery with three masts and a jib boom.

The *Flying Sprite* was the first three-master ever built at Newaggen, and the last. People shook their heads over the experiment. "No good can come of sech a critter," they said. "It's contrairy to natur. Two masts is masts enough." The *Flying Sprite* began its career of base improbity at the very moment of its birth. Instead of launching decently into the element for which it was designed, the three-masted schooner slumped through the ways into the mud and stuck there for three weeks, causing great expense to the owners, of whom Captain Trumbull Cram was one to the extent of an undivided third. The oracles of Newaggen were confirmed in their forebodings. "Two masts is masts enough to sail the sea," they said; "the third is the Devil's hitchin' post."

On the first voyage of the *Flying Sprite*, Captain Cram started her for Philadelphia, loaded with ice belonging to himself and Lawyer Swanton; cargo uninsured. Ice was worth six dollars a ton in Philadelphia; this particular ice had cost Captain Cram and Lawyer Swanton eighty-five cents a ton shipped, including sawdust. They were happy over the prospect. The *Flying Sprite* cleared the port in beautiful shape, and then suddenly and silently went to the bottom in Fiddler's Reach, in eleven feet of salt water. It required only six days to float her and pump her out, but owing to a certain incompatibility between ice and salt water, the salvage consisted exclusively of sawdust.

On her next trip the schooner carried a deckload of lumber from the St. Croix River. It was in some sense a consecrated cargo, for the lumber was intended for a new Baptist meeting-house in southern New Jersey. If the prayerful hopes of the navigators, combined with the prayerful expectations of the con-signees had availed, this voyage, at least, would have been suc-cessfully made. But about sixty miles southeast of Nantucket the *Flying Sprite* encountered a mild September gale. She ought to have weathered it with perfect ease, but she behaved so abomi-nably that the church timber was scattered over the surface of the Atlantic Ocean from about latitude 40° 15′ to about latitude 43° 50′. A month or two later she contrived to go on her beam ends under a gentle land breeze, dumping a lot of expensively carved granite from the Fox Island quarries into a deep hole in Long Island Sound. On the very next trip she turned deliberately out of her course in order to smash into the starboard bow of a Norwegian brig, and was consequently libeled for heavy dam-ages.

It was after a few experiences of this sort that Captain Cram erased the old name from the schooner's stern and from her quar-ter, and substituted that of *Judas Iscariot*. He could discover no designation that expressed so well his contemptuous opinion of her moral qualities. She seemed animate with the spirit of pur-poseless malice, of malignant perfidy. She was a floating tub of cussedness.

A board of nautical experts sat upon the *Judas Iscariot,* but could find nothing the matter with her, physically. The lines of her hull were all right, she was properly planked and ceiled and calked, her spars were of good Oregon pine, she was rigged taut and trustworthy, and her canvas had been cut and stitched by a God-fearing sailmaker. According to all theory, she ought to have been perfectly responsible as to her keel. In practice, she was frightfully cranky. Sailing the *Judas Iscariot* was like driving a horse with more vices than hairs in his tail. She always did the unexpected thing, except when bad behavior was expected of her on general principles. If the idea was to luff, she would invariably fall off; if to jibe, she would come round dead in the wind and hang there like Mohammed's coffin. Sending a man to haul the jib sheet to windward was sending a man on a forlorn hope: the jib habitually picked up the venturesome navigator, and, after shaking him viciously in the air for a second or two, tossed him overboard. A boom never crossed the deck without breaking somebody's head. Start on whatever course she might, the schooner was certain to run before long into one of three things, namely, some other vessel, a fog bank, or the bottom. From the day on which she was launched her scent for a good, sticky mud bottom was unerring. In the clearest weather fog followed and enveloped her as misfortune follows wickedness. Her presence on the Banks was enough to drive every codfish to the coast of Ireland. The mackerel and porgies were always where the *Judas Iscariot* was not. It was impossible to circumvent the schooner's fixed purposes to ruin everybody who chartered her. If chartered to carry a deckload, she spilled it; if loaded between decks, she dived and spoiled the cargo. She was like one of the trick mules which, if they cannot otherwise dislodge the rider, get down and roll over and over. In short, the *Judas Iscariot* was known from Marblehead to the Bay of Chaleur as the consummate schooneration of malevolence, turpitude, and treachery.

After commanding the *Judas Iscariot* for five or six years, Captain Cram looked fully twenty years older. It was in vain that he had attempted to sell her at a sacrifice. No man on the coast of Maine, Massachusetts, or the British provinces would have taken the schooner as a gift. The belief in her demoniac obsession was as firm as it was universal.

Nearly at the end of a season, when the wretched craft had been even more unprofitable than usual a conference of the owners was held in the Congregational vestry one evening after the monthly missionary meeting. No outsider knows exactly what happened, but it is rumored that in the two hours during which these capitalists were closeted certain arithmetical computations were effected which led to significant results and to a singular decision.

On the forenoon of the next Friday there was a general suspension of business at Newaggen. The *Judas Iscariot*, with her deck scoured and her spars scraped till they shone in the sun like yellow amber, lay at the wharf by Captain Cram's fish house. Since Monday the captain and his three boys and Andrew Jackson's son Tobias from Mackerel Cove had been busy loading the schooner deep. This time her cargo was an extraordinary one. It consisted of nearly a quarter of a mile of stone wall from the boundaries of the captain's shore pasture. "I calklet," remarked the commander of the *Judas Iscariot*, as he saw the last boulder disappearing down the main hatch, "thar's nigh two hundud'n fifty ton of stone fence aboard thet schoon'r."

Conjecture was wasted over this unnecessary amount of ballast. The owners of the *Judas Iscariot* stood up well under the consolidated wit of the village; they returned witticism for witticism, and kept their secret. "Ef you must know, I'll tell ye," said the captain. "I hear thar's a stone-wall famine over Machias way. I'm goin' to take mine over'n peddle it out by the yard." On this fine sunshiny Friday morning, while the luckless schooner lay on one side of the wharf, looking as bright and trim and prosperous as if she were the best-paying maritime investment in the world, the tug *Pug* of Portland lay under the other side, with steam up. She had come down the night before in response to a telegram from the owners of the *Judas Iscariot*. A good land breeze was blowing, with the promise of freshening as the day grew older.

At half past seven o'clock the schooner put off from the landing, carrying not only the captain's pasture wall, but also a large number of his neighbors and friends, including some of the solidest citizens of Newaggen. Curiosity was stronger than fear. "You know what the critter," the captain had said, in reply to numerous applications for passage. "Ef you're a mind to resk her antics, come along, an' welcome." Captain Cram put on a white shirt and a holiday suit for the occasion. As he stood at the wheel shouting directions to his boys and Andrew Jackson's son Tobias at the halyards, his guests gathered around him—a fair representation of the respectability, the business enterprise, and the piety of Newaggen Harbor. Never had the *Judas Iscariot* carried such a load. She seemed suddenly struck with a sense of decency and responsibility, for she came around into the wind without balking, dived her nose playfully into the brine, and skipped off on the short hitch to clear Tumbler Island, all in the properest fashion. The *Pug* steamed after her.

The crowd on the wharf and the boys in the small boats cheered this unexpectedly orthodox behavior, and they now saw for the first time that Captain Cram had painted on the side of the vessel in conspicuous white letters, each three or four feet long, the following legend:

THIS IS THE SCHOONER *JUDAS ISCARIOT*
N.B.—GIVE HER A WIDE BERTH!!

Hour after hour the schooner bounded along before the northwest wind, holding to her course as straight as an arrow. The weather continued fine. Every time the captain threw the log he looked more perplexed. Eight, nine, nine and a half knots! He shook his head as he whispered to Deacon Plympton: "She's meditatin' mischief o' some natur or other." But the *Judas* led the *Pug* a wonderful chase, and by half past two in the afternoon, before the demijohn which Andrew Jackson's son Tobias had smuggled on board was three quarters empty, and before Lawyer Swanton had more than three quarters finished his celebrated story about Governor Purington's cork leg, the schooner and the tug were between fifty and sixty miles from land.

Suddenly Captain Cram gave a grunt of intelligence. He pointed ahead, where a blue line just above the horizon marked a distant fog bank. "She smelt it an' she run for it," he remarked, sententiously. "Time for business."

Then ensued a singular ceremony. First Captain Cram brought the schooner to, and transferred all his passengers to the tug. The wind had shifted to the southeast, and the fog was rapidly approaching. The sails of the *Judas Iscariot* flapped as she lay head to the wind; her bows rose and fell gently under the influence of the long swell. The *Pug* bobbed up and down half a hawser's length away.

Having put his guests and crew aboard the tug, Captain Cram proceeded to make everything shipshape on the decks of the schooner. He neatly coiled a loose end of rope that had been left in a snarl. He even picked up and threw overboard the stopper of Andrew Jackson's son Tobias' demijohn. His face wore an expression of unusual solemnity. The people on the tug watched his movements eagerly, but silently. Next he tied one end of a short rope to the wheel and attached the other end loosely by means of a running bowline to a cleat upon the rail. Then he was seen to take up an ax, and to disappear down the companionway. Those on the tug distinctly heard several crashing blows. In a moment the captain reappeared on deck, walked deliberately to the wheel, brought the schooner around so that her sails filled, pulled the running bowline taut, and fastened the rope with several half hitches around the cleat, thus lashing the helm, jumped into a dory, and sculled over to the tug.

Left entirely to herself, the schooner rolled once or twice, tossed a few bucketfuls of water over her dancing bows, and started off toward the South Atlantic. But Captain Trumbull Cram, standing in the bow of the tugboat, raised his hand to command silence and pronounced the following farewell speech, being sentence, death warrant, and funeral oration, all in one:

"I ain't advancin' no theory to 'count for her cussedness. You all know the *Judas*. Mebbe thar was too much fore an' aff to her. Mebbe the inickerty of a vessel's in the fore an' aff, and the vartue in the squar' riggin'. Mebbe two masts *was* masts enough. Let that go; bygones is bygones. Yonder she goes, carryin' all sail on top, two hundred'n-odd ton o' stone fence in her holt, an' a hole good two foot acrost stove in her belly. The way of the transgressor is hard. Don't you see her settlin'? It should be a lesson, my friends, for us to profit by; there's an end to the long-sufferin'est mercy, and unless— Oh, yer makin' straight for the fog, are ye? Well, it's your last fog bank. The bottom of the sea's the fust port you'll fetch, you critter, you! Git, and be d—d to ye!"

This, the only occasion on which Captain Cram was ever known to say such a word, was afterward considered by a committee of discipline of the Congregational Church at Newaggen; and the committee, after pondering all the circumstances under which the word was uttered, voted unanimously to take no action.

Meanwhile, the fog had shut in around the tug, and the *Judas Iscariot* was lost to view. The tug was put about and headed for home. The damp wind chilled everybody through and through. Little was said. The contents of the demijohn had long been exhausted. From a distance to the south was heard at intervals the hoarse whistling of an ocean steamer.

"I hope that feller's well underwrit," said the captain grimly, "for the *Judas*'ll never go down afore she's sarched him out'n sunk him."

"And was the abandoned schooner ever heard of?" I asked, when my informant had reached this point in the narrative.

The captain took me by the arm and led me out of the grocery store down to the rocks. Across the mouth of the small cove back of his house, blocking the entrance to his wharf and fishhouse, was stretched a skeleton wreck.

"Thar she lays," he said, pointing to the blackened ribs. "That's the *Judas*. Did yer suppose she'd sink in deep water, where she could do no more damage? No, sir, not if all the rocks on the coast of Maine was piled onto her, and her hull bottom knocked clean out. She come home to roost. She come sixty mile in the teeth of the wind. When the tug got back next mornin' thar lay the *Judas Iscariot* acrost my cove, with her jib boom stuck through my kitchen winder. I say schooners has souls."

THE FLYING WEATHERCOCK

There were two peculiar things that I remarked about the little brick meetinghouse on the hill at Newaggen. The first was the fact that it had once been chained to the ground, as are some structures on mountain summits. Big iron eyebolts were to be seen in the ledge on each side of the meetinghouse, and to one of them was still attached a rusty link of heavy chain. The hill was not high. A steep path led down to the harbor, and you could count the shingles on the roofs of the square, old-fashioned houses. On the other side of the hill was a boggy meadow, with scattering ricks of salt hay, bonneted with aged canvas. The front of the church breasted the wind that blew in across the islands from the ocean.

The second unusual feature was the vane on the stubby steeple. The vane was a great gilt codfish, evidently very sensitive to atmospheric influences. Its nose wavered nervously between south-southeast and southeast by east.

"Why was the meetin'house tied down to the rock?" repeated my companion, Deacon and Captain Silas Bibber. "Well, I'll tell ye. Because the congregation allowed that this here hill was a fittiner location for a house o' worship than the salt ma'sh yonder."

The deacon and captain paused to shy a stone at a disreputable sheep that was foraging among the gravestones.

"Why do we fly a weathercod instid of a weathercock?" he continued. "I'll tell ye. Because the rooster's the Devil's own bird."

He stooped for another missile just as the excited sheep, which had been surreptitiously flanking him while watching his movements with vigilant eyes, cleared the stone wall at a plunge and disappeared over the edge of the hill.

"Durn the critter!" remarked the deacon and captain.

The unwritten legends of the coast of Maine are kept by a generation that is rapidly going. Men and women are pretty old now who were young in the golden age of the seaport towns; when not only Portland and Bath and Wiscasset and the places to the eastward but also all the little settlements wedged in between rock and wave enjoyed a solid prosperity, based on an adventurous spirit and keen commercial insight in the matters of Matanzas molasses and Jamaica rum. Between the Maine towns and the West Indian ports there was and is a straight ocean way. Time was when direct communication with foreign parts brought sharp and increasing contrasts into the daily life of the coast people. This was the time, too, when the prevailing orthodoxy in theological doctrine still left room for a curious and in some respects peculiar supernaturalism that concerned itself chiefly with the malevolent enterprises of the Enemy of Mankind.

I

It appears from Captain Silas' narrative that about fifty years ago Parson Purington was the chief bulwark of the faithful against the Devil's assaults upon Newaggen. The parson was a hard hitter, both in petition and in exhortation. It was generally believed at the harbor, and for miles both ways along the coast, that nothing worried the evil one half so much as Parson Purington's double-hour discourses, mercilessly exposing his character, exhibiting his most secret plans, and defying his worst endeavors.

It was partly this feeling of triumph and pride in the prowess of their champion that led the congregation to construct a substantial church edifice, conspicuously situated on top of the hill, and possessing both a steeple and a bell that could be heard as far out at sea as Ragged Tail Island, with the wind favorable. The parson himself chose the site. He eagerly watched the progress of the workmen, and his heart was in every additional brick that went into the walls.

At half past eleven o'clock one moonlight Saturday night, just after the last touch of gilt had been put on the fine rooster vane —the donation of an unknown friend—Parson Purington ascended the hill on purpose to delight his eyes with the completed structure. Imagine the astonishment with which the good man discovered that no meetinghouse was there! No weathercock, no steeple, no belfry, no brick walls and wooden portico, not even the faintest trace of foundation or cellar!

The parson stamped his feet to see if he was awake. He wondered if the three tumblerfuls of hot rum toddy with which his daughter Susannah had fortified him against the night air could have played his senses such a trick. He rubbed his eyes and stared at the moon. The round face of that luminary presented its usual aspect. He gazed at the village under the hill. The well-known houses in which his parishioners slumbered were all distinctly visible in the moonlight. He saw the ocean, the islands, the harbor, the schooners at the wharves, the streets. He even made out the solitary figure of Peleg Trott, zigzagging home from the tavern, as if beating against a head wind. The parson tried to shout to Peleg Trott, but found that he had no voice for the effort. Everything in the neighborhood was as it should be, except that the new meetinghouse had disappeared.

Dazed by that tremendous fact, the parson wandered aimlessly about the summit of the hill for fully half an hour. Then he perceived that he was not alone, for a tall individual, wrapped in a black coat, sat upon the stone wall. The stranger looked like a Spaniard or a Portugee. His elbows were on his knees, his chin was in his hands, and he was watching the parson's movements with obvious interest.

"May I venture to inquire," said the stranger, "whether you are looking for anything?"

"Sir," the parson replied, "I am sorely perplexed. I came hither expecting to behold the sacred edifice in which I am to preach tomorrow morning for the first time, from a text in thirteenth Revelations. Not longer ago than this afternoon it occupied the very spot on which we stand."

"Ah, a lost meetinghouse!" said the stranger, carelessly. "Pray, is it not customary in this part of the world to send out the crier with his bell when they stray or are stolen?"

There was something in the tone of voice which caused the parson to inspect his companion more closely than before. The tall foreigner withstood the scrutiny with perfect composure, twirling his black mustachios. His eyes were bright and steady, and they seemed to grow brighter as the parson gazed into them.

"Well," said the stranger at last, "I fancy you would know me again."

"I think I know you now," retorted the parson, "although I do not fear you. If I am not prodigiously mistaken, it is you who have destroyed our meetinghouse."

The other smiled and shrugged his shoulders. "Since you press me on that point, I must admit that I have taken a trifling liberty with your property. Destroyed it? Oh, no; I have simply moved it off my land. The truth is, this hill is an old camping ground of mine, and I can't bear to see it encumbered with such a villainous piece of architecture as your brick meetinghouse. You'll find the whole establishment, to the last pew cushion and hymnbook, down yonder in the meadow; and if you are a man of taste, you'll agree with me that the new site is a great improvement."

The parson glanced over the edge of the hill. True enough, there stood the new meetinghouse in the middle of the marsh.

"I know not," said the parson resolutely, "by what diabolical jugglery you have done it, but I do know that you have no just claim to the hill. It has been deeded us by Elijah Trufant, whose father and grandfather pastured sheep here."

"My pious friend," returned the other calmly, "when Adam was an infant this hill had been in the possession of my family for millions of years. Would it interest you to peruse the original deed?"

He produced from beneath his cloak a roll of parchment, which he handed to the parson. The parson unrolled the document and tried to read it. Strange characters, faintly luminous, covered the page. They grew fiery bright, and as the parson's hand trembled —for he afterward admitted that it did tremble—they danced over the parchment charring the surface wherever they touched. At last Parson Purington's hand shook some of the fiery hieroglyphics quite to the margin of the sheet, the edge curled and crinkled, a thin line of smoke went up, and presently the entire document was ablaze.

"Rather awkward in you," said the stranger, "but it's of no great consequence. I happen to have a duplicate of the deed."

He waved his hand. The same flaming characters, enormously enlarged, danced now all over the ground where the meetinghouse should have stood. The parson's head swam as his eyes sought in vain to decipher the unhallowed inscription. There lay the claimant's title, burned into the top of the hill. The dry grass caught fire, the twigs and blueberry bush stems crackled in the heat, and for a moment the tall stranger was enveloped in smoke and flame that cast a lurid light over the features of his forbidding countenance. He stamped his feet and the unnatural conflagration was immediately extinguished.

"You perceive that my title is perfectly valid. Nevertheless, I am not a hard landlord. You have set your heart upon this location. Suppose you occupy it as my tenant at will. It will only be necessary, as the merest form, to sign this little—"

"No, sir," shouted the parson, now thoroughly aroused. "I make no compact. Whether you be indeed Beelzebub in person, or only one of his subordinate devils, your claim is a lie, your title of fire is forged, and I shall defy you and all your works in the sermon which I shall preach tomorrow morning in that brick meetinghouse, no matter if it is on the hill or on the marsh, no matter if you have meanwhile spirited it away to the bottom of the bottomless pit!"

"I shall do myself the honor to listen to your discourse," replied the stranger, with an exasperating grin.

When the parson reached home his daughter Susannah heard his story, gave him another glass of hot rum toddy, tucked him comfortably in bed, and then dispatched the hired help to the other end of the village with instructions to arouse Peletiah Jackson, first mate of the hermaphrodite brig *Sister Sal*.

II

After beating through all the streets of the little settlement, and sailing in great circles over several of the outlying pastures without making a port, Peleg Trott found himself about an hour after midnight halfway up the hill path, with a heavy sea on and the wind still dead ahead.

He sat down on a rock to take his bearings. "Peleg!" he shouted from his lookout on the forecastle deck.

"Aye, aye, Cap'n Trott!" he responded from the wheel.

"Howz hellum?" he demanded from the forecastle.

"Har' down, Cap'n Trott," he reported from the wheel.

"Makin' much starnway?"

"Beat's nater, the starnway, Cap'n Trott."

"Shake down the centerboard a peg, Peleg."

"It's clean drapped now, Cap'n Trott."

"Lez hear box ze compash. Believe ye're drunk agen; ye clapper-clawed—"

"Sartainly, Cap'n Trott. Cod, codcodfish, codfish becod, *cod*-fish; codfish-befish; fishcodfish, fish becod, FISH, Cap'n Trott."

"Whazzat light, Peleg, bearin' codfish becod, half fish?"

"Make it out for the moon, Cap'n Trott."

"Orright, Peleg. Head's she is till the moon's astarn, then make a half hitch an' drap anchor to low'rd new meetin'house to take 'zervation' ze wezzercock."

"Aye, aye, sir," and the difficult navigation was resumed, with Peleg and Trott both on deck.

At the brow of the hill Trott encountered the same surprising fact which had stupefied the parson an hour or more earlier in the night. The meetinghouse was not there.

"Salt me down ef the gale hain't blowed her off her moorin's," he muttered.

After carefully scrutinizing the horizon on every side, he continued:

"I'll be salted an' flaked ef she hain't adrift yonder on the ma'sh!"

Peleg studied the situation attentively. In none of his nocturnal voyages had he run against anything so extraordinary. His spiritual interest in the new edifice was perhaps less than that of any other inhabitant of the harbor, since he never went to meeting. Yet he had transported several cargoes of brick for the church from Wiscasset in his celebrated four-cornered clipper, the scow *Dandelion*, and his interest in the progress of the building had been greatly enlarged by an incident which happened several weeks before the night of which we are speaking.

One afternoon a tall, dark man, in an outlandish cloak, stood on the wharf at Wiscasset watching Peleg as he thrust bricks into the capacious maw of the *Dandelion*. "What's building?" asked the foreigner in excellent English. "Meetin'house," said Peleg. "Orthodox?" persisted the inquiring stranger. "No, Parson Purin'ton's at N'waggen," replied Peleg curtly. "Ah!" said the man on the wharf, "I have heard of that eminent divine. I am glad he is to have a new church. Have they everything they need?"

Peleg was about to say yes, for that was the last cargo of bricks and the other material was already on the ground. But his eye happened to wander to the steeple of the Wiscasset church, and an idea struck him. "Ef you're minded to contribute," said he, "they're desprit for a rooster vane like the there." The mysterious benefactor smiled. "I'll send them a bird," said he. In due course of time there arrived by schooner from Portland a fine wooden weathercock, properly boxed and ready for mounting and gilding. Peleg's story had been received with some incredulity at Newaggen, but now he found himself a hero. His presence of mind was highly commended by the deacons of the church, and they presented him with half a barrel of Medford rum. By the time the weathercock went aloft the half barrel was empty, and Peleg was chock full of rum and theological enthusiasm.

There was the meetinghouse fully a quarter of a mile off its anchorage. There was the well-known chanticleer—Peleg's especial joy and pride—resplendently conspicuous in the moonlight. But what strange spell was on the world that night? As Peleg gazed upon the bird, it appeared to him to be disproportionately large. There was no wind, and yet it began to revolve violently. Peleg distinctly heard a prolonged crow and the gilt rooster flapped its wings as if about to assay a flight into the upper air. True enough, up it went, carrying the meetinghouse with it, the church swaying and the bell tolling sadly as it rose, until the brick walls of the structure actually eclipsed the moon. Then the weathercock and its quarry slowly settled back to earth, hovering an instant over the waters of the harbor, and finally landing not in the meadow, but on top of the hill, not a dozen yards from where Peleg stood, his knees shaking, his teeth chattering, and his heart a-thump like the flat bottom of the *Dandelion* in a chopping cross sea.

"You may split me, salt me, and flake me!" ejaculated the mariner when he had partially recovered from his stupefaction. "Am I Peleg Trott, marster 'n eighth owner of the skeow *Dandy-line*, or am I a blind haddock, a crazy hake, or a goramighty tomcod?"

Thus it happened that the people of Newaggen Harbor had information, more or less trustworthy, as to what occurred on the disputed territory that memorable night between the time of Parson Purington's departure and the arrival of the army of relief, led by Susannah and Peletiah Jackson.

III

When Peleg's somewhat incoherent story had been told, the parson's daughter turned to the first mate of the *Sister Sal*. "Peletiah," said she, "what is to be done?"

"My idee," remarked Deacon Trufant, "is that the adversary purposes to sperrit away the parson and the whole congregation. He is subtile and fule of wiles."

Peletiah Jackson was not a theologian, but he was a practical young man and very fond of Susannah. He took off his coat. "My idee," he said, "is that if we cut away the mainmast, the ship'll weather any gale the Devil can send. Somebody fetch a hatchet."

In ten minutes Peletiah Jackson's head was seen to emerge through the window opening above the bell deck. Two minutes later he was clasping one of the four little pinnacles that surrounded the base of the steeple. In a surprisingly short time he had a running noose around the stubby spire, high above his head. The story of his ascent is the heroic episode in the annals of Newaggen. A dark cloud threatened to obscure the moon. The group of eager spectators on the ground below watched with breathless interest the slow progress of the first mate up the steeple. If he should lose his hold? If the running knot in his rope should slip? If the moon should go behind the cloud? Worse than all, as Peleg Trott suggested, if the weathercock should choose this moment for another flight?

Up went Peletiah, hand over hand, until his arms, and then his legs, encircled the steeple. Now he scrambled aloft with the agility of a monkey. The free end of the rope was thrown around the very apex of the steeple, and in no time at all Peletiah, seated comfortably in a sling, was hacking vigorously at the woodwork under the gilt ball on which the diabolical rooster was perched.

Blow after blow resounded in the still night air. Down in the harbor settlement windows were thrown open and nightcapped heads appeared. The racket was infernal. The edge of the cloud covered the moon, and it was difficult to distinguish Peletiah's form, except now and then when a flash of lightning lit up the weathercock and its bold assailant. The strokes of the hatchet ceased. It began to rain and blow. The hatchet strokes were heard again. The people huddled together. "My idee," said Deacon Trufant, "is that the adversary will presently come in a cherriat of fire and—" A clap of thunder interrupted the development of the idea. Thud, thud, thud, thud went the hatchet, more viciously persistent than before. Another brilliant flash—was the weathercock toppling at last? Peleg Trott declared in an awestruck whisper that he saw the cock's wings flapping, as a preliminary to another flight, with meetinghouse, Peletiah, and all. At that instant the storm burst in full fury. There came a blinding glare, a deafening peal, a blast of thunder and hurricane combined that shook the church and the hill itself, a wild shriek overhead, half a human yell of triumph and half a chanticleer's defiant cry, and with a tremendous crash something like a ball of fire fell to the ground not a dozen yards from the affrighted group by the meetinghouse portico.

A moment later, Peletiah came down the rope on a run, dripping wet. Susannah put her arms around his neck and gave him a kiss which could be heard even above the uproar of the elements.

They searched the hill all over next morning for some trace of the flying weathercock. Not a splinter of wood nor a spangle of gilt was ever discovered, but on the ledge near where the fiery ball must have fallen there was found a mark like this, burned deeply in the granite:

On the highest point of Ragged Tail Island, seven miles out to sea, they still show you another footprint, also deeply indented in the rock. It is precisely similar to the first, and it points the same way. Taken together, the two tracks are held by the local demonologists to indicate a flying stride from the mainland to the island, a hasty departure from the latter point, and—who knows?— either a final flight into the upper air, or a despairing plunge into the deepest depths of the Atlantic Ocean.

THE LEGENDARY SHIP
A Tale of the Early Days of New Haven Colony

An unexpected and very profitable growth of our business made the immediate purchase of a piece of land necessary. My partners requested me to negotiate for a few acres in the vicinity of New Haven, and I at once began to do so. An annoying delay occurred owing to the illegibility of an ancient record which made it impossible to obtain a perfect title. I was about to abandon the attempt to buy the property, when I was reminded that a gentleman well known to me might be able to give the information that could not be deciphered from the record. This person was a professor in the college, a man of wide repute as a scholar, and an ardent student of the Colonial epoch of the town.

I found him in his library, and he, without any hesitation, gave me the information which I sought, and told me where I would find such legal proofs of clear title as I desired. I was impressed with the accuracy of his learning and the readiness with which it responded to his demands, and I ventured to say to him that the acquisition of such a mass of names and dates must have cost him great labor. To my surprise he replied that I was mistaken, the truth being that he mastered such incidents with ease. His great mental efforts, he said, were required by the processes of analysis and comparison which were necessary to separate truth from the rubbish and chaff of tradition and record, and by the reasoning necessary accurately to trace causes to those results which, when grouped, constituted trustworthy history.

"For instance," said he, "I have here a document which will cost me the most severe application before I am through with it."

I had observed that there lay upon the table a roll of manuscript. The table was littered with pamphlets, documents, aged and worm-eaten books, and I do not know why my attention was specially fixed upon this particular roll of paper. It was plainly an aged manuscript. The paper was ribbed and unruled, like that in use a century or more ago; and if it once was white, the years had faded it to a dull buff leathery hue, while the care with which he afterward handled it indicated that it had little tenacity of fiber. I knew that he referred to this old roll of manuscript, and, as I expected, he took it up.

"I have here," he continued, "a remarkable historical narrative which I found among some refuse in a garret, where it had lain for more than a hundred years. It is an account of a strange, unnatural occurrence, of which I have heard by tradition, and which is even casually mentioned in Mather's *Marginalia*. I have, however, always regarded it as unworthy of serious consideration, believing that there was either no foundation for the tradition or else that it could be traced to the hallucinations of a disordered brain. I now, however, have an account of it which I cannot ignore. It was written by a clergyman of the most godly character, a man who could not, even in jest, speak falsehoods, and he asserts that he was almost an eyewitness of what he describes. How, then, can I refuse to accept this record? It gives all that a historian requires to satisfy him of the authenticity of any alleged occurrence. It is the genuine manuscript of a man whom I know to have lived, and it is not a hearsay account. If we are to put faith in any of the records of the past, we must accept this one. I do not know of an established fact of history that has any better basis than this document gives to substantiate the wonderful phenomenon which it records.

"I confess," continued the professor with some animation of speech, "that such a problem as is presented by this manuscript has never before been given to me to solve. As a historian, I am compelled to accept as true what I here read, while as a physicist I must regard the record as the wildest and most improbable of romances. Were it based on the testimony of one person it could easily be rejected as a vision or alienation of mind, to which the austerity of the Puritans seems to have rendered some of them peculiarly liable. I am confronted, however, with the assertion of this writer, as well as with the inherent proof of the assertion, that he was one of many witnesses. It is, indeed, an interesting problem, and the difficulty of reconciling an account that must be accepted as truthful history with the fact that it must be denied as physical possibility makes the task fascinating."

Doubtless Professor M—— observed that he had awakened a pleasing interest in me. Indeed, I took no pains to conceal it, and told him that I would gladly hear the story that had so puzzled him. He at once unrolled the manuscript.

"This appears," said he, "to have been written by the Reverend Dr. Prentice, and in the year 1680. I judge it was a letter to a friend, although the ravages of time have made the first few sentences illegible. I have other manuscripts of the clergyman, a few sermons, and having thus been enabled to make comparison, I find the handwriting of all to be identical. I will not read it in full, and will paraphrase some of the text, for it is written in the stiff, formal manner of that day, many of the words found in it now being obsolete.

"'There had come,' began the professor, 'upon the tradesmen and those engaged in commerce a season of adversity in the year 1646, such as they had not known even in the earliest days of the settlement of the New Haven Colony. The vessels lay idle in the harbor, trade with the other colonies languished, and as the New Haven colonists were familiar with commerce rather than agriculture, they were embarrassed even for the necessaries of life. But for the energy and determination of some of the men of character, the colony must have found its existence imperiled, for many had determined to depart, some even making arrangements to emigrate to Ireland. A less courageous and tenacious race must have succumbed. It was determined as a last resort to build a ship large enough to cross the ocean, freight her, and send her to England in the hope that the disheartening losses would be retrieved by the development of commerce with the mother country. Overcoming great obstacles they built a ship in Rhode Island Colony.

" 'The frost had closed the smaller streams, and the ground was whitened with snow when the ship entered New Haven harbor. There was great rejoicing at the sight of her, and her size, being fully 150 tons measurement, was a cause for wonder, for such a monster had never been seen before in that harbor. With her sails all set and her colors abroad, she came up to her anchoring place with such grace and speed as greatly delighted the people who had assembled at the water's edge to greet her. Courage was revived by the sight of her, and the people said, "Now we shall again have plenty and add to our possessions, if God be willing." '

"The master of the ship, Mr. Lamberton, was found to be somewhat gloomy, and Dr. Prentice records that Lamberton told him in confidence that though the ship was of the model and a fast sailer, yet she was so wilty—meaning thereby of such disposition to roll in rough water—that he feared she would prove the grave of all who sailed in her. However, he breathed his suspicions to no one else. The ship was laden and ready for departure early in January 1647.

" 'The cold that prevailed for five days and nights before the time fixed for clearing for London was such as the people had never before known. It must have remained many degrees below zero, for the salt water was frozen far down the harbor, and the ship was riveted by the ice as firmly as though by many anchors. There were no lazy bones among the people, and with prodigious industry the men cut a canal through the ice forty feet wide and five miles long to the never-freezing waters of the sound. The vessel was frozen in with her bow pointing toward the shore, and it was necessary to propel her to clear water stern foremost.

" 'This was an unlucky omen. Captain Lamberton avowed that the sea and the conflicting powers that struggled for its mastery were controlled by whims and freaks, which would be sure to be excited by such an insult as that of a ship entering the water stern first. An old sailor, too, informed them all that a ship that sailed stern first always returned stern first, meaning by that that she never came back to the harbor from which she thus departed.'

"You will observe," said the professor, putting down the manuscript for a moment, "that in these gloomy forebodings are to be detected traces of the mythological conception of the mystery of the sea, with which all sailors, even to the present time, are more or less tinctured. I am especially impressed with the manner in which these colonists acted. Believing in predestination in spiritual matters, their lives in worldly affairs conformed more or less thereto. So, in spite of these omens, there was no thought of delay. They had fixed the time for sailing, and they meant to sail. So godly a man as the Reverend Mr. Davenport expressed this feeling in his prayer as reported by this writer. Mr. Davenport, as the ship began slowly to move, used these words: 'Lord, if it be Thy pleasure to bury these our friends in the bottom of the sea, they are Thine. Save them.'

"Men less completely under the domination of their religious belief would never have gone to sea without exorcising in some way the evil influences which these omens seemed to indicate would prevail. There had gathered on the ice all the people of the colony except the sick and feeble, perhaps eight hundred or a thousand souls. On the departing vessel were some of their friends and kin. The farewells were said with the expression neither of grief nor of joy. Restraint, the subjugation, even the quenching of all emotions, was the rule of life with these people, and I gather from one or two expressions in this account that never was there more formal, less demonstrative leave-taking.

When the vessel reached deep water, and just as one of the great sails was beginning to belly with the wind, the people with one accord fell on their knees on the ice and prayed. The ship was five miles away. The air was clarified by the cold, and the vessel could be distinctly seen, and as the people prayed with open eyes that were fixed upon the distant and receding ship, she suddenly disappeared, vanished as quickly as though her bottom had fallen out and she had sunk on the instant. 'Yes,' says this writer, 'more suddenly for whereas at one moment the eyes of all of us were fixed upon her, at the next, as in the wink of the eye, she was not. We rose, gazed fixedly into the vacant space where we last saw her, and then with wonder turned to each other. Yet in another moment she was disclosed to us as she was before, and we watched her until she disappeared behind the neck of land that bounds the harbor to the east. So we dispersed, wondering at this strange manifestation whose meaning was hidden from us. Some there were who were convinced that it betokened that even as she had disappeared only to be seen again, so we should again behold her after her voyage. But there were many who were impressed that though we should again see her, the sight would be but a partial one. With reverent submission to the will of God, the people repaired to their homes.'

"You see," said the professor, again putting down the manuscript, "in all this that inexplicable commingling of hope and fatalism which was, I imagine, one of the inevitable conditions of mind of this austere and intensely religious people. The mere fact of the sudden disappearance and renewed sight of the ship may perhaps be explained by natural and simple causes, but not so the phenomena afterward described.

"In the natural order of events the colonists would have had some tidings of their ship after three months had passed. None came, however. Ships that sailed from England in March, April, May, and even June, brought no word of her arrival. Their suspense could be relieved only in one way. I should have asserted, even had I no evidence of it, that the colonists sought the relief they always thought they found in prayer. I should also have unhesitatingly said that they did not, in their prayers, ask that the inevitable be averted, but simply prayed that they might be prepared to receive with submission whatever was in store for them to know. I should have been justified in so asserting, as I find by reference to their manuscript. The account has it"—here the professor again read from the manuscript—"'The failure to learn what was the fate of their ship did put the godly people in much prayer, both public and private, and they prayed that the Lord would, if it was His pleasure, let them hear what He had done with their dear friends, and prepare them for a suitable submission to His holy will.'

"In all the accounts that we have of prayer," said the professor, "I know of nothing equal to that. It contains volumes of history. With that simple text the ethnologist and historian might construct the history of a people. Observe the human nature of it, that is, the intolerable burden of suspense, and see the religious faith of it, both of submission and the trust that the prayer would be answered.

"These people seem to have rested with the conviction that this remarkable supplication would be effective. Dr. Prentice continues his narrative, after quoting the prayer, with an account of what happened, as though it were the expected answer. He writes, too, with the vividness and accuracy of detail to be expected of the eyewitness, as inherent proof of the truth of his narration. I infer that within a day or two after the prayer the manifestation was received. There arose a great thunderstorm from the northwest, such a tempest of fury as sometimes follows elemental disturbances from that quarter. It seems to have been accepted as the presage of the manifestation that followed. After it passed away it left the atmosphere unusually clear. An hour before sunset the reward of their faith came. Far off, where the shores of Long Island are just dimly visible, a ship was discovered by a man who made haste to tell all the colonists. They gathered on the shore and saw a vessel, full rigged, every sail puffed out by the wind and the hull listed to one side by reason of the strain upon the masts and the speed with which the breeze carried her.

"'It is our vessel,' they cried. 'God be praised, for He has heard and answered our prayer.'

"Yet while they saw her straining with the wind, and seemingly speeding with such rapidity as should bring her to them in an hour, they also observed that she made no progress. Thus she continued to appear to them for half an hour. While they were still astounded by the mystery, they saw that she had of a sudden approached, and was coming with what seemed most reckless and foolhardy speed, for she was in the channel, which is narrow and of sufficient depth only to permit the passage of a vessel of her size with skillful handling. The children cried, 'There's a brave ship,' but the older people were filled with apprehension lest she should go upon the shoals or be dashed upon the shore. They thereupon made warning gestures, although they could see no one upon the deck.

"At last they observed something of which in their excitement they had taken no heed. The harbor lies in a southerly direction, and the channel itself runs due north and south. The vessel was making toward them with great speed, every sail curved stiff with the steady force of the wind that seemed to come in a gale from the south, and yet the wind was actually north. Thus holding her course due north, they saw her sailing directly against the wind. Then they knew that they were witnessing a mysterious manifestation. As she approached so near that some imagined they could easily hurl a stone aboard her, they could see the smaller details, the rivets, the anchor and its chains, the capping of the smaller ropes, and the rhythmic quivering of the ribbon-like pennant that was flying in the face of the wind. Yet they saw no man aboard her.

"The people awaited with sober resignation such further manifestations as were to be given them. Suddenly, and when she seemed right upon them, her maintop was blown over, noiselessly as the parting of a cloud, and was left hanging in the shrouds. Then the mizzentop went over, making great destruction, and next, as though struck by the fiercest hurricane, all the masts went by the board, being twisted as by the wrenching of a wind that blew in resistless circles. The sails were torn in narrow ribbons, whirling round and round in the air, while the ropes snapped and were unraveled into shreds, and beat with noiseless force upon the decks. Soon her hull began to careen, and at last, being lifted by a mighty wave, it dived into the water. Then a smoky cloud fell in that particular place, as though a curtain had dropped from heaven, and when, in a moment, it vanished, the sea was smooth, and nothing was to be seen there. The people believed that thus the Almighty had told them of the tragic end of their ship, and they renewed their thanks to Him that He had answered their prayer. The Reverend Mr. Davenport, in public, declared 'that God had condescended for the quieting of their afflicted spirits this extraordinary account of His sovereign disposal of those for whom so many fervent prayers were continually made.'

"You will see," said the professor, as he carefully laid the manuscript away, "what an extraordinary problem is here presented to me. If I accept any recorded evidence, I must accept this; yet science teaches me that the laws of nature are inexorable, as much so now as ever. What is the truth?"

THE SHADOW ON THE FANCHER TWINS

King Street is a highway that winds along the crest of the sightly ridge in the southeast corner of Westchester County, doubling and curving to conform to the contour of the land, and permitting, in these swervings from right to left, superb views of the distant waters of the sound and of the hazy blue hills of Long Island to be obtained. It is a noble highway, broad—for men, when in colonial days this road was built, were generous of their land— and finely drooping elms and here and there a warty oak stand like sentinels upon each side. It serves not only its original purpose as a means for passing to and fro between the harbor on the sound and the fertile and romantic valley to the north, but has also in some places been fixed upon as a boundary; so that if anyone riding from White Plains to the sea should meet another driving north, and should, therefore, turn to the right, the other turning to the left to permit easy passage, one would be upon the very outermost easterly rim of New York State, while the other would be skirting the extreme western edge of Connecticut. At one point, some six miles from the sea, the road makes a majestic sweep from east to west, revealing a glorious panorama of sea as far east as the bluffs that hem in Huntington Bay, and to the west until the waters appear to be brought to an abrupt halt by the gloomy Fort Schuyler; while a far-reaching view of the

dissolute rocks of Connecticut gives contrast to the scene. Back
from this point, and concealed from the highway by a scrubby
piece of woodland, stand the melancholy ruins of a house set in
the middle of a dreary and deserted field. So fragile and decayed
with age and neglect does it appear that the wonder is that even
the gentlest breeze had not long ago leveled it. Yet it has resisted
tempests and solitude for more than a hundred years, and when
it at last succumbs it will be with sudden dissipation into natural
elements. It seems now like the skull and skeleton of something
once alive. Great gaping holes, which brown and ragged shingles
fringe like shaggy eyebrows, were once windows, and a yawning,
cavernous space below, defined by moldering beams and scant-
ling, articulated with bent and rusty nails, tells where once hung
a heavy oaken door, now fallen upon the stone steps that show
no signs of age except a cloak of greenish moss.

The wind seems always to be moaning about this remnant,
and at night the screech of the owls awakens echoes of a century,
for it is more than a hundred years since any sound was heard
within these walls, except the mysterious tickings and rumblings
with which the forces of nature destroy what man has made and
then neglected, or the fearless twittering or screech of birds that
occupy when men desert. But why so sightly and pleasing a spot
as this must once have been, and might be, too, again, should
have been deserted as though plague-stricken none are now
left to tell. Was it the subtle influences that, like another atmosphere, were ever present with the Fancher boys and led them to
their irresistible fate? If this be the real though perhaps the unconscious reason, may it not be true that even in lands where
superstition is believed to be conquered, and facts alone command, there remain mysterious and unacknowledged tributes
in human nature to the powers which the astrologers and
necromancers of the Orient worship? It is certain that none ever
occupied the place after the Fancher boys had quitted it, and
after reading this tradition of their lives one may judge for him-

self whether reasons are good for thinking that in the olden times people believed there rested an evil spell upon this home.

When the earth was shadowed and palled in that great eclipse in the year 1733, terror seized the people, for nature seemed reversed, and a stifling calm came over all things, so that the beasts in the field gave frightened cries, and the dogs bayed, and the fowls, even at midday, sought their perches. For people were not prepared as now, to the accuracy of a science, to witness this awful proof of the stupendous powers and laws of the Almighty.

Just at that hour there had gathered in the Fancher homestead neighbors, kindly bent on ministering to one in the most sacred of all necessities. And when the midday shadow began to permeate the atmosphere, and to grow deeper and denser, and the ghastly light revealed the other and unusual sights without, the neighbors sat crouched before the great fire in the living room, close together, and speaking only in hoarse whispers, casting half-averted glances from the window into the weird light beyond. But one, a motherly matron, was in the inner room, whence once she appeared with gloomy countenance, saying, "It were better that it were dead, for this will blight its life."

And the neighbors asked in whispers, not for the child but for the mother, and the matron replied, "She does not know that the sun was darkened when the baby came to us."

By and by the matron came into the great room bearing a burden in her pillowed arms and, having lifted the blanket of soft wool, she permitted her friends to peer at the little child.

"Is it—does it live?" one asked.

"Pity it, for it does. It is a boy, and he will be dark, and fierce, and who knows what; for do you suppose that such a thing as that which happened to the sun will not prevail over one who at that moment came to us?"

And the infant even then opened his eyes upon them, and they saw that, though so long as women remembered there had been none of the Fanchers, or the maternal Brushes, whose eyes were not the gentlest blue, yet this one stretched apart lids that revealed eyes that were surely dark and promised, when puerility had gone, to be the deepest black; and even the little tufts of hair were dark, and some of the matrons were sure that their penetrating eyes detected a swarthy undercolor beneath the smooth skin of the cheek.

"He does not cry," said one.

"No, but his fists are doubled," said another.

"They always are: that signifies nothing," said the matron.

"Aye, but not clenched and firm with resistance like his."

"If he would cry, I would like it," continued the first.

"I doubt if he ever sheds a tear," said the matron who bore him upon her arms.

And then the father came and looked for many moments upon his first born, and at length he said, "His name shall be Daniel."

Then, when the shadow on the earth had gone and the women were about to go, there came again a moment when the motherly matron looked from the inner room for an instant, and though she did not speak not a woman there failed to read her thoughts, so fine is women's intuition at such times, and they gathered about the fire again speaking with hushed voices and looking upon each other with anxious glances. And just as the sun was setting behind White Plains hills the matron came again, bearing another burden gently, and, as she lifted the tip of the covering to let them see, she said, " 'Twas when the sun was shining brightly this one came to us, and he will be fair and gentle and comely, but the shadow of his brother's birth will be upon him all his days."

The women, when they saw this infant, said that his eyes were Fancher eyes—that is to say were very blue; and his hair, which was like a little ray of sunlight, was fair, like his mother's and all her kin.

When the father had looked upon this one he said, "He shall be called David."

Of course so unusual was all this that there was much conversation about it, far and near, and the little Fancher twins were observed above all children thereabout, for there was no small curiosity to note what the effect might be upon them of the strange and unnatural event that happened at their birth. As they grew older the people all agreed that rather than Daniel and David their names might better have been Esau and Jacob, for Daniel was dark, like some of the Indians that lived near by, and his head was shaggy with thick black hair. He was fierce, and imperious, and promised to become a mighty hunter or else a warrior, for he talked of war and bloodshed, and before he was ten years old had led his brother far away in search of Indians to conquer. But David was gentle. He loved the farm and the cattle. But he cared for no other mates, because he was content with Daniel. So the twin brothers grew, David dependent upon and yielding to his swarthy brother like a vine to the tree it embraces. They slept together, and they ate together, and learned their letters and did their sums from the same book, so that what one knew the other knew, and though so different as to seem to have sprung from distinct races, yet they had but one mind between them, and that was Daniel's, and all the people said, "The shadow of the brother is upon David and will be always till it puts out his life."

Once their father said as he looked out in the morning upon his farm, "'Twill storm, I fear, before the night. The wind comes from the southeast. Mayhap 'twill bring rain."

And Daniel contradicted, saying, "Not southeast, but southwest."

"You are wrong, my son."

"Not wrong. I am never wrong. I would not have spoken if I was wrong. Ask David. He will tell you."

"David will say as you have said. You are two bodies and one mind, I tell you."

"We are one mind because we say and think the truth."

The father smiled when he heard the imperious little son say this, and then went away; and when he had gone, David said,

"Daniel, we will prevail upon our father that he is wrong and we are right."

"If he will not believe our word he will believe nothing."

"Then he shall see."

"We will make a weathercock."

"It shall not be a cock, David."

"No, it shall not. What, then, shall it be?"

"It shall be a warrior."

"It shall. Can we make one?"

"You shall make the head and arms, for you have skill with the knife, and I will make the body and legs. Then we will join the parts, and if you make the arms with broad swords at the end, then the wind will strike them, and they will point the way it comes from. Our father shall not think we babble when we contradict him."

So the lads went to the shed, and by noon had constructed a marvelous image that they called a warrior, and its arms were elongated into broad swords shaped from tough hemlock shingles, and when one arm was lifted high above its head the other pointed rigidly to the earth, and if there was a breeze the arms were to gyrate with bewildering rapidity.

"A warrior should have color, Daniel," said David, when they looked upon the image.

"He should have a red coat," replied Daniel.

"And his breeches?"

"They should be white, and he should have a fierce beard and a stern eye."

So they thus decorated the image and set it up on the ridge piece of the shed, and when their father saw it its arms and sword were whirling away in a southwest breeze, and it was staring fiercely, though with irregularly marked eyes, away upon the horizon where the Long Island hills touch the sky. And there the warrior stayed, long after the storm had begun, and until the arms had become wounded in battling with the winds until one night it tottered and fell beneath a vigorous blast and lay unburied on the ground until the worms finished it. Daniel said, when his father saw it: "When you look upon it remember that David and I will not be disputed."

The neighbors heard this story of the warrior, and they said, "The shadow is upon the lads. Who can tell what yet may happen?"

When Daniel had come into possession of his strength, his fame as a strong man spread far and near, and they said that he had felled an ox with a blow, and had captured two robbers from the town below and held them with a grip of steel, each by an arm; and no one said yes or no to him until his desire was first ascertained. But David they loved because of his gentleness, and respected because of his skill with tools, and he was of such kindly disposition that he had but to surmise a desire of any of the neighbors when he would try to gratify it. So that when it was their desire that Daniel should do some act or lend some help, the wish was made known to David and Daniel was then overcome. For as they grew older so they seemed more and more closely to be united in common impulses and purposes, though the people asserted that the shadow was more and more potent, and that David's heart and mind were surely being absorbed, and that before many years he would simply be the shadow of his brother.

There lived in the town of Bedford, some miles distant, Miss Persia Rowland, and it was said of her that, fair as all other maids were, there was none like her, and she knew it, and was pleased thereat, and that she coveted not only admiration but the acknowledgment of it, whereby many a stalwart young fellow had favored her wish to his sorrow.

One day Miss Persia summoned one who obeyed her always, and said to him, "There is to be the great assembly of the year on St. Valentine's eve, and the sleighing is fine."

"That will be well, mistress. But whether the sleighing was fine or not the young fellows from miles around would come."

"No doubt. The winter is dull."

"Aye, but 'tis not that, and you know well, mistress, why they come, and why, if you were not there, they would quickly depart."

"But it tires me to see the same faces, with their staring, yearning eyes. There's no spunk to them. I hear of one below who, they say, never even so much as lets his eyes rest on a maid; not from abashment, but because he cares not for them at all, being in love with his own shadow—that is, his twin brother. It would please me to set my eyes upon such a man."

"Ah, he never saw you, mistress, for if he had, the brother would be forgot."

"Have you seen him?"

"Often."

"And what looks he like? Is he strong and fierce, and does he scowl, and does he permit himself a beard?"

"He is all these things, and all men seem to fear him but the brother, and he says nothing to the women."

"If you wish to please me, as so often you assert you do, you will see that this strange being and his brother are present at the assembly. The sleighing will be fine, I said."

So it happened that the young man, being greatly desirous of doing whatever might make this woman smile even for an instant upon him, with caution approached David, and at last won his promise that he and Daniel would attend the assembly. But when David and his brother talked about it, Daniel said, "You have said we would go; therefore we will. But why do they chatter so of this young woman? Is she unlike others? Have they not all eyes that they cast on young men, David, and do they not all pucker their lips that their smiles may seem more pleasing? Fools they be who are bewitched thereby; but you have said we will go, and we do what we say, David."

So, as the young men and women were engaged in the courtly minuet in the great assembly room, there came among them the Fancher twins. They stood side by side in the further end of the room, where the light from the great burning logs revealed them clearly. They were of an even height and tall, but one was muscular and strongly built and his face seemed in the dim light more swarthy than it really was, and his thick black hair stood in shaggy masses, as nature had arranged it, and without the rigid dressing of the time. The other was slight and fair as a maid, and there was a smile upon his face, for the bright faces and the gay dresses and the dance and the twinkling of candles pleased him.

Miss Persia had seen them enter, and though with demure and graceful manner she seemed occupied with the evolutions of the dance, yet she saw them all the while. When the cotillion was ended she summoned her adorer and said, "The dark one, that is he. Why do you permit them to stand there? Will his brother be his partner in the next set? He must not. Why do you not bring him to me?"

And so the youth, in stiff peruke and silken stockings and satin breeches, went to Daniel, and bowing, said, "'Tis dull for you, I fear."

"If so we can go as we came."

"But not until you have been presented?"

"We came to see, not to be seen."

"He wishes to present you, Daniel," said his twin brother David.

"Well, he may do it."

But the youth with some embarrassment perceived that Daniel had no thought of moving when David were by, and he thought how often had he heard it said, "The fair one is the other's shadow." But he led them both to the high-backed chair wherein the fair Persia sat; and though Daniel stood before her staring grimly at her without abashment, and David, with becoming humility, bowed low before her beauty, yet she took no heed of the fair one but spoke to the dark one only.

"We have heard of you, but we have never seen you here before," she said. "Why is it?"

"Because it has not been our wish," Daniel replied with grave dignity.

"But it should have been. Such men as you do wrong yourself and others by living as hermits." She perceived that by bold self-assertion and fearlessness of manner she could alone interest this man. "Come with me," she added. "Your arm, if you would be considerate. 'Tis a strong arm, I perceive. No wonder they tell us of your feats of strength. I wish to hear you talk and it is pleasanter to stroll about. Here, let me present your brother to a fair young woman. For once, sir, give me the preference, and permit him to entertain Miss Nancy Brush."

And before he knew it the fierce Daniel was promenading with the beauty on his arm, while David—Daniel for once forgot him.

"It is a delight for us to see a strong man here," she said. "A woman might almost lose her faith in men, did not such as you appear once in a while."

"My strength is my own, and David's. What is it to you?" he said.

"What to me? The pleasure of novelty. They say there is a war brooding, and troops have fought already on Bunker Hill. It is that to me that gives me and all women sense of safety, for I now know that there are men fearless and brave, and quick to fight an enemy, and we shall, therefore, be safe. Ah! why was I a woman?"

"You talk of strength. It is weak to bemoan your fate."

"Would you not bemoan too had you been born without arms?"

"If you were a man what would you do?"

"Be strong and glory in it. If there were war, I would command an army, as you might, and if there were peace, I would compel the homage and affection of every fair maid."

"To command an army is well; to woo and will is pastime for puerile men."

"So little do you know and realize the power of strength. The greatest victories that a man can win are those which enable him to woo and wed whichever of all the maids he ever saw that he desires. If she be proud, he can subdue her pride, and that is a greater feat than winning a battle; and if she be vain, he can humble her vanity, and if she be selfish, he can make her forget herself, and if she be well favored above all other maids, he can be conscious that, if he wed, the beauty is for him, and that is a conquest of all other men."

As she said this she looked up at him, bending her graceful neck that she might obtain full view of his stern face and compel him thereby to look upon her. And when he had perceived her face and the beauty of it he did not speak, but led her to the remote corner of the great room, and then, unloosing his arm, turned so that he might stand squarely before her. He looked at her steadily for a moment, she not quailing. She asked at length, "What is it? Why do you look so fiercely at me?"

"Because you spoke as you did, and I perceive now what woman's beauty is. Have you not more strength than I?"

"I? I stronger than you?"

"Yes, you think you are. I think you may be, but you are subtle. Is that one form of strength? Is there one of the men here, or whom you ever saw, who would not with joy obey you? And if that be so, is that not due to the very strength you just now complimented in men?"

"There may be some, who knows? I can be as frank as you. There is one who would not."

"I don't know whether I would not, for you mean me."

"Yes, and you don't know? Well, I'll try you. I have a powerful but vicious colt; no man dares approach him. I think you would dare. Will you come tomorrow and break it for me?"

"I will come with my brother."

"Then you dare not come alone."

He looked half angrily upon her a moment, and then said, "I will come alone."

"Now go and fetch your brother to me. He stands there now alone, looking with great eyes at you. Is there some intangible bond between you?"

"My brother is myself and I am he."

"Then bring him quickly, and leave us for a while, that I may perceive how Daniel acts in David's person, as I have already by your strange admission seen how David appears in Daniel's person."

"You are a strange woman," said he, looking almost fiercely upon her with his eyes black as the ornament of jet she wore, and reflecting brighter light. But he brought David, and then stepped aside and watched that supple, slender figure as, on David's arm, she walked, as the swan sails, without apparent volition; and he saw how white and graceful her neck was, as it was revealed above the soft lace about it, and how like a crown her dark hair was gathered upon her head, twinkling like stars in winter's night with the jewels set there; and he could hear the whistle of her silks as she once passed close by him, looking up with serious face at him, and he perceived that her feet in slippers white and supple did now and then peep from her skirt like little chicks that thrust and withdrew their heads from their mother's wing.

"What is my strength and determination beside this power?" he thought. "I could crush, but this supple thing can compel."

While she was walking with David, Miss Persia had said, "Who would surmise that you and he were brothers?"

"Why not?" asked David.

"Have you never surveyed yourselves side by side in the mirror?" she asked.

"Why should we do that? I think the mirror belies, for no reflection would put out of my mind the conviction that I am like him and he like me. We cannot see ourselves."

"But your brother is so fierce and gloomy and imperious."

"Ah, that is but the other side of myself."

"And you, shall I say it? They say you are gentle and kindly and peaceful."

"Ah, but that is the other side of him."

"Being the complement of each other, together you make a man," she said.

He laughed, and she continued, "But you cannot live always thus. There is a better complement even than a brother."

"Tell me what you think it is."

"A fair maid: and there will come the realization of this to you. But you are most unneighborly. We have never seen you before. Come and be better friends. Come for I want to talk with you more. Will you?"

"We will come."

"Not together. You would embarrass me. I should not know to which I spoke. Come you the day after tomorrow and pay me a little visit at my home. My father would be glad to know you," and she looked up, pleadingly with an arch smile, and not serious and demure as she had when she obtained Daniel's promise to come. So he promised her.

On their way home in the still hour before dawn the twins were silent for a long time perhaps because Daniel drove furiously. At length Daniel said:

"She is not like other women, David."

"She is not, Daniel."

"She hath a luminous eye."

"And a cheek like the pink shell in our best room, Daniel."

"And her smile, it pleases, for it hath meaning, David."

"Yes, it pleases, but more her serious face."

"Even more that, and there is great power in her supple motion."

"So I surmise."

The next afternoon Daniel mounted his horse and went flying along the King Street to Bedford and when he returned he limped as though lamed, but he said nothing.

"You are lamed, Daniel," said David.

"Yes, a colt kicked me but I mastered him."

On the next day David mounted the horse and away he went, Daniel paying no heed to his departure. When he came back he said nothing.

"Are you going supperless to bed?" asked his twin brother.
"I have eaten supper with friends," said David quietly.

Then until the winter frosts were yielding to the summer sun Daniel and David ate and slept and worked together, but in silence, and almost every day one or the other went hurrying off toward the north, but never together.

One day after David had gone, Daniel an hour later followed. He drove straight to the door of Esquire Rowland's mansion, and without ceremony, entered, passing to the best room. There he saw David sitting beside the fair Persia, who had not heard Daniel enter.

He stood on the threshold for a moment. Then he said, "David, I sat there yesterday and should tomorrow. Is it to be our curse that we have no mind except in common? Come, my brother; I say come."

He did not speak to Persia but turned abruptly and quitted the house; and David, without one word, arose and followed him.

The girl sat there like one bewildered, speechless; and when at length her wits came she perceived that the brothers were far down the highway.

"Oh were there but one, and that one the dark one," she said, as she stood peering through the little windowpanes and watching until the twins had passed out of sight.

Not a word did Daniel or David speak until they reached their home. Then Daniel said:

"David, in this, as in all things wise, we are agreed. You love the maid, as I love her. If you hated her, I should hate her. But though we may be one, we are to the world as two. We love her, and must be content with that."

"That is true, Daniel. She cannot cut the bond that binds us."

"I love you as myself, David, and you me, for we are indeed in all but body one. Therefore we must see her no more. And, as in men contrary customs part them this way and that, so one of us may be overcome by our passion, and visit the girl again. If so, whichever does shall go to the other and confess, and say, 'What shall I do? What will you do with me?' And what the other says, that will be done."

"There is reason and purpose in this pledge, Daniel, and we will make it."

"David, if it is you who comes to me I shall say what I hope you will say to me if I fail."

"And that is to end my life?"

"That is what it is."

One day some weeks later Daniel came to David and led him to the glen that even to this day may be seen beyond the old house.

"David, I am a poor weakling. I have seen her again yesterday. You know our pledge," and here Daniel drew from his pocket a pistol.

David looked upon his brother with an agonizing glance, while Daniel stood before him grim and fierce, and very dark. His hand was upon the trigger.

"I can't, I can't, Daniel," David said.

"You can, for if I were in your place I could and would command you to keep your pledge and do as I bid. There is no escape, but here," and he held up the weapon.

"No, I cannot bid you do it, though 'twas our pledge," said David, and put his hands to his eyes and shuddered.

"You are a babe," said Daniel, with contempt.

"But, Daniel, there is another thing that can be done. The war has come. Washington is below. You shall enlist, and be a soldier. Perhaps you will become a great commander, as you once felt sure you would."

"You tell me to enlist, I will do it." And that night Daniel quitted his home and within three days was with Washington at Harlem.

Some months later the army was gathering near the natural fortification at White Plains, preparing there to resist the on-coming of the soldiers of King George. It was a time when men were gloomy, but determined, for the shadow of battle was upon them, and their courage was greater than their hopes. One morning the sentry on the extreme left wing that was encamped in the outskirts of the town of Bedford brought in a sad and sullen man. They said to the officer in command that he was a deserter whom they had captured that night.

"Who are you?" asked the officer.

"I am known as David Fancher."

"You heard the accusation?"

"It is the truth. Do as you please with me. But let me say this thing—'twas not from cowardice I went away."

"If not, what then?"

"That is my affair."

"You know the penalty unless there be good excuse?" he was asked.

"I know the penalty. Perhaps I am glad of it. Who knows?"

They led him away, and as he stood sullenly before the officers of the court-martial and admitted his guilt and would say no word in extenuation. They pronounced his sentence—to be shot at sunrise the next morning.

In the evening David sent a communication to the officer, saying that if it were not too late he would like to speak to one of the soldiers who were detailed to execute him, and the officer said, "Let his wish be granted."

So it happened that in the darkness of the night a soldier was brought to the guardhouse and admitted. He stood by the door, for he could not see within, but he said: "Who is it that has sent for me and why?"

"It is I, Daniel."

"That is David's voice."

"Yes, Daniel. Daniel, do you remember how you used, with the musket at fifty paces, to send a ball unerringly through a bit of wood no larger than my hand?"

"That I remember."

"Remember that tomorrow when you see my hand."

"Do not speak in riddles, David."

"You remember the pledge we gave and that you promised that if I came to you and said 'Daniel, I have seen her again,' that you would do what I asked in recompense?"

"I remember that you would not keep your pledge with me."

"But you said you would had you been in my place. Daniel, I have seen her again."

"I knew you would, and so must I if I live. 'Tis a common impulse."

"Daniel, when I am led out tomorrow, and you stand facing me, promise me that you will mark well the spot where my hand is placed. 'Twill be over my heart."

"Is that in pursuance of our pledge?"

"It is."

"Then I will do it. But wait: there is military order about this. The file will be selected."

"It is selected, and you are one."

"How know you that?"

"Because it was inevitable. No one told me, but I knew it."

"Then I will do as you say," and he turned to go away.

"Wait, Daniel. What happens to one will happen to both."

"I know that. We cannot escape that."

"Daniel, in my hand will be a tress of hair."

"She gave it to you. Give me my part at once. No, keep it. What matters whether your hand or mine hold it?"

"When you enlisted I had to follow and though I could not find your regiment yet I knew we should be brought together."

"I knew that."

"We were in camp near Bedford, and, by chance, she strayed with some mates near us. She saw me first, and pleaded with me to return with her. Though I was on guard I could not resist, and I went. They found me and brought me here, and tomorrow morning the mystery of it all, of our lives, will be cut short."

"It is better so, David. I am glad."

"You loved her, Daniel?"

"Better than I loved myself, and therefore better than I loved you."

"And so, of course, it was with me. And I told her in my frenzy that I did."

"As I had the day I came and demanded the fulfillment of your pledge."

"She said that were we one she could have smiled on us. She could not marry both."

"Those were her words to me. We could not escape our fate, Daniel. Together we came into the world, and under mysterious beclouding of nature."

"Together we shall go out, David. And if such a thing is possible let us hope that there may be reunion complete, if so be it happens men's spirits live after them.

"Sit here by me, Daniel for a while. You are not unhappy for I am not."

"No, David, we are content."

They sat there side by side for many moments, until at last the guard came and took the brother of the condemned away.

In the morning they led David out into the meadow beyond the encampment, and there followed a line of soldiers, at the head of which marched a swarthy and stern man whom not one of all that company knew to be the brother of that man who, with bared head, was kneeling, proudly and unflinchingly, some twenty paces away. He had asked that he might give the signal, and the request had been granted, and he told them that he would be ready when he passed his hand on his heart.

The file of soldiers stood before him with leveled muskets awaiting the word, and David looked upon Daniel for a moment— and the soldiers said he smiled—and then he placed his hand upon his heart.

There was a quick report. The swarthy soldier had fired before the word, and then the volley of the others was delivered, but David Fancher had fallen prone before their bullets reached him.

Then the soldiers saw a strange thing. The swarthy companion, unmindful of regulation, went forward to the dead man and seemed to be leaning over him, and then lay prostrate beside him; and when the soldiers went there they found that two were dead instead of one.

Though soldiers are accustomed to things that startle, this was such a mystery that much inquiry was made. At last one came and looked upon the faces of the dead.

"Those are the Fancher brothers. Twins," he said.

THE PAIN EPICURES

Nicholas Vance, a student in Harvard University, had the misfortune to suffer almost incessantly with acute neuralgia during the second term of his senior year. The malady not only caused him great anguish of face, but it also deprived him of the benefit of Professor Surdity's able lecture on speculative logic, a study of which Vance was passionately fond.

If Vance had gone in the first place to a sensible physician, as Miss Margaret Stull urged him to do, he would undoubtedly have been advised that it was mental friction that had set his face on fire. To extinguish the conflagration he would have been told to abandon speculative logic for a time and go a fishing.

But although the young man loved Miss Margaret Stull, or at least loved her as much as it is possible to love one who feels no interest in hypotheses, he had little respect for her opinion in a matter such as the neuralgia. Instead of consulting with a duly qualified member of the faculty of medicine, he rushed across the bridge one morning, in a paroxysm of pain, to seek counsel of Tithami Concannon, the very worst person, under the circumstances, to whom he possibly could have applied.

Tithami was himself a speculative logician. He lived up four pairs of stairs, and his one window overlooked a dreary expanse of back yards and clotheslines. By a subtle process of reasoning he knew that the window commanded a superb view of the sunset, granted only that the sun rose in the west and set in the east. As Tithami was aware, moreover, that east and west are relative terms, arbitrarily employed, and that inherently and absolutely there is no more reason why the sun should travel from east to west than from west to east, he derived a great deal of enjoyment from the sunsets he did notice. Such are the resources of speculative logic.

Tithami owed his education to his name. Thomas Concannon, who thirty years ago taught the Harvard freshmen how to pronounce the digamma, died a month before Tithami was born. Poor little Mrs. Concannon, sincerely desiring to compliment the memory of her deceased husband, named the infant after a Greek verb which the tutor had held in especial esteem, and of whose capabilities she had often heard him speak with enthusiasm. Her family tried in vain to persuade the simple-minded mother to give up the idea, or at least to compromise on Timothy, approximate in form to the heathen verb, but thoroughly respectable in its associations. She would not yield—not one final iota—and Tithami the baby was baptized. This queer christening proved both the making and the marring of the child. A rich, eccentric great uncle, mightily tickled by the unconscious humor of the appellation, offered to give young Tithami the best schooling that money could buy, and he kept his word, all the way from a kindergarten to Heidelberg. At the latter institution Tithami learned so much logic from the renowned Speisecartius, and went so deep into metaphysics with the profound Zundholzer, that he thoroughly unfitted himself for all practical work in life. He came home and speedily argued his benevolent uncle to death, but not before the old gentleman had stricken the logician from his will and diverted his entire property to the endowment of an asylum for deaf mutes.

"My dear Nicholas," said Tithami, when Vance had sung all twelve books of his epic of pain, "you are the luckiest individual in the city of Boston. I congratulate you from the bottom of my heart. Take your hand away from your cheek and sit down in that easy chair and rejoice."

"Thank you," groaned Vance, who knew the chair. "I prefer to stand up."

"Well," said Tithami cheerfully, "stand up if it pleases you so long as you stand still. The floor creaks and my landlady, who is absurdly fussy over a trifle of rent, has a way of rushing in when the slightest noise reminds her of the fact of my existence. You've read how, in the Alps, a breeze sometimes brings down an avalanche?"

"Hang your landlady!" shouted Nicholas. "I came to you as a friend, for sympathy, not to be jeered at."

"If you must walk up and down like a maniac, Nicholas," continued Tithami, "pardon me for suggesting that you keep off that third plank from the fireplace. It's particularly loose. I repeat, Nicholas, that you are a lucky dog. I would give my dinners for a week for such a neuralgia."

"Can you do anything for me or not?" demanded Nicholas, fiercely. "I don't like to exercise intimidation, but, by Jupiter, if you don't stop chaffing, I'll raise a yell that will start the avalanche."

A perceptible tremor passed over Tithami's frame. It was evident that the threat was not ineffectual. He arose hastily and assured himself that the door was securely bolted. Then he returned to Vance and addressed him with considerable impressiveness of manner.

"Nicholas," said he, "I was perfectly serious when I congratulated you upon your neuralgia. You, like myself, are a speculative logician. Although not in an entirely candid and reasonable frame of mind just now, you will not, I am sure, refuse a syllogism. Let me ask you two plain Socratic questions and present one syllogism, and then I'll give you something that will subdue your pain—under protest, mind you, for I shall feel that I am wronging you, Nicholas."

"Confound your sense of justice!" exclaimed Nicholas. "I accept the proposition."

"Well, answer me this. Do you like a hot Indian curry?"

"Nothing better," said Nicholas.

"But suppose someone had offered you a curry when you were fifteen years younger—during the bread and milk era of your gastronomic evolution. Would you have partaken of it with signal pleasure?"

"No," said Vance. "I should have as soon thought of sucking the red-hot end of a poker."

"Good. Now we will proceed to our syllogism. Here it is. Sensations that are primarily disagreeable may become more or less agreeable by a proper education of the senses. Physical pain is primarily disagreeable. Therefore, *even physical pain, by judicious cultivation, may be made a source of exquisite pleasure!*"

"That doesn't help my neuralgia," said Nicholas. "What does it all mean, anyway?"

"I never heard you speak unkindly of a syllogism before," said Tithami, sorrowfully. Then he took a small jar from a closet in the corner and shook out of it a little pile of fine white powder, of which he gave Nicholas as much as would cover an old-fashioned copper cent. This he did with evident reluctance.

"Come here tonight," he added, "at half past nine, and I will try to show you what it all means, my young friend."

II

The apprehension of a new and profoundly significant truth is a slow process. As Nicholas walked home over the bridge he pondered the syllogism which Tithami had advanced. When he reached the front gate of the house where Miss Margaret Stull lived, and saw that young lady in her flower garden watering polyanthuses, it occurred to him for the first time that he had forgotten his neuralgia.

He sat down on the doorstep and lighted a cigar. The kind inquiries and gentle solicitude of his sweetheart made him rather ashamed of himself. It was not dignified that a young philosopher with a heroic malady should be sitting among polyanthuses, forgetful of his misery, and actually experiencing that dull glow of bodily self-satisfaction which a well-fed Newfoundland dog may be supposed to enjoy when he lies in the sunshine. Nicholas felt it his duty to subject the facts of the case to logical analysis.

The first result obtained was the remarkable fact that the pain was still present in all its intensity.

Upon closely examining his sensations, Vance could discover no change in either the frequency or the acuteness of the nervous pangs. At tolerably regular periods the stream of fire ran throbbing through his face and temples. In the intervals of recurrence there was the same dull aching which had made life intolerable for days before. Nicholas, therefore, felt safe in the induction that the powder administered by Tithami had not cured the pain.

The astonishing thing was that ever since he had taken the powder the pain had been a matter of indifference. Nicholas was compelled to admit, as a candid logician, that he would not raise a finger to rid himself of the neuralgia now. So strange was the transformation wrought in his sensatory system that he even felt a sort of satisfaction in the throbbing and the aching, and would have been sorry, rather than glad, to have them cease. Indeed, the more he thought about it the nearer he approached to the conclusion that neuralgia, under the existing conditions, was a luxury and something to be cherished.

When this idea was communicated to Miss Margaret Stull, she at once became alarmed for his sanity, and ran to fetch her aunt Penelope. That respectable and experienced maiden heard the proposition stated without showing surprise or other emotion. Her comment was comprised in a single word.

"Morphia," said Miss Penelope.

"Call it lotus or ambrosia," exclaimed Nicholas, "call it morphia, or what you will. If there is a potency in the blessed drug that can transform agony into joy, torment into delight, make the forenoon's paroxysms of torture the pulsations of ecstasy in the afternoon, why may it not be, as Tithami said, that—but I'll go to Boston and ask him this very hour."

Nicholas paused, for both Miss Penelope and Margaret were regarding him with amazement. Margaret looked bewildered, but on her aunt's face there was a very peculiar expression, which he afterward recalled most vividly.

"Mr. Vance," said Miss Penelope calmly, "the morphia is acting on your head. Suppose you lie down on the sofa in the back parlor, where it's cool and quiet, until suppertime. After a good cup of tea you'll be in better condition to go to Boston, and I shall be very glad of your escort. I'm to spend the evening with some friends at the West End."

III

At twenty-five minutes past nine Vance climbed the stairs that led to Tithami's abode. He found the speculative logician arrayed in full evening dress and just drawing on a pair of tight boots. This surprised Nicholas. He had never known his friend to be guilty of that folly before.

"Neuralgia's not so bad a thing, eh, Nicholas?" said Tithami, gaily. "Something like a hot curry when your taste's educated up to it. Great pity, though, to blunt the edge of your enjoyment with morphine. It's like sprinkling sawdust over a fine raw oyster. However, we'll soon have you educated beyond such crude practices. I want you to go out with me."

"But I'm not dressed," said Nicholas.

Tithami went to the looking glass and complacently surveyed his own rather rusty attire. "That makes no difference," said he; "it won't be noticed. Now, if you'll have the goodness to go downstairs first. If the coast is clear, whistle 'Annie Laurie,' and I'll come right along. But if you observe at the foot of the stairs a she-dragon, a female Borgia, a gorgon, a raging Tisiphone in a black bombazine dress, whistle the 'Dead March' from *Saul*, and I'll climb down the gutter pipe and join you at the corner."

The coast happened to be clear, and the notes of "Annie Laurie" brought Tithami to the street door close upon Nicholas' heels. He led Vance through street after street, and turned corner after corner, discoursing the while upon light topics with the rattling air of a man about town. Nicholas had never seen Tithami display such animal spirits before. He seemed to have shaken off the mustiness of scholastic logic, and walked and talked like a nineteenth-century blade on his way to a congenial debauch.

"You were saying this morning," said Nicholas—timidly opening a subject on which he very much desired instruction—"you were saying that physical pain, being only a relative term, inasmuch as the same sensations in a modified degree often yield us what we call physical pleasure, might be cultivated so as to be a source of exquisite enjoyment. Now it seems to me that this theory—"

"Oh, bother theory," said Tithami, smartly and apparently with purpose rapping his knuckles against a lamp post they were just then passing. "What's the use talking of theory when you'll shortly see the idea in actual practice?"

"But please tell me what you mean," persisted Nicholas, "by pain's being only relative."

"Why," said Tithami, "who can draw the line, for example, that marks the boundary between the comfortable feeling you have after a good dinner, and the uncomfortable feeling you have after eating too much? In one case the sensation is translated by your brain into pleasure. In the other, the same sensation, only a trifle more pronounced, is called pain. Are you as blind as a newborn rabbit that you can't see, after sitting so long under Professor Surdity, that the distinction between pain and pleasure is nothing but a fallacy of words? Didn't your morphine experience today prove that? Throw away the morphine and educate your intelligence up to the proper standard and you get the same result."

Here Tithami, as if wearied of parleying, stopped short and began to dance a vigorous jig upon the pavement.

"Why do you dance if your boots are tight?" Nicholas ventured to inquire.

"Simply because they *are* tight, and my feet very tender," replied Tithami.

Nicholas walked on in silence. Tithami's conduct became more and more astonishing every minute. But Nicholas' surprise culminated when his friend halted in front of a brick mansion which had once been aristocratic. Tithami ascended the steps and rang the doorbell with the air of one who has reached his destination. No wonder Nicholas was surprised. It was to that same door that he had escorted Margaret's aunt Penelope, not half an hour earlier that very evening.

IV

Nicholas had once attended a meeting of the First Radical Club in a private house not far from the one which he now entered. The scene in the parlor recalled the session of the Advanced Thinkers. About a dozen men and women, more or less progressive in appearance, were sitting in chairs or on sofas listening to a paper read in a mumbling voice by a tall gentleman who stood in a corner and held his manuscript close to his spectacles. The essay did not seem to excite much enthusiasm. There were more empty chairs than auditors.

When Nicholas and Tithami were ushered in, nearly all the company arose and greeted the latter silently but with every evidence of profound respect. Indeed, the salutations were almost oriental in their obsequiousness.

"You are quite a rooster here, Tithami," whispered Vance, irreverently.

"Hush!" Tithami whispered in return. "It was I who first

brought this idea from Heidelberg to Boston. It is simply their gratitude for a great boon. But listen to the essay."

The speaker was just then saying: "Let it be postulated that the principle which we hold is the true arcanum, the actual earthly paradise, and let it be also postulated that we shall progress from the material to the intellectual in the development of this principle, and who can escape the conclusion from these premises? As we advance in the self-discipline that already enables us to derive the highest physical pleasure from sensations that have been deemed a curse since Cain's first colic, we shall find still loftier joys in the region of mental pain. I firmly believe that the time is not distant when to the initiated the death of a wife or husband will be a keener joy than the first kiss at the altar, the bankruptcy of a fortune a truer source of elation than the receipt of a legacy, the disappointment of ambition more welcome than the fruition of hope. This is but the logical—"

Nicholas could no longer contain himself. He knew the voice, the style of reasoning, the spectacles. He had listened too often and too intently to the lectures of Professor Surdity of Harvard College to mistake him for another, or another for him. He uttered a low whistle. Tithami checked him on the very edge of another.

"Above all things," he whispered, "show no astonishment at anything you may see or hear. And take special care to recognize nobody you meet, even if it is your own grandmother. The etiquette of the place requires that much of you."

Tithami now arose and beckoned Nicholas to follow him out of the room. "This is slow," said he. "The professor is inclined to be prosy. A few of the old fogies of our number like to sit and listen to him. They are probably trying to carry his principle to the extent of deriving excitement from a painful bore. We mustn't waste time here. Let's go to the symposium."

A passageway, screened by heavy curtains, led to an extension apartment that originally had been built for a painting gallery. It had no windows. The skylight overhead had been removed and the room was as completely sequestered as the inner chamber of one of the pyramids of Gizeh. On a table in the middle of the apartment a repast was laid. The table was surrounded by broad couches, like the *lecti* of the Romans, on which several persons were reclining. A few were eating, but the majority seemed wrapped in the sufficiency of inactive bliss. In the corners of the room Nicholas observed several bulky machines of wood. The place seemed half banquet hall, half gymnasium.

As had been the case in the outer parlors, all the company arose and saluted Tithami with marked deference. This was done almost mechanically, and as if a matter of course. Of Nicholas' presence the Pain Epicures apparently took no more notice than the inmates of a Chinese opium den would have done. There was a dreamy languor upon the company that made the locality seem not unlike an opium den.

Tithami went directly to a sideboard and poured from a decanter a brimming draft.

"It is aqua fortis," he explained, "diluted, of course, but strong enough to take the skin from the lips, and set the mouth and throat a burning. You will try a glass? No? It would be no stronger to your taste than raw brandy is to a child's. The child grows up and learns to like brandy. You will grow to esteem this tipple. Ah, Doctor! A glass with you. How are you enjoying yourself nowadays?"

In the gentleman who approached at this moment, and whom Tithami thus addressed, Nicholas recognized one of the most eminent of Boston physicians, celebrated as a skillful practitioner all through the eastern States. The doctor shook his head at Tithami's polite question.

"Poorly, very poorly," he replied. "The moxa yields me no more pleasure now than a mere cup blister or leeching. I'd give half my income to be able to enjoy a simple neuralgia as I used to."

Tithami gave Nicholas a significant look.

"And yet," continued the doctor, musingly, "the blind, ignorant fools who employ me professionally insist on taking chloroform for a trifling amputation. I suppose they won't have a tooth drawn without anesthesia. What a pity that a luxury like pain cannot be monopolized by those who can appreciate it!"

"With your resources and pathological knowledge," suggested Tithami, "you ought to keep abreast of your pain progress and avoid ennui."

"I try everything," rejoined the medical gentleman, with a sigh. "Did it ever occur to you, Tithami," he continued, with more animation, "that if one could find some stimulant that would arouse the entire nervous system to acuter sensibility than any agent now known, he might make himself conscious of the circulation of the blood. How delightful it would be to actually feel the hot tide rushing along the arteries, oozing through the capillaries, coursing the veins, and surging into the aorta! Why, it would lend a new piquancy to existence."

"He is one of the most advanced of us," said Tithami to Nicholas after the doctor had passed on. "But he goes too fast. I believe in moderation in pain, as in all other enjoyments. By being temperate in my indulgences I keep the edge keen. By using the moxa three or four times a day the doctor killed the goose that laid the golden eggs. He's not enough of a philosopher to be an epicure."

"Have all your friends here advanced as far as the doctor?" asked Nicholas.

"Oh dear no! You understand that as one progresses the dose must be increased. While a beginner may be contented with a toothache, or may satiate himself by eating green watermelons for the colic, like that young man yonder, or by sticking pins in the calf of his leg, as those three gentlemen on the left-hand couch are doing at this moment, there are others, of more cultivated appetites, who must have the higher grades of pain. Yet it's the same thing in all stages. Some are content to be rational in their dissipations; others plunge into extremes. I have in mind a banker, not present tonight, who became so infatuated with the use of an old-fashioned thumbscrew which he picked up in some curiosity shop, that he takes it in his pocket to the office and uses it surreptitiously during business hours. I have no patience with such a man. He must either degenerate into a secret voluptuary or else set a bad example to his clerks."

"I should think so!" said Nicholas.

"Now here's a very different character," continued Tithami, as a burly German approached. "He's satisfied with the simplest pleasures. Good evening, mein Herr. You are all smiles tonight."

"*Ach Gott!*" said the Teuton, "but I have one lovely head woe. I have been—how say you it?—ge-butting *mein kopf* unt de wall."

"And over there," Tithami went on, after congratulating the German on his method, "is one of the rarest examples of besotted folly that I could possibly show you. That man with his hand tied up in a cloth and a serene smile on his face was ass enough one day to cut off the tip of his little finger for the sake of the temporary gratification he had from the smart. He is a lawyer in good practice and ought to know better. Well, the wound healed, and his enjoyment was over. So he cut off a fresh slice, a little further down. Thus it went on, little by little, till now he has nothing but the stumps of seven fingers and a thumb to show for his sport. He's begun on the eighth finger already, and I'll wager that he lays his next case before the jury with a solitary thumb."

A strident creaking now attracted Nicholas' attention to one of the wooden machines in the corner. Proceeding thither, followed by Tithami, he beheld an extraordinary spectacle. The machine rudely resembled an overshot water wheel. It was operated by a crank at which a brawny African of decorous demeanor was laboring. Upon the rim of the wheel, lashed hand and foot, was stretched a fleshy citizen of middle age and highly respectable appearance. He was in his shirt sleeves, and the perspiration stood in great beads upon his brow, but his face bore an expression of ineffable felicity. At every exertion of the darky at the crank the strain upon the fat epicure's muscles and joints increased. The tension seemed to be terrific, yet Nicholas heard him whisper, in a voice almost inaudible, but ecstatic beyond description, "Give her one more turn, George Washington, one—more—little—yank—"

"I was just now speaking," said Tithami, "of the higher grades of pain. Here you have an example. The fat gentleman is a well-known capitalist and also a man of leisure, like myself. He lives on Beacon Street. He is something of an enthusiast in the pursuit of pain novelties. He bought that machine at Madrid and presented it to the association. It is an undoubted original of the instrument of torture known as the rack, and is said to have been used by the Inquisition. At all events it is still in good working order. With a capable man at the crank it affords an amount of refined pleasure which I hope you will some day be able to appreciate."

Nicholas shuddered and turned away from the rack. By this time there were thirty-five or forty epicures in the room. The company had been increased by the party from the parlors, Professor Surdity's essay being at last concluded. There was more bustle and activity among the epicures than earlier in the evening. The intoxication of pain was working its effect and the revel was growing reckless and noisy.

"Let us see what they are doing," said Nicholas.

"Make yourself perfectly at home," replied Tithami, politely. "I told you your presence would not be noticed. Go wherever you please, and if you feel like testing any of our appliances, don't hesitate to do so. But if you'll kindly excuse me for a few minutes, I think I'll take the next turn on the rack."

The revel went on with increasing zest. The hum of delirious voices mingled with the creaking of two or three of the instruments of torture. On one side Nicholas saw a sedate party consisting of two philosophers and half a dozen theological students. They were sitting on a bench cushioned with the sharp points of tacks, and were discussing the immortality of the soul in a most animated manner. Several epicures had taken a hint from the German, and were butting their craniums against the wall. A young man, evidently inexperienced in the luxuries of pain, seemed to derive exquisite pleasure from the simplest form of torture. He had inserted one finger in the joint of a lemon squeezer, and was grimacing with callow delight as he pressed together the handles of the utensil with his other hand. Two doctors of divinity had stripped themselves to the waist, and were obligingly flagellating each other in turn with willow switches. It was creditable to their sense of equity that the reciprocal service was performed with exact fairness, both in regard to time and in regard to the energy with which the blows were administered. Nicholas observed that, as a rule, the intoxication of pain made men selfish. Wrapped in the felicity of his own sensations, each epicure had little concern for the enjoyment of those around him.

That, however, was not the case with a group of men and women who had gathered at the remotest end of the apartment. There was a buzz of conversation there, and a manifest display of interest, as over some great novelty. The crowd was applauding the inventor of a new appliance. Nicholas pushed his way into the group, and then suddenly started back dumbfounded.

A woman of middle age sat on an ottoman, her foot in a basket that was tightly covered over with cloth. A shoe and a stocking lay on the floor. The woman's hair was disordered and her face flushed with unhealthy excitement. With the abandon of a mad bacchante, she began to sing a lively but incoherent song. Her rather shrill voice floated into the uncertain quavers of hysterical rapture. Nicholas turned to a bystander. "What has she in the basket?" he demanded.

"Six nests of hornets," was the answer. "Isn't it beautiful? It's the discovery of the age, and to think that a lady should be the first!"

v

Nicholas was almost stupefied with horror and disgust. He knew the basket, for he had brought it from Cambridge. He knew

the lady, for she was Margaret's aunt Penelope. Margaret's aunt
the central figure in such an orgy! He pushed his way to the front
and stood before the frantic woman. She looked up, and a cloudy
expression of dim remembrance and uncertain shame came over
her face. "Put on your shoe!" he sternly said. Mechanically she
obeyed. Nicholas kicked aside the basket, and there was a fierce
struggle among the epicures for the possession of the treasure.
The young man heeded not their rivalry. He took Miss Penelope
by the arm and led her out of the unholy place, out of the house.
The fresh night air brought her partially to her senses. She hung
her head and accompanied him in silence.

The last car for Cambridge was just starting from the square.
During the long ride not a word was said by Nicholas, and not
a word by his companion. At the door of the house the silence
was first broken. Nicholas looked up from the ground. The moon
lighted the window of the room where Margaret was innocently
sleeping.

"For Margaret's sake and for your own sake, Miss Penelope,"
said Nicholas, in a low but firm voice, "swear to me never to visit
that place again."

Miss Penelope's frame shook with agitation. She sobbed
violently. She looked first at Nicholas and then at Margaret's window. At last she spoke.

"I swear it!" said Miss Penelope.

A DAY AMONG THE LIARS

MY DEAR FRIEND: You will no doubt be glad to hear about the newly established infirmary at Lugville. I visited it a few days ago in company with Mr. Merkle, a Boston lawyer, whom I happened to meet upon the train. On the way down he gave me a most interesting account of the endowment of this institution by the late Lorin Jenks, to whose discriminating philanthropy the world owes a charity that is not less novel in its conception than noble and practical in its aim.

Mr. Lorin Jenks, as you know, was president of the Saco Stocking and Sock Mills. He was a bachelor, and a very remarkable man. He made a million dollars one day by observing women as they purchased hose in a cheap store in Tremont Row. Mr. Jenks noticed that females who hesitated a good while about paying fifty cents a pair for plain white stockings eagerly paid seventy-five cents for the same quality ornamented with red clocks at the ankles. It cost twenty-two cents a pair to manufacture the stockings. The red flosselle for the clocks cost a quarter of a cent.

"That observation," said Mr. Merkle, "was the foundation of Jenks's great fortune. The Saco Mills immediately stopped making plain hosiery. From that time forth Jenks manufactured nothing but stockings with red clocks, which he retailed at sixty cents. I am told that there is not a woman under sixty-five in Massachusetts, New Hampshire, Maine, or Vermont who does not own at least half a dozen pairs of poor Jenks's sixty-cent red clockers."

"That fact," said I, "would interest Mr. Matthew Arnold. It shows that sweetness and light—"

"Pardon me. It shows that Jenks was a practical man, as well as a philosopher. Busy as he was during his life, he took great interest in politics, like all sensible citizens. He was also a metaphysician. He closely followed contemporary speculative thought, inclining, until shortly before his death, to the Hegelian school. Every midsummer, he left the stocking mill to run itself and repaired joyfully to Concord to listen to the lectures in the apple orchard. It is my private opinion that Messrs. Plato, Kant & Co. bled him pretty heavily for the privilege. But at Concord Jenks acquired new ideas as to his duty to the race."

Mr. Merkle paused to hand his ticket to the conductor.

"During the last years of his life, inasmuch as he was known to be eccentric, philanthropic, and without a family, Jenks was much beset by people who sought to interest him in various schemes for the amelioration of the human race. A week before he died he sent for me.

"'Merkle,' says he, 'I want you to draw me a will so leathery that no shark in Pemberton Square can bite it in two.'

"'Well,' says I, 'what is it now, Jenks?'

"'I wish,' says he, 'to devote my entire fortune to the endowment of an institution, the idea of which occurred to me at Concord.'

"'That's right,' said I, rather sharply. 'Put honest money made in red clock hose into the Concord windmill—that's a fine final act for a summer philosopher.'

"'Wait a minute,' said Jenks, and I fancied I saw a smile around the corners of his mouth. 'It isn't the Concord school I want to endow, although I don't deny there may be certain expectations in and around the orchard. But why spend money in teaching wisdom to the wise?' And then he proceeded to unfold his noble plan for the foundation of an Infirmary for the Mendacious."

The train was hauling up at the platform of the Lugville station.

"A few days later," continued the lawyer, as we arose from our seats, "this far-seeing and public-spirited citizen died. By the terms of his will, the income of $1,500,000 in governments, Massachusetts sixes, Boston and Albany stock, and sound first mortgages on New England property is devoted to the infirmary, under the direction of thirteen trustees. How the trust has been administered, you will see for yourself in a few minutes."

We were met at the door of the infirmary by a pleasant-faced gentleman who spoke with a slight German accent and introduced himself as the assistant superintendent.

"Excuse me," said he, politely, "but which of you is the patient?"

"Oh, neither," replied Merkle, with a laugh. "I am the counsel for the Board, and this gentleman is merely a visitor who is interested in the workings of the institution."

"Ah, I see," said the assistant superintendent. "Will you kindly walk this way?"

We entered the office, and he handed me a book and a pen. "Please inscribe your name," said he, "in the Visitors' Book." I did so, and then turned to speak to Merkle, but the lawyer had disappeared.

"Our system," said the assistant superintendent, "is very simple. The theory of the institution is that the habit of mendacity, which in many cases becomes chronic, is a moral disease, like habitual inebriety, and that it can generally be cured. We take the liar who voluntarily submits himself to our treatment, and for six months we submit him to the forcing process. That is, we encourage him in lying, surround him with liars, his equals and superiors in skill, and cram him with falsehood until he is fairly saturated. By this time the reaction has set in, and the patient is usually starved for the truth. He is prepared to welcome the second course of treatment. For the next half year the opposite method is pursued. The satiated and disgusted liar is surrounded by truthful attendants, encouraged to peruse veracious literature, and by force of lectures, example, and moral influence brought to understand how much more creditable it is to say the thing which is than the thing which is not. Then we send him back into the world; and I must say that cases of relapse are infrequent."

"Do you find no incurables?" I asked.

"Yes," said the assistant superintendent, "once in a while. But an incurable liar is better off here in the infirmary than outside, and it is better for the outside community to have him here."

Somebody came in, bringing a new patient. After sending for the superintendent, the assistant invited me to follow him. "I will show you how our patients live, and how they amuse themselves," he said. "We will go first, if you please, through the left wing, where the saturating process may be observed."

He led the way across a hall into a large room, comfortably furnished, and occupied by two dozen or more gentlemen, some reading, some writing, while others sat or stood in groups engaged in animated talk. Indeed, had it not been for the iron bars at the windows, I might have fancied myself in the lounging room of a respectable club. My guide stopped to speak to an inmate who was listlessly turning the leaves of a well-thumbed copy of *Baron Münchausen,* and left me standing near enough to one of the groups to overhear parts of the conversation.

"My rod creaked and bent double," a stout, red-faced gentleman was saying, "and the birch spun like a testotum. I tell you if Pierre Chaveau hadn't had the presence of mind to grip the most convenient part of my trousers with the boat hook, I should have been dragged into the lake in two seconds or less. Well, sir, we fought sixty-nine minutes by actual time taking, and when I had him in, and had got him back to the hotel, he tipped the scale, the speckled beauty did, at thirty-seven pounds and eleven-sixteenths, whether you believe it or not."

"Nonsense," said a quiet little gentleman who sat opposite. "That is impossible."

The first speaker looked flattered at this and colored with pleasure. "Nevertheless," he retorted, "it's a fact, on my honor as a sportsman. Why do you say it's impossible?"

"Because," said the other, calmly, "it is an ascertained scientific fact, as every true fisherman in this room knows perfectly well, that there are no trout in Mooselemagunticook weighing under half a hundred."

"Certainly not," put in a third speaker. "The bottom of the lake is a sieve—a sort of schistose sieve formation—and all the fish smaller than the fifty-pounders fall through."

"Why doesn't the water drop through, too?" asked the stout patient, in a triumphant tone.

"It used to," replied the quiet gentleman gravely, "until the Maine legislature passed an act preventing it."

My guide rejoined me and we went on across the room. "These sportsman liars," he said, "are among the mildest and most easily cured cases that come here. We send them away in from six to nine weeks' time with the habit broken up and pledged not to fish or hunt any more. The man who lies about the fish he has caught, or about the intelligence of his red setter dog is often in all other respects a trustworthy citizen. Yet such cases form nearly forty per cent of all our patients."

"What are the most obstinate cases?"

"Undoubtedly those which you will see in the Travelers' and Politicians' wards of the infirmary. The more benign cases, such as the fishermen liars, the society liars, the lady-killer or *bonnes fortunes* liars, the Rocky Mountain and frontier liars [excepting Texas cases], the railroad prospectus liars, the psychical research liars, and the miscellaneous liars of various classes, we permit during the first stage of treatment to mingle freely with each other. The effect is good. But we keep the Travelers and the Politicians strictly isolated."

He was about to conduct me out of the room by a door opposite that through which we had entered when a detached phrase uttered by a pompous gentleman arrested my attention.

"Scipio Africanus once remarked to me—"

"There couldn't be a better example," said my guide, as we passed out of the room, "of what we call the forcing system in the treatment of mendacity. That patient came to us voluntarily about two months ago. The form of his disease is a common one. Perfectly truthful in all other respects, he cannot resist the temptation to claim personal acquaintance and even intimacy with distinguished individuals. His friends laughed at him so much for this weakness that when he heard of the establishment of the infirmary he came here like a sensible man, and put himself under our care. He is doing splendidly. When he found that his reminiscences of Beaconsfield and Bismarck and Victor Hugo created no sensation here, but were, on the contrary, at once matched and capped by still more remarkable experiences narrated by other inmates, he was at first a little staggered. But the habit is so strong, and the peculiar vanity that craves admiration on this score is so exacting, that he began to extend his acquaintance, gradually and cautiously, back into the past. Soon we had him giving reminiscences of Talleyrand, of Thomas Jefferson, and of Lord Cornwallis. Observe the psychologic effect of our system. The ordinary checks on the performances of such a liar being removed, and, no doubt, suspicion, nor even wonder being expressed at any of his anecdotes, he has gone back through Voltaire and William the Silent to Charlemagne, and so on. There happens to be in the institution another patient with precisely the same trouble. They are, therefore, in active competition, and each serves to force the other back more rapidly. Not long ago I heard our friend in here describing one of Heliogabalus' banquets, which he had attended as an honored guest. 'Why, I was there, too!' cried the other liar. 'It was the night they gave us the boar's head stuffed with goose giblets and that delicious dry Opimian muscadine.'"

"Well," I asked, "and what is your prognosis in this case?"

"Just now the two personal reminiscence liars are driving each other back through ancient history at the rate of about three centuries a week. The flood isn't likely to stop them. Before long they will be matching reminiscences of the antediluvian patriarchs, and then they'll bring up square on Adam. They can't go any further than Adam. By that time they will be ready for the truth-cure process; and after a few weeks spent in an atmosphere of strict veracity in the other wing of the infirmary, they'll go out into the world again perfectly cured, and much more useful citizens than before they came to us."

We went upstairs and saw the scrupulously neat bedrooms which the patients occupy; through the separate wards where the isolated classes are treated; across to the right wing of the building and into a lecture room where the convalescent liars were gathered to hear a most interesting dissertation on "The Inexpediency of Falsehood from the Legal Point of View." I was not surprised to recognize in the lecturer my railroad acquaintance, the Boston lawyer, Merkle.

On our way back to the reception room, or office, we met a pleasant-looking gentleman about forty years old. "He is a well-known society man," the assistant superintendent whispered as the inmate approached, "and he was formerly the most politely insincere person in America. Nobody could tell when he was uttering the truth, or, indeed, whether he ever did utter the truth. His habit became so exaggerated that his relatives induced him to come to Lugville for treatment. I am glad to have you see him, for he is a good example of a radical cure. We shall be ready to discharge him by the first of next week."

The cured liar was about to pass us, but the assistant superintendent stopped him. "Mr. Van Ransevoort," he said, "let me make you acquainted with this gentleman, who has been inspecting our system."

"I am glad to meet you, Mr. Van Ransevoort," I said.

He raised his hat and made me an unexceptionable bow. "And

I," he replied, with a smile of charming courtesy, "am neither glad nor sorry to meet you, sir. I simply don't care a d—n."

The somewhat startling candor of his words was so much at variance with the perfect politeness of his manner that I was taken aback. I stammered something about not desiring to intrude. But as he still stood there as if expecting the conversation to be continued, I added, "I suppose you are looking forward to your release next week?"

"Yes, sir," he replied, "I shall be rather glad to get out again, but my wife will be sorry."

I looked at the assistant superintendent. He returned a glance full of professional pride.

"Well, good-by, Mr. Van Ransevoort," I said. "Perhaps I shall have the pleasure of meeting you again."

"I hope not, sir; it's rather a bore," said he, shaking my hand most cordially, and giving the assistant superintendent a friendly nod as he passed on.

I could fill many more pages than I have time to write with descriptions of what I saw in the infirmary. Intelligence and thoroughness were apparent in all of the arrangements. I encountered and conversed with liars of more variation and degree of mendacity than you would believe had distinct existence. The majority of the cases were commonplace enough. Liars of real genius seem to be as rare inside the establishment as they are outside. I became convinced from my observations during the profitable afternoon which I spent at Lugville that chronic mendacity is a disease, as the assistant superintendent said, and that it is amenable, in a great number of cases, to proper treatment. On the importance of the experiment that is being carried on at Lugville with so much energy and apparent success, it is not necessary to dilate.

I sincerely hope that you will not misconstrue my motives in laying the matter before you; and I cannot too strongly urge you to go down to Lugville yourself at the earliest opportunity. You ought to see with your own eyes how admirably Lorin Jenks's bequest is administered, and what a prospect of reform and re-generation the infirmary's system holds out to unfortunates. The regular visitors' day is Wednesday. No doubt they would admit you at any time.

OUR WAR WITH MONACO

When I last visited Monaco I found that enlightened community in a state of exasperation against everything that is American. I even detected covert hostility in the manner of M. Berg of the Beau Rivage Hotel, who had formerly received me with so much politeness. After breakfast, during which meal the waiter glared at me with undisguised hatred, I went to pay my respects to our diplomatic representative, an acquaintance of old in Ohio. The consul's face was haggard, as if from protracted anxiety. He was putting the final touches to an elaborate toilet.

"What is the trouble, Green?" I demanded.

The consul sighed repeatedly while he was framing his reply. The excellent fellow had a habit of adorning his ordinary conversation with the phraseology of an official dispatch. This process required more or less time, but the effect was impressive.

"I must inform you," he said, "that the relations between the United States and the Independent Principality of Monaco, cordial as they have been in the past, are approaching a crisis full of peril. Recent events justify the apprehensions which I have from time to time expressed in my communications to the Department of State at Washington. It would be folly to conceal the fact that the present attitude of the court of Prince Charles III is anything but friendly to our own government; or that the situation is one which calls for the utmost watchfulness and the most delicate diplomacy. I have the honor to add that I shall be both prudent and firm."

"Yes," said I; "but what is the row about?"

"The complication," he replied, emphasizing that word, "arises partly from the dark intrigues of the crafty statesmen who surround the prince, and partly from the behavior of Americans here and at Nice, particularly Titus."

"And who the deuce is Titus?"

"George Washington Titus," he replied, with a look full of gloom, "is a man whose existence and acts embitter my official career; yet I am constantly yielding to the remarkable influence which he exerts over me, as over most people with whom he comes in contact. George Washington Titus is a perpetual source of danger to the peace that has been maintained so long between the United States and Monaco; yet when he is with me I cannot help being carried away by the reckless enthusiasm of his nature. To employ a colloquialism, he has kept me in hot water ever since he arrived. Pardon me; but, privately and personally and apart from my official capacity, I sometimes say to myself, 'Confound George Washington Titus!'"

"Now," I remarked, "I am just as wise as I was before."

"The story is a long one, and, as in every affair of international moment, the details are many and complicated. I am about to have an interview with the hereditary prince, and shall officially request an explanation of certain things. Come with me to the palace. I will give you the facts as we walk."

It is only a step from the American consulate to the palace, and the consul's narrative advanced slowly, owing to the dignity of its periods. For convenience, I had better join what he told me on this occasion with what I afterward learned respecting the difficulty.

Since 1869, when Prince Charles III abolished taxation, the revenue of the government of Monaco has been derived exclusively from the gaming tables at the casino. The prince's subjects, nearly six thousand souls, have been prosperous and happy, having no taxes to pay and plenty of travelers to fleece. The income from the casino has been large enough to meet all administrative expenses, to support the court in a style befitting the importance of the oldest reigning family in Europe—for Prince Charles traces his line of descent directly back to the Grimaldi of the tenth century—and to leave a handsome annual surplus, part of which has been wisely devoted to a system of internal improvements.

In pursuit of this policy, it had been determined about a year before to blast out the large rock at the mouth of the cove behind the palace. The prince's Navy, which consists of a steam launch of about twelve tons burden, armed with a swivel gun, is accustomed to ride at anchor in this cove when not actively engaged. The rock seriously impeded the free ingress and egress of the Navy. The contract for the work of removal was awarded by Roasio, Minister of Marine, to Titus, an American engineer.

Up to the time of Titus' arrival in Monaco, the Americans had been popular with the subjects of the prince. They were liberal in expending money, rarely disputed reckoning at the hotels, cafés, and shops, and contributed largely to the revenue of the casino. The official pathway of my friend, the consul, had lain over rose beds. Titus himself won much applause at first. He was a tall, good-looking Baltimorean, who had been major of Engineers in the Union Army. A genial and sometimes roistering companion of men, gallant in his bearing toward the ladies of the court, skillful in his attack on the obnoxious rock, he had enjoyed for a time a pronounced success in Monaco. The people watched with pride the operations of his divers, the work of his steam dredge, the arrival and unloading of the square tin cans of dynamite which came consigned to him from Marseilles. He was in a measure identified with the mysterious forces of nature, and therefore a little feared; but it was generally conceded that he deserved well of the inhabitants.

Soon, however, he was unfortunate enough to incur the displeasure of several very influential personages; and although he himself cared not a copper for the frown of any dignitary on the peninsula, the consul, who felt more or less responsible for him, thenceforth trod on thorns. Titus' decline in prestige was due to several causes.

One night, being in his cups, he had knocked down M. De Mussly, the generalissimo of the Army, who had ventured to remonstrate with him for practicing the war whoop of the American Indian in the public square in front of the palace. On receiving a challenge the next morning from the outraged warrior, Titus had laughed, and offered to swim with De Mussly due south across the Mediterranean until one or the other should be drowned. The affair was brought to the attention of the Tribunal Superieur by M. Goybet, Advocate-General, but Consul Green succeeded in having the charge suppressed.

Then followed another misadventure, far worse than the De Mussly incident. At a grand ball at the casino, Titus deliberately excused himself from dancing a fifth polka with the Princess Florestine, sister of the reigning prince. This august lady is a widow, who, in spite of her fifty years and two hundred pounds, has managed to preserve the impulses and tastes of maiden youth. If rumor was to be credited, she was not unkindly disposed toward the good-looking American engineer. When Titus was asked by a friend why he chose to fly in the face of Providence, he replied, "I had already danced four times with the princess. The old lady ought to remember that people go to balls for pleasure." This remark, of course, came to the ears of the princess, and thereafter she devoted every energy to the accomplishment of Titus' ruin.

The unlucky American next provoked the hostility of the all-powerful authorities at the casino, by introducing the game of poker as a rival, in private society, to the public attractions of roulette and rouge et noir. The new heresy spread like wildfire. In Monaco and in Nice people lost money to each other, instead of to the bank, as formerly. Receipts at the casino fell off more than one half. In vain the Administration procured a deliverance from the ecclesiastical authorities, declaring the game immoral. People still played poker. Worse than all, Titus and his disciples turned the terrible new engine against the subjects of the prince, and won *their* money. This was a startling innovation, and it awakened deep resentment. It was said that no less a personage than Monsignor Theuret, the Grand Almoner, having won thirteen thousand francs at roulette on a succession of three seventeens, lost the entire amount the next night at poker to Titus, and as much more besides; and that he was obliged to give his note for a large sum to the American. This was a specimen case.

As the prosperity of the people of Monaco rested wholly upon the prosperity of the casino, popular indignation rose high against the Americans, especially Titus. The poker question found a place in politics. Titus' enemies were unceasing in their efforts to undermine him at the court and neglected no means to inflame the prejudices of the populace.

II

Such, then, was the situation when I accompanied Consul Green to the palace.

At the threshold of the mansion inhabited by the descendants of the Grimaldi, we encountered a gorgeous usher wearing a heavy gold chain upon the breast of his crimson velvet robe. He led the way across an inner court and up a flight of marble steps, at the top of which he surrendered us, with a magnificent bow, to the keeping of M. Ponsard, Commandant of the Palace. Ponsard, in his turn, conducted us along a corridor and through a series of stately apartments to the office of the First Chamberlain, who after some delay ushered us into the presence of the Grand Almoner of the prince's Household. This eminent individual was seated at a desk writing. He greeted Green ceremoniously. He was aware that Monsieur the American Minister had audience that morning of the hereditary prince; but His Serene

Highness was just now reviewing the Army in the piazza before the palace. His Serene Highness would soon return. If Monsieur the Minister and his friend would like to witness the pageant, there was an admirable view of the piazza from the balcony of the *Salon des Muses,* the third apartment to the left. The chamberlain would show the way.

"A polite old gentleman," I remarked, as we followed the chamberlain to the *Salon des Muses.*

"That extraordinary man," whispered Green, with a touch of awe in his voice, "is Monsignor Theuret, one of the most astute statesmen in Europe. His influence at court is practically boundless. He combines ecclesiastical with secular functions, being apostolic administrator and bishop of Hermopolis, and at the same time Grand Almoner of the household and superintendent of the third *Salle* of the casino. Being one of the chief leaders of the anti-Titus party, he both hates and fears me; yet did you observe how well he dissembled?"

"It strikes me," said I, "that this doubling up of offices is rather droll."

"It is necessary," returned Green, with perfect gravity, "in Monaco, where the total population is not large. The First Chamberlain, ahead of us here, as well as the Commandant of the Palace, and the usher with the gold chain act at night as croupiers at the casino. Chevalier Voliver, Minister of Foreign Affairs, leads the casino orchestra. He is an excellent musician and rather friendly to our interests, inasmuch as I have on several occasions rendered him trifling services of a pecuniary nature. But I must admit that, in statecraft, the Chevalier is weak and irresolute. He is hardly more than the tool and creature of Monsignor Theuret, whose ambition is as limitless as his ability is diabolical."

The First Chamberlain left us on the balcony. Thence we commanded a view, not only of the piazza below, but of nearly the entire principality. One could have fired a pistol ball into the Mediterranean, either to the west or to the south, and to the north the French frontier was within long rifle range. The palace itself shut off the eastward view, but Green informed me that the sea boundary on that side, with the cove where the Navy rode at anchor, was scarcely a stone's throw away. Opposite us were the grounds of the casino, the long stuccoed façade, the round concert kiosque, the theater, the restaurants, and the shops of the bazaar. Above this seductive establishment floated a captive balloon, in which visitors might ascend to the length of the rope for twenty francs the trip.

From the balloon overhead I turned my attention to the spectacle in the open piazza in front of the palace. Sidewalks, steps, doorways, and windows were thronged with loyal subjects of Charles III. Directly beneath us, on a fine black stallion, sat the hereditary prince, motionless as a statue. The Army of Monaco, commanded by the intrepid De Mussly, marched and countermarched before him, exhibiting its proficiency in all the evolutions known to modern military science. In their smart red uniforms and white cockades, the thirty-two carabineers, who constitute the effective force under De Mussly, presented a truly formidable appearance, wheeling to and fro. The generalissimo had drilled them to march with that peculiarly vicious fling of the legs which is taught in Prussian tactics; and when they came kicking across the square in fours, wheeled suddenly into a sixteen-front line, halted before the hereditary prince, and grounded arms with a simultaneous clang of thirty-two carbine butts against the pavement, bravo after bravo arose from the delighted spectators, while a smile of proud gratification rested for an instant upon His Serene Highness's countenance.

Just then I observed the eccentric actions of an individual halfway across the square, who seemed to be trying to attract our notice. He whistled through his knuckles, waved both arms in the air, and then, apparently dissatisfied with the result of these demonstrations, snatched a gun from the nearest soldier and raised his own silk hat on the muzzle high above the heads of the crowd. Having restored the gun to the astonished warrior, he expressed his low opinion of the Army, for our benefit, by means of a derisive pantomime, and began to elbow his way through the ranks toward us.

"It is Titus," groaned Green. "He is continually compromising me in some such way."

The consul endeavored in vain to discountenance our fellow citizen below, by staring fixedly in another direction. Titus was not to be snubbed. He shouted, "Hi! Green," and, "Oh! Green," until he obtained the full attention of my embarrassed companion.

"Be sure to be at home by two o'clock, Green," roared Titus. "I have important news." Thereupon he gleefully flourished before our faces what looked like an official document and hurried away.

When the First Chamberlain came to summon Green to his interview with the hereditary prince, I returned to the consulate to await him. He rejoined me at a little before two o'clock. "Well, what luck?" I inquired.

"The outlook is gloomy," he replied, nervously. "The interview was most unsatisfactory. In order to commit the government of Monaco to some definite form of complaint, I requested His Highness to say candidly in what the American people had offended him. The prince regarded me steadily with his dark, piercing eyes, and at last replied, 'Pouf! You Americans talk loudly at our *tables d'hôte*, bully our croupiers, browbeat our gendarmes before our very face, and make yourself generally obnoxious.' I perceived, of course, the disingenuousness of this answer, but managed to control my indignation. His Highness next asked me a good many questions about the financial and material resources of the United States Government, the efficiency of its military and naval forces, its debt, annual revenue, and so on. I need not say that my answers to all these questions were guarded and discreet. I then pressed the prince to tell me if there was any truth in the report that a personage high in the court had a pecuniary interest in fomenting trouble between the United States and Monaco. I thought the prince winced a little at this home thrust; but he replied in the negative, referring to the story as an 'idle *bruit.*' The interview then ended; but as I came away I observed on the face of the crafty Monsignor Theuret an expression which I could not fathom. It seemed very like mirth, untimely as—"

Here the consul was interrupted by the precipitate entrance of Titus, followed by three or four other Americans.

"Hallo, Green!" said this brusque individual. "Are you in the dumps? I'll enliven you presently."

There was something in his tone, careless as it was, that fairly startled Green out of his official dignity.

"Merciful heavens!" exclaimed the consul; "what has happened now?"

Titus winked at the rest of the company. He took a pipe from his pocket and reached for the tobacco box on the table, upsetting, as he did so, the contents of the consul's inkstand over a pile of official papers. This accident did not discompose him in the least. He coolly filled his pipe and occupied himself for some minutes in emitting large rings of smoke, one after another, and then shooting little rings through the series.

"We are all of the Yankee persuasion, I suppose," he said at last, casting a glance of inquiry at me. I nodded in reply. Then Titus produced the document which we had seen him waving in the piazza.

"Here's a lark," said he. "I took this down from the bulletin board in front of Papa Voliver's Foreign Office this forenoon. Lord forgive the theft! I did it for my country's sake."

Then he proceeded to read, rapidly translating the French into English. We listened, dumfounded. Great beads of perspiration stood upon Green's forehead. He clutched mechanically at the papers on the table and inked the ends of his fingers.

The document was an edict, signed by Charles III himself, countersigned by the Chevalier Voliver, Minister of Foreign Affairs, and sealed with the great seal of the principality. Stripped of verbiage, the edict decreed:

First, that it should be unlawful for any subject of the prince, or any foreigner sojourning within the boundaries of the principality, to engage in the American game called poker, said game being dangerous to the public morals and subversive of existing institutions.

Secondly, that all obligations contracted by subjects of the prince to subjects of the American President, through the game called poker, *or otherwise,* be thereby repudiated.

Thirdly, that thenceforth no American subject be permitted to enter the Principality of Monaco, for business or for pleasure; that American subjects then in Monaco be allowed twenty-four hours from the promulgation of this edict, within which time they must leave the principality, under penalty of imprisonment at the discretion of the Tribunal Superieur and confiscation of their effects.

All eyes were turned upon Green. It was some time before the consul recovered the faculty of speech. "But this is unprecedented!" he exclaimed. "It is not only outrageous in a general way, but it is specifically discourteous to me, personally and officially. I am the diplomatic representative of the United States, duly accredited to this court. Here is an important paper, seriously affecting the relations between the two governments, which, instead of being conveyed to me in the proper manner, *has been tacked on a bulletin board,* like a miserable writ of attachment. Furthermore," he added, as the enormity of the outrage grew upon him, "I have not only been ignored, insulted, but I have been trifled with. This edict must have been posted before my interview with the hereditary prince. It is infamous!"

"Well, fellow citizens," said Titus, with a light laugh, "what are we going to do about it?"

"There is only one thing to do," replied Green. "Dispatch a full and carefully worded statement of the affair to the Department of State at Washington, in order that Congress may take appropriate action."

Titus sent forth a roar of laughter along with a cloud of smoke. "And meanwhile?" he demanded. "I am inclined to think that in the present condition of our glorious Navy it will be about two years and six months before we can expect to have a fleet of iron-clads here."

"I suppose we must leave Monaco," said the consul, sadly. "We are at the mercy of an absolute and remorseless power."

"LEAVE?" thundered Titus.

"Let us have your ideas, Mr. Titus," said I.

"Well," said Titus. "I propose to try my hand at a state paper. I've undertaken tougher jobs in my day. Get a sheet of clean foolscap, Green, and a good, sharp pen. Now write down what I say."

He then dictated the following manifesto:

To Charles Honoré, Prince of Monaco:

When in the course of human events, it becomes necessary for a mighty nation to avenge an injury sustained by her in the persons of some of her most valued citizens, the visitation of her wrath upon the offender is apt to be sharp, sudden, and overwhelming.

Unless your edict of this date be revoked before nine o'clock tomorrow, and due apology made for the same, we, the United States of America, do hereby declare war against the Principality of Monaco on land, sea, underground, and in the skies; and God have mercy upon your soul!

(Signed)

GEORGE WASHINGTON TITUS,
Commander in Chief
JOHN J. GREEN,
Minister Plenipotentiary

"There! Green," said Titus, complacently, "now tell your man Giovanni to go and tack this little composition upon the bulletin board of the Foreign Office, and leave the rest to me."

"But this is very irregular," protested the consul. "The power to declare war is vested by the Constitution in Congress. *We* can't declare war. Besides, there are always certain formalities to be observed."

"Damn your formalities!" rejoined Titus. "In times of great national emergency like the present there is a higher law than the Constitution. In such a crisis men of action must come to the front. You can come in with your protocols and preliminary drafts, and all that solemn rot, when we get to the negotiations for peace. I'm commander in chief just now. You and these other gentlemen must go around among the Americans here and tell 'em not to be alarmed, but to act precisely as if nothing had happened. That's General Order number one. Hold on a minute, though. Is there anybody who understands the army signals?"

I respectfully informed the commander in chief that I was familiar with the code.

"Good!" said he. "You've got grit. I like the build of your chin. Stay here with me. I constitute you chief of staff."

"Now," he continued, after the others had departed, "take four of the consul's red silk handkerchiefs and make some little signal flags. I have another important letter to write."

The composition of this missive seemed to give him considerable trouble, for I had finished the flags long before he stopped writing. Finally he tossed me a sheet of note paper. "I hate infernally to do this," he said, giving his mustache a tug, "but, hang it all, everything is fair in love and war."

The letter bore no address or signature:

MADAME: I have read your eyes, and my heart is full of joy. I have also read the black looks on the faces of your jealous and powerful relatives. If I have seemed cold and indifferent, it is because I cared for your peace of mind—not because I feared for myself, believe me, Madame.

And now the cruel edict has gone forth. Exile from Monaco is nothing, for the world is wide. Exile from you is death; for my poor life is in your adorable smile.

If you are as bold as you are beautiful; if wide difference of rank weighs less in the balance than an absorbing passion; if you can dare everything for the sake of one who has suffered and been silent, be at the pump behind the equestrian statue of your noble ancestor, Vincenzio Grimaldi, one hour before sunrise to-morrow morning, and be alone.

"It's a confounded shame," remarked Titus, half to me, half to himself, "to bring her out into the damp early air at her age; but it can't be helped."

The consul's valet now returned. He had nailed the document upon the bulletin board, as Excellency had commanded, and there was already an immense crowd collected around it.

"*Buono!*" cried Titus. "Now, Giovanni, I have another com-mission for you. You are discreet." He gave him the letter and whispered a few words of direction. The intelligent fellow nodded.

"And, by the way, Giovanni, you are on pretty good terms with the Army?"

"Yes, Excellency."

"How much will it cost to get the Army drunk tonight?"

"Very drunk, Excellency?"

"That is what I mean."

Giovanni made a rapid calculation with the aid of his fingers. "About sixty francs, I think, Excellency," he replied, with a broad grin. Titus handed him five napoleons.

An hour later I walked with the commander in chief along the western rampart—the fashionable afternoon promenade in Monaco. Few Americans were to be seen, but on every hand there was evidence of an unusually excited state of popular feel-ing. We encountered scowls and audibly whispered insults at every step; but my companion walked on unconcerned, with his long, swinging gait. "The Council of State is in session. There will be hot work tomorrow," I overheard one subject of the prince remarking to another. A rattle of drums, and De Mussly marched briskly past us, at the head of a detachment of four carabineers. Ladies waved their handkerchiefs at the military. "The generalissimo is posting his sentinels," said Titus. "Luckily there

are two cafés in Monaco to one soldier." Some of the shopkeepers
were putting up their shutters, early in the day as it was. Suddenly Titus modified his pace, and his countenance assumed a
singularly pensive expression. Three ladies were approaching us.
I had only time to see that one of these, walking slightly in advance of the others, was a very stout person of middle age,
ostentatiously dressed and heavily rouged. As she passed us Titus
took off his hat and made a profound and rather melancholy bow.
The fat lady bent her eyes to the ground. I thought I detected
traces of a blush on those parts of her face which were not
factitiously red.

"It's all right," Titus whispered in my ear. "The battle's ours."

III

At half past five o'clock on the morning of the momentous day,
a strange thing happened near the casino. The captive balloon,
set free from the moorings that tied it to the earth at night, began
to rise slowly and majestically through the mists of the early
twilight. With a plunge or two to the right and left, and a flutter
as if of astonishment at being disturbed at such an unwonted
hour, the vast spheroid settled its course straight toward the
zenith, as rapidly as the paying out of the rope permitted. A
single individual operated the brake of the cylinder from which
the rope unwound. That individual was myself. The car of the
balloon carried two passengers. One was Titus; the other, a
woman muffled in many wraps and closely veiled.

"*Carissima!*" Titus had whispered to his trembling companion
as he helped her into the basket. "It is our only chance of flight.
We should certainly be arrested at the frontier if we attempted
to escape by land." A gentle gurgle of tenderness and helplessness was the only response.

I watched the vaguely outlined bulk as it ascended to the
length of the rope. The light breeze from the west carried the

balloon directly over the palace, where it rested motionless at a height of five or six hundred feet.

When I left the casino grounds I stepped over the prostrate form of a sentinel, snoring lustily upon the pavement. The streets were deserted, but I passed one café which had been open all night. Glancing through the doorway, I saw a dozen of De Mussly's red-uniformed veterans in various stages of intoxication. Those who were still sober enough to sing were shouting a war song, the refrain of which menaced my native land with unutterable doom. Giovanni's five napoleons had done their work.

Three hours later I finished a comfortable breakfast at my hotel and sallied forth to find the consul. The situation had changed. The city was wide awake now, and indescribable confusion prevailed. The entire population surged through the streets leading to the palace and the casino. Business was everywhere suspended. A few carabineers were seen here and there, seedy in the face and shaky in the legs. The generalissimo was making desperate efforts to collect his demoralized army. On the balcony in front of the palace, whence we had witnessed the brilliant review of the Army on the day before, stood the prince and several members of his family, surrounded by Ministers of State. Among the latter I recognized the sinister visage of Monsignor Theuret. The piazza and the adjoining streets were thronged with people. All eyes were turned upward to the balloon, which still floated over the palace, the only tranquil object in the tumultuous scene.

As soon as Titus had shown his face to the crowd below, there had been a rush to the windlass with the intention of winding in the rope and recapturing the balloon. But Titus, leaning over the side of the basket, had brandished a long bowie knife in a way that left no doubt of his purpose to cut the balloon free if any attempt should be made to haul it down. He was thus far master of the situation. The enemy remained inactive, undecided what course to pursue; the dignitaries upon the balcony were earnestly engaged in conference.

In the piazza, just under the balcony, I espied the consul in the center of a little knot of Americans. With some difficulty I elbowed my way to the spot.

A murmur from the crowd drew my attention to the balloon. Titus was making certain motions with two small red flags. I produced two similar flags from beneath my waistcoat. Communication was thus established between the two divisions of the United States Army. The *Duomo* clock struck nine.

"Ask if the edict is revoked," signaled Titus.

I translated the message to the consul, who put the question to the balcony in a loud voice and in the most approved terms of diplomacy.

Monsignor Theuret, speaking for the government of Monaco, replied with a sneer: "The edict is not revoked. Its provisions relating to the arrest of Americans found within our territories will be carried into effect in precisely one hour." This answer was conveyed to Titus.

"Declare Monaco in a state of siege!" was his prompt rejoinder.

The cool audacity of this announcement produced a visible effect upon the populace. What mysterious power had this man in the sky, who talked with little flags and calmly defied a prince with an Army and Navy? What was coming next?

Theuret retained his presence of mind. "Let the rope be cut," he shouted. "Then the wind will blow this impudent American scoundrel over into Italy. We shall be well rid of him at the price of a balloon."

Again there was a rush toward the rope and a hundred knives were ready to do the work. But Theuret, who had been steadily gazing upward, was seen to turn as pale as death and to grasp at the balustrade for support.

"*Basta! Basta!*" he cried. "Cut not that rope, if you value your lives! The princess is in the balloon!"

Sure enough, the round, red face of the princess was visible over the wickerwork of the car. A howl of astonishment and dis-

may went up from the crowd. The little knot of Americans answered the howl with a cheer.

"Titus has won the game!" said the consul.

But the agitation of Monsignor Theuret was even greater than
circumstances appeared to warrant. The sight of the princess in
the car seemed to drive him to madness. He tore his hair, shook
both fists at the balloon, and shrieked as if he expected Madame
to hear. "Ah, Florestine, faithless! I suspected as much. Monster
of perfidy! *Cuor' mio!* Wretched, wretched woman!"

"I suspected as much, also," said the consul, in an undertone.
"We diplomats have eyes everywhere. Look at Theuret! What a
scandal!"

The prince was regarding Theuret's manifestations of jealous
frenzy with searching eyes. Then he summoned De Mussly and
gave him a command, inaudible to those below. Two soldiers removed Monsignor Theuret from the balcony. "The bishop is arrested!" cried the crowd, all agape at the unexpected incident.

"Now, monsieur," said the prince, addressing Consul Green,
"what are your demands? It seems that in some inexplicable way
you have succeeded in kidnaping our sister. What ransom do you
require of us?"

After some signaling, Green reported the ultimatum which Titus propounded: The revocation of the edict, the restoration of
American citizens to an equality with the subjects of the most
privileged nation, the re-establishment of the game of poker, the
prince's own guarantee for the payment of all debts due to American citizens, and an indemnity of ten thousand francs for the
expenses and anxieties of the war.

There was a long consultation upon the balcony. At last the
prince was seen to shake his head, as if in reply to arguments intended to dissuade him from some settled plan of action. The
Chevalier Voliver stepped forward from the group and said,
"His Serene and Most Christian Highness has wavered between
the natural affection which he entertains for his sister, Madame

the Princess, and his duty toward his subjects. The struggle is now at an end. Bitterly as he regrets one result of his decision, he feels that he must place the interests of the people of Monaco above family ties. He sacrifices Her Highness to duty. The edict will go into effect at ten o'clock. He commands that the rope be cut, and the balloon set adrift."

That is the diplomatic way of saying that he is rather glad to get rid of the foolish and troublesome old lady," I remarked to Green after I had reported the speech to Titus.

But the consul and the rest of the Americans had fallen from hope into dejection. They felt that the commander in chief had played his last card and lost.

Not so Titus. His flags were plied vigorously for a brief space of time, and then, reaching his arm at full length from the network of ropes around the car, he held forth a large tin canister that glittered in the sunlight.

The effect of this simple act was marvelous. It paralyzed the arms of those who were about to cut the rope. It carried consternation to the group upon the balcony. It created a panic in the crowd, which scattered in every direction. A cry of horror went up from a thousand throats. In all the noise and confusion only one word was distinguishable:

"Dynamite!"

The people of Monaco had learned, from Titus' own teaching, how terribly potent, even in small quantities, was this agent of destruction. Now they felt that an unknown quantity of the awful, mysterious thing was suspended, so to say, by a single hair, over their heads and homes. The prince himself blanched at the possibilities of the next moment.

"He says," I yelled at the top of my voice, "that if his conditions are not accepted in three minutes by his watch, and without further parley, he will drop the can and blow your principality into smithereens."

In two minutes peace was re-established.

IV

The war was over. Secured by the most explicit guarantees from the government of Charles III, the victorious commander allowed himself to be pulled down from the skies. Still holding the dreaded tin can in one hand, with the other he gallantly assisted his lady captive from the car of the balloon, and led her to the balcony of the palace.

"Serene Highness," he said, as he respectfully consigned the Princess Florestine to the care of her august brother, "I regret that the necessities of war compelled me to make a prisoner of Madame the Princess, who was abroad early this morning on a mission of charity."

The prince bowed in silence. The princess's eyes were fixed upon the floor.

"And, Serene Highness," continued Titus, "I implore you to believe that I would not risk the precious life of so exalted a lady by putting her in proximity with a dangerously large amount of dynamite."

So saying, he tossed the can over the balustrade. It fell upon the pavement with an empty rattle.